It had been more than four thousand years since Ullikummis had spoken anything other than one word

That word was a name, the name of his hated father.

He instructed them with a look, the apekin farmer and his apekin wife. His eyes, molten pits of lava that glowed fiercely in the darkening evening gloom, held them in his thrall, for the apekin were such simple creatures compared to him, compared to a god.

Alison and Peter Marks rose from the ground, their heads still bowed before their new master. Peter Marks had never so much as visited a ville, and he had never submitted to another man in anything. Yet this strangely beautiful being that stood before him in his own field, the same field his father had plowed fifty years before—here was something that he would bow to without question. Deep down inside him, he knew that here was something supreme.

Other titles in this series:

Doomstar Relic	Sun Lord
Iceblood	Mask of the Sphinx
Hellbound Fury	Uluru Destiny
Night Eternal	Evil Abyss
Outer Darkness	Children of the Serpent
Armageddon Axis	Successors
Wreath of Fire	Rim of the World
Shadow Scourge	Lords of the Deep
Hell Rising	Hydra's Ring
Doom Dynasty	Closing the Cosmic Eye
Tigers of Heaven	Skull Throne
Purgatory Road	Satan's Seed
Sargasso Plunder	Dark Goddess
Tomb of Time	Grailstone Gambit
Prodigal Chalice	Ghostwalk
Devil in the Moon	Pantheon of Vengeance
Dragoneye	Death Cry
Far Empire	Serpent's Tooth
Equinox Zero	Shadow Box
Talon and Fang	Janus Trap
Sea of Plague	Warlord of the Pit
Awakening	Reality Echo
Mad God's Wrath	Infinity Breach

James Axler

Outlanders®

OBLIVION STONE

A GOLD EAGLE BOOK FROM

WORLDWIDE®

TORONTO • NEW YORK • LONDON
AMSTERDAM • PARIS • SYDNEY • HAMBURG
STOCKHOLM • ATHENS • TOKYO • MILAN
MADRID • WARSAW • BUDAPEST • AUCKLAND

Recycling programs
for this product may
not exist in your area.

First edition August 2010

ISBN-13: 978-0-373-63867-3

OBLIVION STONE

Copyright © 2010 by Worldwide Library.

Special thanks to Rik Hoskin for his contribution to this work.

Printed in U.S.A.

The most difficult thing is the decision to act,
the rest is merely tenacity.
　　—Amelia Earhart
　　　1898–1937

A capacity for going overboard is a requisite for
a full-grown mind.
　　—Dawn Powell
　　　1896–1965

The Road to Outlands—
From Secret Government Files to the Future

Almost two hundred years after the global holocaust, Kane, a former Magistrate of Cobaltville, often thought the world had been lucky to survive at all after a nuclear device detonated in the Russian embassy in Washington, D.C. The aftermath—forever known as skydark—reshaped continents and turned civilization into ashes.

Nearly depopulated, America became the Deathlands—poisoned by radiation, home to chaos and mutated life forms. Feudal rule reappeared in the form of baronies, while remote outposts clung to a brutish existence.

What eventually helped shape this wasteland were the redoubts, the secret preholocaust military installations with stores of weapons, and the home of gateways, the locational matter-transfer facilities. Some of the redoubts hid clues that had once fed wild theories of government cover-ups and alien visitations.

Rearmed from redoubt stockpiles, the barons consolidated their power and reclaimed technology for the villes. Their power, supported by some invisible authority, extended beyond their fortified walls to what was now called the Outlands. It was here that the rootstock of humanity survived, living with hellzones and chemical storms, hounded by Magistrates.

In the villes, rigid laws were enforced—to atone for the sins of the past and prepare the way for a better future. That was the barons' public credo and their right-to-rule.

Kane, along with friend and fellow Magistrate Grant, had upheld that claim until a fateful Outlands expedition. A displaced piece of technology…a question to a keeper of the archives…a vague clue about alien masters—and their world shifted radically. Suddenly, Brigid Baptiste, the archivist, faced summary execution, and Grant a quick termination. For

Kane there was forgiveness if he pledged his unquestioning allegiance to Baron Cobalt and his unknown masters and abandoned his friends.

But that allegiance would make him support a mysterious and alien power and deny loyalty and friends. Then what else was there?

Kane had been brought up solely to serve the ville. Brigid's only link with her family was her mother's red-gold hair, green eyes and supple form. Grant's clues to his lineage were his ebony skin and powerful physique. But Domi, she of the white hair, was an Outlander pressed into sexual servitude in Cobaltville. She at least knew her roots and was a reminder to the exiles that the outcasts belonged in the human family.

Parents, friends, community—the very rootedness of humanity was denied. With no continuity, there was no forward momentum to the future. And that was the crux—when Kane began to wonder if there *was* a future.

For Kane, it wouldn't do. So the only way was out—way, way out.

After their escape, they found shelter at the forgotten Cerberus redoubt headed by Lakesh, a scientist, Cobaltville's head archivist, and secret opponent of the barons.

With their past turned into a lie, their future threatened, only one thing was left to give meaning to the outcasts. The hunger for freedom, the will to resist the hostile influences. And perhaps, by opposing, end them.

Prologue

They had thought them dead—the Annunaki, for whom forever is but the blink of an eye.

It was said that *Tiamat,* their mother, had committed suicide.

Ultimately, her graceful form, shaped like a dragon of ancient myth, had been consumed by a fireball so glorious that it had lit the firmament above and shaken the Earth below. Some thought that the fireball had been of *Tiamat*'s own making, that she had chosen to expire in that dazzling tumult of flame.

Enlil knew better.

Enlil was one of *Tiamat*'s children, the Annunaki. They had called her mother, the spaceship womb. Her offspring were the rightful overlords of the planet Earth and all of her resources, the kings of all of her people and all of her things.

It was said that *Tiamat,* the spaceship womb, had taken her own life when she had seen the bitter disputes, the spite and viciousness that her own offspring had exhibited as they squabbled among themselves. For it was true that the Annunaki were never willing to compromise, even when carving the Earth up between themselves.

But in his heart, Enlil knew better.

The Annunaki had suffered their most devastating defeat at the hands of the apekin, the humans. *Tiamat* had been consumed by fire, her essence fragmented across the skies high above the Earth in a final display of brilliance. And some had thought her destroyed, that the final chapter of the Annunaki legend had been written.

The Annunaki, whose dominion over the Earth had lasted millennia, had controlled the nine fabled baronies that had emerged from the Deathlands to bring security and a future to humankind—a security and a future that man himself had been unable to achieve.

"Such fools these apekin be," Enlil muttered to himself as he sat on the banks of the timeless Euphrates, gazing out across the great river as the sun played across its glistering surface. Around him, the land was a windswept plain of sand, lifeless but for Enlil himself as the sun's heat pounded down, baking the dusty earth as it had for millennia.

But it had not always been so. Enlil remembered a time, not so very long ago, when his brother had had a city here—a city called Eridu, the first and most glorious city that the Earth had ever seen. Enlil had had his own city, too, a place called Nippur, located not far from Eridu's walls, those scant millennia ago. And yet Enlil had chosen to return here, to Enki's city rather than his own, recalling how its establishment had been a bold statement, the first acquisition of alien ground on the planet that would become their own, a flag in the dirt of foreign soil.

Enlil's reptilian skin shimmered as the sunlight played across his scales, their color that of richest sunset, the color of gold bathed in blood. His form was mighty, a muscular, tall figure, imposing even now as he sat in the sand, gazing out across the shimmering surface of the water through his arrow-slit, crocodile's eyes.

Tiamat was not dead. She had simply been changed, altered, readied herself for rebirth like everything else Annunaki. To change from one form to another, to enter the chrysalis state and be reborn, that was the Annunaki way.

Enlil himself had taken other forms over the centuries. He had been Dagon and he had been Kumarbi and C. W. Thrush and, most recently, he had been Sam the Imperator until, like a snake, he had sloughed his skin and emerged wearing another, each more glorious than the one that came before. All these lives were like a dream, one life told from differing viewpoints, a single life seen through different eyes.

Beside Enlil, resting on the sand at the banks of the river, was the tiny seed from which *Tiamat* would grow once more. The tiny seed that would form the heart of his mother, and which, in turn, would begin the cycle anew.

Enlil glanced up to the heavens, eyeing the cloudless cerulean sky, and slowly a grim, purposeful smile formed on his alien lips.

It was all beginning again.

Chapter 1

Snakefishville stank of death.

Thick clouds of flies swarmed about the ruins, their furious buzzing echoing like an angry symphony of dying lightbulbs between the debris of collapsed buildings. The remains of bodies—and they could only be described as "remains" now, as most of them were no longer truly recognizable as human—lay in the streets and occupied shadowy corners of the rubble scattered at nightmarish angles within the wrecked circle of the ville's high walls.

The walls themselves were destroyed almost beyond recognition, just a few jagged concrete struts remaining here and there, like the last few tenacious teeth in a crone's rotting mouth.

Towering above the devastated streets like a two-fingered salute from some blank-faced god sitting in silent judgment, the last struts of the central Administrative Monolith remained, their jagged peaks clawing at the rain-heavy clouds that trundled disinterestedly over the inconstant sky. The Administrative Monolith had once been the radiant jewel in the city's tiara of lights, but it was now hardly a shadow of its former self, just a few spindly posts all that remained as though marking the place where once there had been high walls. The struts leaned sideways like some ruddy-faced drunkard trying to find his bearings, a few smashed windows and chunks of masonry clinging to its otherwise lost structure as though the building's body had been eaten away by cancer. The smaller structures around it had fared little better; it was as if the whole fabric of the ville had been struck by some virulent disease, an architect's cancer.

Swooping down from above, circling through the jagged shards of buildings, carrion birds cawed their bitter cries of possession as they spied new morsels to feast upon among the rotting flesh that still clung to the bones of those most recently deceased.

Three living figures trudged among the ruins, masks over their faces to protect them from the corrupted air and the stench of death that hung all about.

The shortest of the figures looked somewhat like the Angel of Death herself. Her skin was a pallid shock of chalky whiteness, like something carved of bone, her eyes a ruby red like the flaming depths of Satan's realm. Like her skin, her hair was white as a specter, cut short to accentuate her feral eyes. She was a petite figure, dressed in a protective shadow suit of a light weave that clung to her lithe body like a second skin, drawing attention to the bird-thin limbs and small, pert breasts that jutted from her diminutive form like some perfectly imagined china doll. She had added a light jacket over the shadow suit, reaching down past her hips but still loose enough to allow ample movement, its material the black of the Grim Reaper's shroud. Her name was Domi and she was one-third of a field team sent out by Cerberus to investigate the remains of the destroyed ville.

Snakefishville had been one of the nine great baronies constructed across North America under the instruction of the hybrid barons. Once the barons had been revealed to be the chrysalis state for the higher, godlike beings known as the overlords, their baronies had been left leaderless, struggling to fend for themselves. Just a few weeks ago, a terrible earthquake had struck Snakefishville and several other communities, mortally wounding them like an assassin's final blow. Operatives from Cerberus, a military-style group dedicated to the preservation of humanity in the face of the rising threat of the Annunaki, had been present during Snakefishville's destruction. But it was only now, a few weeks after the event, that they had returned to survey the full extent of the damage and to scout for salvage.

Domi hated jobs like this. Though an operative for Cerberus, she was a wildling at heart, a child born of the Outlands. Being cooped up in a ville, even one as utterly scragged as this one was, set her teeth on edge. She looked around her, swatting flies away from her face as she took in the chunks of masonry, the cracked metal ribs of the broken buildings. If there was a Hell, Domi thought, it would probably look something like this—a ville with nothing left to offer but its own festering corpse.

Clambering over the fractured remnants of the main street came Domi's two partners. Both of them were dressed in loose clothes with masks over their mouths. The first was a man called Edwards, whose shaved head and wide shoulders made him an imposing form even with his features obscured by the mask. Edwards's hair was cropped so close to his scalp that his head shone in the sunlight, drawing attention to his bullet-bitten right ear. Edwards had the bearing of a military man and the patience of a raging inferno. Beside him came a man called Harrington, with pince-nez glasses and dark hair streaked with white that fell past his shoulders in a series of neatly layered steps. Harrington was consulting a handheld Geiger counter as the three of them made their way across the wrecked ville, scouring the rubble.

"Radiation's at normal," Harrington confirmed, stumbling for a moment as his foot got caught in a rut in the ruined roadway.

"Careful there, Poindexter," Edwards growled, grabbing the scientist's elbow and yanking him out of the pothole.

A few paces ahead, Domi stopped in her tracks and stared up at the spindly struts of the Administrative Monolith, watching as tar-feathered carrion birds circled around in its updrafts, nesting in the jutting metal bones that had once held a nearby structure together. Domi's ruby eyes scanned the broken glass of the last remaining windows, searching for movement among the wreckage. As if on cue, a gull came swooping out of one of the shattered windows, its feathers a smoky gray, its impressive wingspan reaching almost three feet. The gull shrieked its ugly call as it took off, a pinkish morsel of bloody meat held in its claws.

As Domi watched, a trio of black carrion birds swooped down at the gull, chasing it through the jagged teeth of buildings that were all that remained of the once-proud ville. The birds flew around one of the lopsided building shells, disappearing from Domi's sight in a clamor of ugly squawks.

Harrington peered up from the plate of the Geiger counter at the noise, taking in the abandoned ville as if for the first time. "This is weird," he commented.

"What's that?" Edwards asked, glancing back at the scientist as he climbed a mound of rubble that had once been a residential block.

"This place," Harrington said. "Like walking through a cemetery."

Domi shot Harrington and Edwards a look, hushing them immediately. "People coming," she said, indicating one of the wrecked structures that abutted the ruins of the Administrative Monolith.

Edwards's hand automatically went to his hip, pulling free the Heckler & Koch USP he had strapped there. "Keep your head down, Harry," he ordered Harrington, his voice low.

A few paces ahead, Domi had pulled her Detonics CombatMaster .45 from its hidden holster at the small of her back. The handgun, finished in silver metal, looked large in her tiny, milk-colored hand. Domi scampered forward, leaping over the potholes that marred the road, making her way toward the crooked doorway of the building shell where she had detected people. She moved like something liquid, each motion blending effortlessly into the next as she sped toward the door. Edwards chased after her, his long strides struggling to keep up with her swift progress.

As Domi reached the open doorway, its lintel hanging at an awkward thirty-degree angle, she saw a figure moving within, its features hidden in the shadows. Warily, Domi waited at the door until Edwards caught up with her.

"On three?" Edwards proposed, mouthing the words without speaking them aloud.

Domi nodded, and watched as Edwards counted down on extended fingers.

When Edwards's count reached zero, the two Cerberus warriors rushed through the doorway, guns held out before them, scanning the lobbylike room where they found themselves. The floor was littered with rubble and, when they looked up, they saw that the ceiling had almost entirely disappeared. Just its edges remained, clinging to the scarred and pitted walls of the higher stories. The whole structure had sunk by at least two stories, and so they found themselves on what was in fact the third or fourth story, despite being at ground level. There was no one inside the room, and the two warriors made their way swiftly into the next room, Domi taking point as Edwards covered her from beside the doorway.

The movement was so quick that Domi almost missed it. In fact, it most likely would have been missed by anyone else; only Domi's eerily heightened senses caught the motion before it disappeared from her field of vision. The figure was rushing from the room, a foot visible for a fraction of a second as it ran through the crumbling archway of the next door, the dust of rubble puffing up in its wake.

Domi initiated pursuit, shouting, "Stay where you are. We mean you no harm." It seemed a curious instruction. Technically, it was Domi and her team who were trespassing here, and yet they hadn't expected to meet with anyone else after the ville had been destroyed.

Domi dashed toward the doorway, and another of the gray-feathered gulls came swooping out, shrieking an ugly cry as it flew at her. Domi ducked, and the confused bird flew on, flapping its wings and ascending into the open area above through a gap in the broken ceiling. Behind Domi, Edwards tracked his pistol on the bird as it disappeared, before returning his attention to her progress.

Ahead, Domi rushed through the next doorway, leaving the corridor behind her. She found herself face-to-face with a half-dozen people dressed in the ragged clothes of Outlanders. They were huddled around a fire that had been set in an upturned canister, warming their hands as they cooked several rats and birds at the ends of greasy sticks hung over the yellow flames. Domi cursed herself for missing the cooking smells—the breath mask had hidden them from her, obscuring the natural senses that she relied upon.

The room itself was a vast open area. The floor was tiled in terra-cotta, a swirling pattern like sea spray created using a series of darker tiles within the mosaic. The tiles had been cracked by the earthquake that had shaken the ville weeks before, and a number of them were missing, now just crumbled to dust. On the far side of the room stood a counter at roughly chest height, indicating that the room had probably been some kind of reception area just a few weeks before. Now it was simply a corpse, the rotting remains of a once magnificent building.

As Domi dashed forward, she became conscious of something coming at her from behind, and she moved just swiftly enough to avoid a harsh blow to the back of her head. She spun to face her attacker, seeing the tall figure dressed in a dark, hooded cloak with a lighter pattern in the weave. The lighter pattern was almost undetectable now, so much dirt had become ingrained in the man's clothes.

"Submit," the hooded man spat, following through on his first attack.

Domi ducked as the cloaked man lunged at her again, inexpertly driving a heavy fist toward her face. As the man's fist sailed over her head, Domi rushed at him, barreling shoulderfirst into his gut and knocking him off his feet. The man fell backward and became tangled in his cloak even as he struggled to right himself. Leaping back, Domi held her gun on him, instructing him not to move. The whole attack and rebuttal had taken less than four seconds.

Behind Domi, Edwards was making his way through the doorway, the black barrel of his Heckler & Koch nosing into the room before him. "Everything okay in here?" he asked.

"Just peachy," Domi said. "Fuckwit here tried to ambush me."

Edwards glanced at Domi's would-be attacker sprawled on the cracked tiles. "Looks like you had it covered."

Domi's red eyes flicked to Edwards for an instant, and he saw that her expression was one of irritation. He ignored it, turning to assess the other people in the room.

"Now, why don't you nice people tell us what the shit is going on here?" Edwards asked, striding toward the group huddled around the fire.

For a moment, no one answered. Edwards glared at them, his snarl visible through the transparent cup of the breath mask. Then, keeping his movements slow and smooth so that everyone could see just what he was doing, Edwards lowered the Heckler & Koch until he had it held loosely at his side. Still, he left the safety catch off so that he could fire it at a moment's notice.

Then, her voice timid, a woman with ragged ginger hair and dirt-caked clothes spoke to Edwards, her pleading eyes wide. "Are you the new baron?"

"What?" Edwards spit. "Shit, no. The barons have all gone."

"But how can we have a barony without a baron?" another of the ragged figures spoke up, this one a man with stubble darkening his jowls, a woollen cap pulled low over his brow.

Other members of the group muttered their assent as they cooked the vermin over their little, contained fire.

Domi backed across the room on light feet until she was standing beside Edwards, her pistol still pointed firmly at the hooded man sprawled on the floor. Wisely, the hooded man stayed where he was, his eyes locked on the silver barrel of Domi's CombatMaster.

"These guys are looking for a baron," Edwards explained.

"So I heard," Domi replied, her words laced with cynicism. She glanced over her shoulder, turning her attention from the hooded man for a moment while she addressed the group. "Care to explain why your friend here attacked me?" she asked.

"He's a Magistrate," the ginger-haired woman who had first addressed Edwards explained. "You must have broken laws."

Domi spoke to Edwards out of the side of her mouth, keeping her voice low. "The way he attacked me—guy was no Mag. Way too sloppy."

Edwards addressed the ginger woman, his gaze taking in the other people in the group before him. "Has your friend here been a Mag for long?" he asked. When no one answered, Edwards turned to the hooded form lying on the floor, casually turning his gun over in his hand so that it caught the light. "Well?"

The man in the hood groaned as he spoke. "Three days," he said. "Volunteered three days ago. Ville needs Magistrates, right? What the hell did your freak girlfriend hit me with?"

Domi reacted angrily. "What did you call me?" she asked, taking a menacing step toward the self-proclaimed Magistrate, jabbing her gun at his face.

"Mutie, right?" the hooded man asked. "Figures."

Domi looked irritated, but Edwards told her to ignore the man's comments.

"So," Edwards asked, "you're all here building a ville? That right?"

As one, the group of stragglers shook their heads. "No, sir," said the stubbled man in the woollen cap, "we came back. This is how people should live. Within walls. Within rules. There's a place for you here. Can't you feel that?"

Though not a man given to introspection, Edwards was taken aback. "I think you want to be careful what you breathe in around here," was all he could think to say. "Lot of nasty crap in the atmosphere just now. Quake churned up a lot of shit."

The stubbled man nodded. "Thank you, sir. Won't you stay and help us to rebuild?"

Edwards smiled and shook his head. "Not today, ace."

As the people stood watching the strangers in their midst, grease from one of the cooking birds spit and the fire flared brighter for a second.

Wary of the locals around them, Edwards and Domi made their way slowly out of the sunken building, both of them feeling somewhat unsettled by what they had seen.

"Seven of them," Edwards growled, "and they're planning on rebuilding a ville. Waiting for the new baron to appear. Crazy."

"The villes do shitty things to people," Domi told him. "Mangle them." She glanced back, confirming that no one was following them.

"But there's no barons anymore," Edwards pointed out. "They all vanished and became overlords. So what's drawing these people back?"

Domi stopped for a moment, fixing Edwards with her demonic eyes. "Like I said, the villes mangle people. Give them tangle-brain. The Outlanders know this, and that's why we didn't come to the villes unless we had to."

Edwards looked at the petite woman, his brow furrowed in confusion. "Didn't you grow up in Cobaltville, Domi?" he asked.

"No," Domi told him, shaking her head. "Settled there for money. Saw the way people were on the inside."

"Hah." Edwards laughed. "You make it sound like a prison."

Domi said nothing. While she had recognized the differences in ville dwellers from Outlanders, she had never seen anything quite like this—people coming back, choosing to live in the ruins while they waited for the next epoch to begin. It was almost as if the villes themselves had some kind of magnetic pull over their citizens. Domi, who had spent a portion of her life as a sex slave in Cobaltville, knew little of the scientific principles of magnetism, but she understood fatal attraction all too well.

Outside of the wrecked skeleton that had once been a building, Domi and Edwards found Harrington sitting on a mound of rubble that looked out over the ruined streets. He had found three chunks of rubble and was juggling them while he waited for his partners.

"You find anything?" Harrington asked when he noticed Edwards and Domi approaching.

"What do you think you're doing, man?" Edwards barked. "This is a danger zone—gotta keep alert."

"I am alert," Harrington replied petulantly. "You think I can juggle like this when I'm asleep?"

Edwards shook his head, muttering something about eccentric scientists.

"We found a wannabe Magistrate," Domi explained, "and a group of people waiting for the next baron."

Harrington sighed. "And so the system reboots itself," he said. "Are we reverting back to…well, the Deathlands era? Jumped-up little barons fighting it out for their little piece of land?"

"There's no baron," Edwards clarified. "They just think there will be. So they're waiting here, eating rats and setting up a hierarchy of Magistrates to keep the peace."

Domi looked around her, taking in the ruined structures of the ville once more, seeing the mangled struts where its old Administrative Monolith had once stood noble and proud. "Somehow, the villes call to people," she said. "Like boys in heat, hormones drawing them to the honey trap."

Edwards shook his head. "You may be right, but it's all way over my head."

Chapter 2

"They say that the gods came from the sky," Papa Hurbon said as he led the three-strong party through the Djévo room, his wooden leg clomping on the decking of the floor.

Ohio Blue's response was to offer the man an indulgent smile. "I never held much stock in gods," she admitted as they walked through the large room of the wooden shack, its air as hot and as damp as the night sweats.

Ohio Blue had brought two bodyguards with her—a man and a woman—who followed her and Hurbon as they paced slowly through the room, moving just as fast as Hurbon's false leg would allow. As per the rules of the meeting, her bodyguards were unarmed, and in return Hurbon had kept his own people out of sight, though it was understood that they could appear in a moment upon his request.

Blue felt the man's eyes play across her for a moment. She was a tall, slender woman in her midthirties, and her thick, long blond hair was cut in a peekaboo style, leaving only her left eye boldly visible. The eye was a brilliant blue, dazzling as a polished sapphire. She wore loose combat-style pants with a silk vest top that shimmered as she moved. Over this, despite the stifling heat of the Louisiana afternoon, was a neatly tailored jacket that was cut short, reaching barely to the small of her back. Her clothes, like her name, were blue.

"You ever meet one?" Papa Hurbon asked, his voice so low it sounded like the rumbling of distant thunder.

Hurbon was a large man, both tall and corpulent, with the lustrous, dark skin of an octoroon. His skin glistened with free-flowing rivulets of perspiration, which he wiped from his heavy brow as they trudged through the Djévo, passing glass jars filled with herbs, feathers, snail shells and other curios. Hurbon wore a sweat-stained undershirt and cutoffs, with a homemade sandal on his remaining foot. His right leg was missing below the knee, and a wooden strut had been shoved in its place that he used to totter forward with a lunging, rolling gait that looked as though he might overbalance at any moment. Hurbon's shaved head was shaped like a bullet, wide at the bottom and tapering at the top, and when he smiled it was a gap-toothed maw that seemed to engulf the whole width of that impressive, bucketlike jaw. Both of Hurbon's ears were pierced in multiple places, both at the lobes and along the archlike helix of the ear, and what appeared to be two tiny fetus skeletons depended from their bulbous lobes.

"I've never had that pleasure," she admitted, her long blond tresses sweeping across her back as Ohio Blue shook her head.

Hurbon offered his wide, all-encompassing smile. "Ain't no pleasure," he told her. "You can take my word for that. Ezili Coeur Noir came here one time, 'bout a year ago. Mad bitch took my leg. Laughed the whole time she was doing it, too. When she was done she held it up before my congregation, blood spittin' everywhere, and she laughed and told them to do the same. Mad bitch."

Ohio blanched at the story. "And did they?"

Hurbon's brow creased in a frown. "Did they what?"

"Remove their legs?"

Hurbon nodded. "Some did," he said, resignation in his voice. "They wanted her blessing, lizard-skinned vision that she was. That sound crazy to you, Mam'selle?"

"Like I said, I never held much stock in gods," Ohio told the corpulent man as they passed through an arched doorway and into the center of the voodoo temple.

Papa Hurbon stopped for a moment, openly admiring Blue's shapely figure from head to toe. "With the gams on you, that's probably for the best, little peach," he said with a rich basso laugh.

Through the archway, the inner room was much smaller than the Djévo, roughly square and just nine feet from wall to wall. Lit by candles, this was a mirrored room, wherein one side balanced the other. Thus, it featured a door to the far side, precisely opposing the one that Ohio's party had entered. Several figures could be seen milling about in the room beyond that far doorway, and Ohio's bodyguards tensed as they eyed them through the gloom.

This inner room was uncluttered, holding just a few objects. A polished broadsword had been placed horizontally on the wall, resting there on two hooks, ornately weaved tassels drooping down from its leather-wrapped hilt. Two matching hooks had been drilled into the opposite wall and they held what appeared to be a human shinbone of roughly the same length as the sword, polished so that it shone in the flickering light of the candle flames. Two foot-high clay pots filled with the dried stalks of dead flowers sat at opposing corners of the room, placed at diagonals to each other.

A curious-looking chair waited in the center of the room. The chair appeared to be carved of some kind of plant root, and it had a seat and a back but apparently had no legs. Instead, the seat itself had been ignominiously placed atop a stack of house bricks, like some stripped-down automobile.

"Here she be," Papa Hurbon rumbled, indicating the odd-looking chair.

Ohio appraised the strange chair for almost half a minute, pacing slowly around it to view it from all angles before she finally spoke in her soft drawl. "Where did it come from?" she asked, sapphire eye still peering at the chair.

Hurbon pointed to the ceiling. "Tumbled out of the sky," he said, "just like my people told you. Gift from Ezili Coeur Noir. Instructed me to take care of it, tend to its needs. It gives visions in the head, makes you see beyond the Barriè."

Blue looked quizzically at Hurbon for a moment until, finally, he elaborated.

"The Barriè, the spirit world," he said. "So, you want?"

"How does it work?" Blue asked.

"Just sit down," Hurbon encouraged, "and let the visions flow through you. Simple as that. Chair of the gods, you see?"

Ohio Blue looked dubious as she considered the man's strange boast. Finally, she turned to her two bodyguards. "One of my people will test it," she decided, "to verify your claim. If that is satisfactory to you."

Hurbon shrugged. "The gods deserted me. What do I care?"

Ohio turned to her waiting bodyguards, who had assumed positions at either side of the entry door, their expressions grim. "Brigid? Kane?" she asked, addressing each in turn. "If one of you would be so kind…?"

Kane smiled sourly. A muscular man with steel-gray eyes and short, dark hair, Kane resembled a wolf, for his limbs were long and rangy and his body seemed furiously powerful, a coiled spring waiting to release. He was like a wolf in other ways, too, naturally adopting the role of pack leader and equally comfortable striking out on his own. Despite current circumstances, Kane was not a bodyguard, and nor was he an employee of the blond-haired trader, Ohio Blue. An ex-Magistrate, Kane was one of the Cerberus exiles. The Cerberus redoubt was hidden in Montana, and its residents were dedicated to the protection of humanity, tasked with freeing it from the hidden shackles that the alien Annunaki race had placed upon it. Kane's role had taken him across the globe and beyond in his quest to eliminate the Annunaki's nefarious meddling in the affairs of humankind, and his appearance here, as Ohio Blue's bodyguard, was yet another instance of that ongoing struggle for freedom. He wore a ragged denim jacket and pants over the figure-hugging black weave of his shadow suit, which offered protection from radiation, contamination and could even withstand minor blunt-force trauma.

Ohio Blue was playing her own role admirably, Kane thought. An independent trader, Blue had a solid reputation in the Tennessee/Louisiana area and boasted a whole network of contacts through whom she could locate items of value and interest. As such, she had one important asset that the Cerberus team lacked—credibility among the minor players who occasionally ended up with something the Cerberus exiles might need. A recent meeting with Blue had resulted in Kane saving the woman's life, and she had vowed to return the favor should he call on her to do so.

This operation, however, had not come at his urging but at hers. Aware of Kane's interest in alien artifacts,

Ohio Blue had contacted him with information regarding a possible sighting out here in Louisiana. In this case, Papa Hurbon, a *houngan* priest in a small voodoo sect hidden in the swampland, had come into possession of what was rumored to be a section of the Annunaki mother ship, *Tiamat*. It seemed that this odd-looking chair was that item, although Kane couldn't be certain. He had been inside *Tiamat* during that final, frenetic battle that had resulted in the destruction of that incredible Annunaki starship, but he was hard-pressed to remember all of the details of the furniture that he had seen there. Kane nodded dourly toward the other bodyguard, indicating that she was better qualified to examine the chair.

The other bodyguard was a striking woman with an athletic body and vibrant long hair the red-gold color of sunrise. Her name was Brigid Baptiste and she had partnered with Kane ever since the pair had joined the then-embryonic Cerberus operation several years before. Brigid's dazzling green eyes and high forehead suggested intelligence, while her full lips hinted at a more passionate aspect; in truth she was both of these things and more. An ex-archivist, Brigid Baptiste possessed an eidetic memory—more commonly known as a photographic one—with total recall for any item or text that she had seen for more than a few seconds. Dressed entirely in black, including a thin cotton shirt over her figure-hugging shadow suit and a snap-brim hat holding her hair out of her eyes, Brigid stepped forward and reached tentatively for the chair.

As the others watched, the beautiful redhead sat down on the barklike surface of the seat, settling herself until her back rested against the back of the chair itself.

Papa Hurbon leaned close to Brigid's face, his broad smile forming once more on his lips. "Just make yourself comfortable there, little cherry," he instructed. As the large man spoke, Brigid smelled something sickly sweet on his breath. "Let yourself go an' the visions, they will flow through you."

Sitting there, Brigid eyed the chair, confirming that it was of the same design as one she had seen when she had been aboard *Tiamat* with Kane just prior to the great starship's destruction. Up close she recognized it, despite the damp, swamp-ring stain that had bleached away its original color. It was a seat from the bridge, a piece of salvage somehow fallen to Earth after the mighty spaceship had been destroyed. It was incomplete; the base was missing and Brigid was certain that its back part was missing a headrest. But, just as Hurbon himself had said, it was a chair of the space gods, fallen from the heavens, a gift to him from his lizard-skinned goddess.

Brigid slowed her breathing, closed her eyes and let the mysterious power of the Annunaki chair wash over her, waiting for the promised visions to begin. If what Papa Hurbon had said was true, then the visions from the spirit world might in fact be valuable reconnaissance information about their alien enemy. And if that was the case, then the chair itself could prove to be an invaluable asset to Cerberus.

Behind her eyelids, Brigid saw the familiar light-embracing darkness that was always there, a shadow playing across it as one of the people in the room moved across her field of vision. And for a moment there was nothing else. No great revelation, no fantastic visions of another world. She opened her eyes, fixing Hurbon with her emerald gaze. She was about to ask how long before the visions would begin, but he spoke first.

"Give it time, sweet cherry apple," Hurbon said, the conviction in his voice clear. "I seen things there the likes o' which man hain't never seen before."

Brigid smiled indulgently. "Time," she agreed. She realized now what the sweet smell was that wafted off the man's breath—he was high on narcotics, most likely painkillers for his missing leg. This voodoo priest didn't need to sit in an alien chair to get visions—he was probably tripping most of his waking life, and who knew what his dreams were like.

Kane's eyes met with Brigid's momentarily, and he recognized the bubbling disappointment there. But even as he looked, he saw something change in Brigid's appearance.

For just a second, Brigid saw something projected over the candlelit room, pinpricks of light hovering in place. "Do you see that?" she asked, her voice quiet, awestruck.

Hurbon chuckled. "The Barriè. Amazing, is it not?"

Brigid looked at the corpulent man as the pinpricks of light swirled across her vision. Stars. She was looking at the stars. It was a map, a star chart that could only be seen by the person occupying the chair. It was incredible.

Papa Hurbon, meanwhile, had turned back to Ohio, that broad, gap-toothed smile tugging at his lips. "Now, your people said something 'bout an art collector out near Snakefish," he began.

"Ruined Snakefish," Blue corrected automatically. The whole baronial ville had been wrecked by an earthquake recently and rumor had it there was barely anything of the old structure left. Yet another of the nine baronies fallen with the disappearance of the Annunaki.

"Think this might be something that your buyer be after?" Hurbon asked.

"For the right price," Blue said nonchalantly. There was no art collector in Snakefishville; that was simply a lure to disguise the true significance of the item. Ohio turned to

Brigid, looking for any indication that the redhead might give as to the item's value to Cerberus, that she might begin negotiations.

Beneath the wide brim of her hat, Brigid offered a barely perceptible nod of her head, her long hair brushing at her shoulders. Right now, the strange chair was an eyesore that happened to have fallen into the lap of a drugged-up cultist. However, there was value here, and certainly Cerberus would be interested in testing the genetic makeup of the object to find out as much as they could about the Annunaki. If it possessed star charts that could locate the Annunaki's home planet, for instance, such knowledge would be of inestimable value.

"Vision chair like that," Hurbon continued, "visions as big as the sky, that's got to be real valuable to your client. Art collector sees visions like that and he won't need to buy any more art."

Hurbon laughed at his own observation as Brigid began to rise from the strange rootlike seat. As she did so, her hand brushed against the water-stained armrest and something clicked within. Brigid stared in shock as a series of thornlike spikes appeared along the arms of the chair, and several of them pierced the heel of her hand where it still rested against the chair itself.

"Oh, you gone done it now, haven't you, girl?" Hurbon muttered, and a rich laugh came from deep in his chest.

As the four of them watched, the thorns were turning into tendrils, reaching out from the surface of the chair's arms like a plant's shoots emerging from the soil. In a second, the waving tendrils latched on to Brigid as she struggled to get up out of the chair, wrapping around her arms before she could pull away.

"What's it doing?" Brigid asked, an edge of panic in her tone as she found she could no longer rise from the alien seat.

The tendrils continued to pull Brigid's struggling form back down into the seat, wrapping around her wrists and bonding them to the armrests like manacles.

"I can't move," Brigid said as she struggled against the squirming tendrils.

Kane fixed his steely stare on the voodoo priest. "You have to switch this thing off right now," he insisted.

Hurbon shrugged. "Ah, the chair chooses her own lovers," he said, a mellow laugh peppering his words. "I only find them for her."

As Hurbon continued to chuckle, the shoots rushed upward, grasping the underside of Brigid's right arm as her bare skin brushed against them. In a split second, the tendrils wrapped around her arm, more and more of them branching from the first few that snapped around her, spreading to form a network of veins across her flesh. Brigid gritted her teeth as her arms were yanked down toward the armrest, the budding tendrils wrapping over them to lock her in place. Despite her physical fitness, the chair seemed to have no trouble pulling Brigid down, drawing her closer with the viselike grip of those thin, plantlike tendrils.

"What's happening?" Brigid asked fearfully.

"You triggered it," Hurbon stated, laughing once again.

"I just touched it," Brigid said. "You tricked me."

Despite her struggles, Brigid was pulled back down into the seat once more, and she squirmed at an angle as she tried to right herself and get away from the alien chair.

Calmly, Kane bent down and pulled a combat knife from the sheath he wore at his ankle. "Quit struggling, Baptiste," he told her. "You're just making it worse."

Brigid's eyes went wide with shock when she saw Kane move toward her with the lethal-looking blade. "Kane, don't do anything crazy, okay?" she said through gritted teeth, letting out a yelp as the thorns pressed against her supple flesh.

Kane eyed the tendrils as more and more appeared, growing from the arms and back of the chair and then wrapping themselves tightly around his beautiful companion's struggling form. The strange tendrils were already cinched over both of Brigid's arms and had reached around to encompass her pale, slender neck, pulling her so that she sat upright despite her squirming. "Stay still," Kane instructed. "I'll cut you free."

Hurbon laughed louder when he heard that, as though the whole thing was nothing more than a joke.

Ohio Blue fixed the voodoo priest with a fierce look. "Is this your idea of a game?" she challenged. "I had a collector lined up for this piece, but I don't think it's money you're after."

"You're astute for a nonbeliever," Hurbon growled. As if to punctuate his response, Papa Hurbon swung one of his meaty arms at the blue-clad trader, moving fast despite his size and disability. In a second he had knocked her to the floor with a loud, open-palmed slap.

Ohio cried out in pain as she slid across the wooden floorboards, a loose nail tearing the thin cotton of her pant leg.

In the Annunaki chair, Brigid was straining back and forth, shaking her head left and right as the thorny appendages began to burble around her face, covering her eyes. "It hurts," she yelped, and Kane saw the tiny runnels of blood begin to snake across her flesh amid a glistening sheen of sweat.

"Stay still," Kane repeated, pressing his left hand against Brigid's for a moment. Then he swept the knife rapidly through the tendrils, cutting through the first dozen strands that had laced up her arm.

But before Kane could get any further with his task, the vast form of Papa Hurbon reached for him from behind, pulling the ex-Mag away from the chair in a mighty bear hug before flinging him to the floor. Kane slid across the worn floorboards before thudding into the far wall next to Ohio Blue with a bone-shaking crash.

"The chair's chosen," Hurbon barked. "You leave her be now, boy."

Head reeling, Kane struck out from where he lay, sweeping his legs out and catching Hurbon's own wooden leg as the massive figure loomed over him. With a howl, Hurbon's bulbous form fell sideways and he lost his balance, arms reaching out as he slammed against the wall.

"You chose the wrong victim for your little scheme," Kane snarled, pulling himself up off the floor.

"Ain't you been listening, boy?" Hurbon snapped as he struggled on the floor like a beached whale. "I don't choose—Ezili Coeur Noir's chair does that."

Writhing in the chair, Brigid yelped as the weird tendrils squirmed around her face, wrapping around her, covering her eyes. Then she felt the tendrils worming up into her nostrils, pushing between her lips, and she felt as if panic might consume her at that moment.

But something even stranger than that was happening. Within her mind, hovering in her field of vision, a star chart appeared with crystal clarity. Planets rotated in their orbits, and as Brigid's eyes were drawn to them, tags appeared to identify each, written in a script that even she could not decipher despite her incredible base of knowledge.

It was terrifying, that feeling of being trapped in the all-encompassing embrace of the nightmare chair, and a part of Brigid felt the rising panic of claustrophobia as the tendrils snaked over her face. But another part of her, her rational mind, marveled at that star chart playing across her eyes, shifting with the movements of her irises, shifting with her very thoughts themselves.

Across from Brigid in the wooden-floored room, Kane spat a curse at Hurbon as the corpulent priest lay flailing on the floor, unable to right himself without help thanks to the wooden leg he wore.

Papa Hurbon's only response was to look at Kane with defiant eyes as that broad, indefatigable smile formed once more on his lips. Kane dismissed him from his mind, glancing down at Ohio's semiconscious form before returning to Brigid in the chair. But as he did so, three new figures stepped into the room via the far doorway. Each of them was male, muscular and held a vicious-looking blade. They glared at Kane as he stood before the fallen body of their leader.

"I don't make the choices," Hurbon reiterated, cackling a wicked, wheezing laugh, "the chair does. We are just its faithful servants." His next command was addressed to the newcomers: "Kill him."

"I knew it'd come down to this," Kane muttered to himself as the first of the shirtless voodoo worshippers took a step forward and swung a filthy eight-inch blade at Kane's face.

The ex-Mag stepped back just enough to be out of range as his attacker's blade cut through the air. Then he stepped forward once more and delivered a brutal knee to the man's crotch. With a pained howl, Kane's attacker doubled over and dropped heavily to the floor like a sack of coal.

Though the others watched the falling form of their colleague, Kane himself ignored the falling man. Instead, the ex-Mag rushed forward and swung a swift right hook at the nearest of his two remaining foes, his fist slamming into the man's jaw with tremendous force. Even as the man reeled from the blow, Kane was ducking down and whipping his leg out to connect with the kneecap of the other voodoo worshipper. With a sharp crack, the third man's knee snapped backward, bending his leg at an awkward angle, and his arms flailed as he struggled to respond.

Kane was a trained Magistrate, and these penny-ante sec men weren't even enough to make him break a sweat. In six seconds, Kane had eliminated all three men from the fight, leaving two sobbing in pain and the third tossing and turning in semiconscious delirium.

"Now," Kane snarled, turning his attention back to the languishing figure of the priest, "how do I switch off the chair?" He held the knife where Hurbon could clearly see it, menace in his eye.

"Can't be done," Hurbon said defiantly. "Once she starts, the chair takes whatever she wants."

"Screw that," Kane spat, whirling back to his partner, who remained struggling against the clawing grip of the eerie chair.

Brigid Baptiste had almost entirely disappeared amid a cocoon of wavering tendrils. Outside the room, Kane could hear the clomping feet of more voodoo warriors as they ran to investigate the sounds of battle that had come from this inner sanctum.

Biting back a curse, Kane leaned down and began working once more at the tendrils, snapping them aside as rapidly as he could with his combat knife. As he did so, he activated his Commtact—a tiny communications device embedded beside his mastoid bone that allowed him to speak with his teammates in real time via satellite linkup. "Grant? We're making a hasty exit and we'll be needing some covering fire in two to three minutes. That suit you?"

The rumbling voice of Grant, Kane's longtime partner and equal, responded in Kane's Commtact. "I read you loud and clear, buddy. Just let—" With that, the communication went abruptly dead.

For a moment, Kane waited, his busy knife still working through the swirling mass of spindly tendrils as they reached for Brigid's now static form. Had something happened to Grant? The Commtact shouldn't just go dead. Commtacts were top-of-the-line communication devices that had been discovered among the artifacts in Redoubt Yankee some years before. The Commtacts featured sensor circuitry incorporating an analog-to-digital voice encoder that was subcutaneously embedded in a subject's mastoid bone. Once the pintels made contact, transmissions were picked up by the wearer's auditory canals, and dermal sensors transmitted the electronic signals directly through the skull casing. In theory, even someone completely deaf could still hear, after a fashion, using the Commtact. As well as radio communications, the units could also be used as translation devices, providing a real-time interpretation of foreign languages on the proviso that sufficient vocabulary had been programmed into their data banks. Loss of communication through them, while not unheard of, was exceedingly rare.

"Grant?" Kane asked in a low voice, and he listened for a moment for any indication of his partner from the Commtact. "Grant, you read me?"

Beside Kane, Ohio Blue was just coming back to her senses, her thick blond hair in disarray as she struggled up from the floor. Swaying a little, she looked around the room at the scene of devastation. "Kane, my sweet, sweet prince," she said, urgency in her voice, "I think it's time we were leaving."

Kane turned at Ohio's voice, but his attention was distracted by the people appearing behind her. Two new figures pushed through the doorway, and Kane saw immediately that there was something wrong with them. They were tall and emaciated and they walked with a shambling gait. When Kane saw the way that their eyelids flickered over unfocused orbs, he concluded that they were either drugged or something worse. The word *zombie* flashed through the ex-Mag's mind.

Kane spoke into the Commtact again. "Grant? Do you read me? Please respond." After a moment's silence, he tried patching his signal to home base. "Cerberus? This is Kane. Do you copy? Please respond, Cerberus."

And still the only response from the Commtact was a deafening silence.

Chapter 3

Grant stood well over six feet tall, with impressively wide shoulders, deep chest and a solid mass of hard, taut muscle. His dark skin was a rich shade of mahogany, and he wore his black hair close-cropped to his skull, with a drooping gunslinger's mustache curving down from his top lip. Like Kane, Grant was an ex-Magistrate, and their partnership went all the way back to their time together in Cobaltville, years before the formation of the Cerberus operation. Grant was several years older than Kane, and the trust between them was absolute. They had seen combat across the globe, saved each other's lives on countless occasions and there was an unspoken understanding between them that went as deep as the bond between brothers.

Right now, Grant waited in the mouldering marshes of the Louisiana swamps, hunkering down between the low branches of a tree. Clad in camouflaged greens and browns, Grant peered through the sniper's scope of his SSG-550 rifle where it rested high on its bipod legs. He kept his voice to a low whisper as he spoke into the hidden pickup of his Commtact. "Kane? Please repeat, I didn't copy." He waited a moment, listening for any signal from his Commtact over the humming, squawking and chirping of the swamp fauna. "Kane?" he repeated, his voice just a little louder. "Brigid?"

There was still no answer.

Eye locked on the eyepiece of the sniper scope, Grant watched for movement at the entryway to the dilapidated shack. The wooden structure was just one story high yet covered almost 4,000 square feet. Despite its size, the low roof and rotting nature of the building made it appear cramped and unwelcoming.

Grant had seen Kane and Brigid enter the building in the company of the independent trader, Ohio Blue, about fifteen minutes before. They had arrived here via airboat, transported across the marshland by a dark-skinned woman with a toned body and a scarred face, her left leg missing below the knee. Grant had tracked the airboat via the transponder units that were embedded beneath his partners' skins, using his own uplink to Cerberus headquarters to keep track of his friends as they traveled through the maze of swamps. This had allowed him—unseen—to keep to a roughly parallel route on his own airboat, its huge fan whirling as it carved a new pathway through the dense shrubbery of the sweltering marshes.

"Cerberus, this is Grant out in the field," Grant spoke to his Commtact once more. "Appear to have lost radio contact with Kane and Brigid. Please advise."

Grant listened intently, hearing the humming, squawking, chirruping sounds all around him, but the Commtact itself only offered dead air by way of response.

"Cerberus?" Grant repeated. "Anyone there reading me?"

Yet again, there was no response.

Anxious, Grant turned away from the rifle's scope and reached for the handheld unit he had used to track his partners' transponders. Its tiny screen was functioning, but it showed no evidence of the transponders—not even his own, Grant realized with a start. He wiped the screen with his fingertip, and then pressed the reset button, causing the little portable unit to run through a ten-second reboot sequence.

"What the hell is going on?" Grant muttered as he watched the tracker unit reboot. Comms were down and now the transponders seemed to have gone offline, as well. Not good. Not good at all.

After ten seconds, the tracker unit returned to full functionality, but still showed no evidence of any transponders in the area—not even Grant's.

Concerned, Grant bent down to the rifle's scope once more and focused his attention on the shadowy doorway to the shack, waiting to see what would emerge.

THE HEADQUARTERS for the Cerberus operation was located high in the Bitterroot Mountains of Montana. A military redoubt, it had remained largely forgotten or ignored for the two bleak centuries that followed the nukecaust of 2001. In the intervening years, a strange mythology had built up around the shadow-filled forests and seemingly bottomless ravines of the mountains themselves. The wilds around the three-story concrete redoubt were virtually unpopulated; the nearest settlement was some miles away in the flatlands beyond the mountains themselves, where a small band of Sioux and Cheyenne Indians had settled, led by a shaman named Sky Dog.

The facility itself had not always been called Cerberus. For the brief years of its first life, like all prewar redoubts, it had been named Redoubt Bravo after a phonetic letter of the alphabet used in standard military radio communications. In the twentieth century, Redoubt Bravo had been dedicated to the monitoring and exploration of the newly developed mat-trans network of instantaneous teleportation. However, somewhere in the mists of time, a young soldier had painted a garish rendition of the fabled three-headed hound of Hades to guard the doors to the facility, like Cerberus guarding the gates to the Underworld. The artist—whose signature identified him only as Mooney—was long since dead, but his work had inspired the sixty or so people who had taken up residence in the facility, acting as their lucky—and unquestionably fearsome—mascot.

Tucked within the rocky clefts of the mountains around the redoubt, disguised beneath camouflage netting, concealed uplinks chattered continuously with two orbiting satellites to provide a steady stream of empirical data for the Cerberus operatives within. These links were the source of field communications through the Commtacts, as well as routing the feeds from the subcutaneous transponders that monitored the health of the personnel, and it was these that Grant had used to track his partners in the field. Accessing the ancient satellites had been a long process, involving much trial and error by many of the top scientists at the redoubt. Today, the Cerberus crew could draw on live feeds from both a Vela-class reconnaissance satellite and the Comsat satellite. Or, at least, that was the theory.

Within the operations center, however, a far different story was being played out. Dr. Mohandas Lakesh Singh leaped out of a seat that overlooked the vast control room, his swivel chair whirling off behind him on its little plastic wheels. Lakesh had dusky skin and sleek black hair that was just beginning to turn white at the temples. Lakesh had a distinguished air about him, holding himself straight and poised, with a refined mouth beneath his aquiline nose. Though he appeared to be about fifty years of age, Lakesh was in fact a "freezie," one of a number of military personnel who had been placed in cryogenic stasis when the outbreak of nuclear hostilities began, only to be revived some time after that cataclysmic conflict. As such, Lakesh was closer to 250 years old. A physicist and cybernetics expert, Lakesh was an exceptionally capable individual who served as the founder and was still the nucleus around which the Cerberus operation centered.

"What's happened to the feed?" Lakesh demanded, his eyes flicking from his own computer terminal to those of his colleagues who sat all about him. Every monitor had cut to static in the same instant, their flow of live data lost.

Brewster Philboyd, a tall, sallow-faced, blond-haired man wearing black-framed glasses and the evidence of acne scars on his cheeks, yanked off the comm headset he had been wearing as a burst of static interference cut through the earphones. "Some kind of glitch," he stated, gritting his teeth as he glared at the headset. "I'm not sure what it is."

Lakesh ran over to Philboyd's desk. "Find out," he urged.

Philboyd had been monitoring the incoming communications when the link to Kane's field team had gone down. Replacing his headset, he spoke into the pickup mic, calling to the other CAT teams who were out on assignment. "CAT Beta, do you read?" Receiving no response, Brewster's fingers played rapidly across his computer keyboard before he tried for CAT Gamma. Then he turned to Lakesh, shaking his head. "Nothing. I'm receiving no response from anyone."

Cerberus physician Reba DeFore, a stocky woman with ice-blond hair weaved into an elaborate plait atop her head, called to Lakesh from her own terminal where she had been monitoring the feeds from the transponders. "Everything's gone dead here, too, Lakesh," she stated, looking uncomfortable at her unfortunate choice of words.

"A massive equipment failure?" Lakesh murmured to himself incredulously, but even as he spoke, another dissenting voice was calling from one of the terminals in the vast operations room.

"Monitoring feed just went haywire," said Henny Johnson, a young, petite woman dressed in the regulation white jumpsuit of the Cerberus team, her blond hair cut into a severe bob that ended in line with her earlobes. "I can't see anything. Just static."

Lakesh looked around the ops room with frustration. The room had a high ceiling and housed two aisles of computer terminals dedicated to the monitoring of the outside world. A huge Mercator map stretched across one wall, displaying the globe patterned by a plethora of blinking lights and stretching lines showing the patterns and uses of the mat-trans system, the now-antique military teleportation network whose operation had been within the original remit of the base.

Tucked away in the far end of the room was an anteroom that housed the mat-trans unit, which was surrounded by tinted armaglass. This mat-trans unit was still operational and used frequently to transport Cerberus operatives all across the globe. The vast ops room itself was windowless and indirectly lit, allowing for better observation of the backlit terminal screens. Right now, the majority of those monitoring screens had devolved into static or dead feeds of data showing just the standard base-level defaults.

"What the devil is going on here?" Lakesh said, addressing the question to no one other than himself.

Reba DeFore spoke again from her terminal as a scrolling data readout raced across her screen. "My system is working," she stated, "but it's just not receiving any input data."

"The satellite's down," Lakesh realized, the words leaving his mouth almost before he had acknowledged the thought.

Like fascinated meerkats, the people in the ops room peered up from their terminals, eyes on Lakesh as he outlined his thoughts. "We've lost the satellite relay," he said, his voice more decisive now as a plan began to form in his mind. "I need to know why. Brewster, Henny—backtrack through the logs and locate when we lost contact, both sound and vision, and whether there was an indicator of its imminence."

Lakesh whirled around, his gaze falling on Donald Bry, an operative with a mop of ginger hair and a permanently dour expression on his drawn face. Bry acted as Lakesh's right-hand man, and had been known to run the Cerberus ops room when Lakesh himself was otherwise engaged. "Donald, let's start checking meteorological activity, sunspots, magnetic glitches, anything we can find a record of."

Donald Bry nodded as he reached across from his own terminal to switch on another vacant one that sat unused beside him. "Aye, sir." As the spare terminal went through its boot-up procedure, Bry's fingers began working furiously over his own keyboard, bringing up a stream of data covering the preceding hours leading to the loss of satellite feeds.

Lakesh, meanwhile, was standing in the center of the room, reeling off instructions to the other personnel there. "I want you to manually check our power supply," he ordered Farrell. "See if anything's happened to cause a breakdown in service. Get engineering to run a full systems check, both localized to the ops room and for the whole base itself."

Farrell nodded, his gold hoop earring catching the light for a moment before he briskly walked through the doors and exited the ops room to check the generators.

"Reba," Lakesh continued, turning to address the blonde physician, "I want you to bring up the final reports from the transponders, make sure everything's in order and patch the reports through to my screen so that I can double-check them."

DeFore shot Lakesh a fierce look. "You don't need to double-check me," she told him.

Lakesh offered her a concerned look. "We have three teams out in the field. Kane, Grant, Edwards, Morganstern, others. I'll double- and triple-check everything if it means protecting the life of one person while they're under my command."

"Point taken," Reba submitted. Chastised, she turned her attention back to her terminal and began to run a system history to the point where the live feeds had been interrupted.

Agitated, Lakesh paced across the room until he stood behind Henny Johnson at the satellite-monitoring feed. "What do we have, Henny?"

Henny replayed the feed sequence, watching the locator numbers as they scrolled along the side of the screen in a separate window to the feed images themselves. "They just seemed to pop, vanish," she explained. "Like someone pulled the plug."

"So," Lakesh mused, "let's figure out who or what pulled the plug, shall we?"

Henny nodded. "Time of signal break—15.37.08," she began, and Brewster and Reba both agreed with the time from their desks.

"Complete shutdown on both satellites," Lakesh said to himself as the other personnel continued comparing their data feeds. This could be something very big. Very big and very nasty.

PAPA HURBON was chuckling as Kane spun to face the two newcomers who had stepped through the doorway in their plodding, deliberate way. He watched the grim figures as they approached on heavy tread, their eyes flickering white slits.

"Grant," Kane said, engaging his Commtact once more. "My Commtact's not receiving your signal—"

The first zombie swung a vicious blow at Kane's head, moving far faster than the ex-Mag had expected. Kane ducked the sweeping, meaty fist as the second zombie stepped toward him. Up close, both dead creatures stank, and Kane was reminded of the garbage area of the Cerberus redoubt.

"I'm planning to evac in two minutes via the south exit," Kane continued into the Commtact, hoping that Grant could hear him. As he spoke, his arm snapped up to block the second zombie as it reached for him, emaciated fingers clawing for his throat with jagged, yellow-brown fingernails. "We may have some company in tow," Kane continued as he thrust the blade of his combat knife into the zombie's exposed throat. The zombie simply shook its head, and when Kane removed the blade an off-white pus exuded from the rent in the dead man's flesh. As Kane pulled his blade away, he heard Papa Hurbon chuckling from his supine position on the floor.

"We are surrounded by hostiles," Kane continued into the Commtact feed. "Pick off anyone you don't recognize."

At that moment, the first zombie connected with a hard blow to the back of Kane's head, and the ex-Mag staggered forward. Though Kane's knees bent, he kept himself upright as he slammed against the other lurching zombie.

"I repeat," Kane stated into the Commtact, "we are surrounded by hostiles. Dispatch on sight."

With that, Kane drove a powerful fist into the face of the zombie standing before him. The undead creature didn't move, but its face caved in like a rotten fruit, a cloud of skin dust flaking across Kane's fist. The creature itself seemed to just wait in place, swaying a little as Kane watched it, the remnants of its face splayed across Kane's knuckles.

The zombie behind Kane was moving closer, too, and the Cerberus warrior realized that he was hemmed in. Even as he backed away from his twin attackers, he saw that Ohio Blue was finally on her feet once more and had made her way over to the wall where the sword had been mounted. Blue pulled the sword from its twin clips and spun around to face the monstrous figures of the undead.

The beautiful blonde woman stepped forward, swishing the blade through the air and cutting at the zombie behind Kane. Although her blow struck, it was a pathetic effort, and Kane was reminded of his previous contretemps with the female trader out near Knoxville where she had proved to be far more of a con artist than a fighter.

With a foul stench reeking from its rotting flesh, the shambling form of the struck zombie turned to face Ohio Blue as she readied herself for a second strike.

"Ohio," Kane instructed as he stepped across the small room to her side, "give me the sword."

Blue didn't need to be told twice. She handed Kane the two-foot-long sword as the shambling zombies took another step closer.

In return, Kane handed the blond-haired trader his knife. "I need you to free Brigid," he instructed, stepping away from Ohio to face the zombies once again, sword held upright in a ready position.

The demands of her Outlander lifestyle had made Ohio Blue a very perceptive woman and, although she didn't comment on it, she noticed that Kane had referred to his partner by her first name. That was unusual—very nearly unheard of, in fact—and though Blue didn't know it, was a sign of his concern for the beautiful redhead trapped in the alien chair.

As Ohio trotted past the fallen body of Papa Hurbon, he reached out and snatched her ankle, pulling her down toward him. "Not so fast, pretty peach," he said, that sickly sweet breath exuding from his mouth with each word he spoke. "There are other games we can play, man and woman."

Without a moment's hesitation, Ohio rammed the short blade of the combat knife into Hurbon's crotch, and the man let out a pained shriek. "I'll pass," she told him as she scrambled away from the overweight priest.

A few steps away, Kane swung the length of tempered-steel blade at the approaching zombies, ignoring the howl coming from the floor behind him. The sword itself was the ritual weapon used to cut the curtain between the physical and the spiritual world in voodoo ceremony. Right now, however, Kane was using it in a less metaphorical manner, as he hacked at the looming figures, slicing chunks from their torsos as they silently strode ever onwards at him in the confines of the room. With a downward slice, Kane chopped off the reaching hand of the closest zombie, leaving the undead man with a stump that oozed putrid white pus. The hand itself slapped against the floor, a cloud of dust puffing up in its wake. Kane elbowed the wounded zombie aside and drove the length of the blade at the other figure's torso, spreading the zombie's ribs with the brutality of his attack.

Even as Kane dispatched the second zombie, three more had appeared in the open doorway to the inner sanctum, instinctively obeying the commands of Papa Hurbon as the man himself lay in a widening pool of his own blood. Kane steadied himself and swung the sword at the next wave of attackers.

Just six feet away from the scene of carnage, Ohio Blue ripped the last of the waving tendrils from Brigid's form and pulled her from the savage embrace of the alien chair. A network of veinlike tendrils clung to the woman's face and bare hands, and Blue hastily brushed these aside, feeling their spines snag at her own flesh like nettles.

"Are you okay, Ms. Baptiste?" Ohio asked as she swept the last of the tendrils from Brigid's skin. As she did so, red welts formed and runnels of blood appeared on Brigid's face in a cobweblike pattern.

Brigid's breath came in an uneven, stuttered rush as she spoke. "What the—? Where was I?"

"Right here," Blue assured her. "You were right here."

Brigid rubbed a hand over her eyes, seeing the eerie alien visions still playing there for a moment. "I saw something," she said, groping for the words to describe it, "like alien cartography."

"We need to get out of here," Blue told Brigid, and the words seemed to snap the former archivist out of her daze. "It was all a setup. Or something very much like it."

Brigid saw Kane then, and she saw the horde of zombies shambling toward him through the open doorway of the sanctum. "Kane…" she began.

Without turning, Kane batted another zombie aside as it grasped for him from the open doorway. "We about done here, Baptiste?"

"I think so," Brigid told him, still breathless.

Using the sword's hilt as a club, Kane slammed another of the undead figures in the chest, forcing it to step backward as a cloud of foul-smelling dust burst from the point of impact. Knocked back, the zombie fell into one of its colleagues, and the two slow-moving figures struggled in the doorway for several seconds. As they did so, Kane turned and indicated the far door—the one through which he and the others had entered with Hurbon.

"Let's get moving," Kane instructed.

From his place on the floor, the one-legged priest shouted angrily, "You won't get far. The chair has chosen her lover. You can't escape it now."

As Ohio and Brigid rushed out of the cramped inner room, Kane turned back to look at Hurbon, fixing him with his steely blue-gray glare. "I'll bring your sword back when I'm done," he told the corpulent man, whose hands still held his bleeding groin.

With false bravado, Hurbon laughed for a moment, until he saw the grim look on Kane's face. "I'll be ready," he said, blood pooling beneath him.

"No, you won't," Kane told him as he stepped through the doorway and out of the inner sanctum of the voodoo temple.

OUTSIDE THE WOODEN STRUCTURE, crouched against the bole of a tree, Grant waited, the SSG-550 sniper rifle leveled in the direction of the building's rotted doorway. Approximately two hundred feet from the doorway itself, Grant peered through the lens of the rifle's scope. He had had no further radio contact with Kane since the initial burst when his partner had requested covering fire in two minutes. That had been more than five minutes ago, and Grant was pondering whether he should enter the temple himself and recover his teammates. One thing that was certain was that his Commtact was dead. Not only had he been unable to raise Kane and Brigid, but Grant had also failed to patch through to the Cerberus base. In short, he was out in the field on his own now, with no access to backup.

Irritated, Grant comforted himself with the fact that he hadn't heard any gunfire coming from the voodoo temple itself. Kane, Brigid and Ohio had gone in unarmed at the request of Papa Hurbon—a standard indicator of trust between two trading parties in the Outlands—but there was no reason to suspect that Hurbon's people would remain unarmed if trouble arose. And based on Kane's record, Grant reckoned that trouble would undoubtedly arise.

Grant glanced up over the rim of the sniper scope to check that no one was approaching. All he saw were the clouds of insects that buzzed all about the sweltering Louisiana bayou. He fixed his eye back on the scope and waited; he would give Kane one more minute to show himself. If he didn't appear by then, Grant would have to go inside and find out just what the heck was going on.

"Come on, Kane," Grant muttered under his breath, "let's keep the game in motion."

INSIDE THE SINGLE-STORY TEMPLE, Kane, Brigid and Ohio were running through the large Djévo room, their shoes banging loudly against the wooden floorboards.

"You okay, Baptiste?" Kane asked as he glanced behind them to see a horde of followers, both the living and the apparently undead, clambering through the doorway of the inner sanctum in pursuit. Several of their pursuers were balancing on false legs, Kane noted, recalling the horrific story that Papa Hurbon had told them regarding his deity's awful request.

"I've been better," Brigid replied breathlessly, "but I'll get over it. Just let me breathe some fresh air."

Jogging along beside her, Ohio Blue chuckled. "You'll be lucky, Brigid," she said. "We're in the middle of a swamp—all you'll breathe when we get outside is local stink."

"Stink will do," Brigid assured the blonde woman as the three of them hurried through another doorway and into a corridor lined with shelves. The shelves contained jars filled with fascinating and disturbing items: human ears and pickled fetuses; shrunken heads; a vase full of dyed feathers; a sealed jar brimming with canine teeth.

"What happened in the chair?" Kane asked, eying the shelves with disdain.

"I saw stars," Brigid explained, awe coloring her words.

"Meaning?" Kane asked.

"It's an astrogator's chair," Brigid realized. "It projects star charts for the user."

"Projects them *where?*" Kane asked.

"In your head," Brigid explained. "Inside your eyes. It's an Annunaki navigator's seat. It must operate by physical contact."

"Yeah," Kane growled, "that kind of physical contact I don't need. Hurbon called it Ezili Coeur Noir's chair. Any idea how he reached that conclusion?"

"Lilitu," Brigid said thoughtfully, "the dark goddess of the Annunaki. Not averse to taking on other forms so that she will be worshipped."

"And she's a sadistic bitch," Kane recalled as he thought back to his own meetings with the Annunaki female, whose perverted peccadilloes were boundless. "Instructing her worshippers to remove a leg to prove their devotion isn't out of the bounds of belief."

The three of them stopped short as a figure appeared in the far doorway, blocking the exit from the shack. It was a dark-skinned man, so tall his head scraped the ceiling when he stood upright, and with the widest shoulders that Kane had ever seen. A necklace of animal skulls hung over the man's bare chest. A pair of sweat-stained combat pants ended in ragged cuffs below which his left foot was bare, while his right leg ended at a metal spike that attached to his knee. The man was armed with a thick, curved blade about eighteen inches in length and he smiled wickedly, a sinister half moon across his wide face.

Sword in hand, Kane eyed the brute for a moment. "Step aside," he instructed in his authoritative Magistrate voice.

In response, the brute merely laughed, raising the cruelly curved blade in his hand as he took a single thunderous step toward the three strangers. Behind them, just entering the corridor of odd delights, the first of a dozen voodoo followers were coming to box in Kane and his partners.

Ohio turned to Kane, fear lacing the songbird tone of her voice. "We don't have time for this, Kane."

"Sure we do," Kane said. He began charging forward, swinging the sword in a great, sweeping arc as he approached the dark-skinned giant in the bone necklace.

"Stay close," Kane heard Brigid instruct Ohio as he closed in on the brute.

A second later, the corridor resounded with the echoes of clashing steel on steel as Kane's sword struck the curved edge of the brute's scimitar. The power in the huge man's strike was uncanny, and Kane felt the vibration run up and down his arms as he parried the giant's blows. Even as the towering brute lunged at Kane, thrusting his scimitar forward in a devastating attack, Kane's mind calmed and his Magistrate training kicked in. Although he was a part of the battle, Kane also seemed to be standing to one side of the action, analyzing his opponent's strategies and probing for signs of weakness. As he fended off another attack, Kane shifted his balance, kicking off the floor and spinning around. The giant could only watch in amazement as Kane turned in a low arc and slashed the hard edge of his sword against his adversary's bare leg.

The huge man stood there, rocking in place for a moment as blood began to blossom in red stains across the left leg of his pants. And then Kane was driving forward once more, his left arm powering upward to slam the heel of his hand into his opponent's nose. The brute's nose exploded in a shower of blood and mucus, and the fearsome giant howled in agony.

Kane stepped back and glanced over his shoulder in time to see the first of the rearguard meet with Brigid Baptiste as Ohio cowered behind her. Brigid delivered a swift and brutal kick to her would-be attacker's stomach and the man doubled over the pain.

Trusting Brigid's abilities, Kane turned back to the brute who was standing on unsteady feet, pawing at his ruined nose.

The giant man snarled, swinging his curved blade at his opponent as Kane rushed forward once more. Kane ducked beneath the intended blow with ease, and his free hand whipped out and snagged the necklace of skulls and bones that the hulking man wore about his neck. In a second, Kane had wrapped the necklace over his hand, doubling it around and around until he was tight up against his foe. Struggling to keep from being dragged down, the brute swung his blade once again, but Kane drew his left arm back, pulling the necklace—and his attacker—off balance. The man choked as the necklace tightened against his windpipe.

Ignoring the man's cries of pain, Kane yanked at the cinched necklace again. The huge man staggered forward before falling to his knees, the metal clamped to his right leg ringing against the floor with a resounding clang. The brute's scimitar clattered to the wooden floorboards as he reached up with both hands and tried to loosen the gruesome necklace that was now strangling him. His fearful eyes were wide, their whites turning pink with blood as the man tried desperately to take a breath.

Kane watched impartially as the man danced on his knees, the awful hacking sounds of strangulation coming from his open mouth. Standing over the brute, his left arm wrapped in the hideous necklace, his right still holding the sword, Kane fixed his gaze on the struggling man's desperate eyes. "I won't let you die," he promised in a solemn tone.

The man's struggles were lessening now, as the strength ebbed from his oxygen-starved body, and whether he had heard the ex-Mag's vow Kane could not be sure. With a pained croak, the man finally keeled over and Kane released the necklace as his heavy opponent toppled to the floor with a resounding crash. The huge man had blacked out.

Kane turned back to the others and saw Ohio Blue standing with her back to the wall, fearfully watching as Brigid Baptiste struggled to fend off a trio of male attackers while even more hung back, waiting for their chance. Kane marveled at the economy and grace of Brigid's movements as she dispatched men twice her weight with a series of kicks and rabbit-style punches. She was fluid as a rushing waterfall as she defended herself from the gamut of blows aimed in her direction.

Kane winced as Brigid grabbed one man by the hair and pulled him downward until his face struck her extended knee with such force that three teeth flew from his jaw. She pulled the man's head back and, before he could recover, snapped a savage right hook into his face, obliterating his nose in a burst of blood. When Brigid finally let go of his hair, the man staggered backward as though drunk, crashing into one of his colleagues before dropping to the floor. By that time, Brigid had already moved her attention elsewhere, ducking the swinging arc of a machete before grabbing its wielder's wrist and snapping it in a brutally swift movement. The knife wielder stepped back, screaming in pain as he stared at his broken hand, which now drooped at an awkward angle from his wrist.

"Come on, Baptiste," Kane instructed as he sidled up beside her, the sword held ready. "Door's open."

Brigid didn't need telling twice. She drove her elbow into the face of another of the faithful—this one showing the gossamerlike skin of the undead—and turned to run down the corridor toward the far doorway.

Standing in place, Kane swung the long blade of the sword in a wide arc to fend off their remaining attackers, forcing them to retreat from its lethal edge. Then he turned and sprinted down the corridor after Brigid and Ohio, catching up to them with long, distance-humbling strides.

"Everybody still in one piece?" Kane asked as he leaped over the unconscious body of the brute in the skull necklace.

"I think so," Brigid said, and Ohio nodded in agreement, though the blond-haired trader was clearly shaken up by the rapid turn of events.

Behind them, four more lumbering zombies were making their way through the corridor while their living colleagues strode warily beside them, daggers ready.

Kane engaged his Commtact once again, informing Grant of their location, but his only response was dead air.

WATCHING THROUGH the rifle scope from his hiding place amid the dense undergrowth of the marsh, Grant saw the sunlight flash off a sword blade. A moment later, Kane appeared in the shadowy doorway to the low shack. Grant breathed a sigh of relief in seeing Kane still alive, but he didn't relax for a moment. Instead, his finger rested against the trigger of the sniper rifle, waiting to take out any hostiles.

As soon as Kane had stepped from the building and out onto the raised wooden platform that surrounded it, Grant saw the familiar, svelte figure of Brigid Baptiste as she ran through the doorway accompanied by the trader, Ohio Blue. Even held in place by her dark snap-brim hat, Brigid's fiery red hair was instantly recognizable.

Three for three, Grant realized with relief, a brief smile crossing his lips. The smile disappeared a moment later when he saw a lumbering form come striding through the doorway. Kane spun to face the figure, the sword held high in a two-handed grip.

Kane shouted something to his colleagues, and the words echoed back to Grant amid the chirruping background chorus of the swamp: "Get back!"

That confirmed it. Grant leaned into the SSG-550 and waited for the gaunt form of Kane's attacker to be framed in the crosshairs. Behind the strange, pale figure, Grant could see more figures emerging from the shadows of the doorway. In an instant, he stroked the sniper rifle's trigger and the lead figure's head exploded in a shower of bone and pus.

Grant ignored it, shifting the rifle infinitesimally as he centered the next of the attackers in the scope's crosshairs.

STANDING ON the wooden veranda, Kane leaped back as the zombie's head exploded in a splatter of foul-smelling ooze. Glancing over his shoulder, he ran to meet with the next zombie attacker, but even as he moved, the next attacker's face blew apart in a similar spray of pus and brittle bone.

Kane stood in place, the two-foot-long blade of the ceremonial sword held low to the ground. As the next zombie walked through the doorway and out into the sunlight, Kane heard the crack of the rifle somewhere behind him. Suddenly a messy hole appeared on the zombie's neck, a great gob of flesh blasting from it and splattering the wall. Another gunshot, and the zombie fell to the ground, a gaping wound where its chest had been just moments before.

Grant, Kane realized with a bitter smile.

"Grant has us covered," Kane told the others as he turned from the doorway. "Let's get out of here."

Brigid and Ohio ran ahead while Grant's shots rang through the swamp, felling the eerie, undead men as they emerged from the voodoo temple.

Ninety seconds later, Kane, Brigid and Ohio were reunited with Grant in the undergrowth.

"What the hell happened in there?" Grant asked, his right eye still fixed on the view through the sniper scope. Nobody had attempted to leave the shack in almost a minute.

"Bumped into a girl you know," Kane said obliquely.

"That so?" Grant asked, intrigued.

"Yeah," Kane spat. "Little misunderstanding."

"Oh, her." Grant laughed. "She does like to visit us wherever we go, doesn't she?"

"However," Kane continued, "I have another problem— my Commtact's dead."

"Mine, too," Brigid explained. "We think there may have been a jammer in the temple."

Grant raised the rifle and stood up. "No, it's affected mine, too," he explained wearily. "Can't raise Cerberus and the tracker's scragged, too."

"Shit," Kane growled. Then he turned to Ohio, favoring her with an anxious smile. "Looks like we may have some problems of our own, Ohio. We'll get you back wherever you need to go, as promised, but we won't be able to stick around."

Ohio gave him an up-from-under look through the curtain of her thick blond hair. "Oh, my handsome prince," she cooed. "You're always in such a rush. I'm going to start to think you're only after one thing from me."

"That would make things a lot less complicated," Kane growled as he led the way through the swamp toward Grant's hidden airboat.

From there it would take them almost an hour to reach the hidden redoubt that contained the mat-trans they had used to travel here. For the entire journey, Kane, Grant and Brigid took turns trying to raise Cerberus through the Commtacts, but they received no response.

Chapter 4

"The Hindus believe that everyone should bathe in the Ganges at least once in their lives," Clem Bryant explained, a mischievous twinkle in his clear blue eyes. He was a tall man in his late thirties, with a trimmed goatee and dark hair swept back from a high forehead.

Bryant's companion, Mariah Falk, looked at him dubiously. "You want me to—" she air quoted "—'bathe' in that?" A slender woman in her midforties, Mariah had short brown hair streaked with gray. While not conventionally pretty, she had an infectious smile and an inherent inquisitiveness that made her a delight to be with.

Both Bryant and Falk were Cerberus personnel. He was an oceanographer turned chef, while she was an expert geologist. Like many of the Cerberus personnel, the pair shared an unusual bond—as government employees, they had been cryogenically frozen at the end of the twentieth century and placed in the Manitius Moon Base, where they were protected from the subsequent nuclear holocaust that ravaged the Earth. They had been awoken two hundred years later, and found themselves in a world blighted by the horrors that had superseded civilization in the United States of America in the wake of the nukecaust.

"I've done it," Clem told her as they stood at the head of eight wide stone steps leading down to the flowing, muddy waters of the mighty Ganges River in India. The steps were a pale sandy color and there were numerous other people there, locals going about their business, washing their clothes, filling buckets that they rested on yokes across their shoulders, Brahmans washing the soles of their feet. No one seemed to take much notice of the two Westerners who were dressed in the immaculate clothes of the Cerberus redoubt, and whose skin was so much paler, as if they had never seen the sunlight.

Wrinkling her nose, Mariah looked out over the silty wash that swirled past the foot of the steps. "I don't know, Clem," she said. "How long ago did you do this?"

"I took a gap year after college," Clem told her. "Traveled a little. Many Hindus believe that the Ganges is the source of all life. They hold it in the highest respect. They say that Brahma washed the feet of Vishnu here and they believe that it has the power to wash away an individual's sins."

"I don't have any sins," Mariah said, shaking her head and turning away from the murky water as sunlight twinkled across its surface in dazzling white highlights.

Clem took Mariah's hand and squeezed it, looking into her bright eyes. "I'm sorry, Mariah," he said. "Bad choice of destination. Next time you can choose where we go."

Mariah looked from Clem to the wide river, then back to Clem once more. "You really bathed in it?"

Clem shrugged. "I...paddled," he admitted evasively.

Mariah let go of the oceanographer's hand and crouched down, unlacing the dusty white pumps she wore on her feet. "Okay," she said, "I can do that."

The sun beat down as, hand in hand, the two Cerberus personnel made their way down eight sand-colored steps to the water's edge.

Mariah looked down at the murky water, watching the silt swirl within it as the many activities there churned sand up in little cloudlike bursts. "Am I going to catch anything?" she asked Clem, wincing and gritting her teeth.

"Only enlightenment," Clem assured her as Mariah pulled her hand away from his grasp.

In a final rush, Mariah took the last few paces on her bare feet and waded into the flowing Ganges, letting it lap around her bare ankles and calves as she held her shoes aloft. "Eeeee," she cheered, "it's warm."

Sedately, Clem followed her in, feeling the water flowing over his sandals, splashing around his feet and soaking the bottoms of his pant legs. He turned to Mariah as she held her pumps over the sun-dappled surface of the water and tentatively waded a little deeper, making her way from a group of local women who were busy washing their clothes. To Clem's eyes, she looked happy and, for all the activity going on around her, she looked at peace.

Clem called to her as he made his way over to where his companion was now standing hip-deep in the flowing river. "Can't you feel your sins washing away?" he inquired.

Mariah dipped down and, to Clem's surprise, ducked her head under the water for a moment before resurfacing and shaking the water from her dark hair. "Oh, Clem, how did you ever talk me into this?"

"I don't recall," Clem replied with a laugh. "Did I promise infinite being, infinite consciousness and infinite bliss?"

"No," Mariah said, "you said you'd teach me to scuba dive. And take me dancing."

Clem shook his head. "I can't imagine that I would have agreed to the dancing."

"Are you saying you won't dance with me, Bryant?" Mariah asked coquettishly, reaching her arms around his shoulders.

Placing his own arms around her waist, Clem pulled Mariah closer and together they danced in the flowing waters of the River Ganges, Mariah's shoes still dangling from her crooked fingers, while all around them people carried on with their daily chores, oblivious to the couple's joy.

Mariah was still laughing five minutes later as Clem led her back to shore and they ascended the wide stone steps. "I can't believe you made me do that," she said. "I'm soaked through."

Clem stretched his arms wide and turned his head toward the sky. "The sun will dry you off," he told her. His own clothes—a light ensemble of shirt and cargo pants—had stuck to him from the soaking that he had received in the river. "I can't believe I'm back here. I feel like I'm twenty-one all over again."

Mariah walked barefoot up the steps, her sopping pumps dripping in her left hand. "Me, too," she said. "With everything we go through at Cerberus, it's funny to think that places like this still exist. It feels like they haven't changed in a thousand years."

"India suffered in the global conflict as much as any country," Clem told her. "It's just that New York and Washington, London and Moscow—those locales have been relegated to the history books. While places like this—" he swept his hand about him to indicate the magnificent vista of the wide river "—they're eternal."

"Do you really believe in this stuff?" Mariah asked as she and Clem made their way back onto the dusty road that led down toward the steps. "Enlightenment and the washing away of one's sins?"

Clem smiled. "The belief in a higher purpose, the desire to be a better person—these are universal," he said. "These are precisely the tenets that Cerberus subscribes to."

"I didn't really think of it like that," Mariah admitted, running her hand through her hair. To her surprise she found that it was almost dry already, thanks to the warmth of the pounding sun.

"Speaking of which," Clem said, reaching into a sealed pocket of his pants and pulling free an earpiece with a built-in microphone pickup, "it's about time we were heading back to work. I'll radio in and let them know we'll be entering the mat-trans in about twenty-five minutes."

Mariah nodded reluctantly as she watched Clem place the portable communications device over his ear. Unlike the field teams, she and Clem had decided to forgo the minor operation that inserted the Commtact equipment beneath the surface of the skin. As such, they were both limited to carrying robust, portable units around with them and firing them up when they needed to. Also Cerberus was less easily able to contact them while they were away from home base. On occasions such as this, Mariah reflected, that lack of contact and the privacy it brought wasn't such a bad thing.

It had been a nice afternoon, Mariah considered as Clem patched his signal through to Cerberus and waited for an acknowledgment. Although she had seen Clem around the base in the Bitterroot Mountains on a number of occasions, where the man mostly served as a cook within the canteen, having forsaken his primary discipline of oceanography, it was only in recent months that they had become close. It had started innocently enough—they had been thrown together by chance to investigate the epicenter of an earthquake. But somehow, Clem's easy manner and his dry wit had put Mariah at her ease and, more than that, had reminded her of something that most of the Cerberus personnel seemed to have forgotten—what it was like to live in a world without constant fear. Clem was capable and incisive, and he was renowned among his Cerberus peers as a fiercely logical tactician and puzzle-solver. And yet, at times like this, he seemed almost carefree in his utter enjoyment of the world about him. For Clem, it seemed, being cryogenically frozen and learning of the nukecaust were just minor blips in that delightful adventure he called life. And while the rest of Cerberus were geared up to the discovery of new horrors and the unveiling of new conspiracies concerning the ceaseless subjugation of mankind, Clem's was a very refreshing attitude to have.

"Funny," Clem mused, his rich voice breaking into Mariah's thoughts, "I can't seem to get any response from Cerberus. I hope they're not sleeping on the job."

"With Lakesh in charge?" Mariah asked. "They're lucky they're allowed restroom breaks!"

"Quite," Clem agreed, removing the earpiece and looking it over. "I wonder if perhaps the river water has got into my equipment."

"Aren't they waterproof?" Mariah asked.

"They're meant to be," Clem said thoughtfully, turning the earpiece over on his open palm. "It certainly appears to be sealed tight."

Mariah reached into her own pocket and pulled loose the earpiece that she had stowed there. "Do you want to try mine?"

Clem nodded, plucking Mariah's earpiece from her grip. In a moment he had the earpiece hooked over his ear, and was engaging its pickup mic. "This is Clem Bryant calling home. Come in, home." He waited a moment, stopping at the side of the road as a cart drawn by a donkey and laden with ripe melons trundled past. There was no response from the earpiece.

"Anything?" Mariah asked as a half-dozen chickens went rushing past, herded by a shirtless boy who appeared to be no more than ten years old.

"Nothing at all," Clem mused, and his tone was irked. "It's very unusual for two comm devices to go offline at the same time like this. In fact, I'd estimate the odds are up in the hundreds of thousands against."

"Me, too," Mariah agreed. "That hardware is old but it's military solid. Do you think maybe something else has happened? Perhaps Cerberus doesn't want us back."

Clem looked pensive as he considered what to do next. "I'm going to keep trying them while we return to the mat-trans. If there's no response by then, we may need to consider our options more thoroughly."

Mariah nodded as she replaced the white pumps on her feet, feeling the water in them squelch against her toes. Whatever else you might say about Clem, she thought, he was certainly a man who didn't ruffle easily.

THE MAT-TRANS UNIT at the end of the Cerberus ops center was just winding down, clouds of mist being sucked away by hidden filters beneath the hexagonal chamber. The door hissed back on its hinges, and three familiar figures stepped out into the antechamber only to find themselves facing a veritable wall of armed guards.

"Hey, guys," Kane said, dropping the sword and raising his empty hands as he saw the wall of firepower arrayed before him. "It's us."

Beside Kane, Grant and Brigid were also raising their empty hands to shoulder level where they could be seen, and all three of the Cerberus field team were wondering just what was going on.

A mellifluous voice called to Kane from somewhere behind the wall of armed guards and, a moment later, Lakesh came brushing past the guards to greet the three of them. "I'm frightfully sorry about all this," Lakesh began as he grasped Kane's hand in a solid two-handed shake. "We've had a major glitch with the communications relay, causing us to lose contact with everyone out in the field. Precautions will remain in place until we can track who's entering via the mat-trans, I'm afraid."

Kane nodded as Lakesh made a path through the wall of armed guards toward the main area of the control room. He saw Edwards sitting with his own field team in one corner of the room. The military man's face was red with anger and he was complaining in loud terms to his teammates about having his own people pointing guns at him on his arrival at the redoubt.

"Some welcome this is," Edwards snorted. "If I'd wanted this kinda aggravation every time I walk in the door, I'd've got married."

Edwards's teammates agreed with the man, used to his bluster.

Kane and his crew strode beside Lakesh toward the Cerberus leader's own desk.

"Our Commtacts ceased working about an hour ago," Grant explained. "I was talking with Kane at the time and suddenly—*nada*—the line was dead."

Lakesh looked from Grant to Kane to Brigid, concern marring his features. "Did everything go okay?" he asked.

Kane nodded. "Got a little hairy for a while, but you know us—managed to play things by ear."

"And what about the artifact?" Lakesh quizzed. "An alien chair, wasn't it?"

"It's Annunaki, all right," Brigid confirmed as she removed her dark hat and tossed her lustrous hair back over her shoulders. "I think it's an astrogator's chair, used for navigation in starship travel."

Lakesh stroked at his chin in fascination. "You tested it?" he asked.

Brigid made a sour face. "It kind of tested me," she admitted, still conscious of the tingling feeling on her skin where the tendrils had tried to consume her just an hour before.

"That doesn't sound so good," Lakesh mused. "Would you care to elaborate?"

Brigid began to explain about the strange chair that had held her in its unshakable clutches, but Kane interrupted. "That can wait," he said. "What's going on with the Commtacts?"

"And the transponders?" Grant added. "My tracker's still operating but it couldn't even locate my own frequency blip while I was out in the field."

Lakesh indicated the satellite monitoring and communication desks where Brewster Philboyd, Donald Bry and several others were working in unison on what was evidently a fraught and urgent project. "The satellite feeds went down fifty-three minutes ago," Lakesh explained. "We've lost all external comms, including Commtacts, monitoring and general analysis and prediction software."

"You 'lost'?" Kane asked.

"It's still down," Lakesh told him. "Our best guess is that something has taken out the Comsat and Vela satellites, and Donald and his team are trying to backtrack over the unmonitored feeds to see if we can find any evidence as to what."

Tucking a lock of her red-gold hair behind her ear, Brigid asked hesitantly, "Do you think this was a deliberate sabotage?"

"We haven't ruled out that possibility yet," Lakesh said ominously, "but at the same time it may just as easily be a natural phenomenon or a massive internal failure of the satellites themselves."

"Affecting both of them at once?" Brigid asked, clearly dubious.

"Freak weather conditions, such as a magnetic storm, could result in a block to all our signals," Lakesh suggested. "Until we can locate the specific data, we'll be hard-pressed to give any definitive answers."

"And in the meantime," Kane observed, "you don't know who's coming through the mat-trans, be they friend or foe."

"Hence the security detail," Lakesh said. "Though some people seem less understanding of the need for it than others." He inclined his head toward Edwards, who continued to rant about having a blaster pointed in his face when his team had arrived home.

Kane shrugged. "You know as well as I do that Edwards will be on his feet and covering your back at the first sign of trouble," he said quietly. "Leave the man to let off steam for a while—he'll be there when we need him."

Lakesh looked at Kane and smiled, reminded of the natural leadership qualities that the ex-Mag possessed.

While the men explained how Kane had come into possession of the ceremonial blade and outlined what had happened with Ohio Blue out in Louisiana, Brigid took it upon herself to assist Donald Bry and his brain trust in sifting through the data to verify the nature of the satellite disruption itself. Brigid had been a crucial player in many of the Cerberus team's technical advances, including the understanding and development of the interphaser, a portable teleportational device that exploited naturally occurring geomagnetic energy. With her uncanny memory and natural intelligence, Brigid's contribution of both facts and intuitive leaps had served the operatives of the redoubt well in their continued defence of the people of Earth.

When she joined them, copper-haired Bry was flicking through screen after screen of raw data along with two other computer operators, analyzing each page as quickly as they could, looking for possible errors or glitches. While it was true that Cerberus monitored much of the activities on Earth at any given moment through a variety of data streams, it would be impossible to assign an individual to continuously monitor each of those feeds, particularly given the redoubt's personnel limitations. Instead, the vast majority of the system was automated, requiring staff only to engage in the more time-responsive feeds, such as the real-time communications that the Commtacts offered.

Brigid rested against the side of the desk next to Bry, sitting on its very edge. "What do you have, Donald?" she asked brightly, gazing at the scrolling data on his terminal screen.

"A headache," Bry growled, shaking his head. "Something like this should be obvious, but I just can't pinpoint what it is."

"Looking too hard, maybe?" Brigid suggested as she peered at the data screen for a few more seconds, feeling Bry's frustration. "What time did this happen?" she asked.

"We have it as 15.37 and eight seconds," Bry responded. "But I've looked through all the satellite footage and data leading immediately up to that point and nothing is showing up."

"Both satellites went down at the same time?" Brigid asked.

Bry shook his head. "There's three seconds in it," he explained. "The Keyhole sat went first."

Brigid considered this for a moment. "What if you flip the search?" she asked. "Look outwards instead of in?"

"We've checked sunspot activity," Bry told her. "In fact, it was one of the first things that Lakesh suggested—but there's nothing."

"Do you have footage?" Brigid asked.

At a nearby desk, lanky Brewster Philboyd overheard Brigid's request and called up something on his own computer monitor with a quick tapping of the keys. "This is what we've got," he told her.

Brigid dropped down from where she perched by Bry's desk and stepped over to watch the footage playing on Philboyd's monitor. It was a fairly standard satellite photo, showing an unspecified terrain of yellow-brown color, coupled with the dark blue edge of water to one side, and a white blush of clouds drifting across the center. Brigid watched for a few seconds, noticing the slightest movement of the shadows of the clouds on the terrain beneath, confirming that it was not simply a static image. After fifteen seconds, the image abruptly cut to static.

"15.37.08," Brewster told her.

"Play it again," Brigid instructed, her eyes still on the monitor's recorded satellite feed.

Brewster tapped at his keyboard for a moment, and then the image seemed to reset itself before the sequence repeated. He ultimately played it a further seven times before Brigid caught what it was she was searching for.

"There's a shadow," Brigid told him.

By this stage Donald Bry and several of the other techs had joined them to watch the sequence for themselves, wondering at what Brigid's eerily insightful mind might discover that they had missed.

Brewster ran the fifteen-second sequence once more, and Brigid closed her eyes and counted it down in her head. "Sun's roughly overhead. Watch the cloud to the bottom right of the screen," she instructed, not bothering to open her eyes. With her exceptional memory, Brigid was able to reconstruct the sequence with incredible accuracy in her mind, and she used that facility to focus in on the information she wanted, magnifying the image in her head. "Twelve, thirteen," she counted to herself, and then she pronounced in a louder voice, "shadow."

Then the feed went dead once more, the clock indicator showing 15.37.08.

A smile played across Brigid's lips as she opened her eyes and saw Donald, Brewster and the others turning from the static-filled screen to stare at her in openmouthed bewilderment.

"It's there for a second," Bry said.

"Less than that," Brewster corrected. "What is it?"

Brigid's brow furrowed as she thought it over, trying to transform the half-second shadow on the uneven surface of the cloud into a three-dimensional object. "Pass me your notepad," she instructed.

Brewster Philboyd did so, handing her a pen, as well. Still standing, Brigid bent over the table and sketched hurriedly on the pad until she had roughed out a side view of a towering cumulonimbus cloud. Then she drew the shadow that they had seen upon it, recalling the details from her mind while Brewster brought up a static frame for reference for the others. Sketching three quick lines out from the shadow, she extrapolated its form, interpreting the shape of the object that must have cast it. It was roughly circular, fat at its girth so that it appeared to be more like a flattened or squashed circle. The edge seemed ragged, deliberately so, for Brigid's penmanship was precise. When she had finished she showed the others her sketch, and the notebook was passed around the handful of technicians standing around the desk.

"What is that?" Donald asked as he gazed at the ragged, circular object that Brigid had drawn.

"Unless it's been severely damaged, it's almost certainly nothing mechanical or man-made," Brigid said. "It's too irregular. I think it's a meteor."

"Couldn't be," Bry muttered, shaking his head with disbelief. "It would have to be pretty big to knock out both satellites so completely."

When he looked up, Donald Bry found Brigid staring at him with her piercing emerald eyes. "Is there a new rule?" she inquired coquettishly.

"What do you mean?" Bry asked.

"Meteors can only get so big now?" Brigid suggested.

In spite of himself, Bry laughed at her comment. "You're right," he said. "It's just so unbelievable. We've had trouble coming at us from every which way since Cerberus was established—aliens and parasites and insane tribal killers. I just never expected to lose everything so suddenly because of a natural phenomenon."

"Meteors don't always travel alone," Brigid pointed out. "Could be a storm, with two separate rocks knocking into our equipment."

As the discussion continued, Lakesh, Kane and Grant came over to see what the commotion was. When Bry explained Brigid's extrapolation based on the data, Lakesh looked concerned.

Kane sidled up to Brigid as the others discussed the implications of her theory. "You wouldn't have thought a big chunk of rock would cause so much upset," he muttered.

Brigid looked at him. "An impacting meteor could fall into the class of an extinction-level event, Kane," she told him quietly.

Kane made a show of looking at his hands, checking he was in one piece before looking back at her with a lopsided grin. "And yet we still stand."

Brigid shook her head in despair. "A meteor killed the dinosaurs, darling," she told him sarcastically.

"An' if it takes out lizards, I'm all for it," Kane assured her.

Chapter 5

Afternoon was beginning its soft surrender to evening, and the moon could be seen high in the pale sky, a white orb peering down from the curtain of slowly darkening blue.

Peter Marks sat contentedly on the old bench that rested on the stoop outside his front door, his glasses perched on his nose, his faithful hound Barney dozing at his feet. It had been a long day, just like any other, up at 5:00 a.m. to work the fields. Now he was happy just to sit in the cooling breeze and read while his wife toiled in the kitchen to prepare dinner. Today, Peter Marks was reading a dog-eared history book that outlined the establishment of the Program of Unification and told of the horrors of the beforetimes. It was a strange thing to read about, up here in the north, so far from the mighty villes and their sophisticated ways—almost like reading about an alien world. Here in the place that the old maps called Saskatchewan, Canada, the villes and their strictures seemed like something from another planet.

Peter Marks had worked these fields for as long as he could remember, and before that the fields had been worked by his father, who had still called him Junior until the day he died forty years ago. Two years shy of his sixtieth birthday, Peter was still powerfully built with the strength of an outdoors man and the thinning white hair and tired eyesight that came with age. The Marks Farm had stood out here in the middle of nowhere for longer than anyone could remember, yielding crops of carrots and beets and potatoes that Peter and his wife would take to market fifteen miles away and trade for everything else they needed. It was a hard life, but it had an honesty and a simplicity that Peter enjoyed. As his father had told him so many times as they sat down at the dinner table to enjoy the food he had grown, "There's a truth to growing things that won't ever be found in any ville." Peter agreed, though he found himself fascinated by the literature that the villes produced, so caught up in their little worlds and their narrow worldviews.

As Peter's eyes worked over the page, reading slowly and carefully, following the line of his finger, Barney suddenly woke up and let out a bright yip. Peter reached down and stroked the old mongrel on his flank as the dog stood and peered at the sky above the fields.

"What is it?" Peter encouraged. "What is it, boy?"

Barney barked again, standing rigid as he watched the skies. Peter patted the dog's side reassuringly as he peered out across the fields. High in the darkening blue sky, Peter Marks saw the streaks of light appear—shooting stars—a hundred or more. It was beautiful.

"Alison!" he called. "Ally, come quick."

A moment later, Peter's wife, Alison, came bustling out onto the porch, wearing an apron across her wide hips, a wooden spoon held in her hand. "What is it, Pete?"

Peter stood up and pointed to the skies. "Something wonderful is happening," he said. "Shooting stars. A hundred of them. Mebbe more."

"Oh, it's so pretty," Alison cooed. She sidled next to her husband of forty years, wrapping her arm around his strong body. "We should make a wish."

Peter looked at his wife. Her hair had turned white and her frame was stockier than when he had married her all those years ago, but he wouldn't change her one bit. "What do I have to wish for?" he whispered into her hair as the shooting stars continued their wondrous display across the heavens.

Beside them, Barney barked once more, his body tense as a coiled spring. Peter knew that the old dog wanted to run, to get closer to the phenomenon. As they watched the heavenly display, Peter realized that maybe Barney would get his chance. One of the shooting stars grew bigger as it plummeted to earth, and Peter, Alison and their faithful hound all tracked its path as that glowing spark fell through the sky and down, down, down toward the fields. It dropped toward them, disappearing behind the trees at the far end of the field, erupting there in a mighty burst of flaming sparks. Almost a second later, the sound of the impact caught up to them, a low popping against the ears like the effect of high pressure, and the ground itself trembled just a little for a few seconds, shaking leaves and apples from several nearby trees.

"That one was close," Alison said, a little tremor of fear and wonder in her voice.

"It sure was," Peter agreed, and even as he spoke, Barney yipped again and scampered down the porch's wooden stairs, running a dozen frantic steps into the field. Then the old dog stopped, looking back to his master, waiting for Peter to follow, to join him on this new adventure. "Okay, Barney. Let's go see what damage it's done."

As the strange light display continued high above them, Peter pulled his old shotgun out from under the bench while Alison went to turn down the stove. Although much rarer than when his father had been alive, Peter had still seen muties stalking the wilds now and again, most especially once dusk became night. The shotgun was a necessary burden if he was to keep his family alive. Once Peter had checked the breech, he and Alison made their way down the steps to follow the excited old mutt.

"I WANT ITS SIZE CONFIRMED and its path tracked," Lakesh ordered as he strode around the busy ops center of the Cerberus redoubt. "I want to know where it came from, what its orbital path was and—if it *has* entered the atmosphere— I want its landing site triangulated and I want a CAT team out there as soon as possible to investigate."

Donald Bry chased after Lakesh, scribbling down the director's requests as bullet points on the top page of his notepad.

"Furthermore," Lakesh continued, ticking items off on his fingers, "I want to know how many personnel are still out in the field without contact, and I want them located and brought in ASAP."

"What about the satellite?" Bry asked.

"We need to get that back online as soon as possible," Lakesh said gravely, "which means assessing the damage and repairing it as quickly as we can. Can you scramble a team to take a look up close?"

"Grant and I can take the Mantas up," Kane proposed, referring to Cerberus's stratospheric aircraft, "but we'll be pretty lost on what it is we'll be looking at."

"And with the satellites down," Grant pointed out, "we can't radio back."

"Or send photographic scans," Lakesh realized, already a step ahead of his colleagues. "Take two engineers up with you. You'll remain under their command to execute repairs while you're up there."

Kane nodded. "I'll change my clothes and be ready in ten minutes," he said, for he was still wearing the sweat-stained garb he had been in when meeting Papa Hurbon in Louisiana. "Donald, can you assign us a couple of experts for the mission?"

Bry nodded, peering at his checklist and comparing it to the personnel roster he had nabbed from Lakesh's desk. "I'll send them to the hangar bay. Ten minutes, Kane," he acknowledged.

Kane and Grant left the ops room via the main entry door beneath the Mercator relief map, and they found themselves in the large corridor that acted as the central artery for the Cerberus redoubt. Since the redoubt itself was located within a mountain, the impressive corridor was carved straight from the rock itself, with wide steel ribs bracing the ceiling high above their heads. After the energy and hubbub of the ops room, the corridor seemed remarkably quiet and still, its air refreshingly cool.

Grant sighed as he walked beside Kane down the long corridor. "I didn't expect to come back to this," he grumbled.

"Me, either," Kane agreed wearily, stretching his arms out to loosen the kinks he could feel forming in his muscles. "Never a dull moment, huh?"

Grant pushed through the door to the stairwell and held it open for Kane. "What the hell was I shooting back there?" he asked, his change of tack taking Kane a little by surprise.

Kane thought back for a second before he answered. "Beats me," he admitted. "Ohio's contact—Papa Hurbon—said something about being a Bizango. Brigid told me a little about them. They're the branch of voodoo that does all the dark stuff—drugging people to take control of their souls, turning them into zombies, that kind of scary-ass shit."

Grant shook his head. "Then they weren't already dead?" he queried.

"I punched one in the face," Kane said, "and his face came off in my hand. They weren't alive, that's for sure."

Grant shook his head, despairing. "We going back?"

Kane gave him a look. "We'll see."

YIPPING EXCITEDLY, Barney ran ahead of them as the old farming couple crossed the field, turning back every six steps to make sure that his master was following.

"You know," Alison said, laughing, "I haven't seen Barney this excited since the kids were here."

Peter laughed then, too. "He loved those kids," he said. "You remember that time we caught Christopher trying to get him to sit in the swing?"

Alison nodded. "And when Ellie dressed him up in a bonnet and pushed him around in her old pram. He looked so bewildered." She laughed again. "He's always been a good dog, I don't know where he found the patience for our horrible children."

"The same place we did," Peter told his wife as they made their way through a little copse of trees past the field, and out onto the dirt track that lay beyond.

It was getting dark out here now, and with no street lighting they were trusting the light of the moon to guide their way.

Alison glanced above them once more, watching as the display of shooting stars continued to streak across the evening sky. "It's easing up," she decided.

Barney was barking loudly as he stood ahead of them, peering out into the next field that lay past the trees. Ahead of them, Peter and Alison could see flames where one of the trees had caught fire. Peter readied the shotgun before following the old dog through the trees. He wasn't expecting trouble, but it never paid to be unprepared out here in the Outlands. "Go on, boy," he encouraged Barney. "Let's go see what hit."

Barney dashed through the trees, his panting loud in the stillness as he raced ahead to see what had happened. Peter followed, warning his wife to stay a few paces behind them.

There, just a little way past the trees, a huge chunk of rock lay in a crater, embedded in the field. It was as big as the Marks Farm cottage.

"It's a big one," Peter muttered as he followed his faithful hound into the field.

The moon glinted off the rough exterior of the rock, and Peter and Alison could see wisps of vapor drifting from it where atmospheric friction had heated its surface. Flames licked at the base of the rock momentarily before blowing out beneath the evening breeze, and a few leaves from the nearest plants continued to burn where the crashing meteor had clipped them.

The smell of sulphur choked the air, lying in a pocket around the crash site. Barney sniffed at it before rearing away and wrinkling his nose, barking twice in frustration.

Shotgun held steady, Peter Marks took another step closer to the fallen rock.

It HAD BEEN NINE MINUTES since Kane and Grant had left the Cerberus ops room to change their clothes and freshen up. Now, dressed in the standard white jumpsuits of all Cerberus personnel, a vertical zipper down the front of each suit, the two of them entered the hangar bay of the mountain redoubt. As they did so, they saw two people waiting beside the slope-winged Mantas over to one side of the vast room.

"Looks like our dates for the prom are here," Grant muttered.

"And it would be rude to stand them up," Kane responded with a chuckle.

One of their so-called dates was Brewster Philboyd, the lanky engineer who had been monitoring the Cerberus communications network when the system had gone down. He adjusted the black-framed glasses on his nose as Kane and Grant approached before proffering his hand to Grant.

"Sure you'll fit in a Manta, Brewster?" Grant joked, eying the tall figure of the man.

Brewster shrugged. "I'll hunch."

Beside Brewster stood a svelte woman with medium-length dark hair. The woman's head came up to Kane's breastbone, and she was busy studying a set of design plans when Kane approached.

"So, I guess you're my date," Kane said, leaning down to peer into the woman's face, offering an ingratiating smile.

She looked up at him, her stern expression melting to a smile. "I'm sorry, trying to get all this stuff memorized before we lift off. I'm Helen Foster, engineering. You're Kane, right?"

"Yup." Kane nodded.

"Yeah, I've seen you around," Helen said. "Word from the rumor mill is that you're some kind of bungee-jumping, action-hero type."

Kane dismissed the comment with a wave of his hand. "You don't want to listen to the rumor mill." Then he turned from Helen to the others. "Everyone about ready to get going?"

They were.

It took another ninety seconds for the Manta craft to be prepped and take off from the hangar to launch into the darkening Montana skies.

PETER MARKS ESTIMATED that the crashed meteor was as big as his two-room farm cottage, and it towered above him despite being half-buried in the dirt of the field of beets. It was roughly dislike, like a flattened circle, with protrusions of rock sticking out here and there, the wisps of smoke still trailing from them where the flames had stuttered and died. Behind the huge hunk of rock, a trail of churned-up soil ran the length of the field where the meteor had crashed across the crops, and the topmost branches of the trees at the edge of the field were still aflame.

Thankfully, the stench of sulphur was dissipating, carried away by the cool evening breeze, and it was becoming less objectionable to approach the massive hunk of rock.

Peter's faithful dog, Barney, was eagerly running around the fallen meteor now, examining it from all angles, his tongue out and his breathing loud. Now and then the mongrel would look back to Peter and Alison and bark with excitement, enjoying the discovery of something new.

Even here, a dozen paces from the fallen chunk of rock, Peter could feel the heat emanating from its surface, and where it reflected the moonlight, he saw glistening pools of water in its deepest crevices where the ice that would have clung to it in space had been boiled as it smashed through the Earth's atmosphere. The pools spat with bubbling steam as they cooled once more.

Peter turned back to his wife, who waited a few steps behind him, her white hair shimmering like a cloud of mist in the light of the moon. "Stay there, Ally."

"You think it's dangerous, Pa?" Alison Marks asked

Peter shook his head. "Couldn't say for sure, but better to be safe." With that, he strode forward, the shotgun resting in both hands, to meet with Barney where the old hound was happily running back and forth with glee.

Up close, the meteor was even more impressive, towering out of the soil like some ancient carving. "That's a big, *big* rock," Peter muttered, gazing at the cooling, lumpy surface of the meteor.

Barney yipped again and went running around to the side of the meteor, his tail wagging furiously behind him. He stopped then, barking again and again as he looked at the meteor. The old farmer strolled around the edge of the meteor to see what had captured his faithful hound's interest.

There was a gap in the meteor's surface, a crack roughly the length of a man's leg. As Peter peered closer, instinctively pushing his glasses up his nose to secure them, he saw the crack shake a little. Then the shadowy crevice lengthened by another eighteen inches, top and bottom, and the edges seemed to split just a little bit wider.

Peter stepped back and held his shotgun on the crack in the huge rock. "Hello?" he called, wondering if there was something inside the hole.

THE TWIN MANTA CRAFT streaked through the sky like golden fireworks, blasting through the clouds and up into the stratosphere. The bronze-hued craft had the general shape and configuration of seagoing manta rays, flattened wedges with graceful wings curving out from their bodies to a span of twenty yards, a body length of close to fifteen feet and a slight, elongated hump in the center as the only evidence of the cockpit location. Unusual geometric designs covered almost the entire exterior surface of each vehicle, with elaborate cuneiform markings, swirling glyphs and cup-and-spiral symbols all over their graceful wings. The Mantas were propelled by two different kinds of engine, a ramjet and solid-fuel pulse-detonation air spikes. The vehicles were not of human design; instead, they had been built by the alien Annunaki, whose incredible technology was in operation on the planet while the child race called humankind was still cowering in the trees from saber-toothed tigers.

Inside the cockpit of the lead craft, Kane was assessing the readout displays as he piloted the vehicle toward the demarcation line between Earth's atmosphere and outer space. His spherical helmet covered his whole head and was finished in the same color bronze as the craft itself. Inside the helmet, tactical displays alerted him to air pressure and wind speed, besides offering a highly advanced radar monitoring system.

Helen Foster sat in the seat behind him in the two-man cockpit, gazing through the portholes at the skies beyond. It was darkening to evening out there, and with the dark came the clear evidence of an ongoing meteorite storm as shooting stars burst across the heavens.

"Beautiful," Helen muttered as she tracked the bursts of the shooting stars.

"What's that?" Kane asked in a businesslike voice.

"Shooting stars. They look far too beautiful to be dangerous," Helen opined.

Kane toggled a switch on the dashboard, and a further burst of power was driven through the ramjet system with just the faintest tremor. "Beautiful things tend to be dangerous," he told Helen. "One way or another they're usually a lure for the unwary."

Helen smiled to herself. "You have a refreshingly blunt attitude, Kane."

"No," Kane told her, "just a hell of a lot of bad experiences."

"Cheery," Foster muttered, turning her attention back to the incredible view from the porthole.

In the second Manta craft, Kane's wingman was piloting his own engine to a steady cruising speed.

In the rear seat, Brewster Philboyd looked up from a folder of papers that detailed the full design of the Vela-class satellite. "Are we almost there, Grant?" he asked.

"Figure that depends on whether it got badly knocked off course," Grant said. "Might be that the satellite was entirely knocked from its orbit—maybe even smashed down to Earth, in which case we might never find it."

Brewster sucked at his teeth thoughtfully as he looked over the paperwork resting on his knees. "We have the designs," he said. "We could build another."

"Sounds like a lot of work," Grant said.

"Things move on," Brewster told him. "Solutions to problems, change is the only constant in this life, Grant. Are you the same guy you were when you joined Cerberus?"

Grant laughed. "Guess not," he admitted, "but I ain't a satellite."

The Manta craft continued on, fifty miles above the Earth's surface and heading into the mesosphere. The smaller meteors would burn up here, destroyed by the effects of friction on their rocky masses. In fact, the meteor storm was dwindling, almost played out now, with just the last few fragments still pummeling the edges of Earth's atmosphere with bright streaks of light as they burned to nothingness.

Kane and Grant angled their craft toward the last known locations of the two active satellites that Cerberus relied upon for much of its external data. As the two of them split off from each other, Kane grumbled to himself.

"Something wrong?" Helen asked from the rear seat behind Kane.

"Just seems weird not to acknowledge our movements over the Commtacts," Kane told her.

"If we can get the Comsat operating again, we should be able to rectify that," Helen reasoned.

"Yeah, but times like this make you realize how much we rely on tech," Kane said somberly, "and how crippled we are without it."

BARNEY LET OUT three short barks as the crack in the meteor parted a little wider. Peter Marks stood stock-still, his shotgun leveled on the widening rent in the rock's surface.

"What is it, Pete?" Alison asked, her voice coming from somewhere over the old farmer's shoulder.

"I'm not sure, Ally," Peter admitted. "Just keep back, eh?"

Something deep inside the rock was moving, and there was the hiss of escaping gas. Peter sniffed at the air, which smelled stale, like the old air of a long-sealed room. It tickled his nostrils and made the back of his throat feel dry. Barney felt it, too, rearing away from the stench and whining until Peter leaned down and stroked his head to hush him.

When Peter turned back he saw the crack in the rock's surface shifting again, and the opening visibly widened beneath the moonlight.

Suddenly Alison whispered an urgent warning, and Pete looked up in time to see another of the shooting stars drop to the sod on the far side of the field. This one looked smaller, but it still rocked the ground when it struck, a flaming burst like fireworks sparking up with its impact.

Barney yipped with the impact of the second meteor and went galloping off to get a closer look. Peter called to him, but the dog was too excited. Marks watched him go, trying to locate the second meteor in the semidarkness of evening. That one was smaller, probably not larger than a child, just a worthless hunk of space debris.

Peter turned his attention back to the first meteor as a loud cracking noise came from deep within. The noise was accompanied a moment later by growling, a low animal sound. Peter braced himself, eyes fixed on the gap in the space rock.

"Whatever it is that's in there had better show itself or I'm going to be really mad," Marks warned in a loud voice. "I have to warn you that I have a gun right here in my hands, fella."

There was another sound then, a thump like a jackhammer smashing against the hard surface of a tarmac road. The pounding came again and again, repeated at regular intervals for almost a minute. Peter looked across the field, checking that Barney was still okay. The dog barked happily, sniffing around the smaller meteorite that had landed in the field, flames licking at the leaves of the beet plants around him.

"Alison," Peter said, not bothering to look at her, "go get Barney. Make sure he doesn't get himself hurt over there."

Alison did so, giving the larger meteor a wide berth as she walked swiftly across the field calling Barney's name. The dog ignored her, too busy in his investigations.

The thumping noise from the larger rock stopped, and Peter became aware that his heart was racing, thumping faster than the pounding that had just ceased. Then, with no warning, the huge rock split apart, collapsing into the field like the two halves of a broken eggshell.

Peter took another step back from the tumbling sides of the meteor, and he saw the figure standing there, a huge, looming shadow stepping from the gap in the meteor and out into the moonlit field. As the old farmer watched, the shadow seemed to grow as the figure extended to his full height. Within that shadowy figure, multiple lines glowed orange, like the raging lava of a volcano.

THE COMSAT SATELLITE hovered at the wispy blue edge of the Earth's atmosphere, kissing the blackness of space.

"How's it look, Engineer?" Kane asked, his voice slightly muffled by the bronze flight helmet.

Helen Foster gazed out of the Manta's porthole, and there was a note of surprise in her tone when she answered. "From here? Pretty much intact," she said.

"Which would be a good thing," Kane prompted.

"It means it can be repaired," Helen told him. "But I'm just eyeballing. Can you get us closer so that I can make a proper assessment?"

Kane pulled on the yoke and the Manta swooped in a slow, languid arc past the damaged satellite, travelling at its slowest speed shy of stopping dead. As they circled it, Kane saw that one of the vanes that stood out from the body of the satellite like an insect's wings had been bent, its array of solar panels shattered. In the cockpit behind him, Kane heard Helen let out a low sigh.

"Hey," he reminded her, "I thought it could be repaired."

"I know," Helen grumbled, "but we might have to realign the solar array, and that could take a few trips."

Kane pulled the Manta around for another pass at the damaged satellite. "So we make a few trips," he said reasonably. "No big deal."

PETER MARKS HAD NEVER BEEN a religious man. Yet, as he stood there, gazing upon the huge figure that stepped out of the wreckage of the meteor and into the moonlight, he felt certain that he was in the presence of a god.

The figure looked like something that had been carved out of the rock itself. He stood eight feet tall, a great, looming form striding across the ground on legs that were jagged pillars of stone. His body was harsh, a confluence of rocks slammed together, struts and jagged ridges sticking up on all sides, not a smooth edge in sight. Two huge ridges curved up from the shoulders, like the great horns of a stag, and his rocklike body was so dark that it seemed almost as though it was just a shadow, so little of his true form could be seen in the evening gloom. But there were things glowing amid that rocky form, veins of lava, bubbling a furious red-orange as he took another step toward the terrified farmer.

Peter's finger squeezed the trigger of his shotgun, and a bright burst of buckshot blasted out, peppering the rock figure with a rattling noise. The thing didn't seem to notice; he just kept walking forward toward the old white-haired farmer.

His head, Peter saw now, was a roughly chiseled rock, not so much carved as weather-beaten, with the merest impression of a face. The eyes glowed with that same fierce magma that veined his body. The eyes were slits that rent his cheeks as though the lava would burst free. Beneath them, an ugly slash of mouth also bubbled with that lavalike fury.

Seeing the hideous face, Marks had forgotten the shotgun he held in his hands, such was his awe at seeing this huge being emerge from the meteor. "W-w-wha—?" he stuttered. "What are—? Can I help you?"

Taking another pace forward, the towering rock god reached for Peter Marks, placing his huge paw on the old farmer's head. The hand was cold and rough, feeling for all the world like a rock grazing against the farmer's forehead. The rock thing spoke, issuing words that came as gibberish from his burning mouth.

Beneath the pressure that the rock creature exerted upon his head, Peter Marks felt his knees buckle and he began sinking into the soil of the field. As he sank into the ground, Marks heard that gibberish transform, become words that he could understand.

Then the monster from the meteor said three words in a voice that sounded like stones chipping at stones. "Yes, you may."

Peter felt the thing pulling at his head then, wrenching something from deep inside him, pulling at his brain like a spoon immersing itself in honey.

Chapter 6

Peter Marks knelt down as the stone giant pressed one mighty hand to his head. He felt the memories flash before him, Eleanor and Christopher and beautiful baby Francine, who had died before her third birthday. Their dogs, Digger and Barney, their cats and the fish that had only lasted one season. The time that he and Alison had tried to raise chickens and the fowl had been taken by some wild animal or other, leaving just a coop full of feathers. Meeting Ally for the first time, and when his father had died and when hers had, and how his parents had loved her from the second they met her. The time they had painted the kitchen together and found the penciled writing under the old wallpaper. And all of it was flooding out of him, being pulled like someone tugging on his hair. It felt like eating an apple, the way that crunching into it goes through your whole head, only there was nothing to eat. There was nothing but memory.

Something burned for a moment in Peter's mind's eye, a symbol, a pictogram that he didn't recognize.

The pressure abated as abruptly as it had begun, the monstrous hand lifting from Peter's head and the creature stepping away. Peter's heart was racing, pounding against the walls of his chest as loudly as the thing's thudding had been on the walls of the hollow meteor, and his knees ached where they had been pressed down into the soil.

The rock thing looked at him for a moment, his eyes burning with the intense glow of lava. "Bow down and call me master," he instructed in a voice like gravel.

Peter Marks bowed his head, certain now that he was in the presence of a god.

DONALD BRY WAS AGITATED. He paced the Cerberus ops room, immersed in his thoughts, as Brigid and Lakesh spread out detailed maps of the northern part of the American continent. Striding over from his own desk along another aisle, mathematician Daryl Morganstern passed Lakesh his calculations of the possible landing site. Morganstern was an average-looking man with short brown hair and brown eyes, whose rounded cheeks showed dimples when he smiled. Recently, he had been spending a little time in Brigid's company, and she gave him a cheeky wink as he made his way back to his desk.

Lakesh read through the calculations before turning to Brigid.

"Judging by the position of the satellites, the meteor had to have fallen somewhere in this region," Lakesh proposed, sweeping his hand across the northwest of the continent.

"Meteors," Brigid corrected. When Lakesh looked at her quizzically, she raised a thin ginger eyebrow. "Could be more than one," she explained.

Lakesh placed the tip of his ruler down on the map, angling it as though it were an object falling from the sky. "It's a large area to cover," he decided.

"We could wait for the monitoring satellites to come back online," Brigid suggested, "but that could take some time."

Lakesh nodded his agreement. "We can do both," he said, glancing up as Donald paced by the desk. "We'll map out our best guesses for landing sites, send a team to investigate each. Once the satellites come back online, we can backup that investigation with—" He stopped, turning to Donald Bry with frustration. "Donald, will you please sit down."

Bry looked at the Cerberus director, that permanent scowl of consternation furrowing his brow beneath his mop of copper-colored hair. "I'm sorry, Dr. Singh," he apologized. "It's just so frustrating to suddenly find ourselves completely devoid of contact with our people in the field."

"It's happened before," Lakesh reminded him, "albeit to a lesser degree. Did you make up that log of personnel still out there?"

Donald reached for the notepad he had shoved into the back pocket of his pants. "I did. The CAT teams are back. We're just short two of our people now."

Lakesh enquired as to whom, and Donald read the names from his pad: "Mariah Falk and Clement Bryant."

Now it was Lakesh's turn to furrow his brow. "That's an unusual combination to send out in the field without some, um, muscle to back them up. What's the story, Donald?"

"Do you know, I'm not sure," Donald admitted after a moment's thought. "They both had some free time, and they asked to book the mat-trans for some personal business."

"Together?" Lakesh enquired.

"I...think so," Bry said slowly, as though he hadn't really thought much about it before. Then he read off some coordinates that referred to a mat-trans journey. "Do you recognize it?" he asked.

Lakesh had worked with the mat-trans network since its earliest days, and could often recognize the units just by their old code numbers. This one, however, meant nothing to him. "It's not a U.S. military designation," he said, shaking his head.

Brigid looked from Lakesh to Bry. "Overseas, then?"

Nodding, Bry edged past the guards who remained waiting before the doors to the man-trans unit and strode across to Farrell, who was back at his position monitoring the computer terminal that logged its usage. Swiftly, Bry tapped a few keys on the terminal and called up the logs for the past few hours.

"Calcutta," Bry announced, turning back to Lakesh and Brigid. "Clem requested they be routed to an old military base in Calcutta."

"Nice," Brigid said. "It's still afternoon there."

Lakesh was pensive. "I'm wary of sending more personnel out knowing that we'll be out of touch. We'll give Clem and Mariah another hour before we start chasing them."

Donald nodded. "One hour," he said.

"CLEM? CAN WE STOP a moment?"

Clem Bryant turned around and saw his companion, Mariah Falk, reaching down to loosen the white pumps she wore on her feet. "Is everything okay?" he inquired.

Mariah wrinkled her nose. "My shoes are squelching."

"Paddling will do that," Clem told her with a smile. He glanced around them, taking in the tall, leafy stalks of vegetation that grew at the side of the dirt track. He estimated that they were just five minutes away from the redoubt now, and while Mariah adjusted her shoes, Clem took the opportunity to try to patch through to Cerberus once again.

Mariah glanced up and saw Clem's mouth moving as he spoke quietly into the Commtact's pickup mic. "Anything?" she asked.

Clem shook his head and put on a brave face. "Not yet," he admitted.

"Do you think...?" Mariah began, but Clem stopped her with an upheld hand.

"That we shouldn't speculate until we are in full possession of the facts?" he finished Mariah's query. "Absolutely."

With that, Clem took a firm step onto the dirt track and began leading the way once more to the old military base on the outskirts of Calcutta. Mariah trotted after him, hurrying to catch up.

By the time they reached the old military bunker, Mariah was feeling a little more buoyant about the whole situation. "Do you know," she said as Clem tapped in the electronic code that would open the magnetic lock that sealed the underground bunker, "it wouldn't be so bad if Cerberus was gone."

Turning back to the geologist, Clem raised his eyebrows in surprise. "If sixty people had just up and disappeared, you mean?"

Blushing, Mariah laughed nervously. "No, of course not," she clarified. "It's just, if it was... I don't know—if we couldn't get back. That wouldn't be so bad."

Clem had finished tapping in the code and he stepped back as the door opened before them on its silent rollers. "You like it out here in India?" he asked without turning back.

"Not really," Mariah said thoughtfully. "No junk food."

Clem stopped on the threshold of the bunker and turned back to Mariah, perplexed.

Mariah looked at her handsome, dark-haired companion. "I like being with you, Clem," she said. "If I had to be lost somewhere far from home, I can think of worse fates than being with you." She turned away as a rising blush burned at her cheeks and neck.

Clem stood there, blocking the door as he gazed at Mariah. "Well," Clem replied, "the feeling is quite mutual, I can assure you."

A swagger in his stride, Clem led the way into the old bunker toward the ancient mat-trans units, with Mariah at his side.

THE WORLD ROTATED SLOWLY below them, a beautiful marble rolling on the black velvet curtain of space. Kane had docked the Manta craft against the side of the Comsat satellite, and now he was suited up and floating on a lifeline attached to the craft as he assisted Helen Foster with her repairs. She had confirmed that full repairs would take three or more trips just to supply the full gamut of tools and equipment that she would need to do the job properly, but Kane had urged that they get started regardless.

"The way I see it," he had said, "we're up here with Cerberus blind and deaf until we change things. The sooner we get started, the sooner we can tell them what we need."

Foster had argued with his logic, but ultimately she had agreed to suit up and spacewalk out of the Manta, if for no other reason than to study the damage up close. Now she was busy examining the broken wiring that jutted from a damaged panel on the main body of the satellite itself, while Kane worked at realigning the solar arrays by a combination of careful hammer work and not-so-careful brute force. As Foster looked up, gazing at the marvel of the Earth below their feet, Kane caught her eye. He gave her a wink through the clear faceplate of his spacesuit, before engaging the shortwave radio that was built into the suit itself.

"You about done?" Kane asked.

"No, not at all," Helen responded over her own short-wave radio, her voice sounding tinny and immersed in a low hum of static from the background radiation. "Why do you ask?"

Kane grunted as he pushed against the crossbar of one of the solar panels. The crossbar had been bent out of shape with the meteor's impact, and it refused to budge despite his best efforts to make it conform. "You'd just stopped is all," Kane told her.

"Just taking a break," Helen replied, "admiring the view."

Kane glanced over his shoulder, seeing that slowly turning blue-green marble that hung below and beneath him. "The Earth?" he asked. "Beautiful, isn't it?"

"Yes, it is," Helen responded. "It's hard to believe all the terrible things that happen down there when you see it from up here."

"Perspective's a funny thing," Kane mused. "What seems important to folks down there kind of washes over you when you get far enough away."

"Do you like it out here?" Helen asked over the short-wave. "In space?"

Kane took a long, slow breath before answering. "It's peaceful. But it reminds me of where they came from."

"They? The Annunaki?" Helen asked him.

"Yeah," Kane said. "You look down and you see that beautiful, unsullied little planet we call home. They see it as a trophy, something to be held in the tightest of grips until all life is strangled out of it." He glanced back at Helen and he saw that she was encouraging him to continue. "What possessed them to come here, to do that to people, to herd them and brand them like cattle?"

"I don't know," Helen said.

"My whole life as a Magistrate was geared toward keeping people in line, forcing them to conform to a system that held them back, held them down," Kane told her with an edge of bitterness in his voice. "They set up nine villes across America, their little baronies, bases for their experiments, their games. Worthless, evil scum."

Kane peered down at that beautiful, rotating ball of dirt and water once more, thinking about the way the Annunaki had carved it up for their own sick pleasure. And to Kane, in that moment, the Earth looked very small.

BRIGID PEERED AT THE MAP of North America that was spread out across the desk between her and Lakesh.

"Here," Lakesh said, pointing to an area to the north of the Cerberus redoubt. "Here is where it would have landed."

Brigid looked up at him dubiously. "Are you sure?"

"It's mostly guesswork," Lakesh admitted, "based on an extrapolation of the facts we know. Still, do you notice anything interesting about that landing site?"

Brigid looked at the map once more, seeing where Lakesh had marked his proposed landing site beside the letter *n* in the word *Canada*. After a moment, Brigid shrugged. "You got me."

"It's away from the old baronies," Lakesh told her. "See? We have Ragnarville here, Palladiumville across to the east, Cobaltville to the west. But this is farther north than all of them."

"The baronies are dead or dying," Brigid reminded him. "Snakefishville's fallen, Beausoliel went a while ago now. Without the barons, they lost their integrity. It's like they couldn't hold together."

"It's curious, isn't it?" Lakesh pondered. "The way that the Annunaki set up nine villes to rule America, as though they cared little for the world beyond."

"They sure made up for it once they mutated into their true forms, though," Brigid said. "They were just playing a long game, I guess."

Lakesh nodded, turning his attention once more to the map. "Did you ever wonder why they set up nine villes, Brigid? Why—specifically—nine? Why not eight, or ten? Why not one megaville smack-dab in the middle of the Deathlands?"

"The policing would be impossible," Brigid said dismissively. "You'd need hundreds of Magistrates to judge the lawbreakers of a single megacity in the heart of the dreadful cursed earth."

Lakesh laughed, accepting her point with good humour. "But why nine?"

Brigid leaned back in her seat and rubbed at her nose beneath the clips of her square-framed spectacles. "Numbers are power," she said, "just like names."

BARNEY WAS BARKING EXCITEDLY, his tail wagging, as Alison Marks led the way back to the larger meteor. She had heard the shotgun explosion and the deep voice coming from its far side, and she hurried to find out what was going on.

"Pete?" she called. "Pete, was that you?"

As she came around the fallen meteor, Alison saw that it was split in two now, a narrow, two-foot-wide gap between each half. And then she saw the rock figure standing over the bowed form of her husband, like some colossal statue of yore. For a moment she took it to be a statue, in fact, no matter how illogical that might seem, for it was so clearly made of stone.

Beside Alison, Barney whined, hunkering down between the row of beets as he eyed the shadow-drenched form. "It's okay, Barney," Alison assured the old hound. "It's okay."

As the white-haired woman spoke, the towering figure turned and pierced her with his fiery glare. She saw the molten lava behind those eyes, saw the glowing veins of fire that covered his rock body. *His* rock body, she concluded—definitely his.

"What are you?" Alison asked.

"Everything you knew is prologue, Alison Marks," the rock giant told her, finding her name in his head among the data he had withdrawn from the male farmer. He spoke with a familiar accent, Alison realized, though the voice was markedly different, rougher. It was the accent of her husband, spit through new lips, horrifying lips, lips carved out of weather-beaten rock. "I am Ullikummis. I am the all, I am the future."

Without consciously realizing, Alison Marks fell to her knees before the tenth lord of the Earth, Barney barking behind her.

Chapter 7

The air smelled different from how he remembered. In his mind, it had been sweeter, fuller, somehow *more* than this wispy, emaciated thing that he breathed in now, as though it had been tainted in his absence.

It had been more than four thousand years since Ullikummis had walked the Earth, and yet he remembered everything.

Not that he needed air, of course. He had been born here, raised here, but he had spent the intervening years trapped in an airless prison, hurtling around the farthest reaches of the solar system in punishment for his failure, in his father's eyes, and also in punishment for trusting his father to begin with. Perhaps, he realized, he had misremembered the smell of the air in his time away, it had been so long.

The meteor should not have returned. Its path had been plotted by the finest Annunaki scientists, but Ningishzidda had done something before the launch, placed a bribe so that the orbit of the prison would not stay true. And thus Ullikummis had waited, 4,500 years in solitary confinement, thinking of nothing but his revenge.

Ullikummis turned his mighty head to observe the leafy moonlit field of beetroots. The sound of grinding accompanied the movement of his heavy head, an ancient sound like shifting tectonic plates, as his neck muscles scored against his shoulder blades. The rows of crops in the field were neatly ordered, and his intense eyes could see now that the field was surrounded by others, stretching around in all directions, their own rows of crops arranged in strict, long lines. Order.

The bureaucratic ordering of nature was something that the Annunaki had always approved of, even before they had left Nibiru to conquer the stars. So, like all of the people of his race, Ullikummis was gratified to see such order. Although he had never walked upon the soil of Nibiru himself, he knew all that he needed to know of the home world, for the Annunaki shared their memories and so became bored with them, and thus with one another.

He saw, too, the two figures who knelt in the dirt of the field before him. Apekin, a male and a female. They were old, he realized, older than any apekin that he could recall. Their bodies shifted into themselves, and the color was bleached from the fur atop their skulls with age. The male's head had been full of knowledge, and Ullikummis had bonded with him momentarily so as to access that information, scooping what he needed out of the man's mind. It was a mass of contradictions—everything that the apekin, the human, understood had an exception, a caveat, an *i* before *e* except after *c*. The male's knowledge was a whole series of *i*'s before *e*'s except after *c*'s, as though these apekin could never accept absolutes. As an Annunaki, Ullikummis could only really place his trust in absolutes; everything else was simply a mystery to be ordered into its rightful place, like the rows of crops, the hordes of people.

Ullikummis had lifted language from the male's brain, taken his voice that he might speak and be understood. It had been more than four thousand years since Ullikummis had spoken anything other than one word, and that word was a name, the name of his hated father.

He instructed them with a look, the apekin farmer and his apekin wife. His eyes, molten pits of lava that glowed fiercely in the darkening evening gloom, held them in his thrall, for the apekin were such simple creatures compared to him, compared to a god.

Alison and Peter Marks rose from the ground, their heads still bowed before their new master. Peter Marks had never so much as visited a ville, and he had never submitted to another man in anything. Yet this strangely beautiful being that stood before him in his own field, the same field his father had plowed fifty years before—here was something that he would bow to without question. Deep down inside him, he knew that here was something supreme.

Rising beside her husband, Alison looked at the wonderful, stony body of Ullikummis, so ugly that it seemed perversely beautiful. He towered over her, nine feet tall, an escarpment weathered by the elements. His face was a craggy rock face, the face of a cliff, its glowing mouth lopsided, eyes uneven. And yet Alison saw now that the god was beautiful, as all gods must surely be.

Under Ullikummis's instruction, the farmer and his wife led the way across the field, back toward their sturdy old farmhouse. The dog, Barney, remained wary of the newcomer from the stars, and he kept back, following but only from a distance, growling low in his throat. Ullikummis ignored the cur, surmising it to be something less even than the pathetic apekin whom he would turn into his devoted subjects on the planet Earth.

Like those around him, Ullikummis was a creature of the Earth. He had been born here, a second-generation immigrant, a being of two worlds. Despite his Annunaki heritage, the Earth had always been his home.

Ullikummis had been a weapon in his father's hands, an assassin from the day of his birth, poised to strike in a scheme not of his making. His father had used the Annunaki's supreme command of genetic engineering to change his son, to make him the lethal engine of destruction that he needed for his plot of insurrection against Teshub, the ruler of Heaven. Where the others of his race had scales as strong as metal armor, his father had grafted living stone to the DNA sequencing of Ullikummis's young body, forcing him to grow in agony as the rock bonded with him and ultimately became him.

Even now, with millennia passed, Ullikummis remembered the pain. For he had endured years of pain to become what he needed to be, the cat's-paw of his father's devious scheme.

He had grown big and strong, and the things that had been pumped into his system caused him to tower above the other Annunaki, a great stone pillar of a thing, sturdy as a rock. In legend, they said that Ullikummis touched the sky, such was his size, but that had never truly been so. He had, however, reached for the sky, as he had gone to execute his father's final plan. He had been just eighteen years old.

IT HAD TAKEN Ullikummis two full days to climb the rocky ravines and snow-caked paths of the Semien Mountains. He had considered taking a skimmer or one of the Manta craft, but this was to be a stealth mission, and the use of a vehicle would have alerted his prey to his presence. On the way to the summit, Ullikummis had had to avoid or silence forty Nephilim warriors before he could enter the palace, and each had had to be dispatched without alerting Lord Teshub to his presence.

Teshub's palace stood high in the Semien Mountains, vast doors open on two sides that Teshub might watch the clouds passing around and below, the clouds that were believed to be his to control. Teshub himself lounged on his throne, his scaled skin rippling in the breeze, colored the yellow-white shade of the lightning he was so famous for. Without music, young women danced for him in the silent throne room, naked with taut brown bodies and small breasts, their ribs showing where Teshub had failed to feed them. The cold air made their rosebud nipples stiffen, and they cast their breath from their lungs in foglike clouds that streamed from their mouths to hang around their faces as they glided and swirled daintily around the floor of the temple for their master. Teshub barely cast them a glance as they swayed in the chill air for his pleasure, for he was more interested in the cotton-wool clouds that passed languidly by the open doors of the vast room.

Casting aside the last of the Nephilim guardsmen, his throat slit in a single, silent strike, Ullikummis strode the small flight of steps that led to the palace doors. He stepped behind the shadow cast by one of the grand pillars that supported the roof, trusting his rock-covered body's natural camouflage to hide him from a casual glance. Hidden by the pillar, Ullikummis watched for a moment as Teshub lounged against his high-backed throne. The throne room itself was sparse, with just a few items of furniture to decorate it—here a brazier burning incense, there a carved stone ornament. The enormity of the space was left free for the slowly freezing dancers to dip and twirl in the bitter air. Pillars ran the full length of the room in two parallel lines, and off to the side was a low doorway that led into the private quarters of Teshub himself.

Like the others of his kind, Teshub had many domiciles, palaces and temples full of hidden rooms and places where he might go to conduct his experiments or to investigate the nature of the many species that littered this strange new planet. It was a misapprehension to think that the Annunaki were a curious race simply because they liked to experiment, to alter the DNA combinations that they found. No, Teshub, like all of the Annunaki, was supremely bored, feeling a boredom to a level that a simpler race such as humankind could never begin to comprehend. Any experiment that Teshub conducted was done purely in an attempt to relieve the boredom of his existence. Even now, Ullikummis suspected, the dancing girls were but another of Teshub's cruel and senseless experiments, for his tongue flickered past his lips occasionally as his arrow-slit eyes lit upon the sheen of ice that formed on the women's breasts and legs as one collapsed to the floor from exhaustion.

One might say, then, that the Annunaki were cruel, but that too would be incorrect. For a god can never be cruel; a god may only be vengeful. To be cruel would suggest that the Annunaki had emotions for these apelike beasts who worshipped them, and that had never been true. But once, during the flood, Enki, a rogue member of the royal family, had shown compassion and he had helped the apekin to survive.

The wind whipped through the open throne room, and one of the virgin dancers fell to the floor, her coffee-colored skin covered in a glistening sheen of frozen sweat. Teshub laughed, a braying sound like the whinnying of a horse, echoing in the vastness of the room. The remaining half-dozen dancers turned to their fallen colleague, concern in their bright eyes. Teshub merely clapped his mighty hands together, commanding them to leave her, to continue with their dance of exhaustion.

As Teshub clapped his hands together, Ullikummis stepped from behind the pillar and revealed himself, head bowed, his burning eyes on the great god of the heavens.

"Lord Teshub," Ullikummis acknowledged, his gravel-like voice carrying the vast length of the enormous room.

"The boy," Teshub said, surprise in his tone. "What brings you to my abode?"

It had been his father's request, of course. His father wanted more control over *Tiamat,* the spaceship womb, that he might hold sway over the Annunaki's rebirth procedures and thus rule this outpost that the locals called the Earth. But Ullikummis did not tell Teshub that, for Teshub could never agree to such a request. Instead he merely smiled, a frightful thing in his mask of stone.

Caught between the two Annunaki, the dancers had stopped moving, their own attention now drawn to the freakish newcomer in their midst. Ullikummis strode powerfully forward, ignoring the glistening forms of the apekin whose teeth chattered with the cold, his eyes affixed on the resting form of the lord of Heaven. His rock feet slammed against the marble floor of the palace, sounding loud in the silence of the vast room.

"I asked you a question," Teshub spoke, irritation in his voice. "Enlil's boy, isn't it? Ullikummis."

Ullikummis nodded once in response, still striding through the static dancers, his eyes fixed on the seated god.

"Can I get you something?" Teshub enquired, gesturing at the room around him. "Wine? A virgin, perhaps?"

Still silent, Ullikummis shook his head, striding onward through the great hall, nearing Teshub with each echoing step. "You have but one thing for me, Lord Teshub," he said, "and I am here to take it."

With those words, Ullikummis revealed the object he had hidden in his hand, a blade of more than twelve inches in length, carved from stone. The stone was a glistening black in color, like onyx, and its surface seemed to shimmer in the light. An incantation was carved along the length of the blade, a warning to all who dared touch it, written in ideographs along both sides of the fearsome weapon. The writing continued in a pattern that wrapped around the hilt. The knife's incantation promised many things, including the eradication of its victim's family line from history. I Am the Blade Godkiller, the carving concluded. Gaze Upon My Bloodwork and Lament.

The weapon had been formed from a part of Ullikummis himself, carved from his body and shaped in the fires of a volcano until its edge was like a razor. It was a blade of supernatural density, holding the ability to kill an Annunaki across the multiple planes that their bodies existed on. Ullikummis had spent many long hours charging its power as one might charge an electromagnet, and had spent weeks regrowing the limb that he had lopped off to first create it. As such, its first bloodwork was his own, the loss of his right arm to become the weapon that it now clutched. The arm had re-formed, his father's technology enough to ensure that his son never need be a cripple.

The virgin dancers started to scream the second that the blade had been shown, and they ran about like headless chickens, desperate to get away from the stone assassin who strode through the mountain palace toward his target. Teshub himself saw the blade flash in Ullikummis's hand, and he reached down to the arm of the mighty throne that he lolled upon.

"Your father put you up to this," Teshub said.

By then, Ullikummis was fifteen feet from the lord of Heaven, and his pace turned from a brisk stride to a dead run. His legs pounded, rock feet slamming against the marble floor, kicking up shattered chunks of the flooring in his wake. One of the dancers had stepped into his path, and Ullikummis swept his huge left arm out, knocking the naked woman aside as though she were nothing more than the overhanging leaves of a tree. Though barely a distraction, the dancer's intervention was enough to let Teshub reach the device that was propped beside the arm of his throne, an electrified prod used to herd farm animals. Suddenly, Ullikummis found himself battered by a blast of electricity, as lightning arced across the room.

"You are your father's child, boy," Teshub snarled as he raked lightning across Ullikummis's jagged form.

Ullikummis slowed under the barrage, but only for a moment. Teshub was the lord of the lightning, more so than Marduk, who had specialized in lightning-strike weaponry. But lightning cannot destroy stone; it can only hope to leave a mark on the stone's surface, to write its lightning name there.

Pure white brilliance bathed Ullikummis's impenetrable body, playing all around him in a cone of fierce light. And still Ullikummis strode on as though caught in nothing more than a fierce gale, his eyes fixed on his target.

A rogue spark from the lightning bolt hit one of the dancing girls, catching her hair and setting it alight. She screamed out, running around the room, her hair a flaming torch above her beautiful face.

Ullikummis lunged forward then, swinging the God-killer blade through the air with a glorious note from its razor edge. The blade sang as it cut the air, a death song for those whom it sought, and Teshub leaped aside. The charge of Teshub's lightning weapon had depleted, and its shaft fizzled in his hands, burping out a last burst of electricity before finally dying.

Teshub thrust the useless weapon at Ullikummis, smashing the shaft into the rocky jaw of his opponent. Ullikummis stood his ground, feeling the metal of the cattle prod glance off his form, dismissing it without a thought. In that scant second, Teshub reached for the vial he had hidden in his skirts, uncorking it with a flick of his thumb.

As Ullikummis swung his blade at Teshub once more, Teshub flung the contents of the vial at him. Droplets of a putrid yellow liquid burst from the vial's mouth, hurtling across the room and lashing against Ullikummis's face, burning instantly. It was acid, strong enough to burn through the armorlike scales of an Annunaki.

Ullikummis's towering form bent over as the acid scarred his face, and he automatically brushed at it with his free hand, burning his fingers with that powerful liquid. Behind him, one of the dancers was screaming, and Ullikummis realized that she too had been caught in the path of the acid attack. Now her skin—once perfect as a ripe plum—was burning away from her shoulder, arm and the top of her chest, billows of oily smoke whirling around her as she cried out in agony.

Teshub drove forward, smashing the clay vial against Ullikummis's face, driving the jagged splinters at his burning eyes. "Die, you ugly freak," Teshub spat, his voice close to Ullikummis's ear.

Ullikummis staggered back, the acid still burning across his face, hissing steam pouring from his features, his head shrouded in its sizzling halo. All he could see was the floor, and he felt a wave of nausea attack him as the surface of his stone flesh bubbled. Then Teshub's knee came up into his field of vision, connecting with Ullikummis's face with a mighty crack, toppling the stone-clad assassin.

Ullikummis staggered backward a few paces before losing his footing and crashing to the floor like a mighty avalanche.

As the bubbling sensation continued against his skin, Ullikummis heard Teshub's braying laughter, mocking the attempt on his life. "You are as pitiful as your father," he stated.

Ullikummis felt the acid pop and hiss on his face, and he shook his head to clear it.

"Your father," Lord Teshub continued, "who was too scared to face me himself. So scared that he sends a child to do his dirty work. A weakling child."

At that moment, Ullikummis lunged at Teshub, leaping from the floor like a coiled spring, the smoke still billowing from his damaged face. Then he was upon Teshub again, grabbing the reptilian god by his scaled arm and yanking him closer, like some strange partner in a macabre dance.

Teshub looked into the face of his attacker, astounded. Ullikummis wore a grim smile as he glared into his opponent's eyes. The acid had burned his rocky face but, like the lightning prod, the damage was minor, irrelevant. As the lord of the lightning reared back, trying desperately to pull away, Ullikummis thrust his blade into Teshub's form, driving it through the armor-plate skin and deep into his body, wedging it between the lord's ribs.

"Your reign is over," Ullikummis stated, his magma eyes glued on Lord Teshub's. "Free your hand from *Tiamat*. Give the codes over to me."

Lord Teshub looked at Ullikummis and he sneered. "To your father, you mean," he spat, "that he might rule the heavens in my stead."

In response, Ullikummis merely twisted the blade, driving it deeper into Teshub's body.

Teshub grunted, feeling the brutal force behind that blade. "You're a fool, boy, an ugly, misshapen thing that your father spawned simply to do his dirty work. And when he's finished with you, when all the bad deeds have been done, do you really think he will give you a cut of his kingdom?"

Savagely, Ullikummis pulled the stone knife from Teshub's body, glaring into the other's eyes as the Annunaki lord collapsed to the floor in a pool of his own rich blood. "The *Tiamat* codes," he instructed.

Though he did not know it then, that day would be remembered in Hurrian mythology as the day that Ullikummis challenged Lord Teshub for control of the Heavens. One of the dancing girls had survived and related it as "The Song of Ullikummis."

Teshub did as he was told, but far worse things would come before the feud between him and Ullikummis's father came to an end.

ULLIKUMMIS RECALLED that moment in such detail, as though it had been just an hour ago, as though he were still there. He could still feel the force in his hand as he drove that stone blade between the ribs of the astonished Lord Teshub, turned the knife to deepen the wound. Though a part of himself, the blade had been fashioned in the depths of the planet, fired by the flames of the Earth itself. There had been another Annunaki there, too, one who had made the underground his home: the dreamer, Upelluri.

Upelluri had taught Ullikummis a great many things about patience, about pursuit of a target. Ullikummis had come to him in the role of learner, student, a vessel in need of knowledge. But, really, he had come at his father's urging. It had only been later, as he hurtled through the bleak vacuum of space in that prison cell, that Upelluri's teachings had come back to him with renewed vigor, their meaning that much clearer, showing new and unexpected facets, a renewed relevance. The whole time in that stone cell, Ullikummis had only said one word—the name of his father, upon whom he would have his revenge.

They had stopped, Ullikummis realized, the thoughts of Upelluri's teachings still resonating in his capacious mind. The stone god looked up and saw that Peter Marks and his wife had stopped before a building that sat amid the carefully tended fields. Approximately the size of the boulder prison he had been trapped in, the building was like nothing that Ullikummis had seen before, and he equated it to a small palace, containing but a few rooms. It glowed from within as though on fire, a brightness shining from its windows like the magma seams that showed across his own body.

The construction appeared to be of wood, raised from the ground on three-foot-high struts, a wooden veranda all around. There was a seat beside the open main door to the building, and on the seat there lay a strange thing that fluttered in the night breeze.

Intrigued, Ullikummis stepped forward, taking the three wooden steps in a single stride. He reached for the fluttering thing, like an insect's wings or a child's toy, and held it in his hand. It contained many leaves that fluttered with the wind, and on each of these white leaves was a pattern, each pattern different from the one before.

Knowledge, he realized.

Each mark, curved as a scorpion's tail, was knowledge. He was holding knowledge.

It was strange, this world. He had expected to see the towering cities of the Annunaki decorating the globe like shimmering jewels, and yet all that he saw were fields and the wooden house, smaller than any temple.

Casting aside the bound leaves of knowledge, Ullikummis turned then, assessing the ordered rows of crops that surrounded the farmhouse. Finally, he turned his burning gaze on the apekin farmer and his wife. "For whom do you toil?" he asked.

"For whom, great one?" Peter Marks asked, confused by the question.

Ullikummis stretched his arm out to encompass all that he saw. "You work these fields, yes?" he stated. "For whom?"

"F-f-for ourselves," Alison Marks stated timidly when her husband continued to struggle with the question.

"And for market," Peter added. "We sell produce at the market."

Ullikummis looked at the man, trying to comprehend what he was saying. "Then to whom do you pledge fealty?" he asked in a reasonable tone.

The aging couple looked mystified, unsure how to answer the question.

"Lord Marduk?" Ullikummis prompted. "Or mayhap Lady Lilitu? Or a compassionate lord—Enki, perhaps?"

"I do not recognize those words, my master," Peter Marks said after some seconds of consideration. Already several feet shorter than his new master, the farmer looked frightened, cowering before the great stone god Ullikummis. "We are just farmers. The people in the south call us Outlanders sometimes. We have no master."

The farmer's final words struck Ullikummis like a physical blow. *No master.* How could this be? Had the Annunaki's grip upon the races of the Earth weakened so in his absence? Was such a thing even possible? In his immeasurably superior brain, Ullikummis dissected the apekin's statement. "Who calls you Outlanders? Which people?" he demanded.

"The people in the villes," Peter replied. "They look down on us for the way we live."

"They think we're simple," Alison added. "Dirty. Inbred. But we're not. Not all of us, anyway."

From his brief bonding with Marks's mind, Ullikummis understood the concept of the villes. They were like the old cities that the Annunaki had scattered across the world, like beautiful Eridu and golden Nippur. "And these ville kin—do they pledge fealty to a master?" he inquired.

Peter Marks nodded. "The barons rule the villes." As he spoke, the old farmer clambered up the wooden steps, his head dipping low in supplication as he passed his new master, and he reached for the book that Ullikummis had discarded but moments before. "I was just reading about them," the farmer explained. "Look."

With that, Peter showed Ullikummis an illustration in the pages of his book on the Program of Unification. The illustration showed the architectural structure of a ville, with its high walls and towering centerpiece. Ullikummis looked at the line drawing for a long time, trying to render it into three dimensions in his mind. He recognized the high walls and the towering Administrative Monolith at its center as a temple. This very design had been used beside the banks of the River Euphrates many millennia ago, its obsidian walls carved and polished by the Annunaki's slaves.

"The barons live in the villes," Marks continued as Ullikummis stared at the drawing, "where they make the world safe, or so they say. There are nine of them in all and they—"

"Nine," Ullikummis interrupted. *The royal family.*

"I c-can read the book to you, my master," Marks said, timid before the new lord of the Earth. The pages of the book rustled in the wind as the farmer held it in his hand, while Ullikummis ignored his suggestion.

Far from the hubbub of the villes in the south, Peter Marks did not know that the barons had disappeared many months before, that they had evolved into their true forms, the nine ruling members of the Annunaki royal family.

But Ullikummis knew then, without even needing to investigate. "This is a temple," he said. "There were nine great temples in the days before, one for each of the royal family, each with its own laws and traditions, and around which a city was built. Nine, the number of solitude, of individual strength."

Peter and Alison Marks peered up at the magnificent stone creature as he pondered this discovery.

"I shall build the tenth," Ullikummis stated. "A city so majestic that it shall dwarf any previous rule. The City of the Tenth. For ten is the number of the uncontrollable. Ten is the number of Ullikummis."

Peter and Alison Marks bowed in unison, eagerly accepting the new world that was promised. "Yes, my lord," they said as one, trusting of this new design that would reshape the planet Earth.

Ullikummis had traveled for 4,500 years, and the only word he had ever spoken in all that time was his father's name. His father, who had betrayed and banished him. And now he would have revenge on his father, and on all the Annunaki who had dared turn their hand against him. The Tenth City was only the beginning in his plan to remodel the planet Earth to satiate his whims and to achieve his bloody goals. Upelluri's teachings had granted him patience and the knowledge of when he must act, of when he must strike like the poised cobra.

First the city, then the army and then the revenge, pure as blood. He would wrest control of *Tiamat,* wrest control of the Annunaki bloodline for the next hundred thousand years. And he would finally have revenge on that one name he had repeated once a day, every day, as he had hurtled through space in his tiny prison cell.

Revenge on his father.

Revenge on Enlil.

Chapter 8

It had been a day of celebration in the palace of Enlil in the golden city of Nippur. Ullikummis had returned from his quest in the Semien Mountains brandishing the key codes to *Tiamat*. Control of the Annunaki bloodline would now rest solely with Enlil. Teshub had gone into hiding, licking his wounds from his defeat at the hands of the young prince, still unaware that the multidimensional knife wound would see him dead in a week. Ullikummis was eighteen years old.

Enlil laid on a great feast to celebrate the return of his son, with delicacies from all across this new world, meats of a hundred different colors and shapes. Among the celebrants were Ningishzidda, the genetic engineer, and Lord Marduk, who ruled over the nearby city of Babylon. Platters of fruit had been arranged in glorious towers all over the room—one stack had been shaped to look like the city of Nippur, another like *Tiamat* herself, her swooping dragon form dominating one whole table. Delicate finger bowls had been positioned beside every place setting, scented rose petals floating in the water so that the celebrants might wash their hands between courses.

Lord Enlil himself sat at the head of the table, as ever, and was served first by the apekin slaves. However, Ullikummis had been invited to take the seat at his left, normally occupied by Enlil's most prized consort. At that time, Enlil's consort was timid Ninlil, whose delicate Annunaki beauty had entranced Ullikummis's father and driven him to acquisition by way of rape. Ninlil was Ullikummis's mother, though they rarely spoke.

"This is a proud day," Enlil announced to the revelers, raising his cup to his stone-clad son.

Ullikummis tore at a strip of antelope flank, its juices dripping down from his mouth. "Thank you, Father."

"Teshub is deposed," Enlil continued, "running for cover. What do you say to that, Ningishzidda?"

The genengineer looked up from his place at Enlil's right, chewing on a leg of chicken as he spoke. "Your boy performed as you asked," Ningishzidda said. "He is something for a father to be proud of."

"On this day, you are as much his father as I," Enlil told the genetics expert.

While there was truth in the statement, for Ningishzidda had altered Ullikummis's body with his genetic manipulations, it was strange for Enlil to be so magnanimous, the boy realized. Usually, his father's arrogance would assure that he took the credit for any and all great works, whether he truly had a hand in them or not. Truly, the dethroning of Teshub had left his father in a generous mood.

As Enlil discussed the new world balance with the genengineer, Ullikummis's fiercely glowing eyes turned to his mother, who sat alone at the far end of the table. Ninlil looked distracted, and she had barely touched the food. As he watched, Lord Marduk—whose scales were a magnificent cobalt blue—moved from the buffet spread and sat with Ninlil, speaking to her in intimate, hushed tones. Ullikummis watched for a moment, until Marduk looked up, almost as though he felt the prince's magma eyes upon him. As Marduk did so, Ullikummis turned away, making as though to cleanse his hands in the rose water of his finger bowl. Then he turned his head and joined the conversation his father held with Ningishzidda, aware that the cold eyes of Lord Marduk were still upon him.

IN A DISUSED MILITARY installation close to the Ganges, Clem Bryant was making one final check of the mat-trans unit. Mariah Falk watched him.

"Everything okay, Clem?" she asked.

Clem stroked his short beard in thought, then nodded. "One can never be too sure, particularly when other technology fails."

"I quite agree," Mariah said, even though she didn't. She was tired and hungry and she just wanted to go home.

Clem walked around until he stood beside her at the door to the ancient mat-trans unit, its armaglass a tinted burgundy. "Shall we?" he asked, holding his arm out for Mariah.

Mariah took his arm and together they entered the mat-trans as though entering a school dance. "You know, Clem, no matter how long I spend with you I don't think I'll ever quite—" She stopped, as though lost in thought.

"Quite what?" Clem prompted.

"Second-guess you," Mariah said with a definitive nod.

"Well now, a little surprise is a good thing," Clem told her as the mat-trans warmed up and the familiar mist filled the chamber.

A moment later they were back at Cerberus, transported instantaneously through the quantum ether to the mat-trans chamber in the anteroom adjacent to the main operations room. Clem and Mariah stepped out of the mat-trans and straight into a wall of armed guards, each one cocking his rifle or automatic pistol as he jabbed it at their faces.

"We give," Clem said, holding his empty hands up in the air in surrender.

From his position at a side desk, Lakesh looked up and approved their entry. "It's good to see you two back on-site," the good doctor said. "We've been having a few problems."

Clem smiled. "So I see. This was hardly the welcome we expected."

"Communications are down," Lakesh told them both as they shuffled past the armed guards, "which means we can't monitor who's coming through the mat-trans."

"Had any unwelcome visitors?" Mariah asked.

"Not so far," Lakesh said, "but it pays dividends to be cautious. With you two back, we can reengage the firewall and block potential intruders from accessing our mat-trans."

Clem nodded. "It always was a curious design, putting what was effectively an open door in the middle of a secure military base."

"Each one was well guarded," Lakesh recalled. "It was a minimal risk."

"But still a risk," Clem mused. "If anyone had overpowered one base they would potentially be able to access anywhere in the network in an instant."

"National armies and their war games are long behind us, I hope," Lakesh told them both with a jovial smile. "Now, however, we have a somewhat different situation to address, and your reappearance couldn't be more opportune. Mariah, I want you suited and ready for travel in thirty minutes."

Mariah looked at her boss, the exhaustion she felt mere moments before replaced with adrenaline. "Just let me wash the Ganges off me and I'll be ready in twenty."

"Good girl," Lakesh said as Mariah rushed out the doors of the ops room to get showered and changed.

"And me?" Clem asked.

Lakesh turned to look Clem in the eye, genially patting him high on the arms. "Clem, my dear and respected friend," he began.

"Yes?" Clem encouraged.

"There is one job to which you, and only you, show such mastery that this facility would grind to a halt without you," Lakesh said with gravity.

"I'm ready for anything," Clem, an expert oceanographer, assured Lakesh. "Just point me where you need me to be."

"I knew I could count on you," Lakesh said with a smile, pointing to the nearest staircase in the corridor beyond the ops room. "It's proving to be a very long and trying day, and an army marches on its stomach."

Clem smiled. "You need me in the canteen," he realized.

Lakesh nodded. "Thank you, Clem." Clem gave a casual salute as he walked briskly down the corridor toward the stairwell door. "Oh, and Clem," Lakesh called after him. "If you could wash the Ganges off yourself, as well…"

"But of course," Clem agreed. It felt good to be back where he was needed.

ULLIKUMMIS STARED around the Saskatchewan fields, looking for the golden spires of the cities, the villes. It amazed him how little progress the Annunaki had made in four thousand years. He had expected to return to Earth and find the whole planet remodeled, taken on the appearance of fabled Nibiru. He had expected the apekin to be long since destroyed, eradicated from the planet like vermin,

their usefulness long since passed. Yet here he stood, at the
edge of a field with two free, masterless apekin and their
pet, as the moon cast its mirror light.

"It must change," he vowed before turning back to the
farmstead. Peter and Alison Marks stood patiently awaiting instructions from their new lord and master. "I shall
use apekin," Ullikummis said. "People. Where can I find
people?"

Alison rubbed her head and screwed up her eyes as
though something inside her hurt. "The market," she announced. "People meet in the market."

"It's about fifteen miles from here," Peter added.

"Show me," Ullikummis instructed.

Peter began to walk down the path that led to the dirt
road, and Barney yipped once before following.

"It's late," Alison realized, still standing on the farmhouse porch. "The market will be empty until morning."

"The journey must be taken," Ullikummis stated simply,
and that was encouragement enough for the party to begin
trekking down the long dirt track that led toward the distant
market town.

Thousands of years before, Ullikummis had learned to
his cost that an inevitable journey was to be started immediately, lest your enemies reach your destination before
you.

AFTER THE CELEBRATORY FEAST at his father's palace, Ullikummis had returned to the cavern dwelling of his teacher,
Upelluri, buried deep beneath the ground. His father's feast
had lasted three full days, and others of the Annunaki royal
family had attended to congratulate Ullikummis on his
victory, including Lord Zu, Lord Utu and the entrancing
Lady Lilitu, who arrived with a slave apekin on a leash
who would do degrading tricks at her bidding. Ullikummis

had accepted their cheer with good grace, but he found his thoughts turning away from the golden palace, feeling enclosed by its walls.

On reaching the cave entrance, Ullikummis made his way swiftly within, down into the network of caverns that led beneath the earth, out of the harsh sunlight that Upelluri so reviled. Upelluri had taught him much about the necessary mental state of a warrior, and it was he who had turned Ullikummis from a genetically modified engine of destruction into a formidable assassin and planner. If the assault on Teshub's mountain palace had seemed easy, that was down to Upelluri's training.

When he had first entered these caverns, six years before, he had perceived nothing but shadow, black on black. He had still had his own eyes then, before Ningishzidda had replaced them with the burning orbs that now sat beneath his rocky brow. His new eyes could see in the dark, lighting his path like a candle's flame. So when he saw the body of Upelluri in the sun room, his breath caught in his throat.

The old Annunaki was lying in a ball beside the astrogator's chair, hands and ankles tied, drool spoiling his moonlight-colored scales. The blackness was there, too, all over his skin like galloping beetles, the disease that had forced him to live in shadow, away from the treacherous sunlight of the planet Earth.

"Upelluri?" Ullikummis asked, his voice so low as to be just another breeze in the windy caverns.

The great master turned and Ullikummis saw the fear in his wide eyes. "You must run," he instructed, his voice a harsh whisper, "before they come for you."

"They who?" Ullikummis asked.

"They're here already, Ullikummis," Upelluri said. "Run while you can."

"I won't leave you," Ullikummis stated, and he leaned down to pick up the Annunaki master, reaching his rock arms around the smaller figure's diseased body. As he did so, there was a noise behind him, and before he could react something heavy collided with the back of his head.

Ullikummis fell forward with the weight, splaying over the body of his teacher and knocking into the telescope that stood in the corner of the cavern. He turned then, shrugging aside the heavy rock that had been used to fell him, lifting himself up. Some kind of powder had burst from the rock, spraying his upper body from behind in a wash of white like flour. Striding out of the darkness, his pristine scales rippling in the breeze, came Lord Enki, a sword in his hand with a fierce blade almost as long as he was tall. Enki was the despised brother to Ullikummis's father, Enlil, and had not been invited to the palace celebration.

"Uncle," Ullikummis acknowledged, his magma eyes watching the Annunaki lord pace toward him.

Enki nodded in response, hefting the mighty sword as he strode closer.

Behind his uncle, Ullikummis saw others of the Annunaki: Lord Marduk, standing in the deepest shadows of the cave, a blowpipe in his hand, and Teshub, whom Ullikummis had deposed just days before, a healing patch strapped to his wounded chest.

Ullikummis struggled to his feet, but he felt woozy. It was more than the blow to his head, he realized. There had been something on the rock, some agent that reacted with his altered constitution, slowing his thoughts. Warily, he turned to face his uncle, balling his mighty hands into rocklike fists.

"My father will kill you for this," Ullikummis spat, swinging a fist at Enki.

Enki avoided the blow easily, stepping aside as it breezed past him. Ullikummis had slowed down noticeably, telegraphing his movements long before he made them. As he lashed out with another punch, Enki seemed to dance around him, playfully avoiding this lumbering behemoth.

From down on the ground, Upelluri was muttering instructions, urging Ullikummis to run while he still could. He had been present when the three Annunaki overlords had discussed their intentions, knew the hideous fate that they had planned for the young prince.

Then Enki stepped close, swinging the huge blade that he held in a two-handed grip. The blade sliced through the air in a low strike until it met with Ullikummis's legs, just below the knee.

Ullikummis grunted, staggering backward under the force of that powerful blow. He looked down and saw blood streaming down his ankles where the blade had hacked into him like an ax at a tree trunk. Remarkably, the blade had cut through his natural armor.

As Ullikummis staggered, Lord Marduk raised the blowpipe to his lips and blew, unleashing another burst of the fine white poison that had covered the rock that first felled him. The cloud of white showered Ullikummis, making his mind reel and his stomach retch.

The young prince reached out, his hand slapping against one of the walls of the cavern with the crashing of rock against rock, his cut leg pumping blood over Upelluri's papyrus notes where the Annunaki lord had tracked the movements of the sun. With his head feeling heavy, Ullikummis struggled to turn to face his attackers, confusion the primary emotion in his mind. "Why?" he asked.

Drawing the sword back, Enki looked at him with sadness. "My brother has made you into a monster to satisfy his own desires," he said. "I turned a blind eye to his squabbling with the other lords, but I cannot ignore what was done to Teshub."

Ullikummis swayed as he tried to gather his thoughts. Was Enki in league with Lord Teshub? But why?

As Ullikummis pondered, struggling with his slowed thought process, Enki swung the mighty blade, cutting into the god-prince's legs once more. Ullikummis cried out as the blade hit, slicing through his legs, removing his feet in a grand sweep. Lopped off, Ullikummis's feet flew across the room, slamming into the far wall with a crash of stone against stone. Blood pouring from the stumps of his ruined legs, Ullikummis tumbled to the rocky ground of the cavern in agony.

Enki was saying something, but his words seemed distant, as though he spoke from behind a screen. "My brother must not take *Tiamat*," he said to Marduk and Teshub. "If we move quickly, we may yet alter the key codes and block his access."

The three conspiring Annunaki strode from the cave together, leaving Ullikummis lying in his own blood as the aged Upelluri struggled with his bonds.

THE CERBERUS TEAM had a variety of ways to travel across the vast distances that their exploration and defence of the planet required. The interphaser was a portable matter-transfer device that, like the military mat-trans units, allowed an individual to be teleported from and to numerous locations across the Earth and even onto other planets. The interphaser exploited an ancient web of powerful, naturally occurring lines of energy stretching across the globe. The vortices were called parallax points, which provided access to the geomantic energy and formed a powerful technology so far beyond ancient human comprehension as to appear magical. The interphaser was a squat, broad-based pyramid of about twelve inches in height finished in a dull metallic sheen. By interacting with the energy within a naturally occurring vortex, the interphaser became the catalyst in temporarily overlapping two dimensions. The system could not be used everywhere, for it relied on the parallax points, the mapping of which had not yet been completed by Cerberus.

The development of an operational interphaser was the combined work of Brigid Baptiste and Cerberus scientist Brewster Philboyd, and had taken many months of trial and error to achieve. Most recently, theoretical mathematician Daryl Morganstern had been working on understanding and refining the system further.

Travel via interphaser was accompanied by an explosion of rainbow light from the top and bottom of the device, as beautiful as the opening petals of a lotus blossom. Right now, that magical lotus blossom had just burst forth in an area of old Canada known as Saskatchewan, where Brigid Baptiste, Mariah Falk and Cerberus warrior Edwards stepped forth from the quantum ether. It was nighttime and they had arrived in an empty field.

As the blossom of light faded, Brigid crouched down and shut off the interphaser, folding it up on itself and placing it in a metal carrying case. Beside her, Edwards had drawn his Heckler & Koch and was scouting around the area. Dressed in camos, Edwards was a military man through and through. Broad-chested, with a stern bearing, Edwards was known for his impatience, a quick temper ever bubbling just beneath the surface. He wore his hair in a crew cut so severe as to appear almost bald, which drew attention to his mangled right ear where a bullet had clipped it less than a year before.

"Area is secure," Edwards announced, not bothering to look back to his companions.

Mariah Falk, who had replaced her shorts and shirt with the more formal outdoor jumpsuit of the Cerberus team, rolled her eyes as Brigid looked at her. "He means there's no one about," she clarified with a resigned sigh.

"I know," Brigid said, smiling. "He may do things by the book, but he means well."

"I guess," Mariah agreed. "Just, you know, I wish he'd calm down. He reminds me of the puppy I had when I was a kid. 'Enough with the excitement already, Bonzo.'"

Brigid laughed, and Edwards turned back and fixed her and Mariah with a stern look.

"Try to keep it down there, girls," Edwards told them fiercely. "There could be anyone just waiting to pounce out here."

Brigid looked around the moonlit fields that stretched away in every direction. They looked empty. "I think we'll be all right, Edwards," she assured him, "but thanks for the tip."

Edwards saluted. "Just doing my job, ma'am."

Under her breath Mariah Falk suggested that Edwards might disarm the scarecrow three fields over if he wanted to guarantee their safety further. Failing to hear her, Edwards continued searching the area in a series of short runs, his pistol raised and ready.

The interphaser had accessed a parallax point marked solely by a half-buried stone of about three feet in height. It looked like a grave marker or a milestone, though Brigid couldn't be sure of its purpose. One of the strange things about tracking parallax points was that sometimes they weren't transported to towering pyramids in Giza or stone circles in Hastings; instead the oddest items turned out to have some ancient and long-forgotten significance.

"We need to head east," Brigid announced, "about a mile and a quarter."

"Route march, people," Edwards stated as he turned. "One, two, one, two…"

While Edwards led the way to the east at a brisk march, Mariah sighed once again. She had been on her feet all day, and hadn't expected to be called on for an eleventh-hour geology consultation. Why, oh why, couldn't she have chosen to pursue zoology instead?

THIRTY-FIVE MINUTES LATER, the Cerberus field team found themselves at the meteor crash site. Although working from sketchy data, Lakesh's boffins had triangulated its location well enough that the team had managed to locate it with reasonable ease. They had split up, with Mariah and Brigid checking the fields to the left together while Edwards scoured the fields to the right on his own. They finally congregated on two meteors in a field of beets and, in hindsight, Mariah laughed that the burned branches of the nearby tree should have set off alarm bells earlier than they did.

The nearest meteor was fairly small, little bigger than a child, and it had carved a niche into the ground, burying itself among the floppy leaves of the vegetables. Mariah bent down to examine it, running the tip of a pen across its surface and testing its strength. "It's igneous," she said, "so we should be able to date it."

"Where's it from?" Brigid asked.

Mariah shrugged. "I'd need to run a proper spectrographic test on it to tell you that."

Brigid nodded and led the way across the field to the second meteor. This one was much larger, as big as two family rooms, and it featured a long, vertical crack across its center, so deep that it seemed to have split the meteor in two.

"Reckon this is what hit us, Miss Baptiste?" Edwards asked.

Looking the meteor up and down, Brigid nodded. "It's big enough," she said. "Even a glancing collision from this would potentially knock a satellite out of whack. As part of the meteor storm that collided with the satellites, this one would have done one doozy-load of damage."

Mariah came over to join them, sealing an evidence bag in which she had placed scrapings from the first meteor before securing it in her backpack. "Phew," she whistled, "that there is a lot of rock."

"It is at that, but it's good to get a professional's take on it," Brigid agreed. "Is it the same composition as the other one?"

Mariah stepped closer, placing one hand on the meteor's surface. It felt cool. "I think it may be from the same rock," she said. "Probably split up when it hit the atmosphere, so little fella over there got lost from his mommy."

"There's another one here," Edwards said, pointing to the ground, "and another. And another there."

When Mariah looked she saw a half dozen chunks of rock, not one of them larger than her balled fist. As Edwards had suggested, they all appeared to be of the same type, and had probably come from the main meteor as it got slammed by the powerful forces of atmospheric friction. "This was a bigger rock to begin with," she stated. "Thank goodness it broke up before hitting the ground. Something that big would have caused a major seismic event."

Brigid was still staring at the main rock, looking at the vertical chasm that marred its surface. "Edwards? You have a flashlight there?"

Edwards handed Brigid a flashlight from his backpack and Brigid switched it on, its bright xenon beam suddenly dazzling in the darkness. She ran the beam over the hole in the rock, peering at a hollowed-out area she could see within.

OVER FOUR MILLENNIA EARLIER, in the darkened cavern beneath the Earth, Enlil stood over his crippled son, stark disappointment on his face. Wearing his night cloak, the god-king had brought six Igigi slaves who carried lanterns that sparkled with flame, as well as Ninlil, his wife and consort. Ninlil stood beside the entrance to Upelluri's hidden sun room, as far from her son as she could be without outright leaving the room.

"The codes that Teshub gave you were useless," Enlil told his son as the eighteen-year-old prince lay hobbled, his feet hacked from his legs.

"Father, please," Ullikummis pleaded from the ground, "get medical help. If not for me, then for Upelluri." The wise Annunaki, Upelluri, remained bound, and his breathing was shallow.

Enlil glared at the bent form of his son as he paced angrily around the dark cave, circling the old astrogator's chair that stood to the side on its plinth. "I have no access to *Tiamat,*" he growled. "What access I had has been revoked. I can no longer change the codings. No longer produce Nephilim warriors."

"Please, Father," Ullikummis gasped, blood congealed on the stumps where his feet had once been.

Enlil stepped toward his son and stood there, glaring down at him. "Marduk was in league with Teshub," he said. "He has the codes now."

"I'm sorry, Father," Ullikummis sniffled. "I did not know—"

Enlil cut him off with a swift kick to his son's face. "Marduk is the Lord of Heaven now," he snarled. "Marduk!"

With that, Enlil strode from the cave, his cloak catching the wind behind him. "Bring them," Enlil said as he passed the Igigi slaves.

As the Igigi worked at stretchers with which to carry Ullikummis and Upelluri, Ninlil walked across the sun room to speak with her wounded son.

"This will go down as a dark day in Annunaki history," she said.

"I'm sorry, Mother," Ullikummis said, his voice little more than a whisper. "I did everything that Father asked of me and yet..."

"Shh," Ninlil hushed him. "You don't need to apologize to me. You are your father's son, Ullikummis—the product of his loins and his hatred, both of which burn brightly. He put eighteen Earth years into creating and nurturing you. Today your father learned that even eighteen years of channeled hatred isn't enough to achieve his desires."

"I'm sorry," Ullikummis said again, unable to think of anything else.

"He will kill you," Ninlil said. "Not because of what you did, but because of the failure you represent, a loose end he cannot tolerate."

"Please tell him—" Ullikummis began, but his mother hushed him with a stern look.

Then she leaned close and whispered so quietly that it was almost as though she hadn't said anything at all. "Your father cannot be told, Ullikummis," she said, "but I will do all I can to make sure that you survive that you might one day do the same for me, as I have foreseen it. I will stop him from executing you. Beyond that, I cannot promise anything else."

Ullikummis thought, lying there in the dirt of the cavern. He thought of his father, and of the lessons that Upelluri had taught him about his foes and their weaknesses and how, even at the start, Upelluri had known that Teshub was never Ullikummis's real foe. It had been his father, and his father's pyrotechnic rage all along. As he thought, one name inevitably came to mind. "Ningishzidda," he said. "Get me five minutes with Ningishzidda, and instruct him to destroy the evidence of the meeting, hiding it even from me, or Father will kill you."

Ninlil nodded once before turning away and following her husband from the darkened sun room. "I shall do my best," she assured her rape-child.

BRIGID CRANED HER NECK as she tried to see through the gap in the meteor's surface, running the beam of the flashlight along its edge. "It's hollow," she stated, not bothering to address her companions. "There's space inside."

"Space for what?" Mariah asked, peering up from where she was taking scrapings from the surface of the meteor.

"Storage maybe?" Brigid said. "Who knows?" And with that, she turned sideways and shuffled through the gap in the meteor. From behind, Brigid heard Edwards voicing concerns, but she ignored him. Being cautious had its place, no doubt, but exploration was the only true way to learn. She was a trained archivist, and complete knowledge must always be her goal.

Inside, as she had observed, the meteor was hollow, the empty space little bigger than one of the shower cubicles back at the Cerberus redoubt. The shell of the meteor—its walls—were more than eight feet thick, leaving just this tiny hollow area in its center.

Brigid ran her flashlight beam over the edges of the gap, seeing the craggy, jutted edges. She had stepped through at its narrowest side, she realized now. On the other side, a gap far wider existed, though it was half-buried in the field. The rock was so heavy it may have been sinking in the muddy ground, so it was eminently possible that that space had been closer to the surface when it had landed.

"This is crazy," Brigid muttered to herself. "What am I doing? Examining a chunk of space debris that we think hit our communications satellite. What does that prove? What do I think I'm going to learn? It's nothing, just random chance that we got hit."

"You okay, Miss Baptiste?" Edwards's voice came to Brigid from beyond the gap in the rock.

"I'm fine," she called back.

"It's just I heard voices," Edwards continued.

Shoulder first, Brigid made her way through the wider gap and out to where Edwards stood while Mariah took more samples from the meteor. "Don't listen to the voices," Brigid told Edwards, tapping the side of her head with the flashlight. "They'll make you do things, wear girls' clothes, burn down your house."

"What's that?" Edwards asked, utterly confused.

"It's a joke, Edwards," Brigid assured him. "Just teasing." Wow, but did she miss Kane and Grant in that instant.

A moment later, Mariah spoke up from where she was chipping at the rock's surface with her little pick, a note of concern coloring her voice. "Brigid?" she said. "You might want to look at this."

Crouching down beside Mariah, Brigid peered where the geologist was pointing, playing her flashlight's beam there. There appeared to be two marks in the rock, both of them roughly square in shape. Though well camouflaged in the rough surface, the marks were almost certainly artificial. They were both small squares of roughly the same size, each about as big as Brigid's palm. Brigid turned her head sideways and she recognized them then as glyphs from the ancient written language of the Sumerians. Brigid's breath caught in her throat as she realized what they were.

"Mean anything to you?" Mariah asked. When Brigid didn't answer, she turned to her and saw how pale Brigid had suddenly become. "Is everything okay? You look like you've just seen a ghost."

Brigid's finger traced over the square symbols, following each intricate stroke that had been carved into the meteor's surface. Brigid remained standing there for a long time, until she noticed that Mariah had stopped chipping at the rock's surface. When she looked up she saw that Edwards was watching her, too. "I've seen this before," Brigid said gravely.

"What is it?" Mariah asked.

"It's a Sumerian pictogram," Brigid explained. When she saw that Edwards was about to ask a question, she elaborated, "Words. Written in an old, old language."

"Can you read it?" Edwards asked.

"Yes," Brigid told them both. "It says 'Son of Enlil' and the last time I saw it it was written on the hilt of a knife that almost destroyed reality."

Chapter 9

Ullikummis walked slowly past the lines of waiting slaves, his head held high despite the manacles he wore at his wrists and the Nephilim guardsmen who accompanied him to ensure he didn't waver from his path. Ahead, he saw the huge rock construct that had been prepared for him, a prison that would sail evermore through the stars, abandoning him to the mercies of the solar winds. He walked slowly for his feet had not fully healed. Instead, he just had stumps there now, ending where his ankles had once been, and he shoved them into the sand with each step like two great walking sticks. They would heal in time, for Ningishzidda had given him incredible powers of recuperation, and Ullikummis's body would adapt to the change. Now, he had only the most glancing awareness of the pain and discomfort that walking on those stumps caused him, and he knew he would be glad when all of this was over, when he could at last rest in his promised solitude.

At the head of the group of onlookers, Enlil sat within a palanquin, its curtain drawn to suggest that he did not care to view the distasteful proceedings. Ninlil, his wife, stood at the foot of the palanquin, her head bowed low with contrition. Now and then, Ninlil would glance up, gazing at the rock prison or at her son, but her expression remained a mask of stoicism in the face of such disappointment and shame as had been brought upon her by the failure of her son.

There was no sign of Upelluri, although Ullikummis knew that that should not surprise him. With the scarabae sickness, Upelluri rarely ventured into daylight, and yet Ullikummis felt that his teacher would choose to witness this. However, Upelluri had been banned from the ceremony, and there was talk that he would be made to take the fall for what Ullikummis had done, publicly exonerating Enlil's role in the attempt on Teshub's life. He was an obvious candidate for this, for the reprisal attack had happened in his underground realm, and he could easily be painted as a conspirator in a fictitious plot to destabilize the royal family, including Enlil himself. There was an irony to that, of course, for Upelluri would end up being the most effective tool in that he played no role at all, the very opposite of everything he had taught his student.

The reptilian form of an Igigu craftsman was working at the head of the rock itself, chipping at it with hammer and chisel, carving a simple marker there that would inform the unwary of its contents. The two-character marker read simply Son of Enlil.

Nusku stood close to the rock prison, reading from a holographic tablet, its words angled that only he might see them. "'For the gross failure that you have committed, purportedly in your father's name, you shall be cast into the heavens,'" he read, his words carrying over the hushed crowd. "'Your name shall no longer be mentioned in this house, nor shall you be recognized as a deity. Your history shall be known as the story of a failure. No glory shall be visited upon the name of Ullikummis, Son of Enlil.'"

Ullikummis listened to the Annunaki vizier with boredom. Nusku had been Enlil's adviser and confidant since they had left Nibiru centuries before, and Ullikummis had sat through many of his long and rambling speeches as a child. This one was no different except, perhaps, that it concerned himself, albeit as a quality he could no longer recognize. It seemed irrelevant now. He felt as if he was watching the events from a great distance, as if it was happening to someone else—the great stone monster who stood in place of the handsome Annunaki prince he might have been.

The hideous stump at the end of his right leg caught in the ground, and Ullikummis struggled for a moment, stuck in place, his rock lips peeling back in a snarl of irritation.

One of the Nephilim soldiers stepped up to him, reaching out to assist him, placing his hand on the prince's arm and pulling him from the rut in the ground. In response, Ullikummis's arm lashed out, striking the Nephilim a fierce blow across the face, knocking the warrior off his feet. "How dare you touch the personage of a prince of the blood, lowly scum," he spat angrily.

The Nephilim warrior wiped blood from his mouth as he righted himself. "Did you not hear? You're a prince no more," the Nephilim stated, a sneer on his blood-drenched lips.

Something inside Ullikummis snapped then, and he turned on the Nephilim, clutching him by the throat before the warrior knew what was happening, lifting him savagely from the ground. Choking, the Nephilim reached for the dirk he wore at his belt as his fellow warriors rushed to assist him, and the rising hubbub of interest came from the crowd. Ullikummis tightened his grip on the lowly creature's throat, thinking of Upelluri and what would happen to his defenseless teacher once this ceremony was over.

The struggling Nephilim pulled his dirk free of its sheath and slashed it toward Ullikummis. Before it could strike, Ullikummis tightened his grip on the warrior's neck, and with a sudden snap the Nephilim soldier was dead, the blade falling from his suddenly slack grip.

Five other Nephilim surrounded Ullikummis as he tossed the limp body of their colleague aside into the sand. Each of the warriors had pulled his own blade, a short ceremonial dagger worn solely for pompous occasions such as this. Ullikummis looked at them pitifully, his burning magma eyes swirling with contempt. He could kill them all, their simple forms and lifeless eyes, their inability to plan or even to comprehend more than basic instructions. But what would killing them prove? That he was superior to such worthless scum, perhaps? His father would be no less angry with him.

But perhaps he might escape, hide, free Upelluri?

As he reached for the closest of the Nephilim warriors, Ullikummis saw his mother watching fearfully. As their eyes met, she shook her head briefly just once, before turning away. It was a warning, Ullikummis knew. She had promised to help him, had promised to talk with Ningishzidda. Perhaps what he did now would only disrupt whatever plans she had set in motion.

Blades flashed in the air, racing at Ullikummis's immutable stone body, and he simply stood there, taking it, his head bowed. The fight had left him as quickly as it had appeared.

For almost a minute, the Nephilim warriors slashed at his body, hacking at it to almost no effect, like trying to cut granite with a butter knife. A ripple of amusement went through the watching crowds, and several slaves laughed openly at the display before being cuffed or whipped by their masters. Then, with a harsh word, Nusku called on the Nephilim to stop, and a hush fell over the crowds once more.

"'Upelluri dared to turn his hand against Lord Enlil,'" Nusku announced, reading once more from his holographic display, "'poisoning the mind of the great god's only son, Ullikummis. He, too, shall be punished.'"

Then it was true, Ullikummis lamented. Upelluri was held somewhere even now, and doubtless being tortured until he accepted the blame for the incident. Yet Ullikummis had only followed his father's instruction, so the real fault lay with his father.

Enlil had meant for him to hear this, Ullikummis realized. He was goading him, reaffirming his power over his worthless son.

Angered, Ullikummis shuffled forward once more on his stumplike legs until he stood before the wide opening in the towering oval of rock. He turned his head to face his father's palanquin, but still Lord Enlil did not deem to show himself. Ullikummis wondered if he might have apologized had his father appeared. Perhaps he would have tried to explain what had really happened, that his failure was a mistake and not part of a wider conspiracy. Enlil saw wheels within wheels, machinations arrayed against him at every turn, and he determined to turn each new twist to his advantage no matter the cost. His paranoia, while understandable, had blinded him to his son's loyalty and love.

With a nod, Nusku instructed Ullikummis to step forward and to enter the hollow. Ullikummis held his gaze for a moment, wishing his magma eyes could burn into the pompous old vizier. The hate was welling again, and he tamped it down, recalling once more the lessons taught by Upelluri. His anger had become like the tides, ebbing and flowing, and that would reap nothing but misery. He must control it, trust in his mother's plans and in the planning of Ningishzidda. What was it Ningishzidda had said?

You are my greatest work of art, Ullikummis.

But where was Ningishzidda now?

Though reluctant, Ullikummis stepped proudly forward and into the stone prison that was to be his home for eternity in the stars. As he did so, one of the Igigi stonemasons who had been working at the carving above the cell looked at Ullikummis and nodded, the briefest, slightest inclination of his reptilian head as he dropped something no larger than a fingernail on the floor of the hollow. Ullikummis looked back, following where the Igigu looked, and he saw his mother there. Meeting Ullikummis's eyes for a moment, she closed her own and bowed her head in resignation, and the thinnest of smiles tugged at her lips. Ullikummis knew then that she had done it; she had been successful. With that, he stepped into the stone block and the vast rock door was sealed behind him, locking him in absolute darkness in a space so small that he could only stand bent or kneel or crouch, but never lie down.

Ullikummis listened as the rock door was sealed behind him, hearing the ASP torches wielded by the Nephilim being run along its edges to ensure that the seal was airtight. He crouched, genetically altered eyes penetrating the darkness, until he found the tiny metal disc that the Igigu has tossed onto the floor of the artificial cave, small as the head of a rivet. Then Ullikummis took the disc in his stone hand and pushed it into his thumb.

Outside, Nusku concluded the ceremony with all the pomp and circumstance that the people had come to expect from their mighty Annunaki space gods. Then the crowd watched in awestruck silence as Ullikummis's prison was launched into the heavens by a great gravity beam, lifting slowly before being shunted up through the clouds and off into space. Not once did Enlil show himself, preferring to hide his face—and his supposed contempt—behind the draped curtain of the palanquin.

THE MOON WAS HIGH in the sky when Brigid, Edwards and Mariah returned to Cerberus via the interphaser. After a brief discussion with Lakesh, Mariah went to test the content of the scrapings that she had taken from the crashed meteor site, while Edwards finally decided to call it a day. "And a bastard long one at that," he muttered as he left the ops room alone.

Remaining in the Cerberus ops center, Brigid herself found a free terminal and began scrutinizing data. "Still no progress on the Commtacts?" she asked when she saw Donald Bry working at a nearby terminal.

The copper-haired man shook his head. "Nothing so far," he admitted, "but I think it's just going to take time."

Unhappily, Brigid nodded her agreement.

"Something wrong?" Bry asked, registering her dour expression.

"There was something I meant to look into a while back," Brigid told him. "But in all the excitement I didn't quite get around to it."

Donald Bry's eyes widened in mock-astonishment. "You mean you forgot," he said.

"No, I…"

Bry was laughing now. "You actually forgot. The infallible Brigid Baptiste."

"I didn't forget," Brigid said. "I just didn't appreciate the significance of it at the time."

Lakesh strode over from his usual position. "The significance of what, Brigid?" he asked gently.

"You remember the knife—Godkiller?" Brigid asked.

Lakesh nodded. "I read your report," he said warily.

The knife had been found by the Cerberus rebels in a strange underground fortress in the Antarctic just a few weeks before. An Annunaki artifact, the multidimensional blade had possessed incredible properties that could fracture the surface of reality itself. Partnered with Kane and Grant, Brigid had been there when the blade split reality, carving a so-called infinity breach, and she had helped prevent a terrible force from overpowering the earth and killing humanity outright in light of that otherworldly rift.

"What of it?" Lakesh prompted.

"According to the inscription on its hilt, the blade originally belonged to someone identified as the son of Enlil," Brigid said.

"So this would be—what?—five thousand years ago," Donald Bry asked.

"Something like that," Brigid said.

"In which case the owner is long since dead…" Donald began, but Lakesh silenced him with a look. The Annunaki were nothing if not long-lived.

"I think he's back," Brigid said ominously.

"What?" Donald yelped.

"How?" Lakesh asked a little more sedately.

"There was a marking on that meteor we just investigated," Brigid explained. "The same marking that I saw on the Godkiller knife. 'Son of Enlil.'"

"Ancient graffiti, perhaps," Lakesh proposed.

"The meteor had been hollowed out and there was a space inside that could have contained a person," Brigid told them both. "I think that person was Enlil's son, and that the inscription was a warning to anyone who might mistakenly try to open it."

"He'd be dead," Donald Bry stated firmly, "after all this time. Very, very dead."

"Not necessarily," Brigid said. "We've seen that the Annunaki live prolonged lives. Furthermore, they have the ability to regenerate. The contents of that asteroid might not even have been the son, just his DNA sequencing so that he can be reborn."

"And do we have any information on the son?" Lakesh prompted.

Brigid turned back to her computer terminal, her fingers tapping at the keys for a few moments before a file opened and information pertaining to mythology and the Annunaki appeared. "Not yet, but I'll find it," Brigid stated with determination. "If it exists, I'll find it."

Lakesh drew up a chair and switched on the computer port beside her. "I'll start my own search," he told her. "Can you remind me of the many names of Enlil?"

Brigid reached for her pen and wrote the names down on a pad in her pleasingly curved and precise handwriting.

UP ABOVE, in the farthest reaches of Earth's atmosphere, Grant and Brewster were working at the repairs of the Vela-class satellite.

Wearing a bulky spacesuit, Brewster gestured for Grant to join him at a long panel. When Grant looked where Brewster pointed, he saw that the panel was dented and a ragged chunk at the far end was missing, torn off by what appeared to be a savage blow. Exposed circuitry could now be seen, but it was outside of Grant's area of expertise to assess its condition.

Grant turned back to Philboyd and leaned his head forward until their bulbous helmets touched. With the Commtacts out of action and the radiation affecting the shortwave helmet radios, the physical conductivity of the helmets was an easy way to communicate out here in space.

"What am I looking at?" Grant asked, pitching his voice at a normal volume.

When Brewster's response came, it sounded tinny and distant thanks to the medium of the space helmets, but it was perfectly audible. "The satellite has been hit a few times, but this is the main area of damage," Brewster explained. "It's thankfully quite minor, compared to what I was expecting. We were just damn unlucky that it blew out our monitoring."

"So you can fix it?" Grant encouraged.

"It can be fixed," Brewster assured him. "Be a lot easier if we could bring the whole thing down to Earth, where I'd have all the components and tools to hand, but I can't see any difficulties beyond the obvious."

"Not a fan of zero gravity?" Grant queried.

"I get nauseous when Clem relates scuba-diving stories," Brewster admitted.

"Oh, boy," Grant muttered. "I guess we head back to base to collect tools, parts and a sick bag for you, then."

"Never a dull moment," Brewster replied, smiling.

HE HAD TRAVELED for 4,500 years through the farthest reaches of the solar system, so to travel a little farther seemed somehow ridiculous.

Still, Upelluri had taught Ullikummis many things, one of which was the need to do things in the correct order. So Ullikummis instructed his first worshippers, Peter and Alison Marks, to lead him to the settlements and the people. Their yapping hound followed at a distance, fearful of Ullikummis but still loyal to his own masters as they were now loyal to him.

When the Annunaki had arrived here from Nibiru all those millennia before, they had brought their own slaves, the doomed Igigi, "those who watch and see." It hadn't taken long for the Igigi to secure their own slaves, shackling the apekin race known as humankind to do the menial tasks that they felt beneath even a slave caste.

Somewhere on this ball of mud, Ullikummis knew, his father, Enlil, was waiting, scheming as he had always schemed. And doubtless Enlil would have a hundred thousand warriors and a hundred thousand slaves at his beck and call, same as it ever was.

And Ullikummis himself? He had two. Two elderly apekin who were already near to death, the stench of the Grim Reaper's hands all over their deteriorating bodies. He stared at the two white-haired ape-things that led the way along the unlit dirt track toward the market town and he thought of the glorious army he would raise in the days to come. For he had had a long, long time to consider this, a long time even in Annunaki terms, and that was thanks to his mother's intervention.

THE PRISON ASTEROID blasted away from Earth and into the silent vacuum of space, Ullikummis crouched inside as best he could in the claustrophobic gap that was to be his home for the next four-and-one-half millennia.

Before launch, Ullikummis had shoved the Annunaki memory stud into his thumb, letting the message there flow into his arteries and pump the information around his system until it connected with the communication centers of his brain. Now as the massive asteroid was buffeted by the forces of friction as it tore through the stratosphere, the recorded memories began to flow into him. Then, as though from nowhere, he saw the delicate face of his mother, Ninlil, hovering before him as though she were standing right there.

"My son," she began, "though we have rarely shown affection for one another, what happens to you today leaves a stain upon my heart. You were born in horror, for your father only knows how to take. Because of that, I have found myself unable to look upon you the way I might a child born in other circumstances. But still, my love for you has always been pure, Ullikummis. Your father's is considered one of the greatest planning minds to ever be gifted to an Annunaki, and your own life has been just one part of those convoluted, never-ending schemes. You must understand that, even as you entered this awful prison, Enlil saw to it that you were playing yet another role in his schemes, and that your ultimate failure was simply another tactical move on his immense game board."

Ullikummis nodded, listening to his mother's words with understanding, the rock prison shuddering all around him as it ripped through the thinning air.

"I couldn't stave off your execution nor ensure that you would live, my son," Ninlil continued, her voice ringing only in Ullikummis's head, "for I knew that appealing to your father's mercy was a pointless gesture. And so I spoke with Ningishzidda as you asked me to, and he came to visit as you waited in the cell beneath the palace."

Ullikummis's breath caught in his throat at this, for he did not remember the meeting.

"Ningishzidda has done something," Ninlil's message continued, "so that you cannot betray him, lest your father learn of your audacious plan. He has altered the direction of the gravity beam by one degree, so slight that Enlil will never know. Thus, you shall be launched into space, as expected, but you shall return to this planet—Ki, in the tongue of your forefathers—after you have completed one orbit of the heavens.

"With love."

Abruptly the message ended.

Ullikummis waited in silence as the message faded from his mind, and he was plunged into the absolute darkness of the cavernlike prison once more. How long will this orbit last? he wondered, knowing that the memory disc was played out and could never answer his queries.

The answer, he would learn through the bitter veil of his patience, was that the orbit would last over four thousand Earth years.

FOUR AND ONE HALF MILLENNIA later, predawn in Saskatchewan, the first rays of the sun were just peeking over the horizon.

Ullikummis had followed Peter and Alison Marks across the fields, along the dirt roads and through the untamed wilds, taking a straight-line path toward the place where the market was held. Alison Marks had begun flagging at about 4:00 a.m., the long trek and the cold night air too much for her aging body. Ullikummis looked at her fragile form with contempt, recalling now how weak all apekin were. They were lazy creatures, he reminded himself, and needed a firm hand to keep them in line.

As he watched, Alison Marks stumbled on a rut in the road and fell to her knees with a cry. Ullikummis approached the farming woman then, his fierce magma eyes peering into hers like something that might penetrate her soul.

"I can't go on," she told him. "I need to rest."

Ullikummis continued to watch her in silence, realizing that his mental grip on her was fading with her exhaustion. She had not addressed him as her lord, had simply told him what she wished to do. In an hour, he knew, she and the farmer would no longer be held in his power, unless he did something to change that.

Ullikummis glanced down the track, and saw that the other one—Peter—continued to trudge along the path, his shoulders hunched resignedly, just plodding along as he had been instructed.

"Stop," Ullikummis ordered the old farmer, and the man stopped and waited, turning to Ullikummis with a vacant expression on his lined face.

Crouching, his hunched body like a rocky outcropping on the pitted track, Ullikummis leaned forward and placed his hand on Alison's forehead. When she felt his touch, it seemed almost as though she had awoken from a dream into a nightmare.

"What are you doing?" Alison screamed. "Get your hands off of me—!"

Behind them, the dog Barney came running up, barking and growling, snapping his jaws angrily at Ullikummis as the great stone god touched his mistress. By contrast, Peter Marks, the woman's husband of thirtysomething years, simply stood there, waiting for the next instruction from his new lord and master.

"This will hurt," Ullikummis told the fearful woman who struggled in the grip of his mighty hand, "but just for an instant."

Alison Marks tried to tear herself away, pulling this way and that, moving in time to Barney's savage barking. Ullikummis felt sorry for her. She had no concept of the glory of the age that was coming. If she had, she would have turned aside willingly, realizing that the only constant must be change, for her own world had become small and stagnant without his influence. And then he willed the thing from himself and he pressed the stone into her, the tiny bud that was himself, as she screamed and screamed beneath his powerful touch, screamed beneath the searing visions of god.

As the stone burrowed into her brain, Alison Marks became the first human to see the future in all its structured glory. If she had still been able to scream, she would have.

Chapter 10

The market itself was a revelation. Despite his bulk, Ullikummis blended with the shadows of the nearby trees, leaving Peter and Alison Marks to mingle with the traders who were busy setting out their wares. There was livestock here, pigs and sheep and cattle, flightless birds that clucked and squawked as they ran around in circles at the feet of their owners, as well as vegetables and fruit, displayed on vast stalls constructed of wood. Ullikummis had not seen its like in millennia, and for a moment he felt overwhelmed. All these people, these living things—they were like a colony of insects the way they rushed about, ignoring and yet interacting with their fellows as they busied themselves at their mysterious tasks.

Standing in the shadow of a tall tree on the outskirts of town, Ullikummis watched. The male farmer, Peter, had told him that the town was called Market, and Ullikummis had smiled at the directness of the appellation. To him, it seemed a tribute to the ways of the Annunaki, their own naming conventions structured by building words upon words, names upon names, a thing's function being its nomenclature.

While the other farmers prepared to go to auction, one stood alone, serving frothy beer that he had brought with him in a half-dozen barrels on the back of a cart. The cart had been pulled by a weary-looking donkey. Ullikummis smiled, recalling beautiful Ninkashi, who would bathe in

the beer that she brewed, back when he had last walked
the Earth. His old life, his memories, these things seemed
more real than this world now. They seemed somehow
more vibrant, more full of color. This world was dour, its
colors leached away, something faded and dying. Whatever
his father had done in his absence, he had left the world in
a lesser state than when Ullikummis had last been here.

Down in the market, one of the farmers—a middle-aged
man by the name of Dylan, the kind of man who seemed
ever angry and convinced he was hard done by—rushed
over and shook Peter Marks's hand, greeting his old friend
enthusiastically.

"How are things going, Pete?" Dylan asked, pleased to
see his friend.

Peter Marks ignored him, his expression blank.

"Everything okay?" Dylan pressed, unsure of what
was going on but suspecting it was one of Pete's infamous
practical jokes. He turned then to look at Alison, who was
standing at Pete's side, and he saw the way her jaw sagged,
and the strange lump in the middle of her forehead, like
the red dot an Indian woman wears in marriage. "Hey,
Ally?" Dylan began. "What is that there? That thing on
your head."

Dylan let go of Pete's hand and took a step closer to
Alison, peering at the thing on her head. It appeared to be
a jagged little stone, somehow imbedded in the skin. "Let
me get that," Dylan said, and he reached forward. When
Alison didn't react, Dylan brushed at the stone fragment
but it wouldn't move, and her skin seemed tight around it.
"What the heck is that thing?" he asked again.

Mouth still hanging open, Alison ignored him and continued to walk through the market area.

Beneath the tree, Ullikummis closed his fiery eyes and
felt the people begin to mill around his first subjects as

they took an interest in their new state. As they did so, his mind went back to that previous lifetime when he had last walked the Earth.

IT HAD BEEN A HOT AFTERNOON, 2,500 years before the birth of Christ. The blazing white sun hung in the sky like the dead eye of a blind crone, the reflections of its searing rays glaring from the waters of the Shatt-en-Nil canal beside the city of Nippur. This was Enlil's city, its golden towers testament to his dominance over the region.

Eight years old, Ullikummis stood in the golden tower of the main temple, gazing out upon the pure waters of the canal, feeling the heat of the sun on his skin. He was still a boy, yet his skin looked like one of the dried clay tablets that had been poorly fired, its surface cracked and pitted.

Down below, the reptilian Igigi rushed about their tasks, ordering humans to move great weights, to sweep the roads and clean the structures of the city. Ullikummis watched them rushing back and forth, like busy insects hurrying about their tasks in the sunshine. Only a few were taller than him now, and then only barely. Soon he would tower over them, thanks to the hormones that Ningishzidda had pumped through him at his father's behest. Already he was a freak among his own kind, but he knew no better, and so a freak he stayed.

There were footsteps from the far end of the room, and then his father's voice came from behind as he approached the lad. "What are you watching, my boy?"

"The workers," Ullikummis said, his eyes never leaving the vista below. Ullikummis did not turn when he replied to his father, for the stone plating of his shoulder blades was still forming, and Ningishzidda had instructed him not to move until its growth was complete. Instead, he wore a hood to keep the bones in place, while the living stone grew there, melding with him, becoming a part of him.

Enlil stopped beside his son and gazed through the open window to the streets below. "My subjects, Ullikummis," he said. There was pride in his voice, but also something else—boredom. "Slaves."

"They look so small from up here," Ullikummis stated, joy in his words.

"They are small," Enlil told him. "Even close up. Small of mind and small of vision." He turned to face his son then, and Ullikummis met his gaze.

Ullikummis could see, even then, that he repulsed his father. The thing he was becoming, under the instruction of Ningishzidda's manipulations, was a creature of nightmare. "I am taller than many of the Igigi now," he told his father proudly, "or at least as tall."

Enlil nodded, proud of this fruit of his loins. "And stronger?" he asked.

Ullikummis pondered that for a few moments before he replied. "I don't know, Father," he told the god-king with sincerity. "I have not tried my strength on them."

"I believe that you are stronger," Enlil stated. "Tomorrow we shall test you against my finest Nephilim. To the death."

Ullikummis was silent. He had no place to reply. His father had given an instruction and it was his task to obey it, even while his shoulders formed and he remained trapped in the hood.

IN THE FARMERS' MARKET in Saskatchewan, the crowds had formed a circle around Peter and Alison Marks and their dog. The dog yipped once or twice, running around fearfully at the attention lavished upon his masters. These people knew Peter and Alison, good farming folks from one of the nearby farms, and they were fascinated to see them changed like this. Neither Peter nor his wife reacted; they just trudged on through the market, around and around as the crowd followed them.

Their differences were too apparent, and the apekin were reacting badly to that, Ullikummis realized. Difference must be hidden, buried beneath the soil, for humans could never cope with difference. To change them he would have to fool them, make them believe that the change was what they wanted all along. Which, in a sense, it was. They craved only order, he reminded himself, recalling the way that Upelluri had been hidden for his differences.

IN THE ANCIENT TIMES, there was the widely held belief among the humans that the Annunaki were invincible. The Annunaki were their gods, after all, so it stood to reason that they must be invincible. Like many of the beliefs about the gods, this was incorrect.

Upelluri had been born with a beautiful hide the color of moonlit silver. Once, his scales would shimmer as he moved, holding the light like the facets of a diamond. Now his once-white skin was covered in dark, rotting patches where it had reacted badly to the golden sunlight of this alien world called Earth. It was called scarabae sickness, for the patches seemed to be shaped like beetles, blotching his skin like living things. Afflicted with skin lesions, Upelluri had set up a domicile in the underground caverns close to Nippur, hiding himself from the deadly rays of the sun and disguising his corrupted flesh from the humans who worshipped his perfect brethren. He spent most of his time there alone, having dismissed the needs and squabbles of the others of his kind, instead investigating a bigger enemy.

Ullikummis was sent to meet with Upelluri by his father. He was twelve years old and he already towered over any of the others of his race, thanks to the genetic manipulation of Ningishzidda.

"Upelluri will teach you patience," his father had said. Ullikummis could not yet appreciate the value of patience. He had been told that he was a killer, that his designated role was to kill. At twelve years old, he could not understand why a killer would need patience.

Ullikummis had traveled across the desert on foot, all the way from the walls of Nippur. It had taken half a day, and his pace had never slowed, nor had his breath ever quickened.

The mouth to Upelluri's caverns was a shadow-filled maw, unimpressed by the efforts of the midday sun. Ullikummis still had arrow-slit eyes then, like his father's, and they widened, struggling to make sense of the darkness as he stepped within.

Inside the cave there were noises, echoes that seemed to come from far away but could just as well be right next to him. His footsteps sounded like the crashing waves of the sea as his stone feet brushed at the shalelike sand beneath them. From somewhere deep within there came the sound of dripping.

Ullikummis spoke, his voice sounding harsh in the echoing chamber of darkness. "Hello? Lord Upelluri? Are you here?"

The only responses were the sounds of dripping water and the echoes of his own voice, reverberating through the network of caverns that led deeper and deeper into the Earth. So Ullikummis strode forward, finding his way in the darkness of the caves by touch and instinct as much as sight and sound.

If offer card is missing write to: The Reader Service, P.O. Box 1867, Buffalo NY 14240-1867

NO POSTAGE
NECESSARY
IF MAILED
IN THE
UNITED STATES

BUSINESS REPLY MAIL
FIRST-CLASS MAIL   PERMIT NO. 717   BUFFALO, NY

POSTAGE WILL BE PAID BY ADDRESSEE

THE READER SERVICE
PO BOX 1867
BUFFALO NY 14240-9952

Get FREE BOOKS and a FREE GIFT when you play the...

LAS VEGAS
GAME

7

7

Just scratch off the gold box with a coin. Then check below to see the gifts you get!

YES!
I have scratched off the gold box. Please send me my **2 FREE BOOKS** and **gift for which I qualify.** I understand that I am under no obligation to purchase any books as explained on the back of this card.

366 ADL E4CE   166 ADL E4CE

FIRST NAME   LAST NAME

ADDRESS

APT.#   CITY

STATE/PROV.   ZIP/POSTAL CODE

7	7	7	Worth TWO FREE BOOKS plus a BONUS Mystery Gift!
🍒	🍒	🍒	Worth TWO FREE BOOKS!
🔔	🔔	♣	TRY AGAIN!

Offer limited to one per household and not valid to current subscribers of Gold Eagle® books. All orders subject to approval. Please allow 4 to 6 weeks for delivery.

It took another two hours to find Upelluri—perhaps longer, it was hard to tell, for the utter darkness of the caverns acted like a sensory-deprivation experiment, forcing an individual to trust only what they felt in his or her mind. In some ways, this was Upelluri's first lesson for the boy.

When Ullikummis found Upelluri, he introduced himself, bowing formally as his father had instructed him.

"Enlil's boy, is it?" Upelluri asked.

"Yes, sir," Ullikummis said, watching the crooked figure that waited in the darkness. His eyes had adjusted somewhat to the lightless nature of the caves, but still he saw mostly shadows and shapes, nothing definite. Upelluri's shape was that of a bent and crooked Annunaki, his proud form twisted in on itself by the disease.

"You have your father's eyes," Upelluri observed, his voice coming to Ullikummis like something whispered right beside him.

"Thank you, sir."

"Tall, though," Upelluri continued. "Taller than your father."

"Yes," Ullikummis agreed, unsure of what else he should say. "My father sent me here to learn. He said that you would teach me."

Upelluri made some hideous noise as he cleared his throat, and Ullikummis wondered at how sick this so-called god really was. Had the scarabae illness affected his insides, as well?

"What is it that you would wish to learn?" Upelluri asked once his coughing fit had come to an end.

"I'm...not sure," Ullikummis admitted. He had been sent here by his father and told that he was to be instructed in the art of killing, and yet it occurred to him that he already knew how to kill. He had killed several times already, sparring with Nephilim warriors and others, hunting humans for sport. "My father wants me to learn how to kill," he stated finally, yet the words were uncertain and lacking in conviction.

"But surely you already know how to do that," Upelluri chastised, as though he had read Ullikummis's unsettled mind, "and so my assistance is redundant, is it not?"

Ullikummis stared into the darkness, watching the dark blotches that seemed to shift and swarm on the other's light skin, shadows on shadows. Upelluri was rotten, Ullikummis realized. He could see it now, the way that this supposed god of the underworld had turned bad. Not evil, nothing so simple as that. No, Upelluri had turned the way that food turns; he had spoiled from too long in the sun. Yet Ullikummis did not simply see this; he felt it. He felt the presence of the other Annunaki, as he had felt the presence of his father and others of the bloodline. And he knew then what it was his father had sent him here for.

"I need to know how to kill a god," Ullikummis stated. "One of our own."

Upelluri laughed at that, and it was a knowing laugh, one full of wisdom.

"Why do you laugh?" Ullikummis asked, feeling annoyed with this pitiful excuse for a hermit.

"Because you begin to see already," Upelluri said. "We are not like other beings, Ullikummis. The Annunaki have ever been so. And we do not die easily."

"Then I need a weapon," Ullikummis reasoned.

"The Annunaki exist on many cosmic levels," Upelluri began. "We are dimensionally more than we seem. So tell me, what would you use to kill one of your own?"

The youth pondered this dilemma, turning it over in his mind. "Something that exists on those same levels, all at once," he reasoned.

"And you have such a weapon?" Upelluri asked, eyes glistening in a face spotted with the darkness of the scarabae.

"I am the weapon," Ullikummis realized. "I am the instrument in my father's hands."

"But what would the instrument in *your* hands be, child?" Upelluri asked.

Ullikummis stilled his mind, struggling to find the answer. It was like some strange riddle, where all the clues were there if only one knew how to look. "I don't know," he admitted.

Upelluri turned away from the youngster and led the way deeper into the underground. "In time you will," he assured Ullikummis. "Be patient."

Over the next three years, what Upelluri taught Ullikummis was how to look deep within himself, to alter his own perspective, the way in which he perceived the world. It was a lesson that Ullikummis would carry with him throughout his subsequent campaign of terror, and one that served him well when he finally found himself imprisoned and exiled by the father he had trusted.

UPELLURI HAD SHOWN HIM a hidden room within the network of caverns, just another cave really, its entrance disguised by a chicanelike mass of rocks. Twelve years old, Ullikummis had followed, letting the older Annunaki set the pace.

"The only true power, Ullikummis," Upelluri explained, "is knowledge of your enemy. The more complete that knowledge is, the more absolute the power you wield. Come."

Ullikummis nodded his heavy stone head in agreement, his arrow-slit eyes peering into the darkness as they made their way through the long tunnel and into the next cave.

For a moment the cave seemed dark, too, but gradually Ullikummis's eyes adjusted and he saw the equipment there. An astrogator's chair had been mounted close to the rough wall of the cave, and a powerful telescope was propped beside it. Records—bound sheets of papyrus—were stacked close to the chair, their pages alive with markings made in a delicate hand. Upelluri walked across to the astrogator's chair and pushed his palm against it until it chirruped to life, the spiny protrusions appearing on its surface for a moment as they registered his genetic imprint before retracting into the shell of the chair at his command.

"Do you need me to sit?" Ullikummis asked.

"No," Upelluri told him as the chair's built-in projector came to life, displaying a holographic map of a blue-green planet floating in the dark embrace of space.

"What am I looking at?" Ullikummis asked.

"This is the planet Earth, the planet upon which we are standing," Upelluri explained. "Your birthplace and the Annunaki's adopted home. Pretty, isn't it?"

Ullikummis nodded a little self-consciously, associating such terms with the ghastly princesses he had shared dining tables with over the years at family functions, and now utterly detesting the connotations of the vile word.

Upelluri waved his hand over the sensor on the chair's arm, and the Earth became smaller as the image appeared to expand. In a moment they could see the asteroid belt, the red planet and others. Upelluri swung his hand around and the image swung, too, moving in the other direction, sweeping around and past the Earth with its banks of white clouds, through the orbits of two other planets before pulling to a halt before the fiery ball at the center of the solar system. "The sun," Upelluri explained.

"I know," Ullikummis said, his voice tentative. Was Upelluri insane? What could this possibly be teaching him that he didn't already know?

Upelluri held up his scarred arms, and Ullikummis saw the beetlelike shapes that appeared to be crawling over his moon-dusted scales. "The sun did this to me," Upelluri said in a solemn voice. "Forced me to hide from it. The sun is my enemy."

Despite himself, Ullikummis stepped back, feeling fearful of the older Annunaki at that moment, so intense was Upelluri's passion.

"I study it every day," Upelluri told him. "I monitor the sun and I record every flare and every shift in it, as best as I can from my hiding place here so that, one day, I may use these things to my advantage and defeat the sun. Then my underworld kingdom will be the only kingdom."

Ullikummis stood silent, wondering at the old Annunaki's sanity.

"The sun is not a static thing," Upelluri told him. "It changes, as all things change. Within those changes lies my salvation."

Ullikummis spoke at last, his voice sounding suddenly too loud in the enclosed space of the cavern. "Could *Tiamat* not repair the damage to your skin?" he asked. "Or Ningishzidda?"

"Perhaps," Upelluri agreed, "but to simply alter oneself is to admit defeat, is it not? So even with the sickness gone, I would still know that the sun was my enemy, and I would still be bound to defeat it."

"My father wants me to kill Teshub," Ullikummis said quietly.

"I know he does, boy," Upelluri said.

"Then what should I do?" Ullikummis said. "I cannot disobey my father, but Teshub will kill me."

"And what do you expect of me?" Upelluri asked.

"I need a weapon to kill Teshub," Ullikummis stated.

Upelluri nodded. "That can be arranged," he said, "in time." Suddenly Upelluri turned to the boy-prince, his eyes burning with intensity. "Have you identified your enemy yet, Ullikummis?" he asked.

"Teshub," Ullikummis stated automatically, wondering once more at the sanity of the hermit Annunaki.

The name echoed in the cave for long moments after the astrogator's chair had shut down and everything else had gone silent.

ULLIKUMMIS TURNED his thoughts back to the present as he stood in the shadow of the trees just outside Market, Saskatchewan. The people of the farming community had surrounded Peter and his spouse, their voices raised in concern as they tried to comprehend what had happened to their friends and why they were acting so strangely. Peter and Alison didn't react, but Barney was going crazy, yapping and growling at everyone who approached, still scenting the familiarity of his masters despite the obvious change within them to the apekin.

With a determined step, Ullikummis broke from cover and strode toward the farmers. Busy with the mystery of their longtime friends, not one of the farmers noticed the stone god approach until he was almost upon them. It seemed somehow inevitable to Ullikummis that the first to look up was Dylan, the younger farmer who had first indentified the change in his old friends.

"What the hell is that?" Dylan yelped, bunching his fists as he strode purposefully toward Ullikummis.

Up close, Dylan was a tiny man compared to Ullikummis, standing just over five feet tall to the Annunaki's towering frame.

"You know about this, mutie?" Dylan snapped, pointing to his altered friends. "Did you do this?"

Ullikummis looked at the inconsequential little man with his fiercely burning magma eyes, and a smile crossed the craggy rockscape that was his mouth. "The future is upon you," Ullikummis stated, reaching for the little man's head with one of his mighty rock paws. "Embrace it, ape-thing."

In the space of a second, Ullikummis's huge hand was clutched around farmer Dylan's head, grasping him where his hairline met with his forehead. And then, Ullikummis applied the pressure, and a bud of stone formed in the palm of his hand, before migrating into the young farmer's forehead, burrowing through his skull and into his brain. One second more, and the stone's work was done, so Dylan could finally let go his preconceptions and see the glory of the new.

Ullikummis stepped onward, his long arms stretching out and his hands grasping for the next farmer and the next. Here was his first encampment. Here was his first army, with livestock to feed them, and the elements to shape them. Here he would lay the foundation stone of Tenth City.

Chapter 11

A long two days had passed.

Coming off shift, Kane stretched his muscles as he entered one of the communal rooms dotted around the Cerberus redoubt. The room had a coffee machine and a half-dozen low tables surrounded by comfortable seats finished in blue upholstery. The upholstery looked worn. Kane had been cooped up in the cockpit of his Manta craft for close to thirty of the past forty-eight hours, and he had spent the remainder either sleeping or suited up doing spacewalks with Helen Foster or Brewster Philboyd, helping them both with the urgent repairs to the satellites that the redoubt relied upon for information.

As he headed for the coffee machine, Kane spotted a familiar head of red-gold hair over in one corner. It was Brigid Baptiste, her nose immersed in a paperback book.

"Hey, Baptiste," he remarked as he punched at the dispense button on the coffeemaker. "No boyfriend?"

Brigid looked up at him, her square-frame spectacles perched on her nose. "Not tonight," she said before turning back to her book.

Kane watched as an empty paper cup was dispensed by the coffee machine before the scalding coffee came blurting out of a tap just a half inch above the rim of the cup. As he watched her, Brigid turned a page of her book.

"What was the name of your boyfriend?" Kane muttered as the dark coffee filled his cup. "Carol? Beryl? Something girly like that, right?"

Brigid sighed and looked up from her book once again. "Daryl. Daryl Morganstern. And he's not. Why? Are you jealous?"

Kane stared at her in a show of wide-eyed innocence. "Who, me? Nuh-uh."

"Good."

Kane chuckled to himself as Brigid turned back to her book. His coffee cup finished filling, and the muscular ex-Mag took the paper cup from the tray at the bottom of the machine. It was burning hot and he pulled his hand away, blowing on his fingers before picking it up again by his fingertips and rushing across to one of the low tables dotted around the room. He sat there for a moment, nursing his hand, blowing on his fingers until they cooled.

It was just he and Brigid in the room, the first time he had seen her since they had gotten back from Louisiana, and Kane wanted to talk to her just to unwind from the hectic nature of the past two days. She, meanwhile, was immersed in her book.

"What you reading?" Kane asked, moving to a closer seat as he blew on his scalding coffee.

Brigid held up the book so that Kane could see the cover. It was an old book entitled *The Bell Jar;* he had never heard of it.

"Is it good?" Kane asked. "All about jars?"

Brigid smiled indulgently. "Something like that," she said, turning another page.

Kane sat watching her as she turned her attention back to the book in her hands. "Seems a pretty odd subject for a book," he said after a few moments of thought. "Jars. Who wants to read about a jar?"

With a resigned sigh, Brigid closed her book and looked up at him. "Something on your mind, Kane?"

Kane took a sip of his coffee. It was still too hot to taste. "Not really," he told her. "Just been stuck in the Manta for a long time, wanted to unwind a bit."

"How's that going?" Brigid enquired.

"The repairs?" Kane clarified. "Fine, I guess. Helen thinks—"

"Helen?" Brigid interrupted, one eyebrow raised.

"Foster, engineering. You know her?" Kane asked.

"No, it's just you and first names. Kind of intimate for you," Brigid said with a laugh. "How long have you known me?"

"What? I don't know, five, six years…" Kane began.

"And yet you still call me Baptiste," Brigid told him.

"Well," Kane told her, lowering his voice to a conspiratorial whisper, "that means you're part of the gang."

"And Helen's not?" Brigid prodded.

"What am I going to talk about with an engineer?" Kane replied. "Circuit boards?"

Despite herself, Brigid laughed.

"Anyway," Kane said, "*Helen* reckons it'll take another two days to bring the Comsat back on line."

"That soon?"

"According to her, the damage was relatively minor," Kane explained, "just bastard unlucky it knocked the thing out of action. Be quicker but we're working out there without, y'know, gravity, air, that stuff."

"I thought you didn't know anything about circuit boards," Brigid teased.

"Oh, I just hand her the screwdrivers and the extra bolts," Kane assured her and they both laughed.

"Look," Kane said after taking another sip of his coffee, "I didn't mean to interrupt your book. Just have a head full of flight protocol and dented satellite casings. I'll leave you to it."

"No," Brigid said as the ex-Mag began to stand, "it's all right. I've been so busy with Lakesh trying to track the impacts and that stuff about Enlil's son that we never got a chance to talk about what happened in Louisiana."

"We got attacked by sorta dead people," Kane said.

"Yes, we did." Brigid nodded.

"Did you think any more about this Ezili goddess that Hurbon spoke about?"

"Ezili Coeur Noir," Brigid ruminated. "Yes, and it's not good. That was an Annunaki astrogation chair, Kane, which probably means that Ezili Coeur Noir is an aspect of the Annunaki, most likely Lilitu in disguise."

"So you said," Kane agreed. "Question is, when did she give the chair to Hurbon? Before or after we last saw her?"

"You mean, before or after we assumed she was dead," Brigid clarified.

"That's about the size of it," Kane agreed.

"The Annunaki do have an irritating habit of coming back from the grave," Brigid reminded him. "It's possible that Lilitu is running around again, perhaps in a different form."

"Finding new followers and delivering furniture," Kane observed, sarcasm dripping from his tone.

"We should find out for sure," Brigid said. "I don't want the Annunaki getting the jump on us while we think they're dead."

"They're not dead," Kane told her. "Marduk and Enlil have shown up pulling the strings on a couple of operations. They're regrouping, planning. We just need to find them and put a stop to it. And we can only do that—"

"With satellite surveillance," Brigid finished for him.

"Guess I'd better learn to speak circuit board," Kane said with a chuckle.

"That will impress your new girlfriend," Brigid said and she began laughing when she saw the irritation on Kane's face.

"So, what is this *Bell Jar* all about?" Kane asked, pointing to the book resting in Brigid's lap. "Something I should know?"

Brigid shook her head. "I'm just reading it for, well, enjoyment," she said. "Can you remember the last time you read anything, Kane?"

"Other than one of Donald's site reports, you mean? It's been a while," Kane admitted. "I think it must have been the *Book of the Law,* back in Cobaltville."

"What about for fun?" Brigid pressed.

"I read *that* for fun," Kane said, and there was no trace of irony in his voice. "It was my father's copy, he being a Mag before me. This big, leather-bound volume, with every penal code and amendment up to whenever it was he started as a Magistrate. It was interesting."

"And you honestly read it *for fun?*" Brigid asked.

"Like I say, it was interesting," Kane said. "All the different ways that the baronial system worked, the ways that the Program of Unification came about and how it operated. What? Is that really so weird?"

Brigid was looking at him in astonishment, her eyes wide. "A little bit," she said. "I guess I never really thought about how narrow our lives have been. We've seen the world and other planets, visited other dimensions, and yet we've been constantly straitjacketed by the world around us."

"Well," Kane said, "maybe we'll grow old and gray and read books for fun one day, but there's a war on right now and that has to come first."

"Even when the battlefront's silent?"

Kane nodded resignedly. "Even then, Baptiste."

As Kane finished his coffee, Brigid got back to her book, flicking through its pages until she found her place. Kane stood up and made his way from the room, tossing his empty cup in the trash as he left. He stopped at the door and peered back at Brigid Baptiste as she sat there alone, knees pulled up to her chest, immersed once more in the writings of Sylvia Plath.

After a moment, Kane turned back, feeling the tension in his muscles, and he strode to where Brigid sat and took the seat beside her. Brigid peered up from her page, her emerald eyes watching Kane as he settled himself.

Kane smiled. "Why don't you read me your book there?" he suggested. "For fun."

"Really?" Brigid snorted, taken aback.

Kane lay with his head back, feeling the ache across his shoulders from sitting in the Manta's cockpit for far too long. "Maybe just a chapter or two," he said, "while I rest my eyes."

Brigid turned back to the start of the old paperback and began reading.

WHEN LAKESH FOUND Brigid and Kane, they were asleep in the communal room, he huddled against her lap. Lakesh smiled, thinking how comfortable the two of them looked together, how easily one might mistake them for lovers, so close was their obvious bond. In actuality, he knew, they were *anam-charas,* soul friends sharing a mystical bond through eternity. It was one of those things that, two hundred years ago when Lakesh had first walked these halls, people would have snorted at and dismissed as New Age. He wondered, for a moment, what one called New Age two hundred years after the term had been coined? Was it now Old Age?

Lakesh held his cupped hand to his mouth and delicately coughed until Kane and Brigid began to stir. Kane woke with the speed of a cat, sitting bolt upright in a second, his eyes narrowing as he located the source of the disturbance. Here was a man, Lakesh thought, who spent every moment in readiness. Had he not been bone-tired from his almost continuous two-day shift in the Manta, there was no possible way that Kane could have been caught unawares.

"Lakesh," Kane said in greeting, stretching his arms and blinking at the harsh fluorescent lighting of the room.

Beside Kane, Brigid opened her eyes and moved on the cushions of the seat before gritting her teeth and taking a sharp breath. "Dead leg, dead leg," she muttered as she rubbed at the place where Kane's head had been resting. She turned to him. "Why do you have to have such a heavy head?"

"It's full of ideas and strategy," Kane said with a lopsided grin, brushing a hand through his messy hair.

Brigid shot him a contemptuous look before offering a cheery "Good morning" to Lakesh as she continued rubbing away the pins and needles in her leg.

In response, Lakesh smiled broadly and said, "I've found him."

Brigid's eyes widened and she leaped from the seat and began to rush over to Lakesh to hear the news. The pins and needles in her leg made her mutter and limp, and she stomped her foot on the ground to disperse the pain.

From his position on the comfortable seats, Kane called to the pair of them. "Anything I should know about?" he asked.

Lakesh nodded gravely, the broad smile disappearing from his face as Brigid skimmed over the printout that he had handed to her. "We may have a new problem," Lakesh explained, "and one you're not going to like."

"Never met a problem I liked, Lakesh," Kane told the man, "so you may as well save the sugarcoating and just tell me."

"Ullikummis," Brigid said, reading from the printed paper that she held.

"Ullik-*who's-this?*" Kane asked.

"Ullikummis was a giant stone monster," Lakesh summarized, "whose story can be found in the Hurrian myth entitled 'Song of Ullikummis' or 'Ullikummi,' depending on which translation you read."

"And what?" Kane queried as he stood up. "You think this stone monster smashed the satellites?"

"We think he came down in the meteor shower," Brigid said, not bothering to look up from Lakesh's printout.

"And you've jumped to this wild conclusion how exactly?" Kane asked, a rising note of irritation in his voice.

"When I investigated the meteor," Brigid explained, "I saw a marking there that I recognized from the knife we found in the Antarctic."

"Godkiller," Kane muttered, recalling the deadly weapon. "Go on."

"You'll remember that Godkiller had the owner's name—Son of Enlil—carved as two glyphs on its hilt," Brigid reminded him. "I saw those same two glyphs carved into the body of the asteroid that smashed into our communications satellite on its way to Earth." She waved the papers at Kane. "According to this, Ullikummis is the son of Enlil."

Kane cracked his knuckles. "We're going to need to get the team together," he stated. "Let's do this in one quick hit up in the cafeteria, bring everyone up to speed."

Lakesh nodded. "My thinking exactly. I've already set the meeting for ten."

Kane glanced at the wall chron above the door, rubbing his hand over his stubbled jaw. "Great, that gives me twenty minutes to try to remember what I looked like without a beard."

"It wasn't any better," Brigid teased him. "Just ask Helen."

Kane growled as he left the room to wash his face and get himself a change of clothes.

TWENTY MINUTES LATER, the Cerberus personnel gathered together in the cafeteria that served the old military redoubt. They had congregated in various groups around the room while they waited for Lakesh to start his address. A skeleton staff of just one man remained in the main ops center, but with the communications and satellite feeds down, that individual's role largely boiled down to making sure that nothing spontaneously combusted or that the mat-trans didn't start up of its own accord.

Grant signaled when he saw Kane come stalking through the cafeteria doors, a scowl on his face. "Hey, man, it's been a couple of days since I last saw you," Grant said.

"Lakesh has had me on constant flight duty," Kane growled.

"Me, too," Grant told him. "How're the repairs going on the Comsat?"

Kane shrugged. "It'll take at least a day yet, but Helen tells me it's getting there."

"Helen?" Grant asked.

Kane shot him a look. "Don't you start that. I had an earful of that from Baptiste last night."

Grant smiled. "Yeah, I know," he admitted.

"She sicced you on me, didn't she?" Kane realized, seeing Brigid waving innocently from her position a few seats over.

In response, Grant gave his partner a friendly cuff to the shoulder. "So, you know what all this is about?" he asked Kane.

"Wait and see," Kane said enigmatically.

Shortly thereafter, Lakesh took the floor. He began by thanking all of the personnel for being there. Then, after briefly outlining the discovery of the writing on the fallen meteor, he ran through the information that he had shown to Brigid.

"Ullikummis is a figure in Hurrian mythology, from the same period as the Annunaki that we have had so much trouble with over the past few years. The Hurrians inhabited the northern reaches of ancient Mesopotamia, and what records of their mythology have survived indicate that they, too, worshipped the Annunaki, often ascribing different names to familiar figures.

"Ullikummis himself," Lakesh continued, "is described as a stone monster, whose story is the best preserved and most complete in an epic cycle of so-called songs concerning the great god Kumarbi. Kumarbi is, in fact, another name for Enlil. During this cycle of myths, Enlil aimed to replace the weather god, Teshub." Lakesh stopped, waiting for that information to sink in. The Cerberus exiles had had many dealings with Enlil, who had proved to be one of the most vicious and unpleasant foes that they had faced.

In fact, it seemed that it was Enlil who was at the ultimate root of all of their problems from their earliest days, like the spider at the center of the web.

"Enlil raped the sea god's daughter, whom we know as Ninlil, prior to their marriage," Lakesh explained. "Ullikummis was the product of that horrific liaison. According to the story, their child was a pillar of volcanic rock, which Enlil hid in the underworld domain of Upelluri, placing the child on Upelluri's shoulder. Upelluri was absorbed in his meditations and failed to notice as the child began to grow. The child grew quickly until he reached the heavens, where Teshub rained and thundered upon him, but ultimately caused Ullikummis no harm. Teshub abdicated his throne, and turned to the god Ea—whom we know better as Enki—for help. Ea visited Upelluri and cut off the feet of Ullikummis the great stone pillar, toppling him." Lakesh stopped reading, peering up from his paperwork to take in the reaction of the crowd before him.

After a few seconds, Grant broke the stunned silence. "I think that's a story we can all relate to," he said, trying to lighten the somber mood that had fallen on the Cerberus team.

"Quite," Clem Bryant muttered from where he sat with Mariah at another of the long tables.

"If what our survey team found out in Saskatchewan is what we think it is, which is to say some kind of space-going vessel," Lakesh stated, "then we may have stumbled upon the reappearance of Enlil's son."

"A pillar that can't stand up doesn't sound like much of a challenge," Edwards pointed out.

"Need I remind you that these legends should be taken with a pinch of salt?" Lakesh challenged. "This could be a very real and very serious danger, Edwards."

Kane held up his hands. "What if we tap Balam and get his take on this? That little freak tends to have the answers when it comes to this kind of bull."

Balam was a long-lived alien from a separate race to the Annunaki, a race known as the First Folk, and his knowledge of the truth behind the Annunaki stories had served the Cerberus team well in the past. However, Balam kept his own agenda and appeared only when it suited him.

"Your suggestion is noted and we'll act upon it if we can," Lakesh said. "Anyone else?"

"I guess we're going back to the crash site," Brigid piped up.

"That would seem prudent," Lakesh agreed. "Let's get our communications feeds up and running again, and we'll go from there."

With that, the meeting was adjourned.

As the crowd dispersed, Grant turned to Kane, a sour expression on his face. "The son of Enlil, huh?" he growled. "Does it get any more sucky than that?"

Brigid joined them, overhearing Grant's words. "I hate to be the one to foster false hope here, but there's a possibility that Ullikummis is the…well, the 'good' son. A caring Annunaki."

Kane and Grant turned to her with astonishment.

"Enki helped humans survive the Flood," Brigid reminded them. "It's not unheard-of."

"Just unlikely," Kane rumbled.

"Hey, I don't like it any more than you do," Brigid said. "I'm just saying that if this Ullikummis has reappeared, then we should pick our fights carefully."

With a grumble of agreement, the three warriors left the cafeteria to return to their own designated tasks.

Chapter 12

It had taken six days.

Now, a little after midday, the mood in the Cerberus ops center was one of anticipation. Lakesh paced behind the twin aisles of computer monitors, waiting for that final, decisive indicator that both satellites were back online.

Sitting at the communications desk wearing an earpiece, Donald Bry peered up at Lakesh and tried to look reassuring. The attempt seemed somehow out of place on Bry's famously fretful features. "I'm sure we'll hear at any moment, Dr. Singh," he said.

Lakesh nodded, and a playful smile lit his face. "I know," he said. "It's just I feel like I should, I don't know, flip a giant switch or something. Like turning on the Christmas lights."

Bry laughed. "It has been a very long time since I last thought about Christmas lights," he admitted. "Did you ever see the Rockefeller Center?"

As Lakesh began to answer, Reba DeFore's voice piped up from across the room as the data stream on her monitor came back to life. "Transponders are online," she said, seeing the blips appear one after another on the onscreen map.

Before Lakesh had turned to him, Donald Bry was passing a microphone up to his hand and flipping the comms signal to speaker. "You're broadcasting," Donald whispered.

Holding the tiny pickup mic before his mouth, Lakesh spoke carefully, enunciating his words. "Hello, friends, this is Cerberus. Do you read me?"

After a few seconds' pause, Kane's familiar voice came piping over the Commtact relay. "Loud and clear, Cerberus," Kane acknowledged.

From all around the room came the sound of a dozen people sighing in relief as the tension evaporated.

"It's good to hear your voice, Kane," Lakesh said as the ops room staff finally began to calm down. "I was just saying to Donald that this feels like a momentous day."

Via the Commtact relay, Kane's voice piped through the room's speakers so clearly that he could have been in the room with them. "You sound like you're expecting me to give a speech," he said jovially.

Lakesh chuckled. "That would be *one small step,*" he said.

A few desks farther along from the communications array, Henny Johnson gave the okay signal with finger and thumb—the Vela-class monitoring satellite had come back to life about two hours earlier, but the comms signal was only now routing correctly so as to allow anything more than a single, static picture. Her signal alerted Lakesh to the fact she could now change the image and focus the satellite's pickup feed as required.

"One moment, Kane," Lakesh instructed, gesturing to Henny to bring up the live monitoring feeds. In a few seconds, Henny had the eye in the sky focused on the sleek, bronze shape of a distant Manta craft perched beside a gull-winged satellite orbiting the Earth. "There, I think we can see you now. Care to wave?"

Henny increased the magnification on the monitoring screen and Lakesh bent closer, conscious that several other of the personnel in the room were doing just the same over their own monitors as they brought up her feed. After a moment, the Manta rolled slightly to the left, then to the right as it hung there, docked to the satellite. It was just a little dipping of the wings, but it was enough to raise a cheer from several of the personnel in the room.

Kane's triumphant voice came over the Commtact speaker. "Did you get that?"

"We did, my friend," Lakesh acknowledged, "and, let me assure you, a prettier sight I never did see."

With that, Kane signed off and Lakesh passed the tube-like microphone pickup back to Donald Bry at the communications desk. "Raise Grant and Brewster and confirm that we're picking up the signal from the Vela," he instructed as he made his way over to his desk. The moment of jubilation had passed, and Mohandas Lakesh Singh knew that it was time to get back to work.

Twenty minutes later, the ops room was running like clockwork once more, with various data feeds all up and running, and an extra shift of personnel wading through the patchy backup data that had been stored during the six-day period where the facility had been effectively deaf and blind.

The first thing that Lakesh wanted to do was check on the meteor site. Its eerie combination of a natural phenomenon coupled with the engraving referring to Enlil's son had been preying on his mind ever since Brigid Baptiste had first reported it. Now Henny Johnson toggled through screens as the monitoring satellite repositioned itself to bring up a clear view of the area where the meteor had landed. Today would mark their first overhead view of the site since the meteor storm had struck Cerberus's satellites. Even now, Brigid was camped at the crash site with Edwards and Mariah Falk, using portable equipment to assess the nature of the fallen rock and try to learn more about the ominous runes that had apparently been carved into its surface.

"Edwards just reported in," Donald Bry confirmed as Lakesh asked Henny to patch the monitor feed to his terminal. "Situation normal."

"Good," Lakesh said absently, his thoughts fixed on the image that was revealed on his screen. Henny had angled the satellite to frame the fields around the fallen meteor, placing the house-size rock itself in the center of the frame. The image on Lakesh's screen showed approximately an area of two square miles around the crash site itself.

"Henny," Lakesh proposed. "Can we bring the view out a little, see what else got hit? Brigid mentioned an abandoned farmhouse."

With an efficient nod, Henny began working the feed, flipping to a wider angle until they were perhaps ten miles out from the crash site, and her information was patched through automatically to Lakesh's screen. Lakesh looked at it silently as the image came into focus, wondering what the meteor truly was. Mariah's spectrographic analysis placed the rock at approximately five thousand years old, and sourced it as originating from Earth, although she admitted that she could only offer a reasonable degree of certainty with reference to that, at least, she said, until she had visited and examined every other planet in the universe. Lakesh had accepted her good-humored caveat, stating he felt comfortable in her presumption that the meteor had originally come from Earth. While he felt comfortable with the presumption, he was decidedly less comfortable with the reality that went with it. The word that kept coming to mind was *launched*—had this thing been deliberately dispatched from Earth millennia ago only to complete whatever vast orbit it had been sent on and finally return to its launchpad? The imperfect rotation of the Earth—the wobble effect—might mean that the meteor had been launched from another area, even another continent, but its collision course with the planet did not bode well. What had it been to see and why had it returned?

All around the fallen meteor were fields and forest, with almost no housing whatsoever other than a couple of small farmhouses. Lakesh looked at the photographic image on his screen, like an old-style relief map, wondering at what he might be missing. It had been a long, long time since Lakesh had been out in the field, but right then he could feel that he was getting itchy feet. Whatever this odd little mystery was all about, he felt that it was important, and that he wanted to be part of it, right there at ground zero.

Sitting there thinking, Lakesh suddenly became conscious that someone was staring at him. When he looked up he saw Henny was watching him from her own desk a few feet away. "Sir?" she prompted.

"A moment please," Lakesh told her, running over whatever it was that was nagging at the back of his mind. Something had come down, crashed to Earth—a hollow meteor that was somehow associated to an Annunaki called Ullikummis who was described as a sentient stone pillar. Could this space rock be a part of Ullikummis? This rock that had crashed to Earth in the middle of the Saskatchewan fields?

With a rapid movement of fingers across his keyboard, Lakesh brought up a map of the local area and set it to overlay the satellite image. He stared at the screen, wondering what it was he was looking for. A needle in a haystack, perhaps?

Henny was growing impatient as she watched Lakesh. "Sir, if that's all," she told him, "I should probably run a full systems check and take a general sweep of the usual hot spots."

He had had six days to come up with a plan, Lakesh realized. Six days to ponder on what he was going to do when the monitoring satellite came back to life, and all he had thought of was to check on the meteor. There had been so much else to deal with while the feeds were down that it had been like trying to plan a chess game, not simply a couple of moves in advance but rather a couple of *games* in advance. His hands played across the keyboard once more, bringing the overlay map into clearer focus, and letting the live satellite feed dim into the background of his monitor screen. Was there a local settlement? Where was the nearest congregation of people? Fields of vegetables and wild forests didn't matter—what mattered was always the people. So where were they?

On-screen, the map became smaller as Lakesh pulled his view out, showing an ever larger expanse of the terrain until suddenly he spotted the thing he was looking for. There, roughly sixteen miles from the site of the crash, off to the north, a medium-size settlement known as Market. Population estimates had it at under eighty, including children, but still it was a real place where people had come together to make their homes.

"Move the satellite camera," Lakesh instructed Henny. "I want to focus on a tiny settlement off to the northwest— it's roughly sixteen miles from the crash site."

With marked efficiency, Henny pushed a strand of her dark hair back over her ear as she turned back to her terminal and widened the angle on the monitor feed, drawing across until the crash site was in the bottom right corner and the village of Market was in the top left. Except there was no village. The image covered almost eighteen miles in total, but there was no village. Instead, what she and Lakesh saw there both baffled them and chilled them to the bone.

"What the hell is that?" Henny muttered, adjusting the satellite feed to bring the village into better focus.

Lakesh recognized it. He knew the pattern that he saw there, even from so high above. "It's a barrier," he replied automatically. "A wall."

"And behind it?" Henny asked, her voice still low with astonishment.

"A ville," Lakesh stated, the emotion draining from his voice.

Even from overhead like this, Lakesh recognized the familiar pattern, the central spire surrounded by smaller towers, just like Cobaltville where he had spent so much of his second life. One week ago, to the best of his knowledge, there had been nothing out there, just a tiny settlement of thirty properties that housed eighty people in all, a simple Outlander market town whose name was all that it would ever be. Now, sprouting from nowhere, a great ville had taken its place, constructed from stone the color of rain-heavy clouds.

Lakesh realized then that while Cerberus's monitoring capability was down, something very, very odd had happened.

WHILE SHE WAS WORKING out in the field, Brigid Baptiste's Commtact came to life, much to her surprise. She was sitting cross-legged in the beetroot field with a laptop before her, skimming over the latest results of Mariah's spectrographic analysis of the meteor. Above, the sky was covered by a blanket of silver clouds, threatening to rain. It had been almost a week since the subdermal communications chip had been deactivated, and Brigid was just a little taken aback to suddenly have someone else's voice running through her head once more.

"Brigid, this is Lakesh," the familiar voice began.

Brigid caught herself with a gasp. "Well, I guess this means the Commtacts are up and running, Lakesh!" she said.

"Ah, yes," the Cerberus chief responded over the medium of the Commtact, "we should have warned you. I thought Donald had spoken with Edwards already."

"Maybe he did," Brigid said. "The big guy disappeared about an hour ago to, I don't know, start a war on the trees or something."

"Is he giving you a hard time?" Lakesh asked.

Brigid sighed. "He's fine. I guess you just get used to having certain people around, and having someone new in the mix can be a little jarring."

Lakesh sympathized. "Kane and Grant will be back on terra firma in the next few hours," he explained. "The engineers are finishing up their final checks to ensure we don't get any more dropouts in our satellite feeds. Until they get back, the change will do you good.

"However," Lakesh continued, "in the meantime I would like for you and your team to take a little detour and investigate something for me."

Brigid looked over to where Mariah Falk was running a pH test on an area of the fallen meteor's surface. "With Mariah and Edwards?" she queried.

There was a pause over the Commtact as Lakesh considered the question. "It's just a little reconnaissance work, Brigid," he decided. "You shouldn't need backup. But I'd take them just in case."

"That sounds awfully ominous," Brigid said, her tone jovial.

Lakesh dismissed her frivolous comment. "The satellite feed is showing what appears to be—brace yourself—a new ville, located roughly sixteen miles to the northwest of your current location."

Brigid was silent for a long moment as she digested what Lakesh had just told her. She pictured the map of the area, just to confirm that there was—or should be—no ville nearby. Even so, when she did respond she found it difficult to keep the incredulity out of her tone. "A new... *ville?*"

"A new ville," Lakesh repeated solemnly. "I'm just bringing up the data from our last global sweep, which dates from Tuesday of one week ago—seven days almost to the minute..."

"And...?" Brigid encouraged

"Brigid," Lakesh began, "if I told you that a complete new ville had appeared in its entirety in just seven days, would you take my word? Or would you think me insane?"

"I'd never think you insane, Lakesh," Brigid told him, aware that she was being manipulated by the Cerberus leader.

"But you would expect evidence," Lakesh suggested over the Commtact, "and there is no more compelling evidence than viewing something with your own eyes."

Brigid sighed once more. "Okay, I'll go," she agreed. "But why me?"

"You're in the area," Lakesh told her reasonably.

Brigid looked up at the overcast sky. "Sixteen miles is still about four hours away on foot," she said, not so much talking to Lakesh as simply thinking out loud. "I'll see if the interphaser can locate a closer parallax point and I'll report back as soon as I can."

"That's my girl," Lakesh said, and then he signed off, leaving Brigid to her new assignment.

IT TOOK BRIGID TEN MINUTES to wind down her tasks at the meteor site and explain to Mariah that they would be taking a brief side trip.

"We'll use the interphaser," Brigid explained, feeling slightly ludicrous at the proposition. The interphaser could transport them thousands of miles in a heartbeat—using it for a journey of just sixteen miles seemed somehow wasteful.

Edwards rejoined them midway through Brigid's final checks of the interphaser, and Mariah brought him quickly up to speed.

"A brand-new ville?" Edwards said, laughing with astonishment. "The hell?"

Brigid looked up from where she was running coordinates through the interphaser to try to locate a closer parallax point. "Let's go find out," she said.

EIGHT MINUTES LATER, just as the skies opened with rain, Brigid, Edwards and Mariah stepped into the beautiful lotus blossom of quantum energy and disappeared from the parallax point located five fields over.

In less than a second, the three Cerberus warriors stepped out into what appeared to be a dark cavern of rocky walls and pooled water. They blinked rapidly as the lotus blossom of light disappeared from view, plunging the cavern into semidarkness.

"Where are we?" Edwards growled, looking around the cavern as the interphaser powered down.

Brigid set to work packing the interphaser back in its little metal carrying case, her movements economically swift from familiarity. "First National burial ground," she explained without looking up.

"First who?" Edwards asked, baffled by her statement. "We're in a bank's graveyard?"

"First Nations," Brigid explained. "You've heard of Native Americans, right?"

Irritated, Edwards nodded. "Red Injuns, you mean?"

"Whatever," Brigid replied, disinterested in whatever two-hundred-year-old point of semantics Edwards thought he was making. "Well, we're in Canada. The First Nations are analogous to Native Americans."

"Canadian American Indians," Edwards nodded. "Got it. And why are we in their boneyard?"

"Parallax point," Brigid said. "These old burial grounds were often considered centers of power, but they generally drew that power from something far more ancient and fundamental."

"You mean a couple of rutting aliens once did the nasty here," Edwards suggested.

Brigid shook her head in despair as she secured the locks on the carry case. "Something like that," she agreed as she stood up, the handle of the bulky carry case in her hand.

A few paces over, Mariah was using a penlight to check the striations in the cavern walls, her professional interest piqued. "These are some really nice gradations," she said as Brigid and Edwards approached. "You can really see the lines where the deposits sit."

"Let's look at them when we get back," Brigid gently prompted. "Okay, Mariah?"

Mariah nodded, just a little self-conscious.

Together, the three Cerberus personnel made their way through the tunnel-like cavern and up into the open air.

What they saw as they exited the mouth of the cave took their collective breath away. It stood over a half mile distant, yet it loomed over the landscape like some crouching insect drinking blood. It was recognizably a ville, and yet it was something else, something oppressive and dead and—simply—wrong.

Brigid looked at it, and it was like seeing something from a dream—so familiar and yet strangely alien and unreal. The ville conformed to the same fundamental layout as any other ville that Brigid had ever seen. And yet, at that moment, it held her in its grip, with all the attraction of the deadly cobra poised for the kill. A single sentence appeared unbidden in Brigid's mind: "I am paralysed with fear," she told herself. And it was true. There was something so indescribably "other" in that seemingly normal collection of rocks that it threatened to overwhelm the senses.

The walls were there, the high walls that surrounded the building structures of every ville. From this distance, and with no frame of reference, it was hard to estimate how tall those walls truly were, but Brigid would guess they were far taller than a man. Their appearance was not one of a wall that is built, but rather one that has been carved by the elements, lines ripped from stone by the wind and the rain. The buildings themselves were made from the same lustreless gray rock, reaching upward in towers that clawed at the clouds overhead. There were several smaller towers, their tops peeking over the highest point of the walls. The most impressive structure, however, was in the center, as Brigid knew it had to be. A towering pyramidal block, as wide as it was tall, with straight sides that seemed uneven, bumps and protrusions along their edges, like the edge of a cliff. Smoke poured from the roof of the pyramidal structure, puffs of dark gray that matched the clouds overhead. Brigid knew what it was immediately—the Administrative

Monolith. Perhaps called by another name, she didn't know yet, but she knew its purpose. It towered over the landscape as a reminder to the people of the ville—and to those beyond its walls—they were being watched; they were being controlled. And control was good; control was something to be welcomed. *Embrace control, for in control there is safety.*

These thoughts assaulted the mind of Brigid Baptiste as she stared at that towering structure, and she recalled for the first time in years the real emotions that she had felt in Cobaltville, and the fear she had harbored at leaving. *Control is good.*

Brigid shook her head, as if she could physically shake the dread from it, before turning to look at her companions who stood to either side of her. Like her, they were dumbstruck by the ugly ville of gray rock. Unlike her, neither of them had grown up in a ville, and yet they too seemed transfixed by the structures before them.

Remembering herself, Brigid engaged her Commtact and spoke in a dull voice, one drained of all emotional feeling. "Cerberus, we have visual confirmation of your rogue ville." The words seemed so tiny when confronted with the enormity of the ville itself, and yet they were all she could think of to say.

Chapter 13

"It's incredible," Mariah muttered, taking several steps from the cave entrance. "What is that? It looks like…slate? Is that slate?" She turned around, repeating her question to Brigid.

"Mariah, come back here," Brigid instructed, suddenly very aware that Mariah's service with Cerberus had rarely placed her in a potential danger zone such as this.

The cave entrance was less like a cave than a rabbit burrow, a hole with a slight ridge on one side before the rocky tunnel disappeared beneath the ground. It provided good cover, but Brigid didn't like the thought of walking out in the open so close to this strange new ville.

"They can't see us," Mariah told her. "We must be half a mile away."

"Two-thirds," Brigid corrected automatically, her ordered mind insisting on producing the facts she had on hand. She wondered if that was partially because she had so few genuine facts to hand in a world suddenly turned upside down.

Mariah had raised her hand to shield her eyes, even though the sky was overcast. "Schist," she said. "I think that's schist, not slate."

Still standing in the warrenlike entrance to the cavern, Edwards spoke up, his tone laced with annoyance. "What the *schist* are you talking about, Falk?" he growled.

Mariah glanced back at him, pointing out the weathered rock formation that had apparently been somehow carved into a ville in the space of a week. "Schist is an incredibly durable stone, Edwards. It's resistant to decay, *et cetera,*" she explained. "It's considered to be a 'dimension stone,' which is to say that it has formed a major part of the construction industry for long-lasting projects from the Industrial Revolution onward. For example, almost all of the building foundations for New York City through the 1920s and 1930s were made from schist rock."

Edwards shrugged dismissively. "I was always more of a *Flintstones* guy," he grunted.

"The thing is, this is not an easy rock to mold," Mariah continued. "Certainly not to the extent that's been done here with such alacrity. Why, merely transporting such a large amount of schist would be a grand undertaking."

Brigid took a step from the shadowy cave entrance, examining that towering ville in a new light. "It's like the pyramids at Giza," she said. "An incredible feat of construction that seems to defy the tools we know to be available."

"This whole area includes a lot of schist," Mariah told Brigid, "so the builders could potentially have mined it." She sounded unsure of the feasibility of such an action. "If they did, then they did so very quickly. This is a fully constructed ville and it's been built in less than a week. Forget the construction expertise required—just excavating that much rock would be a huge operation. And just where did all the trash go? The offcuts that would have to have been discarded?"

Brigid was pensive as she weighed that nugget of information. "Let's look around," she decided, "see if we can find how they did this. If they used big machinery, then it shouldn't be too hard to either locate it, or find evidence of its usage—tracks, stuff like that."

Still standing in the cavern's entryway, Edwards shook his head. "Uh-uh, ain't going to be doing that, Red," he said.

"We're just looking around," Brigid appealed to him.

"Not on my watch, we're not," Edwards told her. "I'm not here as some big brain like you two. My job is to keep you girls safe and make sure you get back to Cerberus in one piece. So running headlong into danger ain't on the agenda."

Brigid let out a little growl of annoyance. Had this been Kane, it would have been her who was holding him back as he "ran headlong into danger" as Edwards had phrased it. But among this group, she was cast as the impetuous one who put the acquisition of further information above personal safety. "Edwards," she reasoned, "we're here now and Cerberus needs this information."

"So they send a fully equipped CAT team," he said, gesturing to the colossal ville that stood on the near horizon. "That shit ain't going anywhere, Ms. Baptiste."

"This thing has expanded at such a rate that going back to Cerberus and waiting for a CAT team to be assigned just to do a recce is a dangerous waste of time," Brigid implored. "Let's look around now, while there are no Magistrates to disturb us."

Edwards looked at her, taken aback. "Magistrates?" he asked.

"Or sec men, or guards," Brigid continued. "It's a ville— it's probably got someone assigned to keep track of strangers, right?"

"That's what I'm worried about," Edwards told her. "Was only a few days ago I was in Snakefish and met with

a jumped-up little would-be Magistrate trying to bring law
to the ruins. And, believe me, they were the damn dictio-
nary definition of 'ruins.'"

"I recall," Brigid said, for she had been there a few
weeks before when Snakefishville had been struck by the
earthquake. "Let's take a look around," Brigid proposed,
"and if there's any sign of trouble we'll bug out, okay?"

Reluctantly, Edwards unholstered his Heckler & Koch
and checked the breech. "Okay, but you two stay behind
me, and if there is any sign of trouble you pop yourselves
straight back to Cerberus. Deal?"

Brigid glared at him, fiery anger in her emerald eyes.
"I can take care of myself."

"My watch, my rules," Edwards snapped at her. "So, do
we have a deal, ma'am?"

Brigid nodded. For all of Edwards's good intentions,
she firmly missed working with Kane and Grant, and the
equality with which they treated her.

BACK AT THE CERBERUS REDOUBT, Kane found Grant sitting out on the plateau by the main entrance, nursing a cup
of coffee as he gazed out across the mountains surrounding
the hidden military retreat. He had changed his Cerberus
uniform for camo pants and a black undershirt that left
his muscular arms bare, glistening with sweat like gleam-
ing, polished mahogany. Beside him, resting on the dusty
ground, sat a carafe that he had snagged from the canteen
area of the redoubt.

"Hey, what are you up to, partner?" Kane asked jovially
as he sauntered out from the shadow of the doorway into
the breezy open area beyond.

Grant looked around, showing Kane his open palm by
way of acknowledgment. "Just chilling," he said. "Trying
to calm down. It's been a tough few days, hasn't it?"

"Not a week I'd want to repeat anytime soon," Kane agreed. Like Grant, he had changed into more casual clothes, a drab-colored T-shirt and slacks. "I hear Brewster went straight to his quarters to sleep when you guys got back."

"That sounds about right." Grant laughed. "What about your mission partner—Helen, right?"

Kane shook his head fractionally, a friendly warning for his friend not to start ribbing him about his relationship with the engineer again. "She's compiling a full report to file with Lakesh for storage on the main database."

"Oh, so she's another little Brigid," Grant said, chuckling to himself.

Kane laughed, too. "It's what these technically minded types like to do, I guess."

Grant picked up the carafe and shook it at Kane as his friend approached across the dusty plain. "You want to grab yourself a cup and join me?"

Kane nodded as he sat down beside his partner. "I'll get a refill in a minute," he said. "So, how many hours did you rack up?"

"This week?" Grant asked. "I don't know. I think Donald had me at fifty-three hours of flying time in the six days."

Kane pushed a hand through his tousled hair as the wind caught it. "I clocked up fifty-six," he said. "If I close my eyes I can still see the stars."

"Tell me about it," Grant agreed. "I am so sick of sitting in that cockpit, and I swear I can still hear the damn thrusters ticking over. That's why I came out here. Listen—all you can hear is the wind."

Kane sat for a moment, listening to the reassuring breeze as it blew through the leaves of the trees, whipping up the dust around the little area beyond the redoubt doors. Then, from his back pocket, Kane produced a pack of dog-eared playing cards and held them out for Grant. "How about the sound of you losing? Fancy hearing that?"

Grant laughed again, taking the cards from their carton and shuffling them. "Never heard it yet, Kane," he said. "Don't plan on changing that today."

"We'll see," Kane replied, a note of friendly challenge in his voice.

BRIGID HAD DECIDED to leave the interphaser in its protective carrying case back in the cave, hidden behind a little mound of rocks close to the cavern wall. Given the limited nature of the interphaser, tied as it was to the invisible network of parallax points, the idea of lugging it around with her seemed folly. While not ideal, she felt hiding it here was preferable to carrying it with her in what was potentially hostile territory, even if they were keeping their distance from the mysterious ville itself.

Fields of long grass surrounded the ominous Saskatchewan ville, long yellow-green blades swaying in the breeze like a ship rolling on the ocean. As they walked through the grass, Brigid, Mariah and Edwards were surprised to find how dry the soil was. When they looked, they found that it wasn't really soil at all. The majority of what one would call earth was in fact shale, tiny scrapings of gray rocks not much bigger than an eyelash forming the surface layer. Beneath, the roots of the grass held their firm grip on the topsoil now hidden below this rough carpet.

"It's schist," Mariah said, leaning down to examine a handful of the sandlike stones. "Like the detritus when you plane down a stone block."

"The ville was carved from this stuff," Brigid said. "Perhaps this is what got left over."

Mariah stood up and let the tiny gray-brown stones trickle through the gaps between her fingers. "It's insane," she uttered. "Like something out of some weird nightmare."

Edwards looked at them both with irritation. "All I'm seeing is a collection of buildings," he growled.

"That appeared so quickly," Brigid reminded him, "that they didn't have time to dump the waste. It's just been spread here, ground to dust and left to kill all the crops and wildlife all around. In three months, this area will be nothing more than desert. This schist dust will have stifled all the life out of it."

"Let's try to make sure we're not still here by then, okay, Ms. Baptiste?" Edwards said, glancing this way and that, checking for anyone who might be observing them.

Brigid nodded. "Point taken."

Together, the three Cerberus teammates continued to circle the ville at a wide birth, using the natural cover of the long grass to camouflage them from casual view.

As they trekked across the ruined soil, Mariah sighed. "At least we know what they did with the waste now. It's everywhere, ground to dust."

When they were still a quarter mile from the stone border of the eerie ville itself, it became far easier to judge the scale of the place. The walls that surrounded it stretched to almost twelve feet above the ground. This close, they seemed rugged, unlike the smooth walls of the villes that Brigid had seen before, more like something beaten into shape by the elements than carved by human hands. The top of the wall was particularly uneven, with spiky protrusions reaching as much as another three feet in the air, while some lower parts of the wall reached barely nine feet in height.

Unlike Cobaltville or the other villes that Brigid was familiar with, this new ville showed no signs of protection other than the walls themselves. There were no sec men patrolling along the top, no gun turrets aimed outside to keep the Outlanders away from its walls; there weren't even any lookout towers, either manned or unmanned. What's more, coming this close, Brigid noticed how little noise was emanating from within. Occasionally, there was a crash or thump of things colliding, the noise of shifting sand, but with no evidence of voices or the general hubbub of human life, it was entirely possible that the noises were simply loose things being tossed about in the wind.

Brigid looked at Mariah, and then to Edwards. "Do you get the feeling it's empty?" she asked in a low voice.

Edwards peered at the schist-made ville for a long pause before he replied. "There's nothing moving in there," he decided.

"Weird," Mariah added, shivering a little. "Like some kind of ghost ville."

All three Cerberus rebels looked at the mystery that stood silently before them, its rocky walls high, its pyramid-topped monolith looming over them like some great, towering statue, the gray smoke still puffing from gaps in its roof.

Finally, Brigid broke the silence that had fallen between them. "This place was constructed somehow," she said. "There's no sign of any machinery out here. I vote that we look around inside."

Edwards turned to her, consternation lining his brow. "With all due respect, ma'am, are you nuts? I agreed to coming out this far under duress. Actually trying to get inside doesn't seem at all smart."

"If it's empty," Brigid argued, "then all we're doing is looking around some weird ruins."

"Very weird," Mariah chipped in, "given that a week ago they didn't show up on satellite surveillance. Like it's *Brigadoon* or something."

"Brigadoon?" Edwards asked, perplexed.

"It was a musical about a Scottish town that only appeared for one day every century," Mariah told him.

"Wasn't really one for musicals," Edwards dismissed.

Brigid took several purposeful strides in the direction of a gap in the wall that marked the ville gates before looking back over her shoulder. "Come on, let's go take a look," she insisted.

The three teammates spread out as they made their way through the long grass toward the ville itself. Their boots crunched as they walked across the schist-covered earth, sounding like breaking bones beneath their feet. The ville simply stood there beneath the darkening clouds, waiting for them as though poised, a puzzle daring to be solved. Occasional puffs of smoke sailed from the central column, as if it was slowly burning.

Together, they walked through the tall gateway to the ville, a space wide enough to let three Sandcat vehicles through, shoulder to shoulder. As they passed through those gates, the skies opened up and the rain that they had left sixteen miles distant finally caught up to them, a thin drizzle that added a shushing sound to their surrounds as it struck the long grass and the shale beneath, and pitter-pattered against the hard planes of the rocks that had been used to form the ville itself.

Within the high walls, they saw several smaller buildings, as well as the smoldering monolith at the center, all of them constructed of the same grayish-brown rock. Each side of the monolith was fifty feet at its square base, with sloped walls working up to a triangular apex, like a pyramid. The apex itself was over forty feet above the ground, encompassing roughly five stories of an average building. The monolith, like the other buildings and the walls of the deserted ville, had rough sides, craggy and unfinished, almost as though they were something that had been grown or spit out from the ground like the debris of a volcano. And, like a volcano, it coughed erratic puffs of dark smoke into the sky.

Mariah rushed ahead on scampering feet, wanting to examine the surface of those walls more closely. Edwards jogged after her, warning her not to run off without them.

As she watched her teammates run ahead of her, Brigid Baptiste engaged her Commtact and presented a report to Cerberus, keeping her voice low. "We've entered the ville through a wide gap in the surrounding walls. The ville itself appears dead, no sign of life here whatsoever. Something's been burning here recently, though. What passes for the Administrative Monolith looks to be on fire somewhere inside."

From her Commtact receiver, Brigid heard Donald Bry's familiar voice acknowledging her communication. "I'll let Lakesh know. Be careful, Brigid," he instructed. "No unnecessary risks."

"Absolutely," Brigid assured him before signing off.

With that, she ventured farther into the eerily empty ville, wondering who would have—and who could have—constructed such a thing. With the lack of inhabitants, the place seemed more like some elaborate monument or museum exhibit, a reconstruction for exploration and enlightenment. But a reconstruction of what? Brigid wondered. Could this be something more than a ville?

Brigid stood at the base of the central monolith, watching the rain sluicing at its ragged sides, and a fragment of memory came back to her. At that moment, Brigid found herself taken aback as the memory tugged at her thoughts, like something just out of reach. Brigid Baptiste, whose eidetic memory had never forgotten or lost track of a single item, found herself recalling something she thought that she had lost.

There had been a step pyramid, a temple on the banks of the Euphrates, surrounded by an obsidian wall covered with glyphs whose moldings caught and trapped the sparkling sunlight that reflected off the water. The pyramid had been a landing pad of some sort, a small covered area at its summit. Brigid had been with Kane as they watched Enlil, along with his wife and brother, stride from the sheltered area, sweeping majestically down those stone steps toward them.

It was the memory trap, Brigid realized, a thing that she had blotted from her mind lest it overwhelm her. Months ago, she and Kane had found themselves caught within the shared uni-mind of the Igigi, escaped slaves of the Annunaki space gods. The memories had kept repeating, threatening to overwhelm Brigid until Kane broke the pattern, focusing their *anam-chara* bond to break the hypnotic spell. In that brief, terrifying moment, Brigid had seen the world as it had been, millennia before, when the Annunaki had first walked the Earth. Kane had recognized the pyramid within the high walls, telling her it looked like Cobaltville, where they had grown up almost five thousand years later.

"The patterns repeat themselves, Kane," Brigid had explained, the knowledge somehow absolute in her mind at that moment.

And now she saw that repetition once again, the ghostly ville following the age-old pattern of those landing sites, those places of worship, like some magical design intended to hold and to focus power.

Could there be more to the villes than they had ever suspected? The Annunaki's knowledge base was incredible, and their planning absolute. What if the villes with their symmetrical designs, their exact rules and their precise population requisites—5,000 inhabitants in each, no more, no less—what if all of that had been part of some kind of grand plan? What if it had been a way to channel their power?

Brigid felt a cold shiver tugging at her spine as she looked around the deserted ville while rain lashed at the rock buildings. There was something deeper at play here, she was sure of it, and it was something that she, Lakesh and the rest of Cerberus had been blind to. Only seeing an empty ville waiting patiently for inhabitants did she begin to wonder at the truth.

Forty-five thousand people spread equally across nine villes, each of the same design. What did it mean?

Chapter 14

The numbers didn't add up.

Lakesh stood in a restroom located close to the ops center within the Cerberus redoubt, staring at himself in the mirror as he washed his hands under the flowing faucet.

He had been born two and a half centuries ago, had aged normally until the nukecaust, been cryogenically frozen, awoken to live another fifty years and, finally, de-aged by Enlil in his guise of Sam the Imperator. He had stood on this same spot numerous times over the subsequent months, never giving much thought to what had happened when Sam had granted him that wonderful gift of youth. But now he looked at his reflection and he saw the signs of age appearing once more, far more quickly than they had before. He had been physically reverted to a fortysomething-year-old man just three years earlier, yet his face was taking on the aspect of someone older once more, someone in his late fifties, and the white patches of hair over his ears were becoming larger, with more white showing in the black every day.

Sam the Imperator's gift had seemed a miracle. But now Lakesh wondered about the gift's hidden strings. To age once was the fate of every man, he told himself, but to age twice, in full knowledge of what was to come—that was a cruel trick to play on any man. And here he was, aging at a faster rate than he should, feeling that slow weight pulling at his flesh. Sam the Imperator's gift was failing before Lakesh's eyes. Those are strings, Pinocchio, he told himself as he stared at the crow's-feet lines at the edges of his eyes.

Suddenly, Lakesh let out a shriek and snapped his hands away from the running water of the faucet. It had turned scalding hot and, with his inattention, he had not noticed until now. He turned the faucet off and reached over to the roll of towels that was attached to the wall of the restroom. As he did so, the door opened and Donald Bry entered.

"Oh, Dr. Singh," Bry said, taken aback. "I was just coming to find you."

"You found me," Lakesh told him reassuringly.

"Brigid just commed us from the new ville up in Canada," Bry explained. "She thinks it's empty. Her team are investigating now."

Tossing the paper towel in the receptacle, Lakesh raised a surprised eyebrow. "They've gone inside?" he queried.

Bry nodded. "They're there right now," he said as he paced across the tiled floor of the bathroom. "If you'll excuse me, I'll be with you in a minute."

As Donald Bry made his way to the urinal, Lakesh left the restroom, thoughts of his strange aging process still playing at his mind. Something was decidedly wrong, he felt sure. Perhaps it was time to speak to Reba DeFore, the team physician, see if she might give him a full physical when she had a free moment.

THE RAIN WAS GETTING HEAVIER, lashing at the symmetrical structures that made up the ghostly ville. Brigid had visited the ruins of Beausoliel, and she had witnessed the destruction of Snakefishville, but walking through a fully formed ville so utterly devoid of life was far more unsettling. For, without inhabitants, it felt more like a prison camp, something designed to snare and entrap people, something designed to hold them in place. Was that all the villes had ever been? A way to pen and control the inhabitants?

Besides the smoking monolithic pyramid there were four two-story buildings, one at each corner of the ville, and a further two set more centrally, placed in diagonal opposition to each other. Each building had gaps for windows and doors, but there was no glass apparent, nor any physical doors.

As the rain became heavier, the noise that it made became louder, clattering against all of the hard surfaces that were all around the Cerberus teammates.

"Who do you think built it?" Mariah asked, addressing her question to Brigid as the red-haired archivist absorbed the details of the eerily empty ville.

"And how?" Brigid replied, a question for a question. "There's no evidence of machinery here."

"So they moved on," Mariah suggested.

Brigid shook her head. "No, these buildings weren't built. Look closely at them. It's like they were beaten into form by the elements, almost like they were grown. Does that even make sense?"

Mariah stepped up to the imposing monolith, running the palm of her hand down its side. It felt rough to the touch. "It doesn't make sense, and yet I think you're right," she concurred. "This feels like the eroded surface of a cliff face. It has that same basic pattern and physical structure."

"The weather can't do this, Mariah," Brigid stated. "It's not unlikely—it is quite simply impossible. To construct a proxy ville from the rock, even if the rock was already here…"

"Which it wasn't," Mariah retorted. "At least not in such abundance above the surface," she quantified after a moment's thought.

"Could this have been excavated from below the soil?" Brigid asked.

"Logistically? Sure," Mariah said. "Honestly, though, this is a lot of work. And I mean 'a lot lot.' With twentieth-century mining techniques, this is still several weeks' work. And, as you've pointed out, there's no evidence of any machinery being used. This stuff has been weathered."

"Or grown," Brigid reminded her.

"You can't grow rocks," Mariah said, wondering that she was pointing out the obvious to someone as smart as Brigid. "Crystals, yes, but not rocks."

Brigid stood there, her rain-soaked hair weighing heavily against her shoulders, looking around at the eerie constructions all about them. "Maybe not in the traditional sense," she agreed, speaking slowly, ordering her thoughts, "but maybe in a more general way. Somehow excavated and shaped."

"Like a 'rock garden,'" Mariah said, then she began laughing in spite of herself, realizing her accidental play on words. Her laughter echoed from the hard surfaces all about them, and she stifled it with her hand.

"Could it be possible?" Brigid asked.

Mariah shrugged. "You of all people should know the answer to that, Brigid," she said. "From what I hear, you've had more and wilder adventures than most of us can dream of. Your tolerance of the impossible would seem to be far greater than that of myself or Edwards."

Brigid smiled. "But there tended to be a logical explanation to every last one, however wild it seemed. What's starting to bother me is why there were only nine villes to begin with. I mean, the Annunaki were supposedly all-powerful, and yet their plan to reconquer the Earth through taking chrysalis form and ruling the villes…it's so convoluted that it doesn't ring true."

"They're devious," Mariah reminded.

"Devious, yes," Brigid agreed, "but the villes are utterly out of place with the rest of their objectives. It's almost like whoever came up with the concept never really thought it through."

"But the Annunaki think everything through," Mariah said dubiously.

"That they do," Brigid agreed. "Which means there must have been something more to the villes than we realized. The existence of this, a tenth ville, screams as much. And it is a ville—there's no doubt about that in my mind."

"Mine, either," Mariah agreed.

As the two women stood in the rain, digesting the ramifications of that statement, Edwards reappeared from his own scouting of the rock ville, sprinting around the corner of the monolith, his Heckler & Koch pistol held high. Brigid saw immediately that there was concern furrowing the brow of his bullet-shaped head.

"Edwards?" she asked. "What's—?"

"We got us some trouble," Edwards said as he ran past, heading for one of the blocks that stood at the four corners of the square enclosure.

Automatically, Brigid's hand went to the holster she wore at her hip, pulling loose the TP-9 pistol she had housed there. The TP-9 was a compact semiautomatic, a bulky hand pistol with the grip set just off center beneath the barrel and a covered targeting scope across the top, all finished in molded matte black.

In a moment, Brigid was chasing on Edwards's heels as the ex-Mag rushed toward the doorway to one of the far buildings.

"What do you have?" Brigid asked.

"Saw movement in one of the windows," Edwards told her. "Looked like a figure."

"You saw him?" Brigid asked.

"I saw something, Ms. Baptiste," Edwards stated, "and I sure as hell don't want to be caught pissing against the wind with my pants down if it's something come to hurt us."

Brigid agreed, and together the two of them ran into the two-story block at the corner wall.

Behind them, Mariah Falk watched the pair rush off. Unarmed, she backed toward the central monolith and crouched there out of the rain, her eyes fixed on the far building. Unlike these two, Mariah wasn't a warrior. At the first sign of trouble, she suddenly realized the danger she had placed herself in by agreeing to search the ville.

Inside, the building seemed as eerily silent as the ville itself, with just the ambient noise of the constant shushing drone of the rain against its hard exterior walls. Edwards held his gun high by his shoulder in a two-handed grip, the little German-made USP pistol looking small in his large hands. Beside him, Brigid raised the TP-9.

Within, the building was dark, dull light spilling through the windows from the overcast sky. The first room, a bland lobby area with undecorated rock walls, seemed full of moving shadows as the rain continued to pour outside. The wind howled through the open windows and doorways, like some awful banshee's wail. The room had a fresh damp smell from the falling rain, but other than that it smelled of nothing much.

Although Brigid considered this to be a lobby—unconsciously relating it to a structure she recalled from Cobaltville—it was a wide area encompassing much of the lower story of the building. There were several bland walls jutting out, seemingly at random intervals, within the space, and several of these seemed poised to create additional rooms. However, it had the feel of something not of human hands, a series of jumbled pathways rather than a dwelling, like a map plotted through some schizophrenic nightmare. As such, the jumble of stabbing walls and twisting curves was disorienting, and even Brigid's exceptional memory struggled to create a workable schematic of the building in her mind's eye.

Edwards crept ahead on stealthy feet, his steps almost silent, gun leading the way as he turned each corner of the eerie, mazelike lobby area. Warily, Brigid followed, her own pistol held before her.

Edwards turned the corner of a wall and found a staircase leading to the upper story. Like the rest of the building, the staircase was uneven and appeared to have been chiseled from schist, and where it met the outside wall it joined perfectly, the two sections shaped from one piece. Edwards turned back to Brigid, gesturing silently to her that he was going up the stairs.

Brigid nodded, stepping back into the shadows and securing a position by the wall from which she could cover the stairwell should Edwards return with someone—or something—following. As Brigid watched, her senses alert to any sign of movement, Edwards slowly ascended the stone steps, the slight sound of his footfalls drowned out by the continual drumming of the rain against the walls and the pained howling of the wind.

The staircase stood flush against one exterior wall, while the other side was open with no balcony, simply exhibiting a sheer drop to the ground as one climbed higher past the jutting wall that stood at the ground level. Edwards made his way carefully to the top, walking heel-and-toe to keep the noise he made down to an absolute minimum. He was sure he had seen something moving in these upper windows, but the nightmarish interior had already confused his sense of direction. Now he couldn't seem to fit the interior into his mental map of the exterior, couldn't settle on which wall was which.

As he touched the higher reaches of the staircase, Edwards ducked, keeping his head and shoulders below the level of the highest step while he listened for sounds of movement or breathing coming from above, or anything else that might give away a presence he felt sure he had seen. The rain lashed against the rough exterior walls, sounding like the rubbing of sandpaper, obscuring anything Edwards might have heard. Warily, he peered over the highest riser of the stairs, turning his head left and right to get a quick view of the room. There were pillars lining the room at odd intervals, each one twisted like the thick branches of a crooked old tree. As he turned, he saw a figure waiting for him across the other side of the vast room, far from the stairwell. Not just one figure—ten, twelve, more than that. All of them were dressed in worn and dirty clothes, standing erect as they stared blankly toward him.

What the fuck? Edwards mouthed, his lips moving but no sound coming out.

Automatically, Edwards had ducked back below the top of the stairs, keeping himself out of sight from the group. He glanced back over his shoulder for a moment, indicating to Brigid that he was going up into the room above.

A moment later, Edwards raced up the last few stone steps in a hurried crouch, the gun ready as he emerged in the upper room. The figures seemed oblivious to him, waiting there in silence as he aimed his pistol at them, covering them.

"You," Edwards commanded. "What the hell is going on? Who are you? Did you build this ville?" He strode closer, recovering to his full height, the Heckler & Koch held before him in a steady two-handed grip. "Do you hear me?" he asked, gesturing with the pistol toward the nearest of the waiting crowd, a white-haired old man with blank eyes and a week-old beard.

They were like statues, utterly unmoving. He saw now that they had arranged themselves in two distinct rows like crops, set at the back of the vast room that encompassed almost the entirety of the top floor. They were dressed in ragged, dirty farm clothes, with stains of blood and other things marking them here and there, several rips showing where the clothes had been roughly torn. Their eyes were open and they were breathing, but their expressions were blank, like sleepwalkers waiting to be awoken. Edwards counted seventeen in all, all of them adults, several quite elderly. Despite Edwards's repeated questions, none of the strange group reacted, let alone provided any answers.

Irritation rising, Edwards scanned the room more slowly, looking to see if anyone else was there to whom he might address his questions. It appeared empty. The windows were small up here, tiny gaps in the walls not much bigger than a man's head, placed roughly at eight-foot intervals along the long wall of the structure, several of them poking out from where crooked pillars had been placed, bent as if with osteoporosis. Water pooled below the windows of one wall, where the rain was being blown through the open gap there and into the building. The tiny windows left the room immersed in gloom, its rock walls a mass of shadowy bumps and lumps, the pillars like figures in the darkness.

As his eyes searched the room, Edwards became aware of another presence, one he couldn't see. He turned, searching the shadows, the walls, trying to find the thing he felt sure was watching him.

Suddenly, like the whirling vision from a merry-go-round, he saw twin burning circles appear close to the far wall, almost nine feet above the floor—they were two flaming eyes watching him from the shadows. Edwards turned his gun at the creature, demanding he show himself. In response, the eyes burned brighter in the gloom, and then, as Edwards tried to make out its form, thin lines began to materialize in the blackness, tracks of molten lava, burning fiery bright in the shadows. Then the giant stepped forward, his head barely ducking the rough ceiling, and Edwards realized why he had failed to notice him on his first scan of the room. The giant was made of rock, perfectly camouflaged for the surroundings here, hidden until he chose to be seen, like one of the crooked pillars that poked from floor to ceiling. A pillar of stone with arms and legs, a pillar that could walk.

And the lines of magma barely visible in the shadows began to glow brighter. Brighter and angrier as the stone giant stepped closer to Edwards's fragile human form.

Chapter 15

Edwards skipped backward, glancing over his shoulder to locate just where the rock stairs were. When he turned back, the stone giant had emerged from the shadows and was walking toward him with heavy, purposeful strides. Nine feet tall with a body of weathered rock, the thing looked like an animated, primitive statue, so imposing that Edwards was reminded of the Easter Island heads.

"Stay back," Edwards commanded, training his gun on the approaching monster. "Stay the hell back!"

Off to his right, Edwards saw that the other inhabitants of the room simply stood there, giving no reaction to the weird scene that was playing out before them. They seemed like statues themselves, statues carved of flesh.

"Stay back," Edwards ordered again, skirting a crooked stone pillar that stood like a tree trunk amid the gloom. He was running out of places to go and, despite his immensity, the rock giant was moving too quickly to let him reach the opening of the stairwell.

As Edwards continued moving away from the monstrous form, Brigid's voice came from downstairs. "Edwards? Everything okay? What's happening up there?"

Before Edwards could answer, the rock giant stopped moving, turning to incline his head toward the opening of the stairwell, listening to the woman's voice. Then, as Edwards watched, dumbfounded, the giant turned to the statuelike people waiting in rows at the far side of the room, and his eyes glowed brighter for a few furious seconds. Edwards watched in awe as the creature's jagged slit of mouth opened and the burning fires of a volcano seemed to play within that gaping maw. And then, in a deep, basso voice that sounded rough, like rocks being pounded together, the thing spoke one single word: "Recruit."

On that instruction, the seventeen still forms sprang to life, as if clockwork automatons that had been wound up and let loose across the room, marching in file toward the rough-edged hole in the floor where the stairs began.

Shit, they're going for Brigid, Edwards realized. And after her, he knew, Mariah would be next.

His attention turned back to the stone colossus as the ragged-clothed farmers made their way down the stairs in hurried single file.

ONE FLOOR BELOW, Brigid could hear the sounds of frantic movement above, the shuffling feet and Edwards's shouted orders. Her own shouted query had been as much to check on Edwards as it had been to scare off any potential attacker once they realized that Edwards had backup.

Brigid's Commtact burst into life a moment later, and she heard the slightly disconcerting double voice of Edwards as he spoke above her while his voice was channeled through the subdermal pintels into her skull casing.

"You have incoming, Ms. Baptiste," Edwards said, his voice urgent. "Seventeen potential hostiles coming down the stairs right now."

Brigid shifted a little farther back into the shadows, holding her TP-9 automatic steadily at the gap in the ceiling. "*Potential* hostiles?" she queried over the Commtact link. "What's going on, Edwards?"

"I got me a moving statue up here," Edwards chimed back, "and he's just ordered your potentials to go 'recruit,' whatever the hell that means."

"That means we're in trouble," Brigid muttered as a booted foot appeared at the top of the stone steps.

A moment later, the first of the farmers stomped down the stairs, with more following, walking in unison just one step between each figure. Seeing their blank expressions and single-minded movements, Brigid was reminded of the zombies she had faced at Papa Hurbon's voodoo temple less than a week before. In their dirt-caked clothes, these old sod busters moved faster and with far more uniformity, and yet there was that same unnatural gait to their manner, as though they followed a mental compulsion rather than a voluntary instruction. Hurbon used herbs and drugs to alter the minds of his victims, placing them into a trance-like state where they would follow his orders. As such, the voodoo zombies were effectively living people, albeit so underfed and mindless that they appeared to be dead. By contrast, the people before Brigid seemed healthy, but the rigidity of their movements was so unnatural it sent shivers down her spine. Here, then, were zombies in their earliest stages, before they had lost the compulsion to eat and had begun decomposing while still alive.

Even as Brigid realized what she was facing, she engaged her Commtact once again, calling to Cerberus. "There are people here," she stated in a harsh whisper, "and things are turning strange."

Donald Bry's voice piped back over the Commtact a moment later. "Please expand, Brigid."

The fourth of the zombielike farmers had reached the bottom step and they were spreading out, searching for Brigid among the shadows.

"No time, Cerberus," Brigid subvocalized, trusting the remarkable technology of the Commtact to pick up and relate her voice. "Will report in as soon as I'm able." With that, she disengaged her communication link before it became a distraction to the matter at hand.

In an instant, the first of the farmers—a well-built, dark-haired man in his early forties—turned in Brigid's direction and stopped. While his bland expression didn't really alter, there was a look of recognition about his body language, as though he had found what it was he had been sent for. "She's here," he stated, his voice low.

Like flocking birds, the others in the group turned their heads to where the first farmer was indicating, spying Brigid among the shadows. In response, Brigid moved the automatic slowly, tracking across the group.

"Keep back," Brigid warned them. "Keep back or I'll shoot."

In less than a second, the dark-haired farmer lunged at Brigid, his hand reaching out and snagging the extended muzzle of her TP-9. Even as the farmer grabbed the gun, Brigid squeezed the trigger, and a stream of bullets arrowed forth, the explosive propellant lighting the room in a staccato burst.

The dark-haired farmer was tough. He yanked at the weapon in Brigid's hand, pulling off her aim even as the first of the bullets struck him, clipping his shoulder and turning his right ear into a fountain of spurting gore. He pulled powerfully at the muzzle of the gun, yanking Brigid two steps forward before his other hand lashed out and struck her forehead with a hard slap. Brigid found herself being pulled forward and knocked back at the same time, and she felt her feet go from under her, kicking forward as

she toppled back. Reluctantly she released the TP-9, and
its fire-bright stream of bullets came to an abrupt end,
plunging the ill-lit room back into shadow.

With a crash, Brigid struck the unforgiving floor—just
dirt sprinkled with chipped fragments of schist like the soil
outside the ville. A second later, she was righting herself,
sweeping one of her long legs outward to hook her dark-
haired attacker by his ankles. The man staggered forward
before losing his balance and crashing to the floor beside
Brigid, still clutching the hot muzzle of the TP-9.

Brigid shifted her body, swinging a bladelike hand into
her attacker's wrist, forcing him to let go of her blaster. As
he did so, her other hand came at him, balled into a fist,
striking the man in the face, just above his right cheek.
Each of Brigid's blows landed with a resounding crunch,
but the man made no sound in reaction. Instead, he just
seemed to shake his head, shaking off the pain of Brigid's
punch as she reached for the discarded pistol.

Swiftly adopting a crouch position, Brigid turned,
swinging the recovered TP-9 at the approaching farmers
as they continued to file down the stone stairs and swarm
toward her. They paced toward her as one, sixteen forms
looming over her as she selected her first target.

"Keep back!" Brigid shouted, her voice loud in the con-
fined area of the stone room.

Brigid didn't want to kill these people, convinced they
were innocent victims in some scheme she had yet to
divine, but as they approached her she became frustrat-
ingly aware that she was running out of options.

ONE FLOOR ABOVE, Edwards continued to back away from
the looming stone giant as he stalked across the vast room
toward the ex-Mag.

"I'm warning you, pal," Edwards said, his Heckler &
Koch pointed at the giant, "stay back. I know you can
understand me now, and I won't have any compunction
about shooting you if you make me. Now, back off and
let's talk."

The great stone monster ignored Edwards's plea, con-
tinuing to stride forward, solid feet slamming against the
rocky floor with loud reverberations, herding the Cerberus
warrior to the far side of the room, well away from the
stairwell exit.

"The hell with it," Edwards growled. With that he aimed
the gun at one of the winding, tree-trunklike stone pillars
that littered the room and pulled the trigger. There was a
flash of gunfire in the gloom, and a single 9 mm bullet
whipped past the stone creature's side and slammed into
the pillar.

The stone creature gave no reaction to the blast, con-
tinuing to stride toward the little man who stood before
him. Edwards shifted his aim, centering the gun on the
monster's rocky chest.

"That's your only warning shot," Edwards advised. "I'm
not playing games here."

The monstrous rock thing continued onward, and suddenly Edwards found himself pressed against the far wall
between two of the well-spaced windows with nowhere
left to run.

"Screw it," Edwards spit. Gritting his teeth, he blasted
three rounds into the creature's chest, roughly where he
presumed his heart would be. The bullets struck the rock
hide before pinging off in different directions, leaving no
discernible damage on the creature's body.

"Oh, it's like that, huh?" Edwards growled as he shifted
his aim, targeting the creature's head.

The gun spit again, bullets lancing out of its muzzle in a rush of tiny detonations. The shots lit the room in momentary flashes like a faulty neon sign, before the room was plunged back into darkness, the acrid smell of cordite heavy in the air. The bullets cut through the air, slamming against the creature's head like angry insects, before simply bouncing off his rock face and whizzing off into the room accompanied by rising notes.

As the smoke cleared, Edwards saw the monster was still coming, now just four feet from him, and he leaped forward, ramming the gun upward and pointing it at the thing's glowing eyes. The eyes themselves seemed to be just sockets, the magmalike orange glow swirling beneath them as if in some deep volcanic pit. Edwards blasted through the clip of his Heckler & Koch, loosing shot after shot into the creature's face at point-blank range. In five seconds, the clip was empty and Edwards found himself standing there, just inches from the monster's wide, rough-skinned chest.

Emotionless, the great creature reached forward, and Edwards turned aside as a mighty rock arm reached out for him, huge hand open. The heavy arm missed him by three inches, and Edwards ducked down and ejected the empty magazine of his Heckler & Koch USP. The used magazine bounced off the stone floor with a clattering sound, while Edwards's left hand found the spare clip in his ammo belt and hastily reloaded as the monster stood over him.

When he looked up, Edwards saw the huge rock thing standing over him, his head inclined downward as if fascinated by what Edwards was doing. Hastily Edwards brought up the pistol, his finger pumping the trigger as he blasted half a dozen shots into the creature's groin and belly. The bullets whirred against the monster's armored flesh, sparking as they struck the hard surface before ricocheting in all directions. One bullet zipped past Edwards's shoulder, while another whizzed by his feet, popping against the stone floor there. The whole time, the creature gave no visible reaction, merely standing there as bullets slapped against his skin.

Edwards kicked out, throwing himself backward across the hard floor, scooting along on legs and buttocks as he continued his assault on the towering rock thing. Bullets slapped against the creature's hide with no effect until, inevitably, Edwards's gun clicked once more on empty.

His anger and frustration rising, Edwards ejected the magazine and leaped out of the way as the creature bore down on him. Swiftly, Edwards was back on his feet, fumbling with the useless gun as he struggled to reload it once again. As he looked up, he saw the giant rock creature standing over him, his arm reaching outward, right hand enveloping Edwards's forehead.

Edwards felt something then. Not pain, but something more akin to elation. The fear seemed to drain from him, to be replaced by a sense of comfort, of security.

The pistol dropped from his hand as Edwards was lifted, both physically and spiritually, by the great stone god that stood before him.

FROM HER CROUCHING POSITION, Brigid Baptiste sprayed a quick burst from her TP-9 in a low arc at the legs of the approaching zombified farmers. Clothing was shredded under the barrage, and chunks of bloody flesh ripped from the legs of the three who were closest to her, but none of them stopped moving. It was as if they were possessed, immune to the damage and the pain that Brigid's bullets must have caused.

They were in a trancelike state, Brigid realized, like a firewalker, unable to be affected by external considerations like pain.

Reluctantly, Brigid raised her pistol, thrusting it in the direction of the lead member of the group. "Don't make me kill you," she ordered, knowing it would do no good. Her options had just run out. For a second she hesitated, wishing for some sign that she didn't have to kill these people to stay free.

As her finger squeezed at the trigger, a hand to her side swept out of the shadows, throwing off her aim and intercepting the paths of that first volley of shots. Brigid turned, remembering the dark-haired farmer whom she had brought down. He had a swelling redness over his eye and there was blood in his mouth now where she had punched him, painting his teeth a reddish-pink as he snarled at her. Foolishly, she had thought him dispatched because of his serene state, but of course all of these "firewalkers" exhibited serenity.

Even as Brigid cursed her oversight, the dark-haired farmer slapped the TP-9 upward so that its burst of fire drilled into the ceiling above them in a loud rattle of shots. His arm was wounded, Brigid saw, the flesh exposed and bloodied where he had placed it in the path of fire for the briefest of instants. Yet the farmer didn't seem to care.

And then he was upon her, lashing out with his bloody arm, knocking Brigid so hard in the breastbone that her breath came out in a great burst and she began to splutter. Before she could react, train the pistol back on her attacker, the other farmers had moved in and began repeatedly kicking and punching her as she squirmed in place, struggling in vain to avoid their brutal blows.

STANDING OUTSIDE by the monolith that dominated the eerie ville, the rain splashing all around her, geologist Mariah Falk heard the echoes of gunshots carrying across the vast courtyard. She took three steps forward, out into the rain and toward the building that Brigid and Edwards had entered, then thought better of it.

Mariah activated her Commtact. "Cerberus, this is Mariah Falk," she said, keeping her voice low as she tensely watched the doorway of the building into which her colleagues had disappeared. "Repeat, this is Mariah Falk. Come in, Cerberus."

There was a pause, and Mariah heard the muffled sounds of more gunshots through the hiss of the falling rain.

Then Donald Bry's voice came through over Mariah's earpiece, as clear as if he had been standing beside her. "This is Cerberus, Mariah—what's happening?"

"We have a—" Mariah's words went dry in her mouth as she saw the figures step from the building and march purposefully toward her through the rain.

IN THE CERBERUS COMMAND CENTER, Donald Bry, who had pulled comm duty for the whole afternoon, was monitoring three other feeds as Mariah's voice came through. After a moment, she went quiet, and Donald recognized the fear in her tone.

"Mariah?" he asked. "Are you still there?"

When Mariah's voice came over his earpiece, it sounded breathless, and he realized that she was running. "Oh, my gosh, Donald, there are loads of them."

"Loads of what, Mariah? Please expand," Donald requested, remaining calm and businesslike.

He heard Mariah's panting as she continued to run, and the Commtact picked up a crashing noise which Donald realized must be either very near or very loud.

"Mariah?" he urged again, the trace of concern now coloring his tone.

"Something's happening here," Mariah reported. "The ville wasn't empty. We're outnumbered and…and…"

"And what, Mariah?" Donald prompted when she left the sentence hanging.

"Send help," Mariah said, urgency and fear in her tone. "Send help now!"

"Mariah? Mariah?"

Abruptly, her communication cut out and Donald Bry was left speaking to dead air.

Chapter 16

There was no record of Enia.

She had been Ullikummis's first—the first to taste his blade.

Enia had been a minor dignitary in Enlil's court in the golden city of Nippur, with responsibilities in maintaining diplomatic relations with the other Annunaki cities spread across the fertile lands of the Euphrates basin. Essentially it was her job to ensure that the simmering rivalries between the Annunaki didn't erupt into open warfare. Though an unimportant player in the royal household, Enia, like all Annunaki, was viewed as one of the gods by the simple-minded humans.

One day, Enlil had come to Ullikummis with a mission. There had been a liaison, Enlil explained as he stood with his son in a private room of his palace located far from prying eyes, between the girl and himself, and the liaison had resulted in a pregnancy. Since Enia was oviparous, there now existed a fertilized egg that Enia had stored away where it would hatch in due course. Enlil had grave concerns about what might happen should news of his by-blow child become public.

Enlil intimated that the young goddess had threatened him with blackmail, that he was to leave Ullikummis's mother, Ninlil, for her or she would tell the world of their tryst.

"In short," Enlil had explained to Ullikummis, who was then sixteen years old, "Enia's loose lips would disrupt this household beyond repair. I need her to be quietened, and evidence of her and the pregnancy erased. Do you understand?"

Ullikummis nodded solemnly, recognizing the true nature of the request that his father dare not voice. He was to assassinate the goddess and obliterate all evidence of her existence from the Annunaki records.

"It is a delicate situation, Ullikummis," Enlil pointed out. "Once you are finished, there should be no record of this. None anywhere."

Ullikummis nodded again, his hand running along his right arm as he subconsciously felt for the wound there that had healed long ago, the wound that had produced the knife Godkiller.

Two weeks later, as the sun was setting behind the horizon, Ullikummis waited in the branches of a tall tree close to Nippur's market square. He had been observing Enia without her knowledge ever since his father had made his request, and he had already memorized her routine. Each evening, as the sun set, she would pass through this street on the way to her living quarters in the east of the city. Ullikummis had searched for the location of the fertilized egg, hoping to eradicate it before he revealed himself to Enia, but his search had proved fruitless. The goddess could not have hidden it in many places, but Ullikummis had stopped short of drawing attention to himself, concluding that his best course of action was to question her before killing her. Thus, the prince waited, the blade Godkiller held tightly in his grasp.

Ullikummis's rock flesh had no sheen, and so he blended into the shadows of the tree, a strange, looming thing amid the branches, like some weird insect hive constructed solely of stone. The only indicator of his presence, should Enia look, were his glowing eyes, for he had learned now to dim the lavalike veins that ran over his body, the way a normal man might quieten his breathing.

Ullikummis waited, watching the street as the sinking sun painted it the pink of the salmon's flesh. Up ahead, a towering pyramid dominated the skyline of the city, central to everything that happened within Nippur's high walls. When Enia turned the corner of the market, making her way past the stalls that were being packed up, Ullikummis closed his eyes, that he not reveal his hiding place, and he listened to her footsteps, filtering away all other noises from his mind.

Enia was small for an Annunaki female, barely five feet in height and svelte, like a miniature or a child. Her scales seemed luminous in the dying sunlight, a deep crimson flushed with pink. She was beautiful, and Ullikummis could see immediately why his father had been attracted to her; she had a natural grace and an economy of movement that went beyond that of most Annunaki. With his eyes now closed, Ullikummis listened to her gentle footsteps on the paving stones, their familiar rhythm, slightly hurried in compensation for her shorter legs.

Killing her would be like killing a child, Ullikummis realized. Perhaps that was why his father had assigned him this task as his first mission. To kill a full-grown Annunaki took merciless power. It was not like killing the feebleminded Nephilim or the worthless apekin who inhabited the planet. To kill an Annunaki was to kill a god. But, even so, Ullikummis mused, there were gradations of godhood.

As Enia passed beneath the tree, Ullikummis moved, just a silent shifting of his weight, and suddenly he was dropping from the high branch, plummeting toward the ground, the rushing air singing past his ears.

Despite his size, Ullikummis landed with near silence, just the lightest of footfalls like a cat, his knees bending to absorb the impact. Even so, Enia heard—or perhaps sensed—him and she turned to see what it was that had fallen from the tree. Crouched there in the dwindling light, his knees still bent, Ullikummis looked to her like a pile of rocks, something discarded from one of the construction sites that were dotted all about the golden city. But as she began to turn away, dismissing her momentary concerns, Ullikummis opened those brightly burning eyes, and Enia's heart began to race faster, thudding in her chest.

Ullikummis was a monster, a thing to be hidden by his family, so his freakish appearance was not something often seen by those outside the royal circle. Enia had never seen him, and she struggled for a moment to comprehend what it was that she was looking at. As Ullikummis stretched to his full height—nine feet tall and of monstrous proportions to one so small—the fight-or-flight instinct inside of the diplomat kicked in, and Enia began to run, turning from the monster and heading for her home. This, too, was as Ullikummis had planned it, for he suspected that the germinating egg was hidden somewhere in her property. To have her there, to lead him to it, would make the final transaction easier.

Enia ran ahead of him, her short legs pumping, her foot claws clattering on the stones. Ullikummis paced after her, his long strides more than capable of keeping up. As she turned the corner into her street, Enia finally began to shout for help, as though she had not thought up until now that she had that option in her weak arsenal. Perhaps she had believed she was in no danger until she had confirmed that the rock thing was following her, for his appearance was one of nightmare, not of something of her reality. No matter—Ullikummis took to running, reaching for the female as she ducked into the canopied doorway of her domicile. His hand reached around her mouth, stifling her cries before she could pull herself away.

Enia struggled in his grip, shrugging this way and that as she tried to free herself. She bit down on his fingers, trying to hurt him, but it was like biting at rock, not only pointless but painful.

Ullikummis kicked at the door and it collapsed before them both, the wood splintering beneath his single powerful blow. The accommodation within was simple: a room of four walls with a single table at which to dine, two small chairs arranged at opposing sides. Beyond that, Ullikummis saw the doorway leading to other parts of the dwelling, the sleeping quarters and an area set aside for the preparation of food. He let go of Enia, shoving her ahead of him, watching as she staggered and fell.

"I am here for the by-blow," Ullikummis told her, keeping his request simple. There was no need to tell her that he was to execute her, not yet. Better that she believe she might survive, that she play along.

Sprawled on the stone floor, Enia turned, wiping at the blood that had formed on her scaly lips. "I don't know what you're talking about," she spat.

Ullikummis kicked out, brutally knocking the female in the face. "The egg," he repeated as Enia collapsed before him, slipping across the floor under the power of his savage blow.

Defiant, Enia looked up at the towering form of Ullikummis, her dainty mouth forming a sneer. "He sent you, didn't he? Lord Enlil."

"The by-blow egg," Ullikummis replied, his eyes glowing fiercely in the darkness of the room.

"Did he tell you what happened?" Enia asked. "Did he tell you that he came to me? That he raped me?"

Ullikummis looked at her, feeling her anger and, beneath that, her sadness. But it was not his place to judge, or to weigh the pleas of his victims. He was the instrument of his father's focused rage and that was all he must ever be. "The egg," he instructed once again.

Slowly, her movements strained, Enia stood up and led Ullikummis through the house and into the pantry that sat below the kitchen under a wooden trapdoor. Below ground, the larder was kept cool the better to store food. Its dimensions were tiny, barely enough to fit the both of them in, and Ullikummis had to duck to prevent his head from scraping against the clay brick ceiling.

Two days before, Ullikummis had been here, had scoped out the whole house, but he had been unable to locate the egg itself. Knowing he would need to kill the female, he had concluded then that it was easier to wait and let her take him to it than to disrupt things and potentially alert her to the danger she was in.

Ullikummis watched as Enia pried open a metal container with her long, delicate fingers, the container's golden sides flashing in the sliver of light from above. Within was a key, and she brushed jars from another shelf to reveal a strongbox slotted within a gap in the wall. Placing the key in the lock of the strongbox, Enia opened it to reveal an egg barely larger than her hand, its shell glistening a washed-out green in the light from above. She pulled the egg from its hiding place and brought it close to her breast, rocking it for a moment before she handed it to Ullikummis. So small, the egg was dwarfed when it sat in his huge palm.

"Did he tell you?" Enia pressed, as Ullikummis weighed the egg in his hand, staring at this potential half brother or half sister. "What did he say? That I'd asked for help? Or that I'd threatened him, perhaps?"

Ullikummis looked at the egg, wondering at the forming sibling that slept within, letting the female's words wash over him.

"I didn't ask for anything," Enia told him. "I merely applied to leave Nippur, but he declined my request. I don't know why. I think he was scared I would go to Lord Marduk and reveal his secrets, as if I knew any of them."

Emotionlessly, Ullikummis closed his hand, crushing the egg and the thing that was forming within. As the egg cracked and albumen dribbled through his stone fingers, Enia began to sob, her wails punctuated by long, racking breaths.

As they stood there, pressed together in the tiny, cell-like pantry, Ullikummis rammed his knife into Enia's torso, driving the blade up, pushing it through her naturally armored skin. Enia cried out for a second, and Ullikummis watched her, his face as expressionless as the stone he resembled. It was the first time that Godkiller had tasted blood, the first time that the multidimensional blade destroyed an Annunaki on all the frequencies of the universe, preventing their return to life.

As he withdrew the blade, Ullikummis felt the thick, sticky blood running down its edge, filling the engraved runes there before trickling over onto the hilt and onward, oozing over his hand. Enia's body sagged but there was nowhere for her to collapse, no room in the pantry. She said something then, before she expired, six words forced breathlessly through clenched teeth: "I would never have hurt him."

Ullikummis turned then, and Enia's body collapsed to the floor of the underground room as he ascended the steps and returned to the kitchen. He left her there, the last of her life seeping out of her amid the shards of broken eggshell of her would-be child.

It had been like plunging a part of himself into her, a part of his own body. The vibrating molecules of the knife echoed across dimensions, slicing through the Annunaki at something even deeper than the cellular level. But truly the blade was a part of him. It had been created of his body, shaped with his own hands. When it tasted first blood, it did so with Ullikummis, and he tasted the blood, as well. The words, like a magical incantation written across its surface, channeled through him then: gaze upon my bloodwork and lament.

Ullikummis used the table in place of the broken door, standing it on its side so that it blocked entry into Enia's domicile. On its surface, he painted the symbol for the scarabae sickness, warning others to keep away. No one would enter the building until that sign was removed, and Enia's body would be left to decompose in peace beside the crushed remnants of her unhatched child.

In all the Sumerian myths and stories, there is no mention of Enia, nor of her tryst with Enlil and the progeny it almost produced. Instead, her existence was purged from the records, as if she had never been.

ONE MONTH BEFORE HIS sixteenth birthday, Ullikummis was spending an increasing amount of time with Upelluri, often disappearing into the labyrinthine caves for whole weeks at a time. Ningishzidda had finished with his genetic alterations. Now, so far as the fabled Annunaki genengineer was concerned, Ullikummis was complete.

"You are my greatest creation, Ullikummis," Ningish-zidda had said when they had last met, to check that the prince's new eyes were fully functional.

Ullikummis had felt strange at the geneticist's choice of words. He made it sound as though Ullikummis was a temple or a work of art, not a living, breathing being, a member of the exalted Annunaki here on Earth.

You are my greatest creation, Ullikummis.

A creation. Nothing more.

Over their time together, the underworld hermit Upelluri had taught Ullikummis about the physical attributes of the Annunaki, shown him detailed diagrams that combined anatomy with string theory, explaining how the Annunaki existed across multiple planes. If the humans were mistaken in their belief that the Annunaki were gods, their error was forgivable, for, compared to the humans, the Annunaki were dimensionally more complex than they could ever appreciate. Tesseracts in humanoid form, their physical bodies as true a representation of their being as a puppet is of its puppeteer. As such, the Annunaki were exceptionally hard to kill. They could be hurt, their physical bodies might be wounded or even broken beyond repair, but to truly kill an Annunaki required a weapon that could cut multiple dimensions at the same time.

Ullikummis had pondered the riddle for a long time, researching with Upelluri a device that crossed all the planes at once. In later times, naive and shortsighted philosophers would call these planes "casements," but that comprehension was simplistic, treating the different vibrational frequencies as one would the rooms of a house. Instead, Upelluri had compared it to looking in a mirror. "You see your reflection, and behind it you see the reflection of the room beyond," he had said, "and the room in the mirror appears to have depth. But in reality, the whole thing is but a picture on a flat, reflective surface, with no more depth than the surface of a blade of grass. This world, this galaxy with all its depth and color and difference—this is but the image on the surface of the mirror to the Annunaki. You must go much deeper if you are to hurt one of your own."

With hindsight, the answer had been obvious. To kill an Annunaki would take that most fundamental of all weapons, the very first weapon—the body. The first Annunaki victim had not been killed by sword or lightning beam; he had been killed by the hands of his own brother.

Ullikummis looked at his hands. "These are the weapon," he realized, but he needed something more. He alone was special among the members of his godlike race, his DNA bent so far out of shape that he resembled no other. When he spoke of himself, he spoke of something alien, something altered.

Upelluri understood that, for his body suffered with the scarabae wounds. He, too, was an outcast from his own people, living alone below the ground, mistaken by humanity for a god of the underworld.

"What if I were to make a weapon from my flesh?" Ullikummis asked him.

"How?" Upelluri asked.

"If I were to take a part of my body, forge it into something," Ullikummis suggested excitedly. "A knife. A knife that could kill gods."

Coughing, Upelluri nodded, his own excitement clear on his scarred and marred face. "There are fires below," he said, "powerful rents that reach temperatures far in excess of anything on the Earth's surface. They would be your forge, where you might shape your godkiller blade."

Ullikummis smiled, a hideous line across his jagged rock face. "Godkiller," he said, reveling in the feel of the word as it left his mouth.

FOUR AND A HALF THOUSAND YEARS later, Brigid Baptiste was struggling to open her eyes against the immense pressure she felt there. It was like trying to wake up from a fever dream or a coma; all she knew was that she wanted to be awake, yet for a moment her body resisted her.

She was lying on the ground and her face was wet. Rain, she realized, feeling its tickling pitter-patter against her skin. Everything seemed dark because of the overcast sky, the sunlight obscured by dark clouds. It felt like a metaphor.

Even open, her eyes wouldn't focus for a few moments, and her left eye stung as though it was infected. Through the blur she saw figures pacing up and down, marching in step. The blurry figures became larger as they got closer, and Brigid saw that they were carrying something—a body. Before she knew it, the marching figures stopped and tossed the body at Brigid, and she flinched as it slapped against the ground, its damp hair the color of straw. It was Mariah.

"Merr—" Brigid began, her voice low. The word wouldn't come out right, and she could feel now that her lip was cut and something stung inside her mouth. She probed around with her tongue for a few seconds, felt that there were abrasions inside her mouth, a swelling around two of her molars near the back right side. She tried again, careful to enunciate the word: "Mariah?"

Mariah didn't answer. Brigid tried calling to her again, but there was no response. Mariah just lay there, unmoving as the rainwater coated her body and soaked her muddy clothes, leaving her wringing wet.

Someone had hit her, Brigid remembered, piecing together the last few moments before she had lost consciousness. People, farmers—seventeen, Edwards had said—ganging up on her, punching and kicking her as she lay on the floor of the stone building, her gun yanked out of her grasp.

Edwards! The thought went through Brigid's brain like a physical blow. He had been upstairs, where the zombie army had emerged from. Had they already killed him?

Still lying on the shale-caked ground, Brigid looked around frantically, her emerald eyes darting this way and that. She spotted a pair of mud-spattered boots lying down on their sides. They were Edwards's and she perceived from their shape that they contained legs and feet. He was probably lying next to her, just out of immediate sight. If only her head weren't so heavy, if only she could move.

She struggled then, trying to move her body where it had gone numb in the cold rain. There were bruises all over, she felt, things aching and muscles screaming inside her where she had suffered punishment at the hands of the trancelike attackers. But she wasn't bound, it seemed. She had just been tossed on the ground like Mariah, like so much dead meat.

Subtly, Brigid stretched her muscles, trying to bring life and movement back to them. As she did so, her eyes watched the crowd through the indistinct curtain of falling rain. Among the farmers in their ragged clothes she saw another figure, one much taller than the others. Not just tall—immense. She blinked back the pain in her left eye, willing herself to focus on the towering figure. It appeared to be a crude statue, constructed of a similar rock to that used for the buildings of the new ville, a sand color turned dark with the rain.

And then, to Brigid's surprise and horror, the statue began to move.

Chapter 17

Carrying an ax with a cutting edge of heavy iron, Upelluri led Ullikummis deeper below the ground, until they came upon the volcanoes, burbling in place, their fires glowing in tune with the prince's new eyes. The open volcanoes were like craters, low to the ground, their furnacelike innards bubbling with molten lava that lit the whole inside of the vast cavern and filled the place with the stench of brimstone.

Ullikummis followed his mentor through the winding passageways to the cavern, a toolkit filled with rags and smelting equipment held in the crook of his arm.

"This is for you," Upelluri said, handing Ullikummis the ax. Long handled, its head was made of solid iron, heavy and unwieldy, an instrument of viciousness rather than delicacy.

Now towering over Upelluri, Ullikummis took the tool from his teacher, judging its weight in his hands. "How am I to use it?" he asked.

"The blade will achieve what you require," Upelluri explained, "but I cannot do it for you. You understand?"

Ullikummis nodded, letting the ax slip in his left hand until he gripped it by the very end of the handle. "Will it be enough?" he asked.

"It will cut through stone," the old Annunaki assured him. "The rest is up to you and your own strength, both physical and mental."

Ullikummis peered at the bubbling volcanic bowls, felt the weight of the ax in his hand. "Leave me," he instructed quietly.

Without a word, Upelluri shuffled from the cavern, and Ullikummis heard his mentor coughing as he ascended through the mazelike tunnels of the network of caves.

Once Upelluri was gone, Ullikummis sat upon the floor, crossing his legs and steadying his breathing. Then he stretched his right arm out before him, resting it on a natural ledge formed in the rocky ground. Stretched out, his arm looked like just another part of the ledge, a hunk of rock with five fingerlike protrusions at its end.

Ullikummis gritted his teeth, feeling the tension in the muscles of his arm. The voice in his head was telling him that he must do it now.

Around him, vapor swirled from the boiling pits of lava, filling the air with that sulphurous stink.

Do it now.

His left hand tensed around the handle of the ax, extending it as far from him as he could.

Now. Now. Now.

The volcanic craters bubbled, spitting gobs of fire on the ground, lighting the cave with their unbridled fury.

Now.

Ullikummis felt his heart hammering in his chest, felt it pound against his ribs, hidden now beneath the plates of genetically engineered rock. He must do it; it was what his father would expect.

Now. Now. Now. Now. Now.

The ax swung, its thick blade swishing through the air, its momentum giving it more and more power as it hurtled down toward his arm. And then it struck a single blow, and his right arm was no more.

Ullikummis did not cry out, for the sickly Upelluri had taught him to befriend pain. He simply let out his held breath, almost as though he was relieved of a great burden. Where his right arm had been, from just below the joint of the elbow, there was a stump, blood spurting from the open wound there. The severed arm itself rolled from the ledge, falling to the ground, the fingers moving as the blood drained from them, making the rock hand open and close, open and close.

This would be his weapon. This part of him, this limb, would become his blade. This would be the thing that did his bloody work. This would be the Godkiller.

As blood pooled around him, Ullikummis reached into the toolbox and pulled free a strip of rag, wrapping it around the jutting stump that had once been his arm. The rag darkened as blood seeped into it, but Ullikummis ignored the wound, certain that it would heal in time. Ningishzidda had made him, his greatest creation—Ullikummis would not bleed forever. Even now microscopic nanites were racing through his system to staunch the flow of blood.

A wave of faintness washed over Ullikummis as he stood, and he wondered that he might fall. But he recovered, stumbling this way and that as he reached down for the freed limb, his vision doubling with the beat of his heart. Now he could heat it in the volcanic fires, cut it and shape it, carve it into the weapon he required.

Alone in the cavern of furious volcanoes, Ullikummis held aloft his severed limb, fierce determination on his rough stone face. Here was Godkiller. Here was the blade that would kill Annunaki.

THROUGH SLIT EYES, the rain playing down the side of her face, Brigid watched the monstrous statue as it paced the length of the ghost ville. It was strange to watch it move, this thing that looked as if it had been carved from rock. It seemed somehow unnatural, a rock thing granted life, or perhaps a life immersed in rock.

There had been the meteor; that was why they had come here. The meteor and its carvings referring to the son of Enlil, Ullikummis, the sentient stone pillar. And now there was this thing, this monstrosity whose eyes glowed like burning magma, whose body seemed to be carved from stone. Could this be him? Brigid wondered. Could this be Ullikummis? She had expected something different. If anything, she had expected an Annunaki, reptilian and graceful, despite his description as a pillar of stone. This thing was a freak, even by Annunaki standards, a living, breathing, walking horror. Or did it breathe? she asked herself. Had it emerged from that gap in the meteor, or had that merely been a safe container for its DNA sequence?

Brigid looked up and around, hoping to see movement in her colleagues. She could run, perhaps even fight, but not without them. She surely wouldn't leave without them.

"Edwards?" she urged sotto voce. "Mariah? Are you awake?"

Again there was no response.

Except...except...

There, in the back of her skull, a voice. No, not a voice— an emotion. And like a new seed planted inside her brain, it was an emotion that didn't belong to Brigid Baptiste.

KANE AND GRANT HAD JOINED Lakesh in the Cerberus ops center, where even now Donald Bry was playing the recordings of their last communiqué from Mariah Falk. The albino Domi perched atop Lakesh's desk, drinking from a paper cup filled with water, observing the whole exchange in silence.

"Something's happening here." Mariah's voice was clear over the Commtact relay. "The ville wasn't empty. We're outnumbered and…and…"

"And what, Mariah?" Donald's voice, prompting her.

"Send help." Mariah sounded scared. "Send help now!"

Kane and Grant wore grim expressions as they listened, while Donald tracked back through the recording using a wheel-type dial on the main console.

"How long ago was that?" Grant asked.

"Eighteen minutes ago," Donald told him as he lined up the other recording. "This came from Brigid roughly six minutes before that." He flicked the dial to run the Commtact recording.

"There are people here," Brigid was saying, her voice strained, "and things are turning strange."

From her position on Lakesh's desk, Domi snorted. "'Turning strange,'" she mimicked. "Brigid has a gift for understatement, right?"

Donald left the recording running, and they heard his own voice going through protocol as Brigid promised to report in soon.

"So that's—what—twenty-four minutes ago?" Kane asked.

"About that." Donald nodded. "We've had nothing since then."

Standing beside the desk, Lakesh turned to Kane and Grant, grim concern furrowing his brow. "Traditionally, it's been you two working with Brigid," he said. "I thought you would want to hear this."

"Why?" Kane asked, his tone angry.

"Twenty-something minutes out of contact after an inconclusive report is not enough for me to scramble a team, Kane," Lakesh said, "but I think that's what we should do."

Kane looked at Donald's computer screen, which showed the voiceprint as a sine wave as he ran back through the report over his headphones.

"I think you're right," Kane decided. "This is a situation that shouldn't even have begun happening. Edwards should have known better than to—"

"Edwards is cautious as hell," Domi piped up, cutting into Kane's complaint. "I worked with him just a week ago, and you know that as well as I do. They went in because it appeared safe."

Kane began to say something, but Grant fixed his dark stare on his old partner.

"Whatever you're about to say," Grant told him, "had better take into full account every single time you and I have walked into the danger zone and trusted we'd make it out alive."

Glancing from Grant to Domi, Kane shook his head, a lopsided grin forming on his face. "Yeah, but it's different when we do it," he muttered.

Lakesh turned and led the way to the anteroom at the end of the operations center. The mat-trans chamber doubled as a launch location for the similar but more refined functionality of the interphaser. "We can have you there inside of a minute using the interphaser," he explained. "There's a parallax point almost on site."

"Well, whoop-de-do," Kane grumbled. "How soon can the armory get our weapons out of storage?"

"Already on it," Lakesh assured him. "I've ordered your Sin Eaters, Copperhead assault rifles and a stash of grenades if you need them. Henny will be here with them momentarily."

Kane nodded. "Momentarily's good. I have a bad feeling where all this is going."

"So do I, Kane," Lakesh agreed as Henny Johnson came rushing through the main doors pushing a flatbed trolley piled with armament.

Domi jumped down from the desk and snatched a pouch full of flash-bangs, attaching them to her belt. "I'm going with," she announced, checking the barrel of her Detonics CombatMaster before replacing it in its holster at the small of her back.

Kane looked at the strange albino woman. "Are you sure you want a part of this?" he asked.

Domi nodded. "Brigid's my friend," she said solemnly.

TWO DAYS AFTER HIS SIXTEENTH birthday, Ullikummis had emerged from the cavern of volcanoes brandishing the blade that he had forged there. It had taken four weeks to craft the blade from his own discarded limb, four weeks to temper it in the fires, four weeks to engrave every last symbol upon it so it would hold all of his power and reciprocate its power back to the user with each deadly strike.

He found Upelluri in his sun room, working at his detailed calculations as his projector tracked the movements of the great ball of fire in the sky. Upelluri turned at the sound of Ullikummis's footsteps, saw the stone prince standing there in the shadows, the thirteen-inch blade in his left hand.

"You return," Upelluri said, a hint of surprise in his voice.

Ullikummis looked at his revered mentor, awaiting his approval. He had been gone one whole Earth month, working in the cavern of lava pools, and Upelluri had not once come to disturb him or even to feed him.

"You look thinner," Upelluri observed as Ullikummis stepped into the light. "Did you eat?"

Ullikummis shook his great stone head. "No. My system can survive without food for a long time. I've never tested it like this before."

"Perhaps it could survive a hundred years," Upelluri proposed. "Perhaps a thousand."

"Perhaps," Ullikummis allowed. He turned slightly then, showing the older Annunaki the wound where his arm had been. It had healed completely, and a thin limb was forming in place of the missing arm, looking like a skeleton, like something that had withered on the branch. In time, it would grow to become an arm once more, and Ullikummis would be complete again.

"And the weapon?" Upelluri prompted.

Ullikummis held the obsidian blade up before his master, watching as the light played along the cuneiform writing scored along its edge.

Upelluri smiled as he read the inscription, the beetle-like blotches shifting on his animated face. "You named it, then."

"Yes," Ullikummis said. "Godkiller."

KANE AND GRANT STOOD shoulder to shoulder in the six-sided mat-trans chamber, with Domi standing facing them. All three had dressed in shadow suits made of the thin, fibrous material that offered protection from various environmental threats. Besides their armorlike properties, the shadow suits also provided a regulated temperature for any climate, allowing a wearer to keep cool in the desert or do star jumps in the Arctic.

Kane had added a simple jacket over his shadow suit, made of faded blue denim with frayed edges and a worn collar, the better to fit in around the farming area that they were teleporting into. The right sleeve of Kane's jacket showed a lump close to the underside of the wrist, which was where his Sin Eater handgun was stored in its remarkable holster. The Sin Eater had been the official sidearm of the Magistrate Division, and both Grant and Kane had kept them from their days as Mags in Cobaltville. An automatic hand blaster, the Sin Eater was less than fourteen inches in length at full extension and it fired 9 mm rounds. The whole unit folded in on itself to be stored in a bulky holster strapped just above the user's wrist. The holsters reacted to a specific flinch movement of the wrist tendons, powering the pistol automatically into the gunman's hand. The trigger had no guard, as the necessity had never been foreseen that any kind of safety features for the weapon would ever be required. Thus, if the user's index finger was crooked at the time it reached his hand, the pistol would begin firing automatically. This reflected the high regard with which Magistrates were viewed in the villes—their judgment could never be wrong.

At Kane's side, Grant had chosen to wear a long black duster made of a Kevlar weave over his own shadow suit. The coat's tails reached down to Grant's knees, and the voluminous coat had several secret pockets to help disguise the weaponry the dark-skinned man was carrying. Like Kane, Grant had his trusted Sin Eater pistol clipped within its flinch-responsive wrist holster. Along with the Sin Eater, Grant was armed with his favored Copperhead close-assault subgun. The barrel of the subgun was almost two feet long and could be tucked into one of the inner pockets of Grant's duster. The grip and trigger of the gun were placed in front of the breech in the bullpup design, allowing the gun to be used single-handed, and an optical, image-intensified scope, coupled with a laser autotargeter, was mounted on top of the frame. The Copperhead possessed a 700-round-per-minute rate of fire and was equipped with an extended magazine holding thirty-five 4.85 mm steel-jacketed rounds. The Copperhead was a lethal field weapon, thanks to ease of use and the sheer level of destruction it could create in short measure.

Over her shadow suit Domi wore a dark jacket, its dark weave in stark contrast to her alabaster skin, creating a vision of black and white. Domi had tucked her Detonics CombatMaster .45 in the holster at the small of her back, and had secreted a half-dozen flash-bang grenades about her person. The flash-bangs were metal spheres approximately one-and-a-half inches in diameter. When primed, the tiny grenades would create exactly what their moniker promised—a flash and a bang, just light and noise, but often enough to clear an area or startle an unsuspecting enemy.

At the feet of the three Cerberus warriors was an interphaser, its metallic, triangular sides glistening under the lights of the chamber. As Kane, Grant and Domi stood there, all three counted down in their heads, waiting for the interphaser's initiation sequence to begin. The apex of the pyramid began to glow, and the familiar, oil-on-water lotus blossom of colored light burst forth and rapidly spread to encompass the whole of the small room. An identical light seemed to splurge from the base of the pyramid, creating another lotus blossom of light where the floor to the chamber should logically be. As with a lot of alien technology, the interphaser had the ability to shift a viewer's perception, altering how they saw its relationship with the physical world.

Grant looked at Kane and nodded. "Here we go again, huh?" he said.

"Yeah," Kane said as the rainbow of light grew bigger, preparing to engulf them. "Let's make sure all our lambs get there together."

With that, the three warriors were swallowed by the multicolored swirl and disappeared from the Cerberus redoubt.

AN INSTANT LATER, they were standing in the underground cavern in Saskatchewan, the same one that Brigid's field team had been transported to just four hours earlier. For almost ten seconds, the bright shimmer of the interphaser lit the interior of the cave as it expelled the colossal energy required to traverse the quantum pathways, before powering down as the Cerberus warriors waited. Abruptly, the interphaser appeared to be nothing more than a foot-high metal pyramid once more; there wasn't even any smell to indicate that there had been any expulsion of such incredible forces of energy.

Kane leaned down and reached for the interphaser, checking to ensure that they had arrived at the correct parallax point. Satisfied, he placed the interphaser unit, which remained cool to the touch, into the protective cover of its carrying case. As he did so, Grant and Domi made their way up the slope toward the light streaming in from the open mouth of the cavern, the Copperhead subgun held ready in Grant's grip. Despite the remarkable nature of their trip, all three warriors were immediately alert to their surroundings, checking swiftly left and right, ensuring that they were alone in the cavern and that they had arrived unseen.

One of the gravest problems with teleportation, be it by the interphaser or the more clunky system of the mat-trans, was that the traveler was unable to view the destination in the moments prior to arrival. It was alarmingly easy to step out of a quantum gateway and straight into the hands of hostile forces, or to find oneself in the middle of an avalanche or submerged beneath hundreds of feet of water. While the Cerberus facility could provide reasonably accurate insights using their surveillance satellites, the threat of local dangers still posed a problem.

Subgun held high, Grant came jogging back along the tunnel of the cavern to where Kane was sealing the locks on the interphaser's carrying case. "Clear," Grant advised him before making his way more slowly back up the slope of the cave to where Domi was waiting, her ruby eyes scanning the astonishing vista beyond the cave's mouth.

Kane looked around the dark cavern for a moment before spying a clump of large rocks over beside one wall. He hefted the carrying case toward the rocks, leaning down to secure it behind them, out of sight. As he did so, a smile crossed his lips, and he let loose a chuckle. An identical carrying case waited there—Brigid Baptiste's interphaser.

"Great minds think alike," Kane muttered as he placed his own carrying case a little deeper into the cave behind a different clutch of rocks. It wouldn't do to leave them both together; if one was discovered it would mean that they both would be found.

As Kane pushed the carrying case behind a rock, something ran out from cover, rushing across the ground in a fury of moving legs. It was a spider, its leg span as wide as

Kane's hand, disturbed by the movements in the shadow-filled cave where it had made its home. Kane watched its inkblot shape scuttle across the cave and find a new hiding hole in the darkness.

A few seconds later, Kane was making his way up the dirt-covered slope toward the entrance to the burrowlike cavern. He joined Grant and Domi at the mouth of the cave, smelling the rain before he saw it.

"What do we have?" Kane asked in a low voice as he scanned the horizon.

It was pouring outside, heavy, thick lines of water falling from a dark, overcast sky, creating huge puddles across the landscape and obscuring the details of what could be seen.

"There's your ville," Grant stated, gesturing to the shadowy structures that stood less than a mile away, wisps of smoke puffing from its center.

Kane looked at it, feeling his heart beat a little faster in his chest. He had grown up in Cobaltville, and a part of him would always feel drawn to the villes, in the way a child will always seek its mother. Despite everything he had learned since, something deep inside him would always see the villes as a symbol of safety and security, a home that the Cerberus redoubt could never replace. It was hardwired into him, and Grant felt the same.

By contrast, Domi looked at the weird ville with contempt. As with her recent excursion in Snakefishville less than a week before, she felt a sense of discomfort at being near ville walls. Her home was the Outlands.

After a few seconds of consideration, Kane engaged his Commtact. "Baptiste? This is Kane, do you read me?"

There was no answer.

"We're coming to the ville," Kane stated over his Commtact link to Brigid Baptiste, still receiving no response. "Whatever's going on, if you can hear this you hang in there."

With that, Kane killed the comm link. "Let's go," he told Grant and Domi, and the three of them stepped out from the cavern mouth and into the fierce rainstorm.

Chapter 18

Brigid was trying to unpick her brain when she heard Kane's voice coming over her Commtact. As she lay there in the dirt and the shingle, the rain running down the porcelain skin of her face, she ignored Kane's calling voice and tried to imagine her brain, visualizing it in her mind's eye.

The brain was a series of rooms, each one containing knowledge of a given subject, each room freely open to all the others, like one of those surrealist paintings, an optical illusion. But now she was aware that there was something there that didn't belong, like a tiny box that had been hidden within one of her rooms. And Brigid felt that the tiny box was muscling out the other objects, changing them to conform.

Through slit eyes, Brigid watched the seventeen human figures milling about. The statue gave several instructions and there, on the rain-soaked ground, four of the people began to wrestle, to fight with one another as though their lives depended on it. It was strange to witness, the way that they had turned from standing to fighting in a heartbeat, as though the people were automatons to be programmed by the towering rock thing.

As Brigid watched, the great rock creature strode across the courtyard of the ville, making his way to where she lay with Edwards and Mariah. Standing over her, his shadow cast upon their fallen bodies, the creature spoke and, deep down, Brigid knew it was the voice of a god.

"Stand up," Ullikummis ordered.

Brigid struggled, pushing herself slowly from the ground. She felt woozy from her recent beating, and her muscles twinged and burned where they had been savagely struck. Beside her, Edwards was rubbing his head as he lay on the ground, apparently just now waking up. To the other side of Brigid, Mariah Falk remained unconscious, her brown hair wringing wet with rain.

The towering stone god looked at Brigid with burning eyes, their color seeming to match that of her fiery hair. "You will fight," he told her in a voice like a gravel path being crushed underfoot.

No, I won't, Brigid heard herself say, but the words wouldn't come. Swaying a little on her feet, Brigid glared at the immense rock thing that stood before her. Behind this Annunaki thing—this would-be god—she could see the gap in the wall where she had entered the ville with Edwards and Mariah. There was no one guarding it and nothing barring her way. Indeed, the wide space stood there as if silently taunting her.

"Kane," Brigid breathed, recalling the message that had come over the Commtact just two minutes before. Kane was out there, bringing backup to infiltrate the ville. If she could get outside, she could reach him and together they could come back and free Edwards and Mariah once they had awoken.

The voice in the back of her head continued to tell her to stay, to conform, but she tamped it down, ignoring it with grim determination.

Hating herself for leaving her teammates behind, Brigid began to run in the direction of that wide gap in the rocky walls. As the rain sluiced around her, Brigid's arms whipped up and down at her sides, her long legs pumping as she sprinted past the towering stone creature and bolted toward the open exit. It was freedom, wide as three Sandcats, just waiting for her to emerge from this horrible, ghostlike ville.

Brigid's feet slapped against the puddles of rainwater pooled on the ground, kicking up dirty water all about her as she ran on toward that enticing break in the wall. No one else moved. None of the farmers who had reverted to their trancelike state stepped in to intervene, and the wrestlers carried on wrestling. The path to the gateway was clear.

Brigid glanced over her shoulder, saw Ullikummis standing still, his arm raised as he watched her run away from him. Edwards and Mariah were still lying there on the ground close to him, and Brigid saw that Edwards had now woken up and was pushing the rain from his eyes, squeezing and blowing his nose.

If I were to turn back, we might all die together, Brigid told herself as she wondered if she was dooming her colleagues to execution in the name of punishment for her escape.

The stone god Ullikummis held his arm out as though pointing at Brigid, and the fingers of his stony hand spread wide. Brigid ignored him, turning back to the wide space in the wall. There was a rumbling then, and all around her and through her Brigid felt movement, like the deep bass note of an orchestra tuning up. Ahead of her, incredibly, the ground seemed to part, and where the gap had been in the wall a ridge began to grow, pulling itself out of the ground like some burrowing mole surfacing. It was a line of schist, a thick chunk of gray of the same breadth as the wall itself. Brigid continued to run, her feet slapping at the pooling rainwater as she rushed at the gap in the wall, but as she moved the ridge of schist heaved out of the earth, climbing higher and higher like some kind of automated shutter door, filling the width of the gap that stood in the ville wall.

It was almost beautiful, the way that rock wall emerged from the ground, sliding upward and slotting perfectly into place in the hole in the wall, blocking the exit entirely. Brigid's pace slowed as she neared it, for already the rising wall was over eight feet high. When she stopped, her heels digging into the rough, shard-covered ground, the wall stood four feet taller than her, and Brigid watched amazed as it continued to grow, masking the exit completely.

Brigid Baptiste turned back, looking at the courtyard that she had just run across, her breathing deep with irritation. Opposite her, Ullikummis stood, his arm still outstretched, his eyes glowing. This sentient stone pillar of myth, Brigid realized now, could control and grant sentience to stone. That was how he had built this impossible ville in next to no time. He had simply willed it, pulling the rocks from the ground and ordering them to form their familiar shapes. It had likely been the work of mere minutes, each towering husk expanding from the ground like a time-lapse film of a germinating seed.

"You will fight," Ullikummis instructed once again, his gravel-crunch voice calling to Brigid through the rain.

Behind her, Brigid heard the wall cease to move, felt the rumbling underfoot finally stop. There was no way out of the ville now, no way to exit. No, I won't, Brigid heard herself say, but the words didn't leave her lips. Instead she said, "Yes, my lord."

Ullikummis turned and stalked back toward the open area of the ville beside the towering monolith that continued to belch dark smoke into the sky. Despite herself, Brigid found she was following. It was like being pulled by invisible threads, a magnetic force.

Three of the farmers were waiting there, an attractive young woman and the dark-haired man who had tried to deflect her bullet, along with another man with wispy white hair who appeared to be much older. Through the rain, Brigid saw that the dark-haired man had a strange protrusion on his forehead, a ridged scar that looked as if some treasure had been buried there. Plus, where his ear had been shot, the man now wore a bloody square of bandage that was tied to his head by dark thread. The woman, meanwhile, had a bruise marring her forehead, and her left eye was swollen closed, while the white-haired man simply wore the vacant expression of a man whose mind had long departed.

Ullikummis stood to one side, placing his palms together as though to pray. "Begin," he instructed.

The three farmers immediately assumed fighting stances, spreading their feet to lower their centers of balance. This is madness, Brigid thought as she watched them. And yet she found herself compelled to fight. She would fight to please her new master, as he had fought for his own master, thousands of years before.

ENLIL SNAPPED his clawlike fingers, and two fierce warriors entered the vast throne room as the young Ullikummis watched. He was just nine years old.

Dressed in golden armor, the Nephilim warriors were a hybrid of DNA created in *Tiamat*'s bubbling vats, and they possessed qualities of both the local humans and the Annunaki. They were utterly hairless, with dark, scaled skin over their thick hides, high cheekbones and craggy brow ridges over their blank, soulless eyes. They were subservient to

Enlil, and would gladly give their lives if only they were capable of such an emotion as gratitude. Standing upright, the Nephilim were barely taller than Ullikummis's towering nine-year-old form.

"You will now kill my son," Enlil instructed the two warriors. Enlil's voice showed no emotion as he delivered the command. Instead, he said it with the same casual air as he might employ had he asked for a bite of a fig.

Ullikummis tensed, watching the warriors unsheathe their short swords and stride toward him. Naturally he was unarmed—his father had a wicked sense of the absolute, and he had discouraged Ullikummis's early reliance on tools and weapons. "Weapons are for those who are ready to be disarmed," he had explained. At nine years of age, Ullikummis did not truly understand his father's pronouncements, but he still followed the instructions that he was given.

Without a word, the two warriors stalked across the room, their shining blades held ready. The first stepped ahead and swung his sword at Ullikummis, plunging it at the boy's stone-adorned chest. Ullikummis leaped backward and felt the breeze from the passing blade as it whipped through the air.

The Nephilim warrior kept coming, his sword describing an elaborate arc through the air as he pressed onward toward the child.

Ullikummis glanced across to his father. Enlil had settled back in his throne and seemed almost bored as he watched the display of combat before him, chewing on a fat purple grape before spitting its seed at the floor.

"Should I fight back, Father?" Ullikummis asked as he sidestepped the Nephilim's second sword thrust and watched the hybrid creature lunge past him.

Enlil voiced no reply to his son's question, just the hint of a smile playing across his scaly lips as he chewed at the flesh of the fruit.

Ullikummis was fast. Despite his stone exterior, he had been drilled long and hard in the ways of the athlete, and he felt that he could keep out of reach of these murderous warriors indefinitely if necessary even though their blades swished all around him, cleaving the air with heavy strikes.

The second warrior had stepped into the battle now, and his own blade whizzed toward Ullikummis's left shoulder as the boy prince jumped aside. There were ridges on Ullikummis's shoulders now, big spiky things that angled upward, toward his head like the horns of a stag. Each of these spiked horns was made of solid rock, grafted to Ullikummis's body in the heat of Ningishzidda's laboratory. With a shower of sparks and a clang like a struck bell, the Nephilim's sword struck Ullikummis's left shoulder ridge, knocking the boy down until he slapped against the floor on one bent knee.

Ullikummis glared up at the Nephilim who now stood over him, sword poised for the killing stroke. I am hurt, Ullikummis realized, anger in his narrow, slit pupils, but not physically. He was hurt by his father's callousness in setting these, his prized warriors, against him.

The slashing sword of the Nephilim flashed in the sunlight as it swooped down toward the back of Ullikummis's neck, hacking into it in an attempt to decapitate the young Annunaki. Ullikummis felt the blow slam against him, the sharp edge of the sword cut into him. And then the sword stopped, caught in Ullikummis's rocky hide, and for a moment the boy thought that he would topple. Instead, he took it, feeling the sword held there, lodged in his stone-like carapace. Above him, the Nephilim was static, having failed to comprehend what had happened.

Ullikummis's stone hand snapped back in a blur, grabbing the Nephilim by his genitalia and yanking, pulling the dull-eyed warrior down to the floor in an explosion of blood and ruined flesh. Emasculated, the Nephilim lay there shrieking as Ullikummis pounded his heavy fist into the creature's gut, driving it into the armor with such force that the golden plate buckled, splashed with his own blood. Ullikummis brought his fist back for another blow, but in his fury he had forgotten the second warrior, and suddenly he found himself knocked aside by a powerful blow to his ribs.

The other warrior stood there, hopping from foot to foot, sword ready as Ullikummis turned to face him, a snarl on his slash of mouth. The warrior's colleague lay sobbing in a pool of his own blood and urine, the bloody remains of his genitals smeared across the marble floor of Enlil's throne room. The fallen Nephilim's sword was still clinging to Ullikummis's neck, lodged in a crevice in his rocky hide, but the boy ignored it.

Ullikummis charged, head down, blundering toward his remaining opponent like a charging rhino. The Nephilim jumped aside, barely fast enough to avoid being knocked from his feet, and Ullikummis barrelled on several steps before coming to a halt. The warrior was on Ullikummis before he had turned, swinging his short sword toward the prince's side. The metal blade clashed against Ullikummis's rock skin, bringing with it another dazzling burst of sparks as forged metal met genetically altered skin-turned-rock. Ullikummis ignored it, realizing now that the blades could not hurt him. He was armored as no Annunaki had been armored before him, clad in a sheath of near-impenetrable stone.

As the second warrior lunged to stab him, Ullikummis's long arm swung around in a wide arc until it connected, knocking the hybrid Nephilim off his feet. The Nephilim dropped to his flank and skidded across the smooth floor of the room until he came to a halt at the feet of Enlil's throne. Unhurried, Ullikummis strode across the floor in pursuit, the other sword still jutting from the back of his neck.

As the Nephilim began to get up, Ullikummis stomped one of his heavy stone feet against the warrior's head, knocking him back to the floor. Held there beneath Ullikummis's foot, the warrior struggled as the Annunaki prince pushed with increasing pressure, crushing his skull. It was the work of a half minute, but eventually there came a dull cracking noise as something in the Nephilim's skull broke. A moment later, blood trickled from the Nephilim's ears and he shuddered in place like a rutting dog, unleashing a pained whimper. The Nephilim was dead.

Enlil looked at his son, a smile on his thin, reptilian lips. "One," he said.

Ullikummis wondered at what his father meant, then he recalled the other warrior, the one whose genitals he had ripped off. He peered across the room, spying the warrior still lying there in his own blood, curled in on himself as if trying to sleep.

"He is no threat to me now," Ullikummis told his father.

But Enlil shook his head. "Dispatch your enemies with finality," the great lord told his son, "lest they return to seek revenge."

Nodding, Ullikummis strode across the room toward the fallen Nephilim, pulling the warrior's own sword from where it was lodged in the back of his neck. In a moment, he plunged the sword deep into the Nephilim's chest, bursting his heart.

When he turned back to his father's throne to seek approval, Ullikummis saw that it was empty. Enlil was exiting the room in a swish of his colorful cloak, bored of the brief entertainment that his son had provided.

Ullikummis had killed on instruction and in cold blood. That was all that mattered to Enlil.

BRIGID DUCKED as the dark-haired farmer swung his clenched fist at her. His hand had been bandaged, she saw, albeit inexpertly, and the white material was stained with dark blood just like the cloth that masked his missing ear.

As the farmer's fist sailed over her head, Brigid struck out with a ram's-head blow, driving the extended knuckles of her left fist into the man's gut. Before Brigid could follow through, however, the white-haired farmer was upon her, swinging his balled fist downward into her back. Brigid staggered a couple of steps forward under the impact, before turning to face her new attacker. Even as she moved, the pretty woman with the swollen eye came at her, kicking out with her long right leg.

Brigid hurried backward, booted feet struggling for purchase against the shifting surface of the damp shale. These people shouldn't move like fighters, and yet they did, as though they had been trained in the fundamentals of technique.

And Brigid wanted to fight, too. It was crazy, but she wanted to fight. She wanted to hurt these people, for no other reason than to fulfill some conception of destiny, of purpose, that appeared to have welled within her. As her three amateur opponents approached, Brigid tried once more to listen to her brain, to find the anomaly, for she knew it was there—the foreign box in the room.

The woman farmer swung a savage blow at Brigid's head, and again Brigid stepped back, keeping her distance from her attacker. But the white-haired man had doubled around her, and she stepped straight into his clutches. His arms enfolded Brigid from behind, yanking her off balance as she struggled left and right, her wringing-wet hair swishing heavily about her as she just barely avoided two further attempts from the woman to punch her in the face.

Then Brigid stamped her foot down hard into the foot of the man who held her, slamming her right heel into the fleshy part where his toes met his foot. Even through his shoe, the man felt the blow, and his grip faltered as he howled out in pain.

Brigid didn't hesitate. She pulled herself forward at the same time as she swung her angled elbow back into the older man's torso, connecting high in the ribs with a loud thump. The old-timer appeared to do a little dance as he tried to keep his balance, his breath wheezing out of him under Brigid's fierce attack.

Once again there was no time to follow her attack through, however, and Brigid readied herself for the other two as the old man struggled to catch his breath. The dark-haired farmer came first, lips pulled back from clenched teeth as he swung his fists at Brigid. Brigid scooted backward, swiping at the farmhand with her outstretched leg, kicking him low and causing him to topple forward with his own momentum. The dark-haired farmer slammed into the ground, taking the hard knock on his chest and scraping his jaw in the shingle of discarded schist. Brigid rushed forward, stepping on the farmer's prone body and using it as a springboard to throw herself into the air, unleashing a primal war cry as she leaped for the woman who was still standing. The woman held her hands up to defend herself as Brigid flew through the air toward her, and together the pair of them crashed to the ground, with Brigid's opponent taking the brunt of the fall.

Atop her fallen opponent, Brigid drew her fist back and punched her across the jaw, again and again in a series of swift, jabbing rabbit punches. The woman had no time to respond but just lay there taking her punishment as Brigid laid into her, her head repeatedly rebounding with the ground with each blow.

As Brigid drew back her rain-slicked fist for another punch, she felt a hand grasp her and suddenly she was being pulled from the girl's body. She lashed out without thinking, her head spinning around to spy her opponent even as her first blow struck. It was the older man once more, and his nose erupted in a burst of crimson as Brigid's fist broke it, the blood mingling with the falling rain.

The white-haired man stumbled back, his hands reaching up for his ruined nose while Brigid freed herself from his weak grasp. She shifted her attention to the other one, the muscular male with the dark hair. He was just pushing himself up off the ground, sweeping back his hair as water streamed into his eyes. In one fluid movement, Brigid leaned down so that her hand clawed along the ground, then came up and tossed a handful of schist stones at the dark-haired man's face as he took his first threatening step toward her.

Shale and dirt slapped against his face, and he screamed out angrily as the sharp edge of a miniscule particle scratched at the surface of his eye. He was blinking the dirt away when Brigid's roundhouse kick swept into the side of his head, knocking the would-be tough guy off his feet and causing his ear wound to burst open again in a wash of blood that dribbled out from the edges of the bandage he had taped there.

Brigid Baptiste stopped then, her breath coming a little heavier than before, her thoughts whirring inside her head. Around her, lying in the rain puddles that covered the courtyard, her three opponents were struggling to get up, all of them looking pained and moving slower than they had before.

Watching it all, Ullikummis nodded. This new one, the fire-haired woman, had the instincts of a true warrior. More so than these idiot farmers, whose only successful battles had been with the dirt of their fields.

Lying on the ground, his own breath coming in heavy panting gasps, the dark-haired farmer called Dylan looked up at Brigid Baptiste as she turned to face her master. An outdoors man with a lousy temperament, Dylan had spent his whole life thinking himself somehow invincible. Now he had learned that for all his posturing, he was a tiny and insignificant thing—a recruit for Ullikummis's army, perhaps, but not the prime player he had always believed he would be in the new world order. To learn that one was but cannon fodder was a harsh lesson indeed.

Brigid approached the rock god, her feet crunching against the wet schist that carpeted the ground of the eerie ville. Ullikummis was satisfied. This apekin had true potential. This woman could be a work of art, as he had been Ningishzidda's, four and a half thousand years before.

ULLIKUMMIS WAITED in Ningishzidda's laboratory, a windowless room beneath one of the great ziggurats on the banks of the Euphrates. He was just two weeks from his fourteenth birthday.

Ningishzidda peered up from the bubbling concoctions that he had been heating at the side of the room, magnifying apparatus affixed to his face before his eyes. His scales were jade-green, and, enlarged by the apparatus, his vertical-slit irises seemed to match.

"You're looking tall," Ningishzidda observed as he eyed Ullikummis's stone form, up and down.

"Thank you, sir," Ullikummis said, unsure of how else to respond. He was a freak now, towering eight feet high, taller even than his father or the others of the royal family. His flesh had been entirely reknitted, turned into living stone at the hands of the geneticist, and now he was back for his final treatment.

"Has it really been a full rotation of the sun since I last laid eyes upon you, Ullikummis?" Ningishzidda asked, a friendly sort of incredulity in his tone.

"It has, sir," Ullikummis told him. "One Earth year."

"Their years are so short," Ningishzidda said amiably, "one forgets. I miss the long nights on Nibiru, don't you?"

Ullikummis shook his head. "I have never visited the home planet, Lord Ningishzidda."

"Of course." Ningishzidda laughed. "You were born here, among the apes. You should visit Nibiru some day."

"I hope to do that, sir," Ullikummis agreed.

Then Ningishzidda's tone became more formal, a scientist once more. "Now then, how have you been? How are the legs? We stretched them, if I recall."

Ullikummis nodded his great stone head. "We did, sir, and they have been fine."

"No trouble?" Ningishzidda asked.

"For a while they hurt," Ullikummis admitted. "I would get shooting pains deep in the bones. But that passed after the second month and now I can run as fast as the gazelle."

Ningishzidda nodded. "Good," he stated absently, reaching across to a work surface that stood to his left. A liquid bubbled there, thick like mercury and colored like the glowing tails of the fireflies that came out at night.

Ullikummis looked at the liquid warily as Ningishzidda dipped a ladle into the beaker, and he watched as steam poured from its contents.

"It's almost ready," Ningishzidda said. "Lie down on the bench there and try to make yourself comfortable."

Ullikummis did as instructed, striding across the windowless laboratory to the long bench that stood in its center amid the bubbling tubes and beakers. He had been in Ningishzidda's laboratories numerous times over his fourteen years, either here or in one of the Annunaki genengineer's other workshops that had existed across the continent. Under the instruction of Enlil, Ningishzidda had altered Ullikummis, retooling him since before birth. The building blocks had been injected into Ullikummis when he was but an egg grown from Ninlil's womb. Over the subsequent years, Ningishzidda had activated each of those changes, encouraging the child to grow in a certain manner, to form in a certain way. In essence, Ningishzidda had created this freak, this monster that stood apart from the rest of the Annunaki pantheon, feared and loathed in equal measure.

As Ullikummis lay there on the familiar bench, he recalled the horrific experiments that he had been subjected to, terrifying changes that his body had been crafted to endure, each more awful that the last. When he had lain here one year before, it had been to stretch his legs one last time, to force the tight muscles to expand, to make him tall like some animated stone pillar. It had hurt beyond belief.

"Calm yourself, child," Ningishzidda said in his soothing bedside tone. "I can hear your breathing from all the way over here."

"I'm sorry, Lord Ningishzidda," Ullikummis responded automatically. He tried to slow his breathing to bring it under control, remembering the lessons that Upelluri had taught him about meditation and breathing technique.

As Ullikummis regulated his breathing, Ningishzidda came to the bench carrying a syringe filled with the bubbling concoction. The sides of the syringe were steaming from the heat. To Ullikummis, it looked like liquid fire.

"Will this hurt?" Ullikummis asked. "Should I be scared?"

"It will hurt," Ningishzidda responded emotionlessly. "Now quieten yourself."

Ullikummis closed his eyes, trying to ignore the tremors inside him, but Ningishzidda's voice came to him in instruction.

"You must keep your eyes open, mighty prince," Ningishzidda said. "There is no other way."

Ullikummis opened his eyes, and he saw the needle filled with liquid fire plunging toward his left eye. In his nightmares he would replay this moment again and again, almost every night for the next two years, and on and off ever after. The needle pierced the waxy shell of his iris and stabbed deep within, popping his eye even as he watched. And then, worse, the liquid in the syringe was driven into his eye, blasting into it like the burning of a rash, of disease.

Through it all, Ningishzidda just watched calmly, pushing the fiery liquid from his syringe into the prince's pierced eyeball, counting down the procedure in his head. When he was done, and without a word, he turned to Ullikummis's right eye and did exactly the same thing, filling the boy's eye with that fiery pain as Ullikummis lay there, trying desperately to cling to his sanity like some drowning creature in a sea of madness.

By the end of the procedure, Ullikummis was utterly blind, and his skull burned, feeling almost as if his brain were aflame.

But for all the pain, Ullikummis didn't make a sound. He could tolerate and even embrace pain now. Upelluri had taught him that much in their eighteen months together beneath the ground, and he would teach him much more over the next three years.

FOUR AND A HALF THOUSAND years later, Ullikummis stared at Brigid Baptiste with the burning eyes that Lord Ningishzidda had given him on that day.

"Be strong, my work of art," he said. "Building the new world shall need strength."

Chapter 19

It's in my head now, Brigid realized. I'd remember if it had been there before. This is new. This old and seemingly familiar feeling is somehow utterly new to me.

She stood at the edge of the ville courtyard, watching as Edwards was put through the same trial by combat that she had endured, three on one. This time it was two women and a man, and Edwards managed to overpower the women with muscle alone while fending off the man's attack. The first woman fell with a single blow, knocked completely unconscious less than a second after the fight had begun. Edwards was a trained Magistrate and, up against farmhands, he made battle look easy.

It's this place, Brigid told herself, looking around at the towering, empty buildings and the high walls that formed the familiar pattern of a ville. Something about this place is working against me, against all of us, sapping our freewill.

Before her, Edwards spun on his heel and drove two outstretched fingers at his final attacker's eyes, sliding his hand along the man's rain-slicked nose. His attacker, a well-muscled farmhand of perhaps twenty-five, knocked Edwards's hand aside at the last instant, tilting his head back as the rain turned his blond hair dark. Edwards didn't stop but merely changed tack, kicking out at the farmhand in a vicious double kick, first low, then high, before his foot returned to the ground. The low kick missed, but the high one cuffed the farmhand's ear, knocking him flat on his back. Edwards was on him instantly, driving his fist at the man's throat.

Brigid looked away.

Standing to one side, observing the spectacle with evident disgust, Mariah Falk was huddled in on herself, her chestnut-brown hair heavy with rain. "What's happening, Brigid?" she whispered. "Edwards is… It's ghastly."

Brigid glanced over her shoulder, checking to see that they weren't being observed. Hideous choking sounds came from the farmhand as Edwards drove his fist into the man's windpipe while he lay helpless beneath him. Everyone's attention was on the battle, although most looked uninterested, somewhat bored now that the result had clearly been decided.

"When you walk into the arena," Brigid whispered to Mariah, "something takes over, fills your head. The need to hurt, to kill. It's like a flashing light in the darkness—you cannot look away."

Mariah gulped, wiping away rain as it ran down her nose. "Where's the arena?" she asked.

"The whole ville," Brigid said, surprising herself. "Every place within these walls can be the arena, I think."

Mariah was wide-eyed. "You sound different, Brigid," she said.

"Once it gets into your head," Brigid said, "it's like it's always been a part of you. I keep closing my eyes and trying to locate it within me, but I can't. It's too well hidden."

Before them, Edwards's battle finally came to a brutal conclusion as his enemy dropped unconscious under the rain of vicious blows. Edwards looked up, his eyes meeting with the glowing orbs of Ullikummis, awaiting his new master's instructions. Should he kill?

OUTSIDE THE TOWERING WALLS of the ville, Kane, Grant
and Domi were approaching from its northwest corner
when they saw the wide gap in the walls suddenly close
as the gatelike hunk of rock emerged from the ground to
fill the space completely.

"Well, there goes option one," Grant growled as he
watched the rock slide into place.

The trio continued walking through the tall grass that
was bent over with rainwater, searching for another possible entryway. They were surprised that there seemed to
be no guards about. The whole ville gave the impression of
being deserted. And yet, from inside came the occasional
sounds of shifting stones through the muffling blanket of
rain.

"Acoustics are terrible," Grant decided, keeping his
voice low. "There could be anyone inside. Or no one."

Kane nodded, looking at the high wall thoughtfully.
"I've had no response from Baptiste," he confirmed. "We
could go up and over and see what we can find."

"Or we can go straight through," Grant proposed. "We
have enough explosives to make an entrance if we need
to."

Kane shook his head. "That could bring a whole heap
more trouble that I'd just as soon avoid. Let's try to play it
subtle for now."

Domi stood apart from the two ex-Mags, her sharp
eyes darting this way and that, her nose wrinkling as she
smelled the area. Grant noticed and he asked her what she
detected.

"Death," Domi said in no uncertain terms. "Below us,
under our feet."

Kane and Grant both looked down at the ground, seeing the gray schist debris that masked the soil through the long blades of grass. Heavy with rainwater, the grass bowed over.

"Cerberus, this is Kane," the ex-Mag said, engaging his Commtact. "What are we standing on?"

After a moment's pause, Lakesh himself responded. "Would you care to elaborate on your query, Kane?"

"Domi smells death," Kane said. "Reckons we're standing on it. Any ideas?"

Back at the Cerberus redoubt, Lakesh brought up the map and satellite imagery from seven days prior, comparing it to the location of the field team's transponder signals. "One week ago, that was a town called Market," he explained. "Thirty properties, plus a trading area. The ville appears to have been placed on top of it. Can you see any evidence of the original town?"

"Nothing," Kane replied, his gray-blue eyes scanning the area. "Looks like they leveled it and buried the remains. Including the residents."

Domi crouched in the grass, pressed her alabaster hand to the soil and plucked up a handful of dirt. She held it to her nose and sniffed at it, taking in the subtle gradations of its many scents. "Some of this is rock," she said. "Some of it is bone."

"Shit," Grant muttered, digging at the topsoil with the toe of his boot.

"How much?" Kane asked the albino girl.

Domi sieved the flinty mixture through her fingers, letting it fall back to the ground. "Just slivers," she said.

"Looks like they've been cremated," Grant realized.

Kane passed on that information to Cerberus headquarters before signing off. If they were walking on the charred remains of the local populace, then whoever had built this ville was utterly ruthless, and the need to get to Brigid and the others was even more urgent that he had previously realized.

Together, the three Cerberus warriors trudged toward the nearest wall of the ville, watching as the plume of dark smoke poured from the towering monolith beyond.

MARIAH WAS THE LAST to fight. Unlike Edwards and Brigid, Mariah had had very little combat training. As with other personnel of the Cerberus redoubt, she had been shown some basic self-defense moves, but hardly enough to hold her own against three opponents coming at her at once.

A part of Brigid wanted to speak up, to explain to Lord Ullikummis his folly, but she remained silent, unable to form the words with the buzzing inside her head. So instead she turned her thoughts inward, trying to locate and dislodge the thing that waited there, inside her mind.

Mariah Falk walked out to the center of the courtyard between the stone buildings, her shoulders slumped, the heavy rain washing down her face and soaking her muddy clothes. Three more farmers stepped forward, including Dylan, the dark-haired man with the missing ear with whom Brigid had fought less than half an hour earlier.

Watching from a few feet away, Ullikummis instructed them to begin.

Mariah would be the first to admit that she was not a fighter. Her curiosity had placed her in occasionally dangerous situations, but she was not argumentative; she wasn't even forthright. The last time she had been determined to investigate something, it had taken Clem Bryant's prodding to get her to speak up for herself, although the result had been the discovery of a hidden monster-birthing pool beneath the San Francisco mountains. So, to find herself facing three foes, each of whom wanted blood, was—to say the least—an uncomfortable prospect.

Mariah looked from one opponent to the next, sure that she should say something, sure that she *would* say something. Besides the dark-haired one that Brigid had beaten, there was an old woman with a cloud of white hair and a stone embedded in the middle of her forehead, and a young male farmhand of perhaps nineteen, with chiseled jaw and rippling muscles—the kind of guy that a much younger Mariah would have described as "dreamy." Right now, the clenched fists and mean scowl marring the young man's features as rain washed over his square jaw made him anything but dreamy.

"I can probably take the old lady," Mariah muttered to herself, and then she heard her own words in her ears and was faintly horrified. Did she actually want to do this? Was there a part of her that wanted this trial by combat? It was just a case of following orders, wasn't it? Was that so wrong?

Before Mariah could contemplate further, the dreamy-looking farmhand stomped across the ground at her at a slow trot, lunging back to swing a low punch at her gut. Instinctively, Mariah batted the punch aside as she stepped backward, and she felt her arm sing with pain as the swift blow struck.

She didn't want this. She knew that she didn't want this. Yet the command had been given—she was to fight and something burned in her mind, compelling her to obey.

Mariah dodged the younger farmhand's next punch. He was a strong lad, but there was little technique to his attacks. He telegraphed every move, and she could just about get out of the way in time. However, she didn't relish having to stop him once he got up a head of steam. Instead,

Mariah ran, darting out of the young man's reach, then doubling around as he chased her, the scene almost comedic. Head down, Mariah ran as fast as she was able with the handsome young farmhand just two paces behind her, his footfalls loud in her ears.

Suddenly, the young man was upon her, and Mariah did the first thing she could think of—let herself go limp and simply dropped to the ground. The man's hands grabbed for empty air where the thin geologist had been, and then he crashed into her, his feet caught up in her dropping form. Miraculously, Mariah arched her back and watched in amazement as the handsome young farmhand fell over the obstacle that was her body and crashed to the dirt.

Before the man could recover, Mariah was leaping up, jumping over the lad's fallen form. The other two stood before her, arms outstretched to block her path. Mariah didn't care. She continued running, charging at the old woman and throwing her whole body at her in imitation of a football tackle, sacking her elderly opponent.

As the old woman fell to the ground, crying out a sharp bark of agony, Mariah was already spinning, her brain working faster now as adrenaline pumped through it, her bloodlust rising. Maybe she was a fighter, after all? Maybe something about this ghost ville had changed her?

As Mariah thought those words, the dark-haired farmer called Dylan lunged for her, driving a hard fist into the side of her head with such power it knocked the geology expert off her feet. Mariah sank to the ground on all fours, feeling the sharp edges of the stone chips biting at the wet skin of her hands and ripping at the knees of her mud-spattered jumpsuit. She turned, her head whipping around to face the dark-haired farmer as he kicked her in the side, knocking her over so that she rolled onto her back, head thumping brutally against the ground. The man was on her in a second, driving his knee into her gut as she lay there. Mariah cried out in pain, but the farmer ignored her, slapping at her face with his open palm. Mariah's vision swam, and she became suddenly aware of the coldness of the rain as it trickled over her face. She was struggling for her very life, trying desperately to flip the man's weight from her body, to shake him away.

At the edge of the open arena, Brigid and Edwards watched the savage display, seeing their comrade suffer at the hands of the angered farmhand.

"We have to do something," Brigid whispered.

Edwards looked at her. "What's that, Ms. Baptiste?" he asked.

"Mariah's going to be brain-damaged or worse if this carries on," Brigid said out of the side of her mouth. "We have to step in, help her."

"The strong will survive," Edwards muttered, his voice emotionless. His forehead was smudged with mud and blood from his own battle, but he didn't seem to notice— or to care, Brigid realized.

The dark-haired farmer pulled back his hand and slapped Mariah across the side of the face again, first one way and then the other, knocking her so hard that her senses reeled. The younger farmer was on his feet once more, and he ran across the shale of the ground and kicked Mariah in the ribs as Dylan continued to slap her face. Mariah tried to scream, but before she could let out the sound her face was knocked again, this way and that, giving her not a second to recover.

Finally, Ullikummis spoke a single word of instruction: "Stop."

Dylan obeyed, drawing his hand back and pulling himself away from Mariah Falk's sagging form.

"Bring them," Ullikummis instructed solemnly, and the farmhands obeyed, helping Mariah to her feet, as well as the white-haired elderly woman she had knocked off her feet—Alison Marks. Mariah was fearful, worried that they would attack her again, but no one raised a hand.

Brigid and Edwards followed as Mariah was led, along with a number of other people including the white-haired farmer that Brigid had floored and one of the weaker women that Edwards had overpowered, toward the towering monolith at the center of the ville. Brigid's eyes drifted up to the top of the tower as the rain fell about her, seeing once more the puffs of inky smoke that sputtered into the skies above.

GRANT LEANED DOWN beside the ville wall, planting the last of his explosives. "That'll do it," he explained, looking up to meet Kane's icy stare.

Kane nodded. "Nice little surprise if we need it," he agreed before turning to where Domi was making her way through the rain-slicked grass to meet them. "Find anything?"

Domi looked noncommittal. "There's a section of the wall about forty feet along that has what could pass for handholds," she explained. "Looks like they run all the way up, so we could probably use them to climb up and over."

"Show us," Kane ordered.

THE FARMERS MARCHED toward the towering pyramid at the center of the ville, with Brigid, Edwards and Mariah among them.

There was a doorway at the bottom of the structure, hidden among the shadows. Like the other buildings in the eerie ville, this one had no door barring the way. It seemed right to Brigid somehow, for she had grown up in Cobaltville where, by law, doors were never locked. Ullikummis walked through the gap, his head inches from the top, leading the way within as the farmers obediently followed.

Like the others, Brigid's eyes were focused straight ahead, walking in time as she headed toward that open doorway with Edwards at her side. Mariah and a few others had been singled out to enter first, marched as though prisoners, though not one of them complained or rebelled.

Within, the ziggurat was warm, almost unbearably so, and a sheen of sweat appeared on Brigid's brow almost instantly. She turned then, looking at Edwards as he marched at her side, staring straight ahead. His face was flushed and soaked like hers, though whether with sweat or rainwater it was hard to tell.

"Edwards?" Brigid mumbled.

He ignored her, eyes fixed ahead as the group marched through the wide open interior of the pyramid toward a thick column that stood in its center. Like everything else in the ville, the column appeared to be constructed from schist, and it was almost cylindrical, twelve feet across and towering up and up through the chamber until the column disappeared through the roof.

Close to the front of the party, Mariah Falk eyed the towering rock column with trepidation. She could see flames within, located at the base of the cylinder, hear their angry popping as she neared, and the air in the chamber around her was burning hot. What she was looking at what was some kind of oven, she realized, its fires roasting hot, the column a chimney piping the smoke into the atmosphere above the pyramid.

"Stop," Ullikummis instructed, and the group halted, standing stock-still awaiting his next order. "Those who have failed are to step forward," he explained.

Four people took a step forward, approaching the bright fires of the glowing oven.

The first was the elderly man whom Brigid Baptiste had dispatched with such savagery during her test. He seemed to step forward willingly, requiring no cajoling to do as he was told.

The second figure was also elderly, the farmer's wife— Alison Marks—whom Mariah had felled in her own trial by combat.

The third figure to step forward was one of the women whom Edwards had fought with. She had been knocked unconscious by Edwards's initial attack, and had played no further role in the fight. It was clear from her emaciated figure that she had barely eaten in a long, long time, and Mariah was surprised that the woman had had the strength to stand, let alone to fight.

As Mariah looked at the skeletal woman, something else dawned on her. She, too, had stepped forward, joining the others who approached the open doorway of the burning oven. "Not me," Mariah heard her voice cry, but some- how her legs wouldn't stop moving; they simply continued marching toward the flames that popped and burned within the towering column.

Fifteen feet from the opening in the front of the oven, Brigid watched, muddling through the thoughts in her head. Her eidetic memory made her exceptional, and she had spent much of the past hour aware that something inside her head was wrong. Not just her head—Edwards's too, and that of Mariah. She had noticed that some of the farmers seemed to have stones embedded in their foreheads, parts of Ullikummis himself, but this had apparently not been done to her, Edwards or Mariah.

Finally, like something discovered in a thick fog, a word came to Brigid: entheogen.

An entheogen describes any of a number of psychotropic drugs that create a specific reaction in the brain. The word literally translates as "creates god within."

As the word came to her, Brigid realized what had happened. Somehow, an entheogen had been forced into their systems. The feeling of obedience, of euphoria at Ullikummis's commands, was the effect.

At the front of the group, the great god Ullikummis watched proudly as Alison Marks, the elderly farm mistress, walked into the burning fires of the oven. She did so willingly, for she had learned that he was her master, and his disappointment would be something far worse, far more terrible, than the elective incineration of her own body.

Around the oven, the rest of the group, including Alison's husband of forty years, watched impassively, seeing what happened to those who were weak. For Ullikummis had to teach them that weakness was merely a choice.

Eyes wide open, Alison Marks stepped through the high rock door and into the furnace itself, feeling the flames lapping against her body immediately. Lord Ullikummis had ordered it, for she was superfluous to his glorious new world, her ideas old and outmoded, small ideas in a world far bigger than she could possibly imagine. She saw all of this, saw that her weakness was more than physical. And her weakness disgusted her as the flames played across her frail flesh.

She remembered Eleanor then, such a cheerful baby, always a baby in Alison's heart. Always laughing, happy to play, wanting to dress up Barney. And Christopher, who had ultimately grown so big, towering over his father and heartbreakingly handsome to boot. And poor Francine, who had been so young when she was taken from them.

Peter had been a good husband, thoughtful and caring, and he had always provided for her in the old way, the way that had existed before Ullikummis.

For even in those brief seconds that marked the end of life and the start of death, Alison Marks recognized that the arrival of Ullikummis was the start of a new era, and that her place within it was as a saint. And saints can only be saints when they are dead.

With thoughts of the new world order on her mind, Alison Marks smiled and her lips boiled away from her teeth, her eyeballs bubbled away in their sockets and finally her whole body was superheated to ash in the matter of just a handful of seconds, bones crumbling to dust in that relentless, purging fire.

BUT HOW HAD this entheogen been administered? Brigid wondered as the farmer's wife was burned to ash before her eyes. Brigid thought back, trying to recall a time where she might have been forced to take a drug, but nothing came to mind. There had been a period where she had been knocked unconscious, she knew, and she may have been forced to imbibe it then. Several of the others had the stones in their heads that she realized could be affecting their thinking. Brigid touched her head but she could feel nothing physically added there, not even a scar where something might have been buried. It was as if it was something more fundamental than that.

The ville.

It came to Brigid like a bolt from the blue. An answer so obvious as to be hidden in plain sight. This place had sprung up out of nowhere, its structures and appearance the familiar lines of any of the other nine baronial villes that had been dotted across America, the same as the one she had grown up in. They had called it a ville because they recognized the pattern, but what if the pattern was just a pattern. What if the villes had been so formed to take advantage of that pattern?

Suddenly, Kane's voice broke into Brigid's thoughts as he spoke once more over the Commtact. "Baptiste?" he began. "We've just entered your ghost ville via the southeast corner wall. Place looks empty. You care to give me a clue if you're still here?"

KANE, GRANT AND DOMI had clambered over the exterior wall and were jogging across the seemingly empty ville at a steady trot, giving the buildings a swift once-over as they made their way through the sinister quietude. Kane left the Commtact frequency open, hoping that Brigid Baptiste might finally respond. Yet, he was still surprised when she actually did so.

"We're all standing in the middle of a giant sigil, Kane," Brigid's voice piped through the Commtact receiver at Kane's ear. "It's a trick to force us to obey."

"Force us?" Kane replied, clearly dubious of the statement.

"We're in what passes for the Administrative Monolith, where I think Mariah's about to cremate herself," Brigid replied, "and I can't make a move to stop it."

"Hell," Kane spit, and he began sprinting for the central pyramid that dominated the ville that wasn't a ville after all, with Grant and Domi at his heels.

Chapter 20

Pain and disappointment were the tools the Annunaki used to shape those around them. Pain and disappointment and the calculated use of fear—these had been his father's weapons, and now they were Ullikummis's.

He stood before the group of apekin, the remaining farmers who had survived the initial tasks he had set them once he had paved over the town of Market. There had been more than one hundred at first, both the local inhabitants and visitors who had come to the town to trade. Initially he had planted the stone seeds within them, just a dozen people in all, which would act as beacons. Peter and Alison Marks had been the first disciples, and the ill-tempered farmer called Dylan had joined them soon after. They had spread the word of Ullikummis among the others.

"A miracle has arrived among us," Dylan had said, easily drawn to a strong personality, deluded that in supporting it he was somehow a part of it.

Peter and Alison, meanwhile, had trudged around the town, Ullikummis's eyes and ears, as they herded the people into one central spot, their brains slowly melting away within their craniums, evaporating to nothingness.

And then Ullikummis had turned to the ground, placed his hand on the soil and felt through it, reached into it with his mind. His father had granted him one last ability beyond his incredible durability—the power to shape the rock. It had been an accidental thing, one that had remained

unsuspected until Ullikummis had taken his own arm and
retooled it into a weapon. When the arm had begun to grow
back, as he knew it must, Ullikummis found he could shape
it, and through proximity, shape other rocks around him.

He had kept the ability from his father and from Ningishzidda, for their relationship was changing subtly. Ullikummis had worshipped his father almost as much as his
father's lowliest subjects, but he had begun to appreciate
the need to hide things from him.

When he had been blasted into space within his prison
made of malleable rock, Ullikummis had appreciated the
irony. He could control this prison, retool and reshape it
for his needs. When he had finally returned to Earth it had
not been through Ningishzidda's doing, but rather through
his own, the meteor storm a thing of his own making.

So, upon landing he had begun to feel for the rocks,
providing them instructions when he reached the town of
Market. The sigil-form ville had taken three days to raise,
and still it was not complete.

Before their lord, the white-haired farmer stepped into
the flames, requiring no further instruction, and the bird-
thin woman would be next.

As he watched the cleansing flames burn away the
farmer's decrepit body, Ullikummis remembered that
other time that he had observed flames, swirling before
his eyes.

ULLIKUMMIS WAS TWO WEEKS SHY of his fourteenth birthday when he learned how powerful disappointment was
as a weapon.

Enlil looked at his son in the way that a man might
look at a rotting piece of fruit to decide whether it was still
edible. Beside him, Ningishzidda looked impatient.

"The procedure worked," the geneticist told Enlil. "You don't doubt me, do you?"

Enlil dismissed the question with a casual flick of a taloned hand. "I merely wish to see for myself," he said.

"Then I didn't need to be summoned here," Ningish-zidda said petulantly. "I do have other business to attend, you understand. Lord Marduk has asked for me to create a combination of human and fish, to see whether proximity to the water might grant the retarded apekin superior intellect. Relatively, of course."

Enlil turned to the geneticist, piercing him with his fierce gaze. "Lord Marduk will wait," he growled. "This is not another of your playful experiments on the local fauna. This is my son, genengineer."

Chastised, Ningishzidda bowed his head in humility. "Yes, my lord."

Enlil leaned close, staring into his son's face. To Ulli-kummis, his father was just a blurred shape now, a shadow standing amid the burning fires that filled his vision. Ningishzidda had assured him that the eyes would bond with his optic nerves in time, and that he would see far more clearly than he had ever thought possible, but for now, all he could do was comprehend the blurs, affixing the voices he could hear within the laboratory to each of the dark shapes.

"My eyes are burning, Father," Ullikummis said.

Lord Enlil ignored him, addressing another question to the geneticist. "Can he see?"

"This is a radical procedure. Your son's vision will take time to adjust," Ningishzidda explained.

Ullikummis watched the blurs move, wondering at what was going on right before his eyes as he lay on the bench in the center of the windowless lab. "How does it look, Father?" he asked. "Does it make you happy, what I have become?"

No answer came and, after a few seconds, Ullikummis asked again.

"Father? Do I make you happy?"

He was alone in the room. His father and the genetic contortionist had left.

KANE RUSHED THROUGH the tall doorway that led into the pyramidlike structure at the center of the lifeless ville. He had known exactly what Baptiste was referring to when she had said she was in the Administrative Monolith. Even though the structure had superficial differences, its relative height and position made it clear to Kane that this was the place she had been referring to.

Inside, he found the air oppressively hot, as if some heavy weight were pressing against him. It was also quite dark, the only light coming from the flames of a fire he could see located near the center of this single, vast room that seemed to encompass the whole of the structure. As he ran, Kane flinched his wrist tendons and suddenly the Sin Eater was in his right hand, powered there by the special holster he wore just above the cuff of his jacket's sleeve.

A few paces behind him, Domi and Grant were making their own way into the pyramid, holding back a little in case they were needed to provide backup.

The thing in the center of the vast room was a furnace, Kane realized, and before it stood a group of perhaps twenty people. He scanned the figures, searching for Brigid Baptiste by her instantly recognizable, vividly colored hair. Instead, his eyes stopped when he saw the thin brown-haired woman stepping toward the open door to the furnace, her arms stretched out at her sides as if to welcome

an old friend in a cheerful hug. It was Mariah Falk, the
Cerberus team's geology expert. Two steps ahead of her,
another woman, this one with gangly limbs that seemed
so thin as to be just fleshless bones, took a pace forward
and walked into the furnace fire.

Kane watched, horrified, as the woman burst into flame,
her thin silhouette catching light like a shadow held against
the sun. The stench came to Kane's nostrils in a second,
though he could never be quite sure if it was psychosomatic
or if he could really smell the burning human flesh as the
woman was reduced to ash and slivers of bone.

And Mariah was next, unless he did something.

"Mariah—no!" Kane shouted as he ran toward the
group around the furnace.

Suddenly, everyone turned, more than a dozen heads
spinning to face him as Kane sprinted toward them. He saw
Brigid then, and beside her the muscular form of Edwards,
his face and clothes caked with mud. At the back of the
group, standing beside the furnace door, a taller figure, a
rough shape like something unformed, glared at Kane with
eyes of molten lava.

Then the unformed thing spoke a single command:
"Recruit."

Kane realized he was suddenly running headlong at a
group of people who were rushing to meet him, with nothing good in mind.

MARIAH FALK WATCHED as the emaciated woman stepped
into the flames of the cremating oven and was reduced
to nothing but bone fragments in the space of just a few
seconds, her body disappearing in an almighty whoosh of
cleansing fire.

The lord Ullikummis looked to her, instructing her
to relieve herself of her burden to him. A useless recruit

for his new model army, better that she die now than drag the new world down with her repulsive presence. And the driving emotion inside Mariah's head told her she should conform.

She stepped ahead, making her way toward the vaporising fires of the oven.

"IS THAT MARIAH?" Domi asked as she ran with Grant into the gloomy interior of the pyramid, the silver Detonics CombatMaster .45 poised in her hand.

"Where?" Grant asked, then corrected himself immediately. "By the fire. I see her."

"What is she—?" Domi began, but Grant cut her off.

"Double around and stop her," he said. "Kane and I will deal with the locals."

Domi didn't need telling twice. She was already sprinting off around the approaching mob as Grant pulled loose his Copperhead close-assault subgun from his coat and chased after Kane, blasting a warning shot into the sweltering air.

Ahead, Kane found himself weaving out of the way as a half-dozen fists made to hit him, and he felt two blows catch him on his left side.

"Keep back," Kane ordered, his voice recalling the authority he had wielded back in his days as a Magistrate.

The group ignored him, and Kane was reminded of the zombies he had faced out in the Louisiana swamps less than a week before. The big differences, he realized, were that Brigid and Edwards appeared to be a part of this group, and every last one of them appeared to be alive.

"Baptiste?" Kane shouted as a thirtysomething sodbuster with a mullet charged at him. "What the hell is going on?"

Kane stepped aside and kneed the mullet-topped farmer in the guts, making the man double over with a grunt. Kane shoved him aside, letting him drop to the floor, clutching his bruised stomach.

The next farmer was upon Kane immediately, swinging her fist at his head. The ex-Mag had to give it to them—these crazies might only be farming types, but they were fighting with more than a simple sense of survival. Not professionals, maybe, but damn serious amateurs.

As the raven-haired farming woman's fist cleaved through the air, Kane stepped back then forward, so swift as to appear a blur before her eyes. As he did so, his empty hand snapped out and grabbed the woman by the wrist, using her own momentum against her to pull her off her feet. The woman flipped over herself, crashing hard against the floor of dirt and stone.

Suddenly, there was a booming noise behind him, and Kane turned to see Grant holding his subgun aloft, having blasted another warning shot up into the air. "Let's nobody move," Grant ordered.

The zombielike crowd ignored him. In fact, a number of them seemed to move as one to swarm at the huge ex-Mag, knocking Kane aside to reach the newcomer.

As Kane traded blows with the young pretty-boy farmer with whom Mariah had battled earlier, he saw Grant go down beneath a scrimmage of bodies.

It was all getting far too dangerous, Kane told himself, and he drove his fist into the blond-haired farmer's chest so hard that it knocked the lad off his feet. A fraction of a second later, Kane had raised the Sin Eater in his hand and spun to face his next opponent, his finger squeezing at the trigger. Before him, he saw to his horror the porcelain skin and emerald eyes of Brigid Baptiste as the first of the bullets blasted from the barrel of his gun.

DOMI WAS SMALL AND LIGHT on her feet. Where Kane
and Grant found themselves immersed in the savage battle
with the indoctrinated locals, she made her way past them
in a series of whirls and jumps, like some frenetic ballet
performance.

Two of the farmers stepped to block her path as she ran
for Mariah, but Domi didn't slow her pace. As the first
leaned in to grab her, Domi sprang into the air, running
up the man's body in two quick steps. Her left foot slapped
against his chest even as her right smashed into his face,
knocking him backward. As the farmer fell, Domi continued running forward, her left leg racing through the air to
find the floor once more. Two paces behind her, the farmer
was recovering, lifting himself off the ground and turning
to chase her, but she had already gone, a white streak in
the darkness of the crematorium.

The second farmer, a well-built man with what appeared
to be an infection on his lip, leaned forward, determined
not to be caught the way his colleague had. To Domi, however, he was just another obstacle to bypass, and she dived
ahead in a forward roll, sweeping across the ground below
his reaching arms.

As Domi leaped up from the rough floor, she turned
back, her right arm whipping through the air, and blasted
off three quick shots from her CombatMaster revolver. The
first slug drilled into the nearest farmer's left knee, bursting
the kneecap apart in an explosion of blood and gristle. As
the farmer stumbled to the ground, his legs whipping out
under him, his colleague took the next two shots high in
the leg, and doubled over himself in agony as steel-jacketed
bullets ripped through tendons.

Despite the pain they clearly must be in, Domi noticed
that neither farmer cried out. They simply flopped to the
floor like beached fish, the fight going out of them.

Still running, Domi turned back to her destination and saw Mariah Falk stepping willingly toward the furnace door, as though in some kind of trance. Beside her, a great stone pillar of a man watched, jagged rocky structures arcing out from his shoulders like the horns of a stag, his eyes glowing as brightly as the fire itself.

Domi was still fifteen paces from the flaming oven and she realized then that she wouldn't make it in time to stop her colleague sacrificing herself. Mariah was stepping into the flames and there was no time left. Domi's mind raced as she strived for another solution, a way to stop the woman from killing herself in those ferocious flames.

GRANT FOUND HIMSELF swarmed by eight of the farmers, and was surprised to find how combat-ready they seemed. He crashed to the ground under the weight of the attack, batting at his attackers with the length of subgun that rested over his right arm like an armored sleeve.

In a moment, Grant was lost from view, and all that could be seen was the dog pile that had overwhelmed him.

At the bottom of that pile, Grant felt something slam against his face as someone tried to knee him in the eye. Another blow came to his side, then more as the angry farmers held him down.

With a growl, Grant pushed upward, shoving the nearest people off him. Two figures fell backward, tossed from Grant's body. Grant's left fist was a blur, jabbing at the next fighter, slamming the man in the face with such ferocity that his front teeth snapped in two and his head twisted savagely on his neck.

Grant shifted his weight, gaining purchase against the floor beneath him as the remaining attackers continued to pile on him. He struck out, spreading his arms as he brought himself up off the floor. Four of his attackers were thrown from his body, and just one remained, clinging to the huge ex-Mag's back. Now standing, Grant reached behind him and wrenched the woman from his back, throwing her to the side like a rag doll.

As Ullikummis watched the huge, bull-like man make short work of his developing army, the Annunaki prince recalled another warrior he had known long ago, when he had first walked the Earth. "Enkidu," he whispered, the word like ashes on his tongue.

Grant powered forward, knocking aside the recovering farmers as they endeavored to regroup, batting each away with a mighty swing of his arms, blasting shots from his Copperhead to ensure they kept their distance. Suddenly, Grant detected another figure come running at him at high speed, swooping low to the ground as the gunshots blasted into the air. It was Edwards, his old colleague from the Cerberus redoubt.

"Oh, don't make me do this to you," Grant shouted, hoping that his Cerberus comrade wasn't so out of his mind that he was going to attack.

Inevitably, Grant was to be disappointed. Edwards slammed into him, a powerful engine of taut muscle driving the ex-Mag backward and forcing him to the floor. Grant's Copperhead blaster went flying from his hand as he was slammed into the ground.

BRIGID LEAPED ASIDE as the leading bullet from Kane's Sin Eater cut through the air toward her. Off target by just a fraction of an inch, the bullet streaked through Brigid's fire-red hair, clipping off a half-dozen strands as it zipped past her and away.

Kane was swinging his arm aside, shifting the aim of the Sin Eater even as he relaxed his finger on the trigger, a burst of 9 mm bullets uselessly peppering the ceiling far above them. "What the hell, Baptiste?" he shouted.

"I can't stop myself," Brigid told him, the frustration clear on her features. "It's Enlil's son—Ullikummis. You have to stop him before he gets inside you."

Kane shoved her behind him as he continued running through the open area toward the furnace and the colossal rock creature who stood before it. "We'll see," he snarled.

Another of the trancelike farmers stepped in front of Kane, blocking his path to the furnace. Kane didn't even slow. His fist lashed out, knocking the man off his feet as he continued to run toward the impressive creature of stone. Up ahead he saw Domi failing to reach Mariah, too late to stop her from stepping into the fire.

DOMI WOULD HATE HERSELF, perhaps, but she was out of options. Mariah Falk stepped forward before her, walking into the open doorway of the furnace. It was so hot that Domi could even feel it here, fourteen paces away from that opening. There was no time left for subtlety.

Still running, Domi lifted the heavy Detonics Combat-Master in her hand and unleashed a single shot, targeting Mariah's legs. It was a tough shot to make on the fly, and the oppressive heat and the general gloom of the room did nothing to help Domi's effort. Time seemed to stop as the 9 mm slug left the chamber of the Detonics and hurtled across the room on its downward path. Domi shouted a word of warning to Mariah to stop, but Mariah was ignoring her, stepping into the scorching heat of the oven, her brain frozen by Ullikummis's cruel command.

Then the bullet struck, drilling into the back of Mariah's left calf and slicing the tendon that connected to her ankle. Poised on the threshold of the oven, Mariah stumbled and keeled over, sagging to one side as her left leg gave out beneath her.

Ullikummis turned his attention back to his loyal devotee as she struck the ground beside him, and then he looked up in surprise as the albino girl came rushing at him, the CombatMaster blazing in her hand. A fraction of a second later, bullets rained across his stone chest, striking sparks off the hard surface of his skin.

Then Domi was upon him, leaping high in the air and blasting another burst of gunfire at the stone god's face. Ullikummis reached forward, his speed once again defying his apparent size, and knocked Domi out of the air, like a man swatting an annoying insect. Domi was flipped back upon herself, and she sailed across the room before striking the floor beside where Mariah was sprawled in the pooling blood of her own leg.

Immediately, Domi righted herself, balancing in a crouch like a cat, feeling the ferocious heat of the oven at her side as she assessed the stone monstrosity looming over her.

Ullikummis turned his eyes on this curiously colored lesser being, admiring her weird bone-white flesh. "You will submit," he instructed her, bringing the full force of his powerful voice of command into play.

"Never!" Domi spat, loosing another blast from her handgun.

For the first time since his return to Earth, Ullikummis knew surprise. The voice, coupled with the reinforcing power of the architecture around them, should make any apekin yearn to follow his command. Yet this one, with her white skin and ruby eyes, seemed utterly immune to its effects. Had the world changed so much in his absence?

GRANT CRASHED TO THE GROUND as his Copperhead skittered away from his reach. Then Edwards was upon him, swinging his fists at Grant's face, kneeing the man in his groin. Edwards was strong, and his natural ability came through. Unlike the others—the farmers whom Grant and Kane had made short work of—Edwards was a trained military man and a physically tough one, as well. But, right now it was clear that Edwards was following the commands of the enemy.

"I don't want to fight you, man," Grant shouted, deflecting Edwards's increasingly wild attacks.

Edwards ignored him, driving a knee into Grant's side and rapping his knuckles across the ex-Mag's jaw.

Grant shunted Edwards away and pushed himself up off the ground. As he stood, Edwards came rushing at him again, trying for his double-kick attack, low then high. The low kick caught Grant at the knee, but the maneuver failed to pop his kneecap. Then Edwards's leg was sweeping higher, bashing Grant across the cheek and bloodying his nose. Edwards reared back, bouncing on his heels as he readied himself for Grant's countermove.

As blood trickled through his gunslinger's mustache, Grant's lips peeled back, showing his gritted teeth. "Sometimes it's just gotta be so," he growled, and then he rushed forward, his boots pounding against the shinglelike ground as he drove his fist into Edwards's jaw.

The blow connected with a loud crack, and Edwards hurtled backward, careering toward the ground. Grant stood ready as his Cerberus colleague crashed to the floor. The man slumped there, unmoving. Edwards was unconscious.

KANE RAN ONWARD through the vast pyramid that housed the furnace, watching as Domi was slapped aside by the hulking form of Ullikummis. Like a wildcat, Domi leaped up again, blasting a stream of shots at the towering stone creature as he stalked toward her beside the open doorway to the oven. Kane saw that Domi's bullets were having no effect, and he commanded his own gun back into its wrist holster as he ran the last few steps to meet with the stone-clad giant.

As he ran, Kane's hand plucked at one of the grenades he had lashed to his belt, automatically priming it with the swiftest movement of his thumb and finger.

"Domi! Get down!" Kane shouted as he tossed the grenade at the stone god standing before her.

Ullikummis turned at Kane's words and found himself struck in the chest by the hard metal shell of the grenade. Domi dived to one side, hands over her ears, using her own body to protect Mariah's supine form a few feet from the front of the furnace.

Then the grenade detonated, the explosion blasting into Ullikummis's chest and knocking the stone-skinned Annunaki backward. Ullikummis staggered, falling sideways as the blast shook him, and then he was toppling into the open doorway of the furnace like a felled statue.

Kane was knocked back by the power of the explosion, and he found himself falling to the floor almost ten feet from the front of the furnace. He looked up just in time to see Ullikummis struggle inside, a blackened smear across his uneven stone chest, the torches blasting jets of flame across his bizarre body.

Lying beside the open doorway of the oven, Domi dragged herself up and pulled Mariah Falk across the floor until they were a few feet farther from the spitting fires as Ullikummis burned within. Then, the chalk-skinned warrior reached for her own grenades and tossed two back into the opening, turning her head as they struck at the flaming form struggling to emerge from the stone archway.

Kane blinked at the brightness of the explosions as the shock wave from the grenades slammed against the furnace and its lone inhabitant, crumbling one wall as they drove the mighty Annunaki back into the center of those white-hot jets of fire.

Then, with an almighty crash, the whole furnace began to crumble around its singular occupant, and a series of further explosions rippled across its surface as the unleashed flames burst from its breaking walls.

KNOCKED DOWN by the second volley of grenades, Ullikummis lay in the furnace, superheated flames jetting all about him, running along his skin like insects. Beneath his body, he could feel the broken fragments of bones and bodies from the farmers he had burned, the ones who had failed the trials by combat. Beyond the furnace's opening, he could hear the explosions rocking the pyramid at the center of his Tenth City, the incredible ville he had built in imitation of his peers. The furnace itself shook as an explosion racked through it, and Ullikummis's body was showered with fragments as the pyramid's chimney began to collapse in on itself from above him.

The jets of flame grew stronger as the chimney parted and a rush of oxygen was fed to the fire. Ullikummis remained, feeling those yellow-red tongues lick at his body.

Ullikummis, who had forged weapons in the heart of a volcano, closed his magma eyes and thought of his father as the flames charred his rocky hide.

Chapter 21

His head was reeling from the explosions when Kane felt a hand pulling at his arm, and he looked up to see Brigid Baptiste leaning over him.

"Come on, hero," Brigid urged, "we've outstayed our welcome."

Kane pulled himself up, brushing at the debris that had splashed all over him with the destruction of the furnace. There was water on his face, he realized, and he peered upward to see the wide rent that had appeared in the roof of the pyramid through which the drumming rain was now falling. "Is everyone okay?" he asked.

"Let's just get you out of here," Brigid told him, "before the whole place crashes down around our ears."

Behind him, close to the shattered entrance to the furnace, Kane saw Grant leaning down to help Domi lift Mariah from the floor. The geologist's left leg was dark with blood and she was crying.

All around the Cerberus teammates, the remaining farmers seemed to be standing about in a daze, unsure of what to do next.

"What happened here, Baptiste?" Kane asked as Brigid helped him to his feet.

"Something about the ville makes people obey," she explained. "I don't know how it does it, but Ullikummis somehow used it to make us go against our natural instincts.

He was trying to create an army of warriors, I think, using the most brutal techniques in a sort of survival-of-the-fittest contest."

Kane grunted as he shifted his weight. His leg was bleeding where a chunk of masonry from the shattered chimney had struck him, and when the adrenaline rush passed he found himself feeling suddenly exhausted. "Obey, huh?" Kane mused as he walked with Brigid through the milling forms of the farmers.

They were close to the doors now, and Kane spotted Edwards lying unconscious among the rocky debris of the crumbling pyramid. Taking a deep breath, Kane issued a command in the old Magistrate voice he would once have used to intimidate lawbreakers: "Everyone is to follow me and my colleagues out of this building on the double. No stragglers, no questions—that's an order."

It took a few seconds, and Kane watched anxiously as the farmers seemed to sway in place indecisively. Then one, then two more, began to march toward where he stood beside Baptiste close to the stone doorway that led from the pyramid to the outside courtyard. A few moments later, everyone began to march as though a military unit under Kane's command.

Among the survivors, Grant came lumbering through with Mariah's form over one shoulder, the tiny figure of Domi padding along at his side. Grant leaned down to pull the unconscious form of Edwards up off the floor.

Kane snapped his fingers, getting the attention of two of the ragged-looking farmers as they paced through the doorway and out into the cooling rain. "You. You. Go back, help my friend with the unconscious man. Quickly." To Kane's astonishment, the two farmers obeyed, turning on their heels and jogging back to help Grant with Edwards's body.

Kane turned to Brigid, a sly grin appearing on his lips. "Well, this is all very interesting," he said, raising his eyebrows.

"Don't get used to it," Brigid told him. "It won't last long now that Ullikummis has been destroyed. They're just receptive right now."

"What about y—?" Kane began but Brigid placed her hand to his lips.

"It only works on the weak-minded," she told him.

Whether that was entirely true, Brigid wouldn't like to say, but for the moment she felt sure that the alien box that had been inside her head had left, and her thoughts were all her own once more. Besides, it wouldn't do to give Kane too many ideas about bossing people around.

AMID THE WRECKAGE of the crumbling pyramid, the remains of the oven finally crashed in on themselves. There were charred chunks of Ullikummis's stone shell mixed in among that wreckage, now just lifeless hunks of metamorphic rock, shaped and altered by pressure and heat.

DOMI SET A SERIES OF CHARGES along one of the rock walls, blasting a hole in it that the befuddled farmers could make their way through. They seemed to be waking up now, as though from some awful nightmare.

As the farmers made their way out of the eerie stone ville, Kane's team set their remaining charges throughout the structures that made up the place. Brigid had insisted, unable to fully vocalise what she wanted to say, but somehow certain that the ville itself held hidden power that they couldn't see.

"Villes mangle people," Domi said, voicing the feeling that Brigid couldn't seem to express. "Give them tangle-brain."

Kane agreed. "Slash and burn seems the best way to proceed. Just to be sure."

As they finally made their way from the eerie ville, a gap appeared in the clouds and the rain began to ease off to a thin drizzle. At the edge of the ville, they found Mariah sitting with Edwards. The well-built former Mag was looking confused, while Mariah tried to explain what had happened from the few fragments she could recall. She was showing Edwards her bloody leg when Kane, Grant, Domi and Brigid joined them.

"We're about out of here," Kane explained. "How does everyone feel?"

Mariah winced. "My head feels better but my leg is burning like you would not believe."

Kane nodded. "I've taken a few bullets in my time, Mariah," he reassured her. "When we get back home we'll have Reba take a look at it. You should be fine."

"I can't stand up," Mariah responded, bitterness in her voice.

"You'll be fine," Kane reiterated.

"Believe me," Domi added, "you may not remember it, but the alternative was a lot worse."

Still caked in mud and blood, Edwards pulled himself up off the damp ground and gave Mariah a hand up, letting her lean against his shoulder. "Speaking of," he said, turning to Grant, "did we fight, you and me?"

"I wouldn't call that a fight, Edwards," Grant replied dismissively.

Edwards looked at Grant for a moment, wondering what he meant. All around, the dozen or so farmers were discussing their own travails, like abductees from some weird brainwashing experiment.

Brigid took one last look at the strange ville that had sprung up in the space of a week. The central pyramid had already collapsed in on itself, and one exterior wall smoldered where Domi had blasted a hole through it to create an exit.

"It's strange," Brigid said. "Kind of beautiful in its way."

"The charges are primed, Baptiste," Kane told her, putting a comforting arm around her shoulder. "In thirty seconds all it will be is a place to start over."

Brigid nodded, turning her eyes from the gray schist walls and heading for the cavern where they had left their interphasers. "Destruction and renewal," she said. "The same things that Ullikummis touted."

As explosions ripped through Tenth City, the Cerberus warriors headed for the cavern where they had hidden the interphasers.

Chapter 22

Edwards had returned to Cerberus exhausted, and had gone straight to his quarters the very second that his debriefing had concluded. While the others rushed to their new tasks—Kane and Grant in the Louisiana bayou, Brigid working through the fundamentals of the villes with Lakesh—Edwards had slept, crashed on his bed still wearing his mud-caked clothes.

IT WAS MIDNIGHT, cold and raining. Kane and Grant had used the mat-trans to travel cross-country once more from the Cerberus redoubt in the Montana mountains, and they met with Ohio Blue in the murky core of the Louisiana swampland. As ever, Blue was dressed entirely in sapphire, a long dress, tight to her legs with a single split going from the hem almost all the way up to her left thigh, a single ribbon choker around her swanlike neck. Her lips were painted a deeper shade of blue that looked almost purple in the dim exterior lighting of the run-down voodoo temple, and she pursed them as she saw the two Cerberus rebels approach in the airboat she had arranged for their arrival.

"Well, you certainly do know how to keep a girl waiting," Ohio pronounced as Kane climbed out of the airboat and walked up the rotting wooden steps of the temple with Grant just a few paces behind him. As Kane moved, Blue saw that he had the ceremonial sword strapped across his back. "You'll have to work on your timekeeping, sweet prince, if you plan on impressing me."

Kane gave a world-weary sigh. "We had a little business elsewhere, coupled with the mother lode of communications blackouts."

Ohio took a pace forward, leaning so close to Kane that her blond hair brushed against the side of his face. "A true gentleman brings flowers, sweet prince," Ohio whispered, "not excuses."

Kane glared at her as she turned and led the way into the wooden structure. "I'll remember that for next time," he snarled.

When Cerberus had checked through their logs, they learned that Ohio Blue's people had endeavored to make contact two days before, during the period when the communications satellite was still down. The message that had been left advised Cerberus to return to Papa Hurbon's temple as soon as possible, as there had been some developments. Although the message had not been left by Blue herself, it had specifically requested Kane be among the party sent. Kane couldn't quite fathom what was going on in Ohio's mind, but he accepted his role in their skewed relationship insofar as it gave Cerberus a valuable link to the underbelly of the outside world.

Accompanied by the glamorous female trader, Kane and Grant made their way through the wooden-walled Djévo room, where Kane and Blue had been fighting for their lives just a week before alongside Brigid Baptiste. Now the only people in the place were a handful of Ohio's men who were busy sifting through the trinkets and junk for items with possible resale value.

"So, what have you found?" Grant asked, watching as one of the trader's crew tipped another huge jar across the floor and began pawing through its spilled contents.

Ohio glanced back, peering at Kane and Grant through her curtain of shimmering blond hair. "Something you won't like," she said before pushing past her men and into the inner sanctum.

Kane followed with Grant at his back. The room had changed from when they had left it. The walls were the same: the simple decoration of human bones on one wall and the hooks on the opposite wall where the sword had hung until Ohio Blue had snagged it for Kane. And the two pots remained at opposing corners, their dried contents looking as lifeless as Kane remembered.

"What is this?" Grant asked, gesturing to the long leg bone that was mounted on the wall. "A kennel?"

Kane held up a hand to silence his partner. "Where's the chair?" he asked. "The voodoo chair."

"The chair's gone," Blue stated. "It was gone when we came back here."

"You didn't take it?" Kane queried.

Ohio shook her head. "Oh, but that I had," she said. "However, there's more, Kane."

The beautiful blond-haired trader led the way through the far doorway and into the other half of the temple. Like the inner sanctum, Kane saw that the whole place had been built with one side perfectly matching the other, with the same proportions to the rooms and a similar array of junk lining the walls. Here, as with the Djévo area they had passed through to get to the inner sanctum, Blue's scavenger team were working through the trinkets on show, taking anything of value and tossing aside everything else.

It's always the same with these bottom-feeders, Kane told himself as he watched them root through someone else's property. He hated dealing with filth scavengers like these. "What happened to the locals?" Kane asked. "We can't have dispatched more than five or six on our way out, surely."

Stepping over the debris, her heeled blue shoes crunching against the shells and feathers and the dried remains of what appeared to be a bird about the size of a man's fist, Ohio spoke softly. "Eight at least," she purred. "I prefer not to recall. Come."

With that, she motioned them into a side room that served as a bedchamber. The room was surprisingly ornate, with a large four-poster bed in its center and silks of pretty colors draped across the ceiling, pinks and violets that fluttered a little as they caught a breeze. The corpulent figure of Papa Hurbon lay in the bed, his busy hands working at a bunch of rags, winding them around and around to form what appeared to be a child's doll.

"Hurbon," Kane acknowledged, informing Grant who the man was.

Papa Hurbon looked up from his busywork, and his eyes looked tired, their edges rimmed with red. "You back, boy?" he asked. "Didn't think you'd have the stones to come here again."

Kane reached behind him, unhooking the strap that held the ceremonial voodoo sword to his back. "I came to return this, just like I promised," he said, no trace of irony in his voice. "Seems that things have changed some since I last visited."

Hurbon laughed, and the bed creaked as it shook beneath his large form. "Can say that again," he said. "Surely you can."

"What happened?" Kane asked, his senses alert as he peered around the bedchamber.

"I thought that the gods had deserted me, but *she* came back," Hurbon said. "Fuck, but did she come back." And once more, he laughed, a booming noise from deep in his chest.

"She?" Kane prodded. "You mean Ezili Co-no-show-whatever?"

"Ezili Coeur Noir," Hurbon muttered, and he nodded. "Came for her chair, but found she had a little time to kill. Play a little with her devotees."

"What happened?" Grant asked, intrigued.

Hurbon assessed his fellow black man for a moment. "You believe in the path? You follow it?"

Grant shook his head. "Not me."

Papa Hurbon shrugged, disappointed. "Your white friend tell you what happened the last time Mistress Ezili Coeur Noir visited?" he asked. "Mad bitch took my leg, and that of some others. Said it was a sign of devotion."

Astonished, Grant swore, looking at the rumpled bed-clothes that appeared to cover the man's legs.

"Well," Hurbon said, "if it was good enough for her once, why not twice, right?" He lifted back the covers of the bed to show where his body ended at the groin, both of his legs missing. The sheets were stained with blood, but the new wound seemed to have scarred over now. "Mad fucking bitch. Killed most everyone else, and those she missed they run like hell. I'd not seen anyone till your woman here comes to raid the place. She was the one that patched me back together."

"My people," Ohio clarified off Kane's look.

"Figured," he said. Then the ex-Mag placed the voodoo sword on a walnut dresser that stood against one wall, a dust-caked mirror standing over it. "You really lucked out when you chose which gods to worship, huh?" he said.

"People who don't believe in the path don't know the power," Hurbon said, and he lifted the thing in his hands to show to Kane.

Kane looked at the thing he had taken to be a child's doll and he saw now that it was a representation of an individual, a female with lizard skin and penetrating eyes. While crude, the caricature was instantly recognizable.

"Ezili Coeur Noir come and mess me up," Hurbon said, walking the little doll along the bedclothes the way that a child might its toy, "but now I put a hex on her. When she comes next time I be the one who is in control." His hand tightened around the doll's middle until she appeared to bend at the waist, bowing before him.

Kane watched as the little fetch bowed in Hurbon's pudgy hands. Hurbon may say it was Ezili Coeur Noir but Kane knew better. It was Lilitu, dark goddess of the Annunaki. She was alive, just as Brigid had guessed.

"I WOULD NEVER HAVE guessed," Brigid said as she went over her findings with Lakesh.

They sat together in a quiet corner of the Cerberus canteen, drinking coffee as they discussed what had happened out in Saskatchewan. "I still struggle with the concept," Lakesh admitted. "The idea that the very design of the villes can somehow be used to affect the human mind."

"I don't even think it's really the mind," Brigid admitted. "It's something more primal than that—emotion, maybe. The shape, the tower at the center. It's like a magical symbol, a sigil that makes people conform. A very, very subtle form of control. The swastika used by the Nazis was a magical symbol, don't forget. Sigils have incredible power over the human psyche, far more than we frequently credit them. Somehow, Ullikummis just upped the sigil's power, maybe because he controlled the rocks themselves."

A smile crossed Lakesh's lips and he let out a nervous laugh.

"What is it?" Brigid asked as she reached for her cup, only to find it was empty.

"What you've just described, the grouping of buildings with one higher building at their center," Lakesh said, "that is every city that ever existed. The financial district at the center with its towering skyscrapers, the lower buildings all around until it finally peters out into the rural areas of the surrounding countryside. If you were to ask any of the people at this facility, certainly those refugees from the Manitius Moon Base who inhabited the twentieth century, I suspect every last one of them grew up in or near a settlement as you've described it. Not always skyscrapers— sometimes a church, a cathedral. Go back through history and every settlement is the same."

"The Annunaki planned for a long time, Lakesh," Brigid reminded him as she pushed herself up from the table, her empty cup in hand.

Lakesh watched as the red-haired woman made her way to the serving area and helped herself to steaming coffee from a towering silver percolator there. Could Brigid possibly be right? Could it be that whole cities had somehow been constructed to affect people at some emotional level, to make them conform? Lakesh thought back to the Manhattan skyscrapers, Big Ben in the center of London, the pinnacle of the Eiffel Tower in Paris. Each city had the rudimentary design that she was talking about. Was it really a magical design that could somehow affect the way people thought? Lakesh couldn't say.

Brigid returned, her coffee cup in one hand and a plate of cookies in the other. "They've just run out of whitener," she explained. "Clem says he'll bring some over. Cookie?"

Lakesh took one of the almond cookies and held it thoughtfully before him as he weighed Brigid's hypothesis. "Let us assume that there is some credence in your theory of the shape of villes breeding conformity," Lakesh said. "Even setting aside the fact that you, I and others like us broke through the spell or hypnosis or whatever it was. Why, after the nukecaust destroyed civilization, were only nine new villes built?"

"I don't know," Brigid admitted. "That was all the Annunaki we had, I guess. A city for each one. Just nine."

As she spoke, Clem Bryant came across to the table carrying a little bowl of coffee whitener, and he set it down beside Brigid.

"Just nine whats?" Clem asked.

"Baronies," Brigid told him. "Nine Annunaki hiding in nine villes."

"Because nine is the number of the universe," Clem said as though it was obvious.

Brigid and Lakesh turned to him, equally stunned and bemused by his left-field statement.

Clem smiled enigmatically. "In Hindu belief, Ganesh—the source of creation—is five, and the shakti of destruction is four. Thus, nine is the sum of these two facets, creation and destruction—the number of the universe. Nine is energy, and energy can never be destroyed."

Brigid cursed, utterly amazed, while Lakesh shook his head in disbelief.

"Where do you get this stuff from, Clem?" Brigid asked.

"Do you think it's significant?" Clem retorted, clearly a little pleased that he could help.

"It might just be," Brigid said as she added whitener to her coffee, stirring it slowly counterclockwise.

In that moment, it seemed to Brigid and Lakesh that the world of villes and resurrected gods that the Cerberus warriors inhabited had become just a little bit more convoluted, and a little bit more dangerous than they had previously realized.

EDWARDS AWOKE to the gnawing feeling of his empty stomach. He was ravenous; it felt as if he hadn't eaten in a month. He pushed himself up off the mattress and reached for the lamp, a durable angle-poise type that arced over his bed. The bulb popped to life and Edwards narrowed his eyes for a moment against the glare in the otherwise dark room.

He was still dressed, he realized. Worse, his clothes were covered in dried mud and, as he moved, he saw that a whole layer of the stuff had flaked off all over his bed.

"Dammit," Edwards grumbled, brushing at the mud only to realize he was making it worse.

He would get food, then come back and clean up here— strip the bed and sweep the floor of any mud that shook out of it. Even as he thought it, he realized he'd need to get changed before he went to the on-site canteen facility and at least make some effort to wash up.

Irritated, Edwards made his way across the room to the tiny cubicle that served as an en suite bathroom, though was really just a basin with a shaving mirror alongside the toilet. As he stalked across the room, Edwards stripped off his undershirt and tossed it on the floor, and dried mud cracked from the folds and skittered across the floor tiles as it landed. Screw it, he was going to sweep the room anyhow.

Then he saw himself in the mirror and realized he hadn't been kidding about needing to wash. His face was smeared with dried mud and dried blood, and when he reached for the faucet he saw more mud ingrained into his finger-nails. He remembered punching some guy in the throat as they lay together on the ground, and he laughed in spite of himself. It seemed faintly unreal, like recalling a dream. "Crazy shit," he muttered as he waited for the water to run hot.

A moment later, Edwards was splashing water in his face, eyes closed as he used his hands to wipe the dried muck away.

When he opened his eyes, Edwards saw there was still a little dirt by his ear and a smudge on his forehead. With another splash of water, Edwards brushed at the dirt. The smudge on his head wouldn't wipe off.

"What the...?" he began as he rubbed harder at his fore-head. It felt as if there was something there, a hard lump like a callus. He pushed against it, and felt the rock-hard lump disappear, sinking back into his skin.

"Weird," Edwards muttered as he grabbed up a new shirt from the single chair in his one-room quarters and made his way out to get himself something to eat.

Epilogue

It was afternoon in the Middle East. The sun pounded down from a clear blue sky as a lone figure strode purposefully across the fertile lands along the banks of the timeless Euphrates River.

Wrapped in a cloak of heavy fabric that was colored as red as blood, Enlil watched the bright sunlight reflecting from the river's glistening surface. It was hot out here, away from the shadows that he had become accustomed to during his enforced exile after the destruction of *Tiamat,* and he wore the cloak as much to keep the sun off his scales as he did to disguise his unusual appearance from the local apekin.

It had been one Earth week since he had planted the *Tiamat* seed, one week since he had left the tiny seed within the fertile soil on the banks of this river where the first Annunaki outpost had stood thousands of years before.

Far away, a noise caught Enlil's ears, carrying as it did on the wind, and he glanced up, the vertical slits of his pupils narrowing as he peered at the distant horizon. A nomadic trader was making his way across the sand there, two camels following in his wake, each of them weighed down with the trader's wares. Enlil watched for a moment longer, saw the trader turn and begin to approach across the empty plain.

Lord Enlil turned away, his eyes roving along the ground as he sought evidence that the *Tiamat* seed might be germinating. The wind blew the dry topsoil back and forth, churning its particles up in tiny whirls that skirted along just a few inches above the ground before sinking back. There, close to Enlil's left foot, a tiny sliver of green poked from the soil.

It had been but one week, and yet the stubborn spaceship womb was re-forming, re-creating herself from just a handful of cells, as she had re-created Enlil and his siblings just a few years before. *Tiamat* was being reborn from the tiny sliver that he had planted here at First Outpost.

Once the mother ship was large enough, once she was strong enough, Enlil would access her knowledge banks, immerse himself in the dataflow. And then he would pluck the things he needed so that he might finally rule this tiny kingdom called Earth.

Enlil looked up from the single, tiny shoot as the nomadic trader neared, peering at the man from beneath the hood of his bloodred cloak.

"Good day to you, fine sir," the nomad said in the local tongue, pulling at a length of fraying rope that was attached to the two camels who obediently followed him. "Might I interest you in something? A new cloak perhaps, or a blanket to keep yourself warm when night falls?"

His face hidden by the shadow cast by his hood, Enlil smiled. "There is but one thing I require," he said in his eerie duotonal voice.

If the trader was concerned by Enlil's voice he did not show it. Instead he gestured to the many things that hung from the backs of his camels. There were copper pots, drinking bottles made of soft leather, thick blankets and thin silks of many colors, stoles, lucky charms and even, curiously, a woman's parasol, its color long bleached away by the fierce sunlight. "Name it, fine sir, and it shall be yours," the trader gleefully announced.

"The future," Enlil told him. "And you are correct, apekin. It shall be mine."

The Executioner®
Don Pendleton's
THREAT FACTOR

Warlords threaten to turn Somalia into a battle zone...

A Somali pirate attack raises a red flag when the stolen cargo is Russian tanks and ammunition—enough to start a civil war. Called in to seek and destroy the weapons, Mack Bolan knows the only way to head off future bloodshed is to cause some deadly mayhem of his own!

*Available September
wherever books are sold.*

**GOLD
EAGLE** ®

TAKE 'EM FREE
2 action-packed novels plus a mystery bonus

NO RISK
NO OBLIGATION TO BUY

AleX Archer
THE DRAGON'S MARK

For everything light, there is something dark…

Archaeologist Annja Creed and her sword have never been outmatched—until now. An assassin known as the Dragon wields a bloodthirsty sword that should be feared. The Dragon initiates a terrible game of cat and mouse. Eventually the two swords, light and dark, must meet…and only one shall triumph.

Available September wherever books are sold.